The AVENUE of the DEAD

Also by Evelyn Anthony

Valentina
The French Bride
Clandara
Charles the King
All the Queen's Men
Victoria and Albert
Anne Boleyn
Far Flies the Eagle
Royal Intrigue
Rebel Princess
The Rendezvous
The Cardinal and the Queen
The Legend
The Assassin
The Tamarind Seed
The Poellenberg Inheritance
Stranger at the Gates
Mission to Malaspiga
The Persian Price
The Silver Falcon
The Return
The Janus Imperative
The Defector

THE AVENUE OF THE DEAD

Evelyn Anthony

Coward, McCann & Geoghegan
New York

First American Edition 1982

Library of Congress Cataloging in Publication Data

Anthony, Evelyn.
The avenue of the dead.

I. Title.
PR6069.T428A95 1982 823'.914 82-1519
ISBN 0-698-11124-9 AACR2

PRINTED IN THE UNITED STATES OF AMERICA

To Isidore and Blanche
with my deep affection and gratitude

Chapter One

THE DAFFODILS were out in St. James's Park. Brigadier James White walked from his flat in Westminster to his office in Queen Anne's Gate during the fine weather. He looked a typical soldier, striding smartly along with his umbrella swinging in time, smartly dressed in the civilian uniform of dark suit and bowler hat. Passersby, had they noticed him at all, would have been surprised that he was well into his sixties. Even more surprised by the innocuous Ford Transit that idled along the route behind him. Two Special Branch men followed the brigadier during his morning walk to work, and both were armed.

He turned into Queen Anne's Gate and said good morning to the security men on duty. The old-fashioned passenger lift trundled him up to the first floor; his secretary was in the outer office; they exchanged smiles and greetings. He hung up his hat and hooked the umbrella over the arm of an antiquated coat stand and went into his office. A comfortable, unpretentious room, with a leather-topped desk, hunting prints and a watercolor of a lawn meet in front of a large pink house. A Persian rug that crawled across the carpet to the despair of the cleaners; a series of mahogany cabinets against one wall, and a small VDU computer, looking self-conscious among the stolid traditional furnishings. Four telephones and a sophisticated intercom system on his desk. One telephone colored bright green. It gave him direct access through a scrambler to the prime minister.

A man turned away from the window as James White came in. He was tall and thin, with a bony, wax-colored face and light eyes. His demeanor was gloomy.

"Good morning, Humphrey," the brigadier said. Humphrey Grant was his deputy, a title that conveyed some of the power he enjoyed in the secret world of the Secret Intelligence Service. His attendance so early meant trouble, and James White knew it. He settled at his desk, opened a packet of his distinctive cigarettes and lit one. The brand was his private joke; Sub Rosa. The pervasive smell of Turkish tobacco drifted up Grant's nose and he grimaced. He hated the habit; he was fastidious and tidy to the extent of obsession. Ash and the detritus of smoking were filthy enough without the danger to health and the unpleasant smell of tobacco. But not even he, from his position of special privilege, would ever dare to protest to his Chief about anything he did.

"There's the usual Thursday morning pile-up, I see," James White said. "People *will* leave things till just before the weekend—I can't understand it. What have you got for me, Humphrey?"

Grant settled his long body into a chair. "Report in from Hickling in Washington," he said. "I put it on your desk." He settled down to wait while his Chief found the papers and began to read them. Grant was always in the office by eight thirty. He had the United States desk, and the previous day's telexes came direct to him. The brigadier put down the report.

"We've got to do something about this," he said. "The ambassador has coped with it remarkably well but it's got out of hand. If there's truth in what this damned woman says, we'd better find it out before our friends at Langley do."

"She drinks," Grant said, his narrow mouth tight with disapproval. "That makes it dangerous to believe a word of this."

"It's less dangerous than ignoring it," James White said. "Edward Fleming is one of the President's closest personal friends—he's just been made a personal advisor to the President. Any hint of unreliability, any breath of scandal—my dear Grant, Fleming is British-born: if he turned out to be a rotten egg it would seriously damage our relationship with the new administration. I saw the prime minister last week, and she said we had a closer tie with the United States than at any time since the war. She never says anything without a motive, that woman. The message was loud and clear. No meddling in American spheres of influence, no rivalry of any kind. If she'd known about this—" he tapped the report "—she'd have thrown a blue fit. Here's the English wife of one of their top men, going to the British ambassador and accusing her husband of trying to kill her. And of being a Russian agent!" He paused and Grant waited. "If there's any truth in it, we have to deal with it quickly and quietly. Better for us to go to the CIA and tell them Fleming is not to be trusted, than have them find out first."

"We might even have to deal with him ourselves," Grant murmured. "Without telling anyone."

"We might indeed," James White agreed softly. "Depending upon what we discover. And I have a feeling—" his cigarette waved to and fro, sketching an imponderable "—I have a feeling that there *is* something to discover. We have a new man in Moscow. We don't know his signature yet; it's possible that we're seeing it for the first time in this business. The key is that damned woman. Our friend Neil Browning has been chosen to look after her, I see. Well, he won't unlock the puzzle for us. We need an expert for this, Humphrey. Someone who could get a hold on Mrs. Fleming without causing any comment. Someone she'd trust. I was reading through the whole file the other day and I noticed something quite extraordinary. And quite fortuitous." He pressed the switch on his intercom and said to his secretary, "Phyllis, get them to send up Mrs. Elizabeth Fleming's file, will you, please? And we might have some coffee."

Ten minutes later they had finished their coffee, and James White handed the slim beige folder to Grant. The dossier gave the subject's parentage, place of birth, education, and early activities before her first marriage to an Englishman who was now senior partner in a Merchant Bank. Both parents were killed in a plane crash in Kenya soon after the wedding. Beside these facts a name and a few words had been penciled in.

Grant read them and looked up sharply. "Davina! Good Lord!"

"Yes," his Chief nodded. "Amazing coincidence, isn't it. They were at school together. She would be the ideal person to take this on."

Grant shook his head. "She wouldn't lift a finger to help us," he said. "Kidson says she's just as bitter as ever."

"I know," James White said. "I've talked to him about it. He and her sister tried to reason with her, but she wouldn't listen. Which is understandable in the circumstances. She had a terrible shock. These things take time. She's had a year. The wound must have begun to heal, at least."

"I doubt it," Grant said. He didn't like women, but he had been forced into a grudging admiration for his colleague Davina Graham. "She'll never come back to the service," he said.

"She's a very rational person," James White said. "Perspective must have crept in by now. We need her, Humphrey. We need her to go to Washington and find out exactly what the score is. And I think I know how to persuade her. I'm going down to Marchwood tomorrow."

Grant stood up. "I don't think you'll succeed," he said.

White smiled his empty smile. "I have to succeed. No matter how I do it, we've got to have Davina back. Otherwise this Fleming affair is going to blow up in our faces."

Grant was at the door when he hesitated and turned back. "After what's happened, how do we know we can trust her?"

"That is a point, Humphrey," the brigadier replied. "Just bear it in mind."

* * *

Davina had been dreading the spring. When she came to Marchwood in the winter, the chill bleakness of the Wiltshire countryside matched the emptiness of her mind and heart. She grieved in harmony with nature, when all living things seemed dead. Now, with the daffodils blazing in the garden and the trees glorious in their new leaf, she could see Ivan Sasanov everywhere. She heard his step on the stair, saw his shadow in the garden, woke from her uneasy sleep to grope for him in her bed and find her face wet with tears. They had come there in the spring, four years ago, adversaries who had left the old house as lovers. They had shared her narrow bed in the room she had used as a child, and she had discovered for the first time in her life what love was like. Four years ago, at the same time as the countryside burgeoned into life and beauty, Davina had achieved the full dimension of being loved.

She was sitting by the window in the drawing room, a popular novel unopened on her knee, looking out into the garden and seeing nothing but Ivan. Ivan laughing at her, Ivan goading her into a quarrel when he was bored in those early days of their relationship. Ivan brusque in his desire for her, gentle and fond in their companionship. And then the final memory of him, the feel of the dying body in her arms, the last whisper of her name. She got up, letting the novel fall to the floor. It was her mother's idea that she should read; she brought back the latest fiction from the public library, and Davina pretended to read because she could retreat upstairs on the pretext of finishing the books in peace. Her parents had been very thoughtful, very sympathetic; she was grateful to them both, but it was more politeness than deep feeling. They were kind and doing their best to help her "get over it," as her father phrased it, when she first came home.

"You'll get over it, my dear. It's been a terrible shock and these things take time. But I promise you, you'll get over it."

She had heard herself saying cruel, wounding things in reply. "You make it sound like measles—his blood was all over my clothes." And then the helpless, hopeless crying, and her mother taking her in her arms as if she were a child, comforting, murmuring words that had no sense, but a soothing sound. A year ago, and the spring was mocking her with memories. It had been high summer in Australia when he died.

And now James White was coming down to Marchwood.

"I won't see him," she told her father. Captain Graham had learned certain lessons in respect of his elder daughter. He applied one of them then.

"You can't run away, my dear. It's purely social; we've invited him to lunch. Avoid him by all means if you can't face it, but I think you should."

"All right," Davina said. "I'll be here. But I hope he doesn't mention Ivan. Otherwise you'll all wish I'd stayed upstairs."

She watched James White through lunch. They were marvelous, she thought bitterly, exchanging small talk with that earnestness so peculiar to the English, as if the weather or the traffic encountered out of London really mattered. Manners glossed lightly over the ugly things like violent death and an empty life; they veiled the wounds no one wanted to admit existed, because then there would be reproaches, explanations.

James White didn't alter; his hair was no grayer, there were no fresh lines on the face; it looked as pink-skinned and healthy as it was when he said goodbye to her and Sasanov when they left for Perth in Western Australia. "Good luck to both of you. Enjoy your new life. And don't worry. We'll be looking after you."

Davina picked at her food, refused wine, and only answered if she was spoken to directly. She noted at the end that there were little lines of strain around her mother's mouth, and felt sorry for her.

Her father was overreacting to her frigid silence by talking louder and faster than usual. She saw the brigadier glance at her from time to time, the blue eyes always benign and slightly quizzical, like a fond uncle examining a difficult child. She met that glance once with a look of such contempt that he turned away. Her mother got up and said, "Davina and I will have coffee on the terrace; James, you and Fergus come and join us when you're ready."

It was warm outside; the terrace faced west and the afternoon sun was beating down on the mellow red brick; forests of daffodils and narcissi nodded their white-and-gold heads to the tune of a gentle breeze.

"Davina, darling," Mrs. Graham said, "try not to be so angry—James was terribly upset too, you know."

Davina didn't look up. "Like hell he was," she said. "You sit down, Mother. I'll bring the coffee out."

Her mother was not on the terrace when she came back with the tray. The brigadier got up from the garden chair. "Let me take that, Davina. Please sit down. I've asked your parents to leave us alone for a few minutes."

She stood without moving. "I've got nothing to say to you. I've been reasonably polite to you for their sakes. But I'm not going to talk to you alone. Unless you want me to tell you what I think of you."

"If it will make you feel any better," he said calmly. He sat down and poured out two cups of coffee.

He saw the anger in her face, and the sudden flush of color. It made her look younger, less drawn.

"All right," she said. "Perhaps it'll make *you* feel better to be told what a swine you are. A liar and a cheat, who took everything from Ivan and then just dumped him when you'd got all you could out of him. What was it you promised when we flew to Australia? 'Don't worry, we'll be looking after you'—"

She was beginning to shake as the words came rushing out. "You bloody well looked after him all right, didn't you? They put a bomb in the car and blew his legs off."

"Davina." He got up and she felt his hand on her shoulder; she pulled away from him. "I don't want your Judas touch." She almost spat the words at him and then she started to cry. She covered her face with her hands. She hadn't cried like that for a long time.

She heard the brigadier's voice. "We looked after him as well as he would let us," he said. "For three years. We kept them off for three years. But we couldn't protect him properly. You knew that, and so did he. He wouldn't live the kind of life that would have guaranteed his safety." She raised her head and wiped away the blinding tears.

"You didn't try," she said. "You knew he wouldn't stay shut up in some bloody compound with guards round the place—you knew he needed his freedom. You just didn't give a damn whether they caught up with him or not!"

"That isn't true," he said quietly. "I liked and respected Ivan Sasanov; more than anyone who came over to us before or since. And whether you believe it or not, I wanted you both to be happy. But I knew that if he insisted on living on the outside, sooner or later someone would pick up the scent and the KGB would come after him. You were lucky, Davina, that you were able to have three years together. And lucky not to have been in the car with him. I don't suppose you'll agree with me, but it's true."

"No," she said, "I don't agree with you. I lost the baby, I lost Ivan. I've got nothing in the world to live for now."

"You could have," he remarked. "Here, use my handkerchief and drink that coffee. Listen to me for a few minutes. It won't cost you anything and it might help you. How would you like to come back to work for the Office?"

He was unprepared for her laughter. She stared at him, holding the crumpled handkerchief in one hand, and laughed out loud.

"Work for you? So that's why you're here! You've got some dirty job in mind and you think you'll come down here and soft-soap me into doing it! Well, I'll tell you, Brigadier, I'll see you and your Office in hell first!" She dropped the handkerchief on the table in front of him.

"I'm afraid you've had a wasted journey," she said. "I'll go and call my mother and father. They can finish entertaining you."

James White didn't move. He said quietly, "We got the man who killed Sasanov."

She froze, half out of her chair. "You've caught him?"

"About three months ago. He was a Center-trained professional and normally they're hard cases. They don't break easily. But this chap decided to save his skin. The Australians were going to charge him with murder; he thought it better to cooperate with us and come to England. He gave us his controller in Sydney and from him the trail led back to Moscow. Right back to the man who directed the search for Sasanov and organized his assassination. A man of great patience and determination. Would you like to know who he is?"

There was not a sound around them; the breeze had dropped and the ranks of flowers were still as guardsmen. "Who?"

"Igor Tatischev," the brigadier said. "Now renamed Borisov. The new director of state security and head of the KGB. He was concerned with your arrest in Russia, I'm sure you remember the name."

"I remember," she said.

"The old director, Kaledin, promoted him after that. He was in line for the top job when Kaledin retired. The assassination of your husband was his chosen target. The damage Sasanov had done to Soviet plans rankled bitterly with the Politburo. They wanted him punished, and Borisov gave them his head—metaphorically speaking." He ignored the blazing look she gave him. He went on in the same casual tone.

"His reward was Kaledin's job and a seat on the Politburo. I put it to you, Davina, if you work for me, you are working against him. Whatever you feel about my responsibility for what happened, and it's not quite fair, the man sitting in the KGB director's chair is the man who killed Sasanov as surely as if he'd set the bomb himself—

I thought you might like to avenge your husband's death. And the loss of your child. Think it over. I'll go and find your parents, I want a chat with Fergus before I go."

"Wait a minute," Davina stood up. "I'll call them for you." She paused, one hand on the back of the garden chair, her face as white as the white narcissi that were her mother's pride in the garden.

"There aren't any holds barred with you, are there? You'd say or do anything to get your way. My husband and my child. You don't see how I could refuse, do you?"

"Oh, no doubt you can. Perhaps you will. Perhaps your spleen against me is greater than your other feelings. I don't mind that, but I do believe that Tatischev is going to prove a very dangerous opponent. I think there's a real chance that he's set up a key man in America as part of a Soviet operation. It so happens that you're in a unique position to find out, and stop him. As I said, my dear, think it over. If I don't hear from you by tomorrow I'll know you've decided to sit here and feel sorry for yourself. Ah—there's your father! Fergus, come and have a chat for a minute. I've got to go back to London soon. The traffic gets impossible after four o'clock."

Captain Graham walked to the car with his old friend James White. It had taken him a long time to forgive White for involving Davina in the dangerous enterprise in Russia four years before.

He had never understood her love for the Russian defector. He hadn't understood how she could go into Russia and risk her life on the man's behalf. When they left England to live in Australia he had sincerely wished them happiness, but he still hadn't understood his daughter and he never would.

He was grateful to James White for trying to help her return to normal. "It's good of you," he said. "Betty and I really appreciate what you're trying to do for Davy. She needs to pull herself together, but one can't say that, of course. She's very difficult to talk to, even now. I just hope she takes this job."

James White nodded. He placed his hand on the captain's shoulder for a moment. "I hope so too," he said. "Washington's a very social place. She'd meet a lot of new people, and the job is—well, it's just keeping an eye on the domestic situation. This chap's wife has been ill and can't cope with all the entertaining. It would be just what Davina needs to put all this behind her. And Washington is full of attractive men. Don't let her feel she's being pushed. But encourage her, if she talks to you about it."

"Oh, we will, we certainly will. By the way, did we tell you we're going to be grandparents any minute? Charlie's baby is just about due—" Fergus laughed and his face lit up as he spoke of his second daughter. "It'll be late, of course; Charlie's never been on time in her life. She's very happy, I must say. John seems to be absolutely the right person for her."

"Yes." The brigadier smiled. "It's a good marriage, from all I hear. I never thought she'd take a middle-aged bachelor like Kidson. Such a beautiful girl—all the more power to him to have got her!"

"And held on to her," the captain said. "She settled down with him like a lamb. I can't wait to see the baby. Goodbye, James, mustn't keep you any more. Lovely to see you. And thanks again for thinking of Davy."

"Not at all." The brigadier climbed into his car. "We always look after our own." He waved, wound up the window and set off down the drive.

Davina woke while it was still dark. She had slept badly, waking with a pounding heart and the cold sweat of anxiety. She got up, pulled back the curtains and saw the faint rim of crimson on the horizon that presaged the dawn. She dressed and went downstairs, taking care to be quiet. Her mother was a light sleeper, and that evening she had looked tense and tired. Nothing was said about James White's visit. They watched television, had dinner, and her

father settled down to read while Betty Graham worked on her embroidery. Davina had gone upstairs early, and the house was in darkness by eleven o'clock.

She drank a cup of coffee in the kitchen, then pulled on an anorak against the morning chill. She knew where she was going; she didn't question the impulse; she had learned enough about herself in the last five years to let instinct have its way at times. Ivan had taught her that; she was always remembering things he had said. Odd remarks would float back to her, and sometimes they made her smile. "Stop rationalizing everything. Use your intuition—it's not to be despised." And intuition sent her out that morning in the predawn darkness, into her car and off on the deserted road to Stonehenge.

The vast plain was empty; when she began to walk towards the circle of great stones the wind tore at her in gusts. The sky was like an artist's palette, rioting with color. Davina watched as the sun rose in triumph, the rays breaking over the horizon and striking the center of the sacrificial altar stone.

They had come here together, a couple of the tourists shuffling round the barrier of ropes; they were not lovers then, but soon to be, though neither of them knew it.

She felt as close to him at that moment as if he were still alive and would suddenly put his arm around her. The wind dropped and the sky was washed clear of strident reds and mauves and glowed serenely blue in the new morning. And there Davina asked the question of herself. Should she go back and accept the brigadier's challenge? Would Ivan want to be avenged?

She knew the answer as clearly as if he were beside her and had spoken. Revenge was sterile. The brigadier had made a mistake when he suggested that as a motive. But Ivan had given his life to frustrate the evil that was destroying human dignity and freedom. It had not been a vain sacrifice. He had done the Russians and their system incalculable damage. If she went back to work, it must be with the same objective. To frustrate and defeat the system that

had claimed so many lives, besides Sasanov's. To battle with his enemies, for his sake.

She turned away from the ring of stones. He had bought a postcard of them from the little gift shop. That postcard went all the way to Russia to his wife. She had died peacefully in a Moscow clinic, and then Davina and he had married in Australia. They wanted children. In the aftermath of shock and grief she had miscarried. The loss was only a part of that other, greater loss. There was no point in thinking about it.

She drove back to find the household awake, her mother in the kitchen making breakfast, her father running the bath upstairs. Like all old houses Marchwood had vociferous plumbing.

"Darling," Betty Graham said, "where on earth have you been? Out at this hour."

Davina kissed her lightly on the cheek. She wasn't a demonstrative person, and such tokens of affection were rare. "I woke early," she said, "so I took myself off to watch the dawn. Here, I'll make the coffee for you. Why don't you have breakfast in bed sometimes, Mother? You're always running after other people."

"I enjoy it," her mother said. "I'm good at gardening and I'm good at looking after people. I'm afraid it would sound pretty dreary to all those bustling ladies in women's lib. But it's my contribution and I like doing it. Oh, Davy, mind the toast, it's burning—I'll have to get a new toaster, that thing burns the minute you take your eyes off it."

"You've been saying that for the last two years," Davina reminded her. "I'll get you one as a present. A going-away present."

Betty Graham turned round quickly. She was a woman who disliked secrets, and pretending that James White hadn't told them anything made her uncomfortable.

"Going away? Do you mean you're going to take that job James talked about?"

Davina nodded. He wouldn't have told them the truth. Whatever the lie was, she would support it. And typically, it would put him, the old family friend, in a good light. "I thought about it," she said. "And I felt I should pull myself together and get on with life. Ivan wouldn't want me to sit around battening on you and Father any longer. You've been wonderful, seeing me through the last six months. I couldn't have survived without you. But I'm going to take this job and see how it works out."

"I'm so glad," Betty Graham's smile was warm. "I've been so worried about you, Davy. I know how much you've suffered over all this, and I'm not very good at talking about things. Neither is your father. But we just hoped being here would help you. We do love you very much, you know."

"I know," Davina said. "Now don't go on like that or I'll make an idiot of myself and start crying. You make some more toast and I'll call Father. I'll ring the brigadier this morning."

Their conversation was brief.

"I've thought it over," Davina said. "I'd like to come and see you."

"Good." His voice was brisk. "Come up this morning and I'll give you lunch."

"I don't want lunch," Davina said.

"I don't want you being seen near the Office," he answered. "Rules Restaurant, one o'clock. I'll look forward to it. Goodbye."

Elizabeth Fleming looked at herself in the mirror. The light was harsh, rows of bulbs surrounded the glass, as in a theatrical dressing room. They had been installed when she first came to Washington. In those days her face could bear the merciless illumination of two hundred and forty watts.

One pale hand, ornamented with long painted nails, smoothed the hair back from her face. "Oh, God," she said to her reflection. "You look like death warmed up." On an impulse she stuck her tongue out; it was coated with the aftermath of drink and chain smoking the night before. She turned her back on herself with disgust. "You bloody fool," she said to herself. "You got pissed again, didn't you? Eh? All the good resolutions gone down the drain. You look a hag, you know that?" There was no answer to the question. She was still a little drunk; it was a sure sign when she talked to herself out loud. In the bedroom next door her husband heard her, and glanced towards the locked bathroom.

She had been very drunk the night before. He had brought her home before the party ended and undressed her and put her to bed. She was fuddled and thought he was going to make love to her. He left her mouthing and reaching for him and slept in his dressing room.

She opened the bathroom and stood there, draped with five hundred dollars' worth of silk chiffon negligee, and started to shake.

"Eddie? I didn't know you were there—what time is it? I can't find my watch."

"It's nine thirty. Your watch is on the dressing table."

"Why aren't you at the office? Aren't you going to be very late?" There was a shadow in her eyes, a shift of fear that was hidden by her forced smile.

"It's Saturday," Edward Fleming said. "I don't go to the office on weekends."

"Of course, how silly of me. I've lost a day, that's all. Lose a day, gain a friend, haven't you heard that, darling?"

"No," he said, "I can't say I have. Maybe it should be gain a lover."

She took a few steps towards him. They were not quite steady. "Don't say things like that to me," she said. "Please. I don't have a lover. You're the only one I want—last night I thought . . ."

"You thought wrong," her husband said. "I took your clothes off because I didn't want to leave you sleeping in them all night. You were too drunk to undress yourself. You're still drunk, Elizabeth. I'm going to play golf. Try and sober up by the time I come back."

He was a big man, broad-shouldered, very trim and fit. His step was surprisingly quiet. He often came into a room and stood there without her having heard him. When he went out of the door she stood for a moment, one hand groping instinctively for something to hold on to. It dropped back to her side, and her fingers fastened on the filmy material and knotted it viciously. "You bastard," she said. "I'll be sober all right. Don't you worry about that. Go and play your fucking golf . . . I don't care. I don't care about anything." She collapsed on the bed among the crumpled pillows. Her head ached, and there was enough alcohol left in her blood to lull her back into a short sleep.

When she woke it was past eleven o'clock. She rang for her maid, who came up with a tray of coffee and toast. She was a dignified colored woman and she had been in service to senior State Department officials since she was a girl. She wished Mrs. Fleming good morning, settled the tray in front of her, and asked if she would like the morning papers brought up. There was no expression on her face or in her eyes, however hard Elizabeth tried to find one. Neither contempt nor curiosity. Never familiarity. She might work for whites, but she didn't intend to get friendly with them.

It was near lunchtime when Elizabeth came downstairs. She wore a cream linen dress and her blonde hair was brushed back into a coil behind her ears. Her face was heavily made up, and the first impression was very effective. She had lunch by herself in the handsome green-and-white dining room where they entertained, and afterwards curled up like a cat on one of the sofas in the sitting room. She drank a cup of black coffee, smoked three cigarettes while she flipped through the pages of the *Washington Post*, without reading more than a headline or a word here and there, and then threw the paper on the floor. She looked at her watch. He must be playing after lunch. Golf, tennis, racquets; he had stopped jogging when some clever-dick doctor discovered that it was a strain on the heart. He looked so young and well kept. The All-American Male, hero of a hundred thousand macho ads for cigarettes and drink and fast cars and sex. He wouldn't be back till six. She had three hours. She reached for the telephone, pushed the button for an outside line, and dialed the British embassy. Neil said she could always reach him there, day or night, if she needed him. She'd drunk lemonade at lunch and she was quite sober. Her hands were shaking, but that was normal now. And she was frightened, which was also normal.

Neil was at home watching afternoon sports on TV when the embassy switched the call through to him. The girl watching with him switched off the sound. He gazed at the silent-movie effect on the screen while he talked. She had heard similar conversations before and she knew her man too well to be jealous.

"Don't worry," he was saying. "No, listen, it's quite all right, I'm not doing anything—I'll come round in the car and pick you up. We can come back here, or just drive around for a while. I'll be with you in about twenty minutes. And don't worry. 'Bye."

He put the receiver back. "I'm sorry, darling," he said. "Duty calls."

"How long will you be?"

"A couple of hours. She's not in too bad a state, but I know that hysterical undertone. Listen, I'm sorry, but in case I have to bring her back here?"

"I know." His girl had a mischievous smile. "Can I keep out of the way while Mrs. Fleming weeps on your shoulder, or whatever she does? I can, but you'd better call me when she's gone. And you'd better be specially nice to me to make up for having the afternoon screwed up!"

He came and kissed her. "I will, don't worry. I wish to God they'd give her to someone else to look after. It's getting on my nerves listening to the same old rubbish over and over again. If I was Fleming I'd shove her into a home!"

He picked Elizabeth Fleming up at 3:37 exactly. Two separate surveillance reports noted the time of his arrival and her leaving in his car. One was filed in the KGB security section of the Soviet embassy at 1125 Sixteenth Street, and the second came through on the CIA computer at Langley.

"I remember her only too well," Davina said. James White was sipping a brandy and he paused to look at her over the glass.

"That sounds ominous. Didn't you like her?"

"I loathed her."

"Oh. That's a pity. Why?"

Davina said calmly, " Because she was the most conceited, empty-headed, self-centered girl in the whole school. We were not only in the same year but in the same house; we shared a dormitory for two terms and they were the most miserable times I spent at Highfields."

"She doesn't sound like a bully," he remarked. "Why were you so affected by her?"

She hesitated, lit a cigarette. Then she frowned slightly. "She wasn't a bully. She was just too pretty and sweet for words and everyone adored her, from the headmistress down. If she came back with her hair cut short, everyone copied it. People copied her handwriting, even, trying to be like her. She never did a damned thing for herself if she could get somebody else to do it for her. And they always did."

"Except you," he prompted gently.

"Yes, except me. I knew she despised me because I was plain and a bookworm and rotten at games. She was only nice to me when she wanted something, and I knew it. I wouldn't pander to her, and consequently everyone said I was jealous and turned against me."

"Wasn't it partly true?"

"Of course it was," Davina said. "I wouldn't have liked Liz Fleming if she'd been a worthwhile person. I had my beautiful darling sister putting me in the shade at home, and Liz doing the same at school. I met her twice afterwards; once at a party in London, where she was a huge success, with the men dancing attendance on her. And once at London airport. I was meeting someone coming in from the States soon after I joined the Office. There she was in a bloody great mink coat looking like Julie Christie, sweeping out of the VIP lounge. That must have been about eight years ago. She was quite friendly with my sister at one time. I can't imagine that she's in any kind of trouble. Not the kind that I could help, anyway."

"She has told our ambassador in Washington that she's in very great trouble," James White answered. "She alarmed him considerably and he got in touch with us at once. I advised him to calm her down and put an embassy official in charge of her for the time being, till we could sort something out. I gather she drinks—that's a problem, of course."

"I'm surprised to hear it. She must have changed a lot."

"Apparently Fleming knows but has done nothing about it. Which is understandable in the circumstances. He was just about to be given a top job in the new administration, and he couldn't afford a divorce or a scandal at that time. That's how it appears, anyway."

"What did she say to the ambassador?" Davina asked. "What sort of trouble would be his concern, for heaven's sake?"

"Our sort of trouble," James White said quietly. "She arrived at the ambassador's residence in a near-hysterical state, saying her husband had tried to murder her the night before. Naturally, the ambassador suggested the police. Her reply had a nasty ring of truth in it. Her husband is a powerful man, close to the President, with powerful friends. The police could be squared. And then came the punch line. The reason Fleming had tried to kill her was that she had discovered that he was passing information to the Russians."

"Trouble is hardly the word for it! My God!"

"Exactly. So you see why the ambassador was so disturbed. Of course he was in a difficult position. There was this woman, ranting and raving about murder attempts and Russian spies, and claiming sanctuary in the embassy! He coped very well indeed. He persuaded her to go back home that evening and he got in touch with me immediately. You can see the implications, if she's telling the truth."

"It'd blow a hole in the new administration as big as Watergate!"

"And we'd fall right into it," he remarked. "Fleming is British-born. Our enemies on Capitol Hill would make plenty of that connection. He's been publicly pro-British and he's regarded as a very good friend in a very high place. That's why we've got to be extremely careful not to jump to conclusions about Mrs. Fleming and her allegations."

"Meaning you don't believe them?"

"I don't know," he said. "I just hope that Elizabeth Fleming is proved to be lying or mistaken. But we have to find out. You are the person who can do it, my dear. You're the kind, sympathetic friend who grew up with her. If she's genuine, she'll clutch at you for support. If she's lying, we'll soon know."

"No, I'm sorry, Brigadier, that won't do. I don't believe in leopards changing spots. She hasn't the intelligence or the temperament to get mixed up in anything more subversive than a beauty secret!"

"You don't have to be intelligent," he countered. "A lot of stupid people are spies. A lot of frightened people, too. She's an alcoholic, she may have left herself open to blackmail. It wouldn't be the first time Moscow Center used a woman to ruin a man's reputation. If I send you to Washington you've got to have an open mind."

"If she's right," Davina said after a pause, "then Tatischev is running Fleming. He must be, he's at such a high level. She could be in real danger if she's found him out and they know she's talked."

"And so could you when they see you together. But only if she's telling the truth. You don't object to being a decoy duck, I hope?"

"If I get flattened by a runaway truck, you'll know Fleming's working for the KGB, thanks very much."

He smiled at her. "Equally, if this *is* a hysterical fantasy, nobody will take the slightest notice of you." He waited, his thick white eyebrows raised a little, questioning her courage.

"When do I leave?" Davina said.

They faced each other across the table; the pretense was over and they were adversaries. James White accepted the challenge.

"You're doing this for Sasanov," he stated.

"As long as you don't think I'm doing it for you."

"As you like," he said. He beckoned to the waiter for the bill. "Could you be ready to leave at the end of this week?"

He ignored the bleakness in her face when she replied, "I can go tomorrow. I've nothing to keep me."

"The end of next week will do," he said pleasantly. "Why don't you go and do some shopping? Washington is quite hot at this time of year. The department will pay."

"I don't need any summer clothes," Davina said. "Australia was hotter than Washington. And if I did, I'd prefer to pay for them myself. Thank you for lunch."

"Thank you for coming," he said. "We have someone else going out at the same time. A Major Lomax—he'll come down to Marchwood and bring you the ticket and details and introduce himself . . . Ah, there's a taxi—of course, you've got a car, haven't you, so you don't need a lift. Safe journey. Give Betty and Fergus my best."

"You're sure you're not too tired?" John Kidson held his wife's hand and gazed anxiously at her. Charlie laughed. "Not a bit; stop fussing, darling. I'm not ill, I've just had a baby!"

She didn't look tired; he thought she was even more beautiful after giving birth, if that were possible. Her long red hair was tied back with a ribbon, her eyes and skin shone with health, and she radiated the smug contentment of the new mother. The child was a boy, born after an easy labor the day before. John Kidson was so happy he didn't know how to cope with it. He had filled the hospital room with out-of-season roses, and rung everyone he could think of to tell them the news. He had spent more money than he could afford to on a gold bracelet for Charlie, set with little sapphires. Blue for a boy. She had surprised and delighted him by bursting into tears and saying it was the most precious thing she owned. And then she began to smile and hug him and he felt near to crying himself.

She held on to his hand and squeezed. It really was extraordinary how happy she was with him. Nobody had given the marriage a chance at first. Two husbands behind her, fifteen years younger than John, a spoiled young woman armored with devastating good looks, and doting parents to support every folly she committed. People had been unkind, and the Grahams themselves had been full of doubts. They were all proved wrong. Much as he loved her, John Kidson was not a slave to his wife. He was too shrewd to give way to his inclination to spoil and pamper her. He gave her the security she had been seeking unconsciously all her life. Captain Graham finally lost his younger daughter to another man, and the wayward Charlie surprised them all by settling down to married life and starting a family.

She lay back on her pillows.

"He's such a lovely baby," she sighed. "I always thought they were hideous little crinkled monsters but, you know, darling, I think he's beautiful! Do you think he's beautiful?"

"Yes, in spite of being a hideous little crinkled monster—I'm only teasing, sweetheart. He's a cracking little boy. Everyone's thrilled with him."

"I know," she said. "Mummy and Daddy were delighted, weren't they—and poor Davina—I couldn't look at her to start with.

She was so good about it, wasn't she? It must have been awful for her, seeing our baby when she'd lost her own. I didn't make too much of it, did I?"

"No, you didn't," he assured her. "She was all right. She was very happy for you, I could see that."

"We're better friends now than we ever were," Charlie said. "We'll never be close, but at least we like each other. I hope this Washington job works out for her. She looks so drained, as if there was nothing inside her." She turned her head away because her eyes suddenly filled with tears. "I wish she was happy," she said. "Do you think she'll ever get over him?"

"I don't know," Kidson answered. "Some people only love once in their lives. But she's young and time heals. Getting back to work will help."

"It isn't dangerous, is it—this Washington job?"

"It shouldn't be. Anyway the Chief is sending out a minder. Davina will be all right with him around."

"Who is it?" Charlie asked. "Anyone I know?"

"No, darling. Ex-major in the SAS. Very tough and very experienced. He joined us after leaving the army. I don't know what his role is going to be in the long term; at the moment he's going to Washington on the embassy staff. I met him a couple of times. I don't think he and Davina will get on. I said so, but you know the Chief—he just sits there and smiles and doesn't take a damn bit of notice if it doesn't suit him. Anyway, she couldn't have a better back-up than this fellow, if there is any trouble. I'm going to go home now, darling, and let you have a sleep. I'll be back this evening. Anything you want me to bring you?"

She smiled lazily at him. "The latest *Harper's* and *Queen*," she said. "And the *Nursery World*." They both laughed and he blew her a kiss as he went out.

"My name," the man said, "is Lomax. Colin Lomax."

They shook hands in the hall at Marchwood. He was slightly

above average height, dressed in a sweater and faded jeans. He didn't look like a major in anybody's army. He could have come from anywhere and been anything, except that when he spoke it was with an unmistakable Scottish burr. He had short fair hair and gray eyes, a hard mouth that looked uncomfortable smiling. He wore his aggressiveness like after-shave. It hung in the air when he entered the hall, and she was instantly antagonized.

"Do come in," she said, and it wasn't a warm invitation. They went into her father's study. He sat in an armchair, very casually, with his arm draped across the back, and stared at her. It wasn't flattering.

"I've got a lot of bumf for you," he said. "I've left it in the car."

"Then perhaps you'd like to go and get it," Davina said. He didn't move.

"Do you know Washington well?" The question caught her unawares.

"I've never been there."

"I have. I hated the place."

"That's hardly a good way to start your appointment," she said coldly. "Major Lomax, I'd be delighted to offer you a drink or anything else you'd like, but I don't think you should leave confidential papers lying in your car. Would you please get them?"

He got up very slowly. "Mr. Lomax, if you don't mind. I'm a civilian now. If you think your papers are going to be pinched, Miss Graham, right outside your front door—I'll go and get them—I'd like a whisky and water."

He was back very quickly. He dropped the envelope on her lap. She set it aside and then got up to pour him a whisky. She could feel him watching her to see if she poured a mean measure. Irritation made her double the quantity. He half lifted himself out of the chair to take the glass, and gave her his ill-fitting smile. "That's a healthy drop. I haven't had a drink like that since I left Ireland. Thanks."

"When are you going to Washington?" she asked him. The silence was becoming awkward.

"At the end of the week. Same flight as you."

"You're going to the embassy, aren't you?"

"I'll be working in the visa section, of all the godawful postings."

Davina stood up. "Mr. Lomax," she said. "Thank you for bringing me the papers. Now, I've got to read them and do some work. Goodnight."

He glanced up quickly at her, and she saw an angry gleam in the light eyes. He drained the glass. "Thank you for the drink, Miss Graham. I'm sorry if I've delayed you."

"That's all right," she said. "I'll see you to the door. She walked out with him. It was past six and quite dark. He turned to her on the doorstep. "I'll meet you in the departure lounge on Friday."

"That won't be necessary, Mr. Lomax. I'd rather travel alone."

"I don't think it's necessary either. But those are my instructions. See you Friday." He loped off to his car, banged the door and revved up, scattering gravel as he drove away.

Davina shut herself in the study and began to read the long report on Elizabeth Fleming and her husband. It took over two hours to digest it, and by then she had completely forgotten the obnoxious Mr. Lomax. The most important file she left till last. It was the length of a long short story—the kind that used to be included in a Maugham collection. It was the novella of a man's professional life. The man who had hovered in the shadows during her own ordeal by terror in Russia, an influence without a face. The man whose calculated vengeance had caught up with Ivan Sasanov in a quiet residential street in Perth.

They had taken it for granted they were safe. Or at least she had. Ivan loved his freedom too much to exchange it for guaranteed safety. He knew his own people; he had taken a deliberate risk. But she hadn't known. She had lived her brief three years of happiness until the blast from the car bomb destroyed everything.

Igor Tatischev. To English ears it was a tongue-twisting name, soft-sounding. Now Borisov. He had changed it when he took Kaledin's place. Igor Borisov. She opened the file. It was compiled by the experts in the Russian Affairs section of the SIS. Everything known about the new chief of internal security in the Soviet Union had been collected, analyzed, and fed through the computers for cross-checking. He was fifty-one years old, born in a small town some eighty miles from Leningrad. His father was a doctor; his mother had trained as a dentist and worked part time in the local clinic caring for schoolchildren. He had a younger sister who was married, with two children, and lived in the Ukraine. Igor had been a promising student who was selected to go to the special college in Leningrad that trained recruits for the internal and external forces of the KGB. He had proved himself conscientious and able, and was heard of briefly in two overseas appointments, first in Ottawa, where he did a spell of duty as a military attaché, and the second time in Cairo, during Nasser's presidency. The name had been changed each time, but the photographs and personal data matched. In both postings he had been a desk operator, an administrator and a coordinator. He was not one of the socializing front men used to recruit agents or initiate blackmail. He had surfaced next in Moscow, working with Antonyii Volkov. His path had crossed Davina's indirectly, through Sasanov's persecuted family, and when she herself was arrested he had moved behind the scenes, acting for the director himself; Kaledin, close to retirement, a figure as powerful and as shrouded in legend as the fearful Beria and Shelepin.

The time passed and she sat on in the study, the fire dead in the grate, the ashtray spilling over. There were a few photographs of him taken years before. They showed a pleasant, round-faced man, fair-complexioned, with a snub-nosed, rather commonplace face. Nothing to give a clue to the personality that was so full of contradictions. He had been the right hand of the sadist Volkov; yet he had personally protected Ivan's sick wife. Fedya Sasanov had been the victim of his predecessor's illegal intrigues. Illness had been accelerated by her experiences in the Siberian transit camp. There she had become a secret Christian. The man who had become Borisov had been aware of her association with other Christians. He had allowed her the comfort of a priest when she was dying, and no action was taken against any of her friends. So there was a sense of justice; he must have a conscience and a moral code; she paused, confronted by shuddering personal memories of her own captivity.

She put the file aside; a cold sweat made her hands and face damp. She had trained herself not to think about that episode. The moment passed. She lit a cigarette, looked at her watch. It was past midnight. The study was chilly; its dead fire and stillness depressed her. She took the file into the cheerful kitchen, made herself coffee and settled down at the table to go on reading. Her mother's Labradors nosed round her knee; she patted them and they curled back in their baskets near the stove and went back to sleep.

This was the worst part, worse than the pang of terror associated with her own ordeal; this was the story of the systematic, detailed planning of Ivan Sasanov's assassination. They had looked for him in the United States; that occupied nearly two years. Then the hunt began in England. They had searched for clues in London among the safe houses and security flats and found nothing. Then they had moved in on Marchwood itself, where her unsuspecting parents lived, and in the debris of daily life in the household, Borisov's agent had found what they were looking for. He had gone through the dustbins before they were collected once a week. God knew who he was or how he slipped into the deserted backyard of the manor, but he had found a torn-up piece of envelope, addressed to Mrs. Graham in her handwriting. It had an Australian stamp in the top right-hand corner. She had signed for her belongings when she was arrested in Russia; the fragment of the envelope would have been fed into the Center computers and come back with the answer that the handwriting was the same.

Her parents had promised to burn any communication from her; they had grown lax as the time passed. Ironically, they probably would have destroyed the letter itself and merely torn up the envelope. So Borisov knew that Sasanov was in Australia. A continent so sparsely populated is an easy place to find a man in hiding.

There is a bush telegraph in the outback. The arrival of a stranger is known hundreds of miles away on the great sheep stations. A Russian could not settle there without attracting widespread notice. So they had concentrated on Sydney and Melbourne, Canberra and Perth. And in Perth they had found him, married and teaching political studies in the university under the Polish name of Pocklewski.

A top-grade Center killer had made the circuitous journey to Australia via Hong Kong.

Davina read what followed with every nerve end tuned to the agony of what was to come. They had been going out to a party that night. Normally sociable, Sasanov was tired and inclined to opt out. It was Davina, usually the shyer of the two, who persuaded him to go. She had become very fond of a fellow professor's wife, and she didn't want to disappoint her by not going to her party. Always indulgent to her, Sasanov had said, all right, they could leave early. As he went to the door, Davina said suddenly, if he was really tired—she could still ring up and make an excuse. He'd kissed her, and she could see the tender curve of his mouth when he released her. He wasn't tired. He was looking forward to the party. Would she please stop arguing?

It was the last time he ever kissed her. He went ahead to start the car, and she turned back to check that she had locked the back door. They were very security-conscious.

She dropped the file on the floor; one of the dogs woke and raised its head. She didn't need the nicely documented details of the horror that followed. The shattering noise, the splintering glass of windows bursting, her own wild scream and the desperate run to the front door, only to find it swinging on its broken hinges and the twisted, smoldering wreck of the car . . .

He wasn't dead. She had time to hold him in her arms and hear him speak. A whisper, distorted with the agony of his dying. Her name. And that was all. She didn't cry; her loss was beyond tears now. She just spoke his name aloud as he had whispered hers. "Ivan. My love."

And then in the silence of her own heart she made the promise. "I'll fight him every inch of the way. I'll get to him, as he got to you."

She bent down to pick up the file again and lit another cigarette. Kaledin had retired at the beginning of the year. He was old and plagued with heart trouble. His successor was chosen by the members of the Presidium of the Supreme Soviet; Igor Tatischev had become Borisov. He had moved into the office in the heart of the Kremlin itself, the center of a power so immense and so pervasive that only the supreme dictatorship of the party chairman could nullify it. He was comparatively young for such a post. Young and unknown. There was no pattern established by which his operations could be measured in terms of international espionage. Would he concentrate on terror, as his predecessor had done, training, financing and manipulating the Palestinians, the fanatics of the Red Brigade and their affiliates in Holland, Germany, and Ireland? Would his approach match the subtlety and patience of earlier directors, who had recruited from the intelligentsia of the West, content to wait for years till they came into use? The "mole" was a KGB concept, typifying the slow patience of the Slav, to whom time was as limitless as the plains of his homeland. Would Igor Borisov follow a hard or a soft line on the Jews in Russia and the small, courageous group of dissidents—would his weapon be the Lubyianka and the firing squad, or the white-coated torturers in the mental hospitals? The West had a new adversary; the unremarkable administrator whose last photograph was fifteen years old. Until he showed his style of doing battle, they were dueling in the dark.

She closed the file. It was one twenty in the morning. She didn't feel tired; she felt alert and excited. For the first time in a year the pall of apathy and depression had left her. She had something to live for; the void in her life was filled with a new purpose. Through her and her work, some part of Ivan Sasanov's spirit survived. She would prove to Igor Borisov one day that killing the man had not destroyed his ideals.

She switched off the light and went up to her room. For the first time since Ivan's death, she fell at once into a deep, peaceful sleep until the morning.

It was Friday morning when she saw Colin Lomax again; she had been so preoccupied that he had completely slipped her mind until she came through to the departure lounge and a man impeccably dressed in a dark suit and regimental tie, carrying a folded copy of *The Times*, came up to her and said, "Hello, Miss Graham." She said briefly, "Good morning," and turned away. When they boarded the big Pan Am jumbo he settled into the seat beside her. She gave him an unfriendly look. "Have you been told to follow me right through to Washington?"

"Yes." He buckled his seat belt. "Don't ask me why, I don't know. I'm just following orders. I'm a great man for orders, Miss Graham."

"I'm glad to hear it," she said. "I'm a great one for changing them, Mr. Lomax."

"That will suit me, Miss Graham."

She opened the novel she'd bought at the bookstall, and six hours later they landed at Dulles airport.

Sir Arthur Moore had held the Washington embassy post for two years. He was a slight, small man, with a shrewd face like a bird of prey, and bright brown eyes darting at people in a way that some found disconcerting. His manner was affable but sharp; the impression Davina gained on meeting him was that no fool would be suffered at all, let alone gladly. They shook hands; he offered her a glass of sherry, which she refused. Then they sat in his office for a while. He asked about the flight; they paid lip service to the conventions for a few minutes, and during that time they summed each other up. He was surprised to find her attractive. A good figure, unusual hair, like beech leaves with the gleam of red in it. He was fully aware of her record but he hadn't expected someone who looked so young.

"I had a long talk with the brigadier," he said. "I can only say how glad I am that you have come here to take Mrs. Fleming off our hands!"

"I'm going to try," Davina said. "I've read all the reports, but it would help me to hear exactly what happened when she came to see you."

He put down his glass of sherry as if he didn't like the taste.

"She turned up one Sunday morning and my wife saw her first. She was in a terrible state. By terrible, Miss Graham, I mean she was drunk and hysterical. We know the Flemings very well socially; I've had a lot to do with Edward on a professional level. We couldn't possibly turn her away. My wife was thoroughly alarmed, and I thought I had better see her and try to calm her down. I may add that her drinking has been an embarrassment to her wretched husband for some time. She behaved in the most extraordinary way. She asked for a drink, which I thought best to give her; then she burst into tears and said she needed my protection. She said she was in danger from her husband. I found the whole thing too distasteful for words—" he paused, and seeing something in Davina's face he added "—I'm not an unsympathetic person; nor, I trust, an inhumane one. But I found the whole performance repellent. I felt extremely sorry for Edward Fleming."

"You have a high opinion of him, then?" Davina asked.

"He's a most remarkable man. His business record is amazing even in this country where people can achieve so much so quickly. Politically he picked the winning side long before the so-called experts, myself among them, considered that the candidate had a chance. I admire brains, Miss Graham, and Edward has more than just that. He has drive, foresight, and considerable personal charm. I find him very likable. As you can gather, I found his wife quite the reverse."

"Yes," she said quietly. "I can appreciate that. She said her husband had tried to murder her and she asked for protection. I understand it was a form of asylum? Refuge in the embassy?"

"That's exactly right," he said. "She claimed that right as a British citizen. I'm afraid I told her not to be melodramatic." The bright eyes flashed at Davina. "Then she made this most disturbing accusation. I was extremely alarmed. I tried to question her, but she refused to elaborate. I remember her sitting there in our sitting room, slopping her whisky over the carpet and saying to me, 'I'm not saying any more. Your bloody embassies are full of spies. But he's on the other side. And he'll kill me because I know. Just like he killed his first wife!' "

"No wonder you were alarmed," Davina said slowly. "And that was all you could get out of her?"

"Yes," the ambassador answered. "I compromised. I got my wife to take her upstairs and put her to bed. Then I sent a telex to London. I was told on no account to keep her in the embassy or cause any scandal. It was up to me to persuade her to go home, and it was suggested that one of my young officers in the intelligence section, a chap called Neil Browning, should act as liaison. I thought it an odd suggestion, but apparently London knew she had a fancy for young men." He made a faint grimace. "By the afternoon she was sober enough to listen. I made a lot of promises, sent for Browning, who had been told what to do, and he took her back home. Since then he's been in constant touch, and I feel as if I've been sitting on a bomb with the fuse burning away. If this woman causes a scandal with security as the issue, it could damage the new administration very badly. My obvious duty was to inform the U.S. secretary of state of the accusation and let the Americans investigate if they chose. I didn't do so on direct orders from London, because Fleming was born in the United Kingdom. He became an American citizen twenty-two years ago."

"Ambassador," Davina asked quietly, "is there anything you can think of that could cast doubt on Edward Fleming's loyalty to the West? Has there ever been any whisper against him before this?"

"Nothing. The man's background was investigated by a Senate subcommittee before his appointment was confirmed. His first wife's death eighteen months ago was an accident. She was burned to death in a fire at their holiday house in Mexico. There's never been a breath of scandal about him, privately or professionally, so far as I know. And I know most things that happen in Washington."

"So you think Liz Fleming is lying, then?"

"Either lying or acting out some fantasy," he said. "I don't believe her, no. But what disturbs me is London's reaction. If there's no truth in it, why are you here, Miss Graham?"

Davina smiled slightly. "I'm here to find out if there *is* truth in it," she said. "The brigadier may want to clean up the mess himself, if it's a British one. If Fleming joined any subversive organization, it could have been before he became an American. At least that's my theory; I don't really know."

"Well, thank heavens you're here," he said again. "The less my embassy is involved in a thing like this, the happier I shall be. Get this woman off our hands and I'll be eternally grateful." He stood up to end the interview. He saw her to the front door and they shook hands. "If there's anything you need," he said, "just ask. But I'll rely on Peter Hickling for progress reports. It would only call attention to you if we were to single you out from other British visitors."

Davina took a cab to the Hicklings' apartment She felt suddenly very tired after the journey. Questions nagged at her. Why hadn't Elizabeth Fleming returned to England if she was afraid? Why was she still in Washington, unless it was part of James White's devious plans to keep her there? They talked about sitting on a scandal; grave-faced and indignant about the danger to Anglo-American relations and the new President's administration. The simplest solution was to remove the source of the scandal and then investigate behind the scenes.

There was more to this than James White had let her know when he issued the challenge to her at Marchwood. "I thought you might like to avenge your husband's death. And the loss of your child . . ." If Edward Fleming, personal advisor to the President, was working for the Russians, James White would sacrifice anything or anyone to catch him out. Including the wife who insisted that her life was in danger.

Davina had a headache; by the time she reached the Hicklings' apartment, she needed aspirin and privacy. She made an excuse about jet lag to Hickling's wife, Peggy, and retreated to her own room. There was a sharp tingling along her nerve ends that was familiar. She remembered the words of the witch in *Macbeth*, learned by heart when she and Elizabeth Fleming were at school. "By the pricking of my thumbs, something wicked this way comes." The last time she had felt that sense of premonition was five years ago, when she went on her mission to Russia.

Chapter Two

EDWARD FLEMING parked his car in the garage and sped up the steps to the front door; he had bought the elegant house in Georgetown as soon as he was told by the President that he had been selected for office in the new administration. He had been proud of the house and everything it symbolized.

Elizabeth had redecorated it, and it was exactly right. Not too ostentatious; everyone knew he could afford what he liked. The effect was understated and in harmony with its period and surroundings. At least she hadn't failed him in that. He opened the front door and saw the maid, Ellen, in the hall. "Good evening, Mr. Fleming. Mrs. Fleming is out. She said to tell you she'd be back in time for dinner."

Out. Out where and doing what? "Thank you, Ellen."

The grave dark face relaxed in a slight smile. She respected Edward Fleming. "There's ice in the living room; is there anything I can get you?"

"No thanks. I'll just take a shower first. It's been a busy day."

He took off his clothes, showered, and rubbed his lean body with a rough towel to stimulate circulation. He dressed in trousers, shirt, and sweater, moccasins on his bare feet. He had no plans for that evening, whatever his wife might have arranged. She couldn't endure a night spent quietly at home. She fidgeted and talked and found excuses to telephone people who could have been contacted during the day. And she drank, furtively, watching him to see if he was watching.

He went downstairs to the living room, which his wife insisted on calling the study, to the confusion of his fellow Americans. It was a pleasant, homely room, warm with russet browns and olive green. There was a fine Victorian painting of a Highland landscape over the fireplace; Elizabeth had given it to him as a wedding present. There was a large studio portrait of them on their wedding day, silver-framed and dominating his desk. He wished he could have thrown it on the fire. A vase of flowers and foliage was arranged on the coffee table; she was clever with flowers. He had been so proud of everything she did, the way she arranged the house, the perfectionism about her looks and her clothes. But now nothing could hide the puffy skin under the eyes or the sallowness of her complexion without its coat of make-up.

She had been a lovely fresh blonde when he first met her. So sweet-natured, so truly feminine, the kind of woman a man wanted to spoil and protect. She was on holiday in Mexico when he was there with his first wife, Raffaella, staying at their summer house in Cuernavaca. She had been divorced for three years; it seemed inconceivable to him that her husband could have preferred someone else, and left her for one of her best friends. Edward Fleming fell in love with her so quickly and completely that it made his marriage seem doubly miserable. Elizabeth was the total opposite of his wife. Or so it seemed. Within six weeks he was a widower; free from a woman he detested, free to remake his life and persuade his new love to share it with him.

Within three months of their marriage, he had found out that she was having an affair with a senior official in the State Department. She had admitted the one lapse with tears and pleas for forgiveness, but far worse was the addiction to drink, which only came to light when they were settled in Washington. He didn't discover it for some time. She was very cunning, pretending to drink mineral water; the first shock was when he sipped from her glass and found it was laced with vodka. He began to watch her and to recognize the signs when he came home in the evening. The higher pitch of her voice, the latent aggression in her manner and the tendency to lie about unimportant things. Her dislike of Ellen distressed him; so did her criticism of his friends. Reconciliations followed the rows but the breach between them widened as her drinking increased and the fear of disgrace began to haunt him. His love had changed to loathing by the end of their first year of marriage. He didn't want to sleep with her; he could hardly bear to sit in the room with her alone. And he never knew when one drink too many would tip her over the edge of acceptable behavior. His political star was rising; the Republican candidate had been elected and he was rewarding his supporters. Fleming saw his ambitions within reach and his wife as the only threat to them.

He was offered and accepted his job in the State Department. There were rumors circulating that he and Elizabeth were near to breaking up. He admitted to one or two intimates that he was considering a divorce and even the President was sympathetic. But nothing happened and their lives went on as before. Nobody would ever know about the night when he told her their marriage was over. That was when he learned he could never get away from her.

He heard the front door slam and her step on the marble-tiled floor. He tensed, waiting for the door to open. It stayed shut. She had gone upstairs to her room. He poured a second vodka, careful to keep the measure small, topped it with ice. She had spoiled his predinner drink for him as she had spoiled every other aspect of his private life. He kept watch on himself all the time now, limiting how much he drank, what he said and did. He never discussed his work or left papers lying loose. Maybe she wouldn't come down; maybe she'd stay upstairs, lying in the bath, pampering herself, drinking out of a toothglass from the bottle she kept hidden in the bedroom. He had smelled Sen-Sen on her breath so often that it made him sick.

He leaned back in his chair in the quiet room and closed his eyes. There was so much to think about, so many different lines of action to be reconciled, so many eyes upon him, watching and judging. At fifty-one he was several rungs up the ladder, ahead of older men of greater experience. He had everything to gain so long as he didn't miss his step. So long as that particularly fragile bauble, reputation, didn't show a flaw. There was no other city in the world where rumor fed upon itself so virulently. Whispers wiped out careers just as cholera destroyed its human victims. He had things to hide. The only person who could expose him was the woman he had married. An English rose, one sycophantic woman columnist had called her in an early interview.

"Hallo," his wife said. "You're not asleep, are you?"

It gave him a shock; he had wandered so far away in his mind from the house in Georgetown that he started and spilled his drink.

"Do you have to creep into a room like that?"

She closed the door. "You usually complain about me being noisy," she said. "You're the one with the cat's feet. Lucky vodka doesn't stain; I'll get a cloth."

"It's all right," he said. He rubbed the wet mark on his trousers with his handkerchief.

She sat down and gave him a nervous smile. He knew she had been to the British embassy, seeing the man Neil again. He was the latest.

"Had a busy day, darling?"

"Yes. Very busy."

"Who did you see? Did you see the President?"

"For a few minutes, yes."

"What did he say?"

"Nothing that would mean anything to you," he answered. "I can't talk about it, anyway. You know that."

"You never talk about anything anymore," she said. She sighed, and he knew that she was preparing herself and him for the usual ritual involving her predinner drinks. "I'm tired too," she said. "I could do with a sharpener." She got up and he heard the bottles chink and the ice rattle into the bottom of the glass. She sat down opposite him and said, "The Harrises are in town; they asked us to have dinner. I'd said I'd call them back."

"What Harrises? I don't know any."

"Yes, you do," she insisted. "New York—he runs an advertising agency and she was a top model. You remember them. They're great fun."

Edward Fleming looked at his wife and said, "You're right—we did meet them. I didn't like them. You can call back and say we're busy."

"Why?" she protested. "Why can't we go?" The level of the glass of whisky had fallen by half in less than a few minutes. "Why can't we ever go anywhere except with your awful, boring political friends? Don't you think I get sick of listening to the same old things over and over again—who's lobbying for who, who's making deals over what? Why can't we be like normal people and just go out and have some fun for a change?"

"Because we're not normal people," he said suddenly. "Your idea of fun is to go out and get drunk in some nightclub with a cheap little ad man from Madison Avenue and his boring, stupid wife! I'm not going out tonight. And neither are you."

She finished the whisky. "I am," she said. She went to the trolley and filled her glass again. She spoke behind his back. "I'm going out with them. I won't stay here and listen to your insults . . . Why do you do it, Eddie, why do you keep insulting me?"

She was standing in front of him, clutching the drink in her left hand. Never to be free of her. Never to escape that nerve-racking whine of a voice, that deceitful, libidinous look . . . He got out of the chair.

"Don't try and start a scene," he said. "You've had enough to drink already, you can have an early night tonight and tell the Harrises we're not available."

"It's not surprising!" she shouted suddenly. "I only do it because I'm lonely and you're so cold and cruel to me and I've nobody to talk to—and I'm scared . . ." He knocked the glass out of her hand. It happened so quickly that she stood staring at him, the whisky and ice splinters spattering the wall behind her as the glass shattered. He didn't hit her; he didn't dare, because he knew that once he did he wouldn't be able to stop. He pushed past her, and she staggered. He turned at the door. "I'll call them," he said. "You can stay *home* and get drunk for a change."

She put her hands to her face and began to cry. She was shaking. Neil had said she must stay calm. Neil had been full of good advice and comfort, insisting that she must take hold of herself and not provoke Edward. She'd felt calmer and come home determined to persuade her husband to go out to dinner and have a relaxed evening. Maybe Neil was right. Drinking didn't help. He had been very tactful about that. But he wasn't living in the house with a man who looked at you the way Edward Fleming did, when you woke in the night and thought he was leaning over you in the dark . . .

There was a knock on the door; she wiped her face hastily, smearing eye shadow. It was Ellen, the maid. "What time would you like dinner, ma'am? Mr. Fleming says he'll have something to eat on a tray in his office."

Elizabeth saw the quick glance at the broken glass and stains on the carpet.

"I had an accident," she sad. "I dropped my drink. Could you sweep up the glass, please, Ellen? Be careful not to cut yourself. I won't bother about dinner. You just give Mr. Fleming what he wants. I may be going out."

I'll go, she said to herself, I'll call Nicky Harris and say can I come alone because Eddie's full up with paperwork. I won't stay here.

The maid came back and began sweeping the broken glass into a dustpan. The telephone rang. Elizabeth hesitated; it must be the Harrises calling to find out if they were free.

She picked it up and an English voice said, "Can I speak to Mrs. Fleming, please?"

"Speaking," she said. She didn't recognize the voice. "Who is that?"

There was a pause and the voice said, "It's Mousey Graham, Liz. Remember me from Highfields? I'm in Washington—I thought it would be fun to meet."

"Oh, what a surprise—" She sat down, hugging the receiver with both hands. Mousey Graham—they'd been at school together. Had she liked her? She couldn't remember. She couldn't be sure. "Why, how lovely! When did you arrive? Where are you?"

"I flew in yesterday," Davina said. Peter Hickling, the principal intelligence officer, was listening in on a separate receiver. Neil was beside him.

"I'm staying at the embassy. With the Hicklings actually, they're old friends. When can we meet?"

Elizabeth Fleming hesitated; Ellen had finished clearing up and had just gone out of the room. "Well, what are you doing tonight?"

Davina glanced quickly at Hickling. He shook his head. Not to be too eager or too available. A visiting Englishwoman wouldn't have been free at a moment's notice as soon as she arrived in the capital. American welcomes were intensive.

"I'm sorry," Davina said. "I'm busy tonight. But I could make lunch tomorrow. Why don't I take you out? You'll have to choose the place."

"Don't be silly, Mousey," she said quickly. "You'll be my guest. We'll go to the Unicorn. I can get a table if I use Eddie's name—it's the smartest place in Washington and the food's divine. We'll have a real girls' gossip. Come here and I'll give you a drink first. Twelve o'clock tomorrow. Look forward to it." She rang off and clasped her hands to steady them.

Mousey Graham. Memory came to her rescue. She was taking shape fully now. Not a popular girl at school. Not good at games, sharp-tongued, reserved, and exceptionally clever. She went to St. Hilda's and came down with a first-class honors degree. She had a beautiful younger sister who made the gossip columns. She was still Mousey Graham, so she hadn't married. It wasn't surprising, Elizabeth thought. She must have frightened the life out of most men. She took a glass and poured another large measure of whisky. She didn't want to eat. Edward was shut up in his damned office, hating her and knowing she was too afraid of him to defy him and go out with the Harrises.

Afraid. Her fear was so real at times; of course there were days when she could master it, arguing herself into a rational view. Other days when she felt close to panic. Now she would have a woman to confide in. Someone who came from her past, who knew her before she had ever met Edward Fleming or come to live in Washington. She would have to pull herself together. Mousey—what the hell was her real name—something rather esoteric and inappropriate—Davina, that was it. Anyway; she sipped the drink and cuddled the glass, making the ice melt, anyway, it would be a change. She switched on the TV and spent the evening watching it alone.

"She sounded all right." Davina turned to Hickling. "In fact she sounded like the perfect Washington hostess. What's so special about the Unicorn?"

"The prices," a voice said behind her. She had forgotten Colin Lomax. "The food is fattening and tastes of ketchup. Even the ice cream tastes of ketchup. It's full of whores and pimps."

"Oh, shut up, Colin," Peter Hickling said. "Don't take any

notice of him, Davina. He can't find anything good to say about anything. The Unicorn is the *in* restaurant. All the top politicians and their wives go there."

"That's exactly what I said," Lomax remarked. "It's full of whores and pimps." He opened the *Washington Evening Star* and rustled the pages aggressively.

Hickling smiled at her and shook his head. "He's just jealous he can't afford it," he said. "You're off to a good start, anyway. Everyone will see you, and Liz Fleming will make capital out of the old school friend from England."

"I'm sure she will," Davina said. "I can just imagine her doing it. She sounded exactly the same."

"Weren't you friends, then?" Neil questioned.

"No. We had nothing in common at all." Lomax lowered the paper and glanced at her. The tone of her voice was sharp. Not just not friends, he thought to himself. More like enemies. The situation could be interesting. He hummed a tune and went back to reading.

Davina lit a cigarette. Hickling produced a jug of iced martinis and poured four glasses. He set one down beside Colin Lomax.

"No Scotch? I hate that rotgut."

"No Scotch," Hickling said. "Take it or leave it."

The glass disappeared behind the paper. It appeared seconds later empty.

"Ugh," came from the center pages. Nobody took any notice. It was only Davina who minded his comments. They were designed to irritate. Hickling and Neil seemed to think some of the things he said were funny.

She turned to Neil. "Tell me what she said this afternoon." Her expression was chilly. She wanted a serious report. Lomax wasn't going down at all well.

"She made an appointment to see me this afternoon," Neil said. "I met her at the usual place and we went for a drive. We stopped at a motel and had a couple of drinks."

"Why a motel?" she interposed.

"It's on the banks of the Potomac. There's an outside bar with a nice view. A lot of people go there. We didn't go inside," he added, seeing her look. "There's nothing like that as far as I'm concerned."

"No business of mine if there is," she said. "I just want to know the score. What did she say?"

"The same old thing, more or less," he answered. "How unhappy she was, how lonely, and how she wished people would believe her when she told them she was in danger. All good, melodramatic stuff. That's the trouble with her—she's difficult to take seriously. And very often by the time she gets to me she's half pissed from lunch."

"When she talks about danger," Davina said, "what kind of danger? Has she ever been specific?"

"Yes," Neil said flatly. "Several times. Says she's convinced Fleming is going to murder her." He glanced at Hickling, who nodded. "She's hinted that she knows something about him. I tried to get details, but she clams up. It's all hints and intuition—if you press her she starts to cry, or acts up."

"Tell me," Davina said quietly, "do you believe her?"

"No," the young man said. "I don't. I think she's a lush who can't face being out of the spotlight. Personally, Fleming has my sympathy."

"I imagine he has a lot of people's," she remarked. "How many other confidants has she got? Women friends, men friends besides yourself?"

"Nobody close," Hickling answered. "Acquaintances, superficial social stuff, but no real friends. Women don't take to her, and the men are scared to mess with her because Fleming's got such a big job. Nobody wants to get in wrong with him or the Oval Office. They're that close."

"I see," Davina said. She sipped a little of the martini and grimaced. Lomax was right; it was rotgut. "She must be very lonely then. That doesn't help if you are turning a bit paranoid."

"You'll see for yourself."

"I'll try, anyway," Davina said. "Starting with lunch tomorrow."

"Don't have the steak," Lomax mumbled out loud. "It's like old shoe leather."

"Mr. Lomax," she said and her tone was very curt. "I don't think you've ever been to the Unicorn in your life. Goodnight everyone."

The paper came down a few inches. "Goodnight, Miss Graham." When the door closed, he lowered the paper to his knee. "My God—that's a bossy female." Hickling laughed. "She doesn't appreciate your sense of humor."

"So I notice," Lomax retorted. "And how do you like taking orders from a woman?"

"From that particular woman I don't mind. And off the record, I'd be a bit more tactful if I were you. Watch the sexist attitude, or you might find you've made a fool of yourself."

"It doesn't worry me, if she gets her jackboots out. As far as I'm concerned women are a bloody nuisance. If they're not strutting around trying to pretend they're better than we are, they're getting in the way if there's trouble. They should stick at home and mind the babies!"

He got up, stretched, looked at each in turn and said, "If you think I'm a male chauvinist pig, you're damned right!" He went out of the office and didn't close the door quietly.

"Well," Browning said, "this is going to be a happy partnership. Whyever did they send him out here? He ought to be leading the charge of the Light Brigade!"

"He's got quite a reputation," Hickling answered. "Very highly decorated for service in Northern Ireland, all undercover stuff I've met the type before; they can't settle down to civilian life and they grouse about everything. I wouldn't have picked him, though. There must be easier triggermen about."

Browning looked at him. "Is that what he is? Why send him here, for Christ's sake?"

"To look out for Miss Graham. I sometimes think my service

invented oil and water so they could try and mix them. The sparks'll fly between those two before long. Come on, let's shut up the shop and I'll buy you a drink."

Lomax made himself something to eat and settled down to watch the television. American TV offered a bewildering variety of channels and programs. He poured himself a whisky and distractedly pressed the buttons one after the other on the little control panel.

He had been hostile to the idea of his assignment from the moment it was suggested. He had argued unsuccessfully that someone else could do the job far more effectively than he, but his own reputation and skills were used against him, with Humphrey Grant's special blend of logic. Davina Graham was one of their most important operatives. A brief outline of her role in the defection of Sasanov had followed. She had to be watched and protected at all times, and by a man who would pass as a member of the embassy staff and be able to mix in Washington circles, without, as Grant put it, his revolver bulging under his coat. For this particular mission, intelligence as well as muscle was required. It was an opportunity for Lomax to prove to the service that he was worth more than a desk job in London.

He hadn't known what to expect when he drove down to Marchwood to meet her, but the impression gained from Grant had hardly predisposed him in her favor. The affluence of the splendid house offended his stern Presbyterian morality. And from the first sight of Davina Graham he felt antagonized. He liked women to be feminine and uncompetitive; Davina was positive and self-possessed in a way that challenged his sense of masculine superiority. He had reacted by being rude and she was promptly rude in return. There was no give at all, no concession to upper-class concern for appearances; he showed her no manners and she had treated him not as a man, but as a subordinate striking a stupid macho attitude.

She didn't want him in Washington any more than he wanted to be there, and she had made it very clear from the start that she regarded him as an encumbrance foisted upon her by London. His only resort was to annoy her as much as possible, to parry that infuriating chill in her manner by sending up whatever she might take seriously. And this goaded him still more, because it was not what he had been assigned to do. Making her dislike him, if only because it forced her to recognize him as a human being, showed a weakness on his part.

And Grant had been specific on that point. Unlike the armed forces, there was no place for personal relationships in the SIS, either friendly or antagonistic. The more Lomax considered it, watching the glittering Hollywood spectacular on the small screen without seeing anything, the less he felt himself suited to the job or the service. He finished the whisky and snapped the Off button down on the panel. The screen sank to a point of light that vanished. He said aloud, "You've been given a job to do. Get on and bloody well do it." He phoned Hickling's private number.

"Listen, I've been thinking about what you said. Maybe I've been a bit rash—yes, with La Graham. If I'm going to work with her, I'd better know a bit more about her. It may make her a bit easier to take. No promises, mind you," he pulled out a cheery laugh for Hickling's benefit. "Can I come round and take a drink off you? Fine, half an hour, thanks very much."

He muttered a mild curse and picked up the evening paper.

Four thousand miles away it was spring in Moscow, and while Washington slept under the stars, the golden towers of the Kremlin churches gleamed in the afternoon sunshine. The weather was perfect, warm enough to bring the crowds out in cotton dresses and shirt-sleeves. The office of the chairman of State Security was in the KGB complex on Dzerz Square. From its windows on the third floor, Igor Borisov had a view down Marx Prospekt to Revolution Square. Best of all, he loved the interplay of light and color on the red-walled palaces, the gilded onion towers of the great cathedral of St. Basil, the glittering skyscrapers of the modern city beyond. He had a deep reverence for old Russia; to him her ancient buildings, the monasteries and churches, the eighteenth-century townhouses and country palaces of tsarist days were priceless jewels in the crown of Russian architectural and artistic genius.

He loved the Kremlin; as a young officer working for Antonyii Volkov, he had spent his free hours wandering round the museums, learning about his country's past. He had found, in the dark painted halls of the tsar's palace, a history of Russia which was not in the state history books. He had a secret affinity with that past, its glories and its mysteries, which no one suspected.

He was a Russian who saw his political ideology in terms of a fanatical nationalism. No one suspected that either. After he became Kaledin's assistant his ambition had burgeoned from the bud to a flower, but the flower was a fierce carnivore, devouring whatever came in reach. He knew that the old director wanted to propose his own successor. He knew that his chances of being elected by the Politburo were stronger as time passed, and he worked more and more closely with Kaledin. He also knew that a spectacular intelligence coup would tip the balance in his favor.

It had taken a long time and infinite patience to bring the traitor Ivan Sasanov to justice. The need to punish him became more urgent as Soviet policy in the Middle East was frustrated by his betrayal. Years of careful planning, of positioning agents, millions spent on bribes and sophisticated networks were wasted as the West moved ahead of them on Sasanov's information. And not just information. For two years he had guided and interpreted for London, and Washington, and he had been beyond their reach. The Politburo waited, smoldering with rage, and the killers of the KGB stood poised like dogs straining at the leash for the order to speed off in pursuit. The director had given his candidate the task of finding and punishing the archtraitor. That was how General Secretary Brezhnev spoke of him. Not by name, but by that epithet. If Igor failed, his chance of succeeding Kaledin was gone forever. Success would secure him the office on the tenth floor, and the second most powerful position in Russia. And so the bomb had exploded in the neat little suburban street in Perth. Sasanov's crime was punished, and the direction of Soviet intelligence operations throughout the world would undergo a subtle change.

Borisov worked a twelve-hour day; he had inherited Kaledin's palatial *dacha* in the Zhukova complex reserved for Russia's ruling elite. His wife and children were reveling in the cars, the Western clothes and luxury goods available, and the lovely retreat in the forests outside Moscow. There would be a discreet villa on the Black Sea for summer holidays; life for his family was rich with privilege. Borisov reorganized his departments by replacing some of the more entrenched Kaledin men with young, ambitious officers, preferably with some foreign service behind them. Then he set himself to travel the tortuous and complex routes through international espionage and internal security initiated by his predecessor. He attended the weekly meetings of the Politburo, and wisely listened more than he spoke. And he learned. He learned about the men who governed Russia, and smiled secretly to himself, remembering that now he was one of them. He studied their dossiers, and their moods, and he made no obvious enemies in the first six months. He devoted himself to the major KGB operations, and delegated the minor ones to officers he considered loyal to him, because he had promoted them.

Among the six principal assaults against Western security that he decided to run personally was the one concerning Edward Fleming in Washington.

"What a lovely house," Davina said.

"You are kind," Liz Fleming responded. "It is nice, isn't it? This is such an attractive part of Washington."

Davina sat down and accepted a drink. The strength of it surprised her and she sipped it before putting it down. She complimented Liz on the color schemes and furnishings, watching the jerky movements, the nervous responses with the voice pitched a little too high and the smile a shade too bright. Her hand, with its big sapphire ring, was curled tightly round the prelunch vodka, and it shook as it brought the glass to her lips. She was beautifully dressed in dark blue, with a silk shirt and modern jewelry: sapphires matched the superb engagement ring. The first impression was of a strikingly beautiful woman in her late thirties. The second was of a nervous wreck. Davina said, "You haven't changed, Liz. You look just the same as the last time I saw you."

"Oh? When was that?" She swallowed almost half the vodka; Davina wondered whether it was anything like as strong as the one she had been given.

"At London airport, some years ago. You didn't see me but I saw you and I recognized you at once. You disappeared into the VIP lounge."

"Well," Liz Fleming shrugged, "it's nice of you to say I look the same—God, sometimes I feel a hundred and one." She felt the vodka warming the pit of her stomach; it wasn't the first that morning. She felt relaxed and able to assess Davina Graham's clothes and general appearance. She looked younger than she'd expected; a dark green linen dress, expensive shoes, an air of confidence that gave her poise. Beautiful legs.

"How long have you lived here?" Davina asked.

"Just over a year. Edward moved here from New York when he went into politics. He bought this house and I redecorated it. It's marvelous for entertaining. I did the sitting room myself. Would you like to see it? I'm rather proud of it—it's not an easy shape. Long rooms never are, they always tend to look like passages."

Davina followed her out of the study. She had made a mental inventory of the room; there was only one photograph, Liz and Fleming on their wedding day, no personal bric-a-brac, some good modern drawings, a spectacular flower arrangement.

One of the ashtrays was full, the butts all tipped with lipstick.

Elizabeth had chain-smoked before her arrival. Davina helped herself to more ice and noticed that the bucket was half empty. Elizabeth had been drinking before she came and it was still only twelve o'clock. The south-facing reception room was long, high-ceilinged, dramatically furnished with gray silk walls and elaborate yellow curtains; a brilliant Persian carpet ran down its center.

There was a big crystal and ormolu chandelier, and she noticed that it held real candles. The eighteenth-century marble mantlepiece was particularly fine and Davina thought it had probably not been in the original house. There was a rare early painting of the old city, before the War of 1812, hanging above it.

A Bechstein Boudoir Grand piano stood majestically near one of the long windows, with famous faces in silver frames on top of it. The new President and his good-looking wife smiled out at them from the front rank. It seemed like a stage setting, in which Mr. and Mrs. Edward Fleming performed as leading actors in the Washington play. A play without a final curtain, and for some, no safety curtain either. The actors changed but the play went on forever. Its title was Political Power.

"Lovely," Davina said. "You've got a great flair, Liz. You could turn professional."

"Not anymore," she answered. "Now all I can do is hang around the house and be the perfect hostess. Being so close to the Oval Office has its disadvantages, Mousey, darling. You can't afford to get your colors wrong."

"You mean you were an interior decorator?" There hadn't been a mention of that on her file.

Liz shrugged. "Not officially," she said. "I used to help people out with colors and materials. I enjoyed it." She seemed evasive, anxious to change the subject. She shrugged again, and there was resentment there too. "When Edward started climbing up the ladder, he didn't want me mixed up in business. I might do the wrong people's houses." She gave a brittle little laugh, tinkling with malice. "He didn't want to deprive me of an interest, of course, but I couldn't take fees or a present anymore, and naturally if I helped someone for nothing it would look like favoritism. Caesar's wife. That's what I had to be."

"And were you?"

The answer cracked at her like a pistol shot. "No. Let's go and have lunch. We'll take my car."

She was a bad driver, erratic and irritable, cursing others for her own mistakes. It was an uncomfortable journey in heavy traffic. The restaurant was in the center of town, nestling between two gleaming office buildings. It was mock medieval, with a reproduction of the famous Lady and the Unicorn tapestry facing the entrance. There was a dimly lit, overcrowded bar, which Liz Fleming bypassed, to Davina's relief, and a long narrow room, with oak panels and antlers and machine-made aluminum armor. It was full of people and very noisy. Heads turned as they followed the headwaiter; there were waves and cries of greeting, to which Elizabeth responded. They were shown to a table in a corner near the head of the room. The air-conditioning was at full pelt, keeping the atmosphere comfortable. The menu, printed on vellum and unrolled before them, was a cumbersome nuisance. Liz waved it away.

"I'll order for us," she said. "They have some medieval crap for the out-of-town visitors. Do you like oysters, Mousey? Good. We'll have the oysters Mornay to start and chicken Maryland with Creole salad. And the wine waiter, Henry, please." She smiled at Davina. "Don't worry, you won't be getting the old English egg-and-breadcrumb, oven-ready version. This is the real thing and it's delicious. I wasn't going to insult you by suggesting steak."

"Why not? Isn't it good?" The words "old shoe leather" floated impishly to mind. "Yes, it's marvelous, if you like eating half a cow, and you get steak, steak, steak, when you first come to the States, until you never want to see a piece of beef again. Now, let's have something nice to drink, shall we—and two vodkas on the rocks while we're waiting."

She disappeared behind a huge leather-bound wine list.

Davina looked round the restaurant; she recognized one or two Republican senators, a well-known political commentator with an earnest-looking young woman. And right across from her, eating a large steak, was Colin Lomax. The annoyance of seeing him there changed to a cold suspicion. James White had been typically evasive about Major Lomax. Always the half truth behind the kindly smile, and that frostbitten heart incapable of human feeling. "Only in case you need a back-up. He's a good man, he won't get in your way. Just think of him as a sort of insurance policy." White had left Ivan unprotected. There was no insurance policy for him. She hadn't forgotten or forgiven that.

She twisted her chair round so that her back was presented to Lomax; he saw the angry movement and smiled with a sour little twist of the lips. She didn't like being followed. He didn't like following. There were fragments of bomb splinter still floating around in his back. Sometimes they caused pain. This was one of those times. He glanced at the woman Davina was sitting with; made-up, artificial . . . He hated the type. She had emptied her vodka and was beckoning for another, smoking all the time. Leaning towards Davina, talking, talking . . . He cut into his steak. It was superb. He had in fact been to the Unicorn before, during a four-day visit to Washington as part of an SAS advisory group. Unfortunately their advice had not been taken. The attempt to release the hostages had gone ahead and failed, with a tragic loss of American lives. The loss of good men because of bureaucratic, political muddling. He had a professional's admiration for the courage and skill of his U.S. counterparts. He responded to their anger at the humiliation inflicted upon their country and its people. He would have flown out with them, given the chance. He had the soldier's contempt for the soft civilians in places like London and Washington and Paris, playing checkers with the lives of brave men. He not only disliked the U.S. capital, he shunned cities generally. He had felt more at home in the windy, rainswept bandit country of Armagh than he ever did in the manicured countryside of southern England.

Whatever those two women were discussing across the room from him was important to a lot of people. The husband was a personal friend and advisor to the new President. The wife was a drunk and, he used the old Scots epithet, a hoor. Some dirty little scandal was fomenting under the custom-built, electronically operated bed, and that did not excite him. He missed his old life and his comrades with an ache as real as the painful jabs from the loose steel in his back.

Elizabeth Fleming was drunk. Not drunk enough to slur her words or fumble with her cigarettes over the coffee. But drunk just the same. Davina recognized the signs; the eyes were too wide, their stare too concentrated. The lowered voice was almost theatrical. Her words had a peak of exaggeration to them that invited disbelief. One hand lay on Davina's wrist, pinning it in a gesture of affection that had just emerged after a childhood of dislike.

"I'm so glad you've come," she said. "I've been so lonely here—so cut off. Nobody to talk to, nobody I can trust. You'll stay for a while, won't you. Mousey? You won't be going back to England?"

"You're in trouble, aren't you, Liz?" Davina asked the question gently. She could see what Neil Browning meant when he dismissed her as attention-seeking, living in a fantasy world. But there was something in the eyes and the way the painted mouth trembled at the corners that she recognized. Fear. Whatever else she was, Edward Fleming's wife was afraid.

"How do you know?" It was a whisper, exaggerated, silly.

"I know you," Davina said. "You were the most confident girl imaginable. Except for Charlie, of course. You were a pair, you two. You had the world at your feet, like a nice little football, just waiting for you to tip it into goal. You've lost that, Liz. You're scared and you're running. Put the brandy down and listen to me. I came here for a holiday; I thought it would be nice to see someone from Highfields after all these years—you're a celebrity, your husband rates a *Time* magazine article to himself these days. I never expected to find you like this. It worries me."

To her surprise Liz Fleming withdrew her hand. "We haven't seen each other for years. Why should anything about me worry you now?"

For the first time since they had met that morning, honesty flashed like lightning through the murk of small talk and deceit.

"There've been times in my life when I needed a friend," Davina said. "I think you need one now, and it might just as well be me. Perhaps I can be a friend to you, Liz, because I'm not jealous of you anymore. I'm fond of Charlie now, because I'm not jealous of her either." She smiled, and a man glancing at them from a nearby table suddenly thought—that's a pretty woman, with the red hair. "It took me a long time, and a very special man, to become a real person. I'd like to help you, Liz. I'll be here for a few weeks, and you know where I'm staying."

"With the Hicklings—from the embassy." She picked up the brandy glass again. "There's a young man called Neil Browning—trade secretary. He's been very helpful—when things get too much for me, and I get nervous, I call him up and he takes me driving, or just walking sometimes. It helps to talk to him. But I can't really trust him, Mousey. He's just an embassy hack, told to keep me happy and stop me making a fuss."

"What sort of a fuss? You're not being blackmailed, are you?"

Liz Fleming laughed, and shook her head again. When the brandy went down, she might find it hard to walk straight. Two wisps of blonde hair came loose and flapped round her cheeks. "Blackmail? Oh, sweet Jesus, that would be easy! Edward is a power figure now, you know. He could deal with blackmail for me. He can deal with anything. Without ever anybody knowing. That's a scary thought, isn't it?"

"It is, if he's the one you're frightened of," Davina said slowly. "I think we should go now, Liz." She turned round to signal the waiter. Lomax was still there. He had the bill in front of him.

Liz Fleming wouldn't let her pay; she signed the bill and, steered by Davina, made the walk through the restaurant without bumping into anything. Outside the hot, damp air enveloped them like a wet sheet. "I'll drive," Davina said. "Give me the keys."

"I'm not drunk," Liz protested. Her voice had risen. "Edward always says I'm bloody well drunk—"

Davina took her handbag, got out the keys and hustled her into the passenger seat. They swung out into Independence Avenue. The car was soon cool, air-conditioned.

In the driveway of the Georgetown house, she turned to Davina.

"I'm sorry I yelled at you," she said. "I'm a *bit* drunk, but not very. It's become a habit. You drink when you're bored. I made a fool of myself at lunch. Forget it. I can be quite good company at times."

"I know you can," Davina said. "I enjoyed lunch. And you didn't make any kind of a fool of yourself, so don't think that. You go and lie down, and you'll be fine by this evening. I'll ring you in the morning. Perhaps we could go shopping—I'm going to need something to wear for parties. I didn't realize Washington was such a gay place."

Liz Fleming turned to her. She seemed to have sobered, or made a special effort. "San Francisco is the 'gay' place," she said. "Washington is social. Not quite the same thing." She smiled, and there was warmth in it for the first time. "I'd love to take you shopping tomorrow," she said. "I'm really glad we've met again. You take the car back; I'll send Edward a message and he'll have it collected. See you tomorrow."

Davina reversed and drove out into the narrow street; in the driving mirror she watched Elizabeth Fleming open her front door and go inside.

She was a purposeful driver, her reactions razor-sharp. Ivan used to tease her, saying her aggressive impulses took over at the wheel. He came on the wings of laughter sometimes, instead of pain. A very special man, she had said. He would have teased her about that.

He had praised her instincts when she doubted them. And they were clamoring that Elizabeth Fleming was genuinely afraid of something. So afraid that she was hiding from it in drink.

She left the car in the embassy compound and went into Hickling's private office. The scrambled line to London was installed there. She got through to James White.

"I've seen Elizabeth Fleming," she said. "There's definitely something wrong. I'm going to have to stay here for a time. I'll need money. I think it would look better if I rented an apartment."

His reply was smooth; he always ignored her abruptness. "Of course, my dear. An account will be opened for you. Take as long as necessary. And don't hesitate to call on Colin Lomax if you get worried."

"I appreciate your sending me a minder," she said sharply. "I'd appreciate it more if I knew why I needed one."

"We don't know ourselves," he answered. "But he's a very useful chap to have around. What's your next move?"

"Consolidate with her, and meet the husband."

"He's a very able man," the pleasant voice intoned down the telephone. "A very able man indeed. Be on your guard with him!"

"Clever men don't frighten me," she said. She couldn't resist the thrust. "Not after Sasanov." She put the receiver down without saying goodbye.

Chapter Three

DAVINA'S STAY with the Hicklings was cut short. Liz Fleming had helped her find an apartment; it was a studio owned by an artist friend who was going to Europe for three months. Liz's enthusiasm was too high-keyed, and she seemed almost pathetic in her eagerness to keep Davina in Washington. For Davina, the dependence of the other woman was a suffocating experience. She had never indulged in a close relationship with anyone except Ivan Sasanov; the clinging, never-off-the-telephone friendships enjoyed between some women were difficult for her. By nature she was a private person; by long training she was of necessity secretive. Her inner self was her citadel, and it was being battered down by the demands of a woman who had nothing in common with her except need. She found it a strain, and she began to snap at her colleagues.

She wanted information about the Flemings' early life; she wanted to know everything possible about Edward. When Hickling responded that this was difficult and would take time, she lost her temper. He kept his, explaining that without help from the CIA such an investigation would take an outsider months. Davina flared at him. "Hire a private detective! For Christ's sake, that's standard procedure in this country when you want to know anything about anyone! Some firms won't hire an executive here without a confidential report, and how the hell do they get those?"

"Asking for an investigation into a personal advisor to the President isn't quite the same thing as finding out about the sex habits of a marketing director," Hickling pointed out. "There isn't a reputable agency in the States that wouldn't be on to Langley five minutes after you'd made the inquiry."

"Then what am I supposed to do?" she demanded.

"Find out from Mrs. Fleming." Lomax spoke for the first time. "Isn't that the object of the operation?"

She swung round on him. "Mind your own business, please. This has nothing to do with you."

"It so happens it has," he said quietly. "Peter, haven't you told Miss Graham that I've been promoted? No, I suppose she's in such a mood, you thought you'd better wait."

Davina turned back to Peter Hickling. "What is this?" she demanded. "What's he talking about?"

Hickling was a very astute judge of people. He hadn't lost his temper with Davina Graham because he knew that her irritability was due to considerable strain.

"You explain it," he said to Lomax. "Why don't you take Davina out to dinner—isn't it time you stopped snapping at each other, if you're going to work together? I'm going home. Peggy's got a couple coming in for bridge. I know Davina doesn't play. Goodnight." He left the office. For a moment they stared at each other; Lomax took out a packet of cigarettes and offered one to her.

"It's not a bad idea," he said. "If you don't play bridge."

"No, thanks." She didn't take the cigarette. "I'll go to bed early."

"Please yourself." Lomax shrugged. "I'm surprised you haven't had the notification."

"The notification of what? Your promotion? I know what you

are, Mr. Lomax, and I made my feelings on the subject very clear to London. I expect there's something in the diplomatic bag for me, I just haven't had time to go through everything. Whatever this is all about, it won't make any difference to me. I don't intend to work with you. I came here to do this job on my own, and I'm going to do exactly that."

He surprised her then. He didn't respond to the challenge as she expected. He didn't say something rude and walk out. He went on sitting in his chair, smoking the cigarette she now wished she'd accepted, looking at her.

"If I said you looked tired," he remarked suddenly, "I suppose you'd take it as an insult."

"I think I'd say what I said before; it's none of your business." She didn't mean to sit down, but it was a reflex. Since she came to America no one had said she looked well or ill or tired or anything personal, except for that gabbling woman who followed every remark with something about herself. She opened her bag and shut it again. She had no cigarettes left. He got up and gave her one.

"You're the most awkward bloody female I've ever met," he said. "You are a bloody woman," Sasanov used to say when they quarreled in the early days. As Lomax lit her cigarette, she turned her head away because her eyes had filled with tears. He saw them, but he said nothing and strolled to Hickling's desk. "I know that canny sod keeps a bottle somewhere," he said.

"It'll be gin." Davina was fumbling with a handkerchief. "He only drinks martinis."

"I have a decent bottle of Scotch at home," Lomax said. "I think you'd better come round and help me drink it."

Long afterwards, she was to remember that moment when her life changed its direction. It was not predestined; she had a choice. Or it seemed that she had. To accept or refuse. To take one turning down the crossroads to the future or another. But this would be hindsight, and time always mocked truth. "All right," she said.

It was a pleasant three-room flat in the embassy-owned apartment block on Massachusetts Avenue. An impersonal place, as all such government-issue places are; standard decor, furnishings, the stage left bare for the occupant to install the scenery of his life, the photographs, books, oddments from a past outside the neat little Washington pad. There was nothing. Lomax had put nothing of himself on a wall, or a table. Nothing but whisky, bottles of soda, and packets of English cigarettes. They didn't talk much to start with. He gave her a drink, and they sat quietly.

"Why did you rip into poor Peter Hickling?" he asked her. "It's not like you."

"Isn't it? I thought I had a reputation for being sharp," she said.

"That wasn't sharp. That was more like someone who's at the end of their rope and had to let fly at someone."

"I'll apologize tomorrow," she said. "I think I've let Liz Fleming get on my nerves."

"Neil said she was a handful," Colin remarked. "Dealing with drunks isn't easy; a drunken woman is the bottom of the well, as my father would say."

She hadn't intended to discuss it with him. She didn't know what made her start.

"She drives me mad at times," Davina said slowly. "When we were girls, I hated her. She didn't hate me, she just despised me. Now the boot should be on the other foot. But it isn't quite. I'm sorry for her, you know that? There's something pathetic and awful about a woman who's let herself down. And she's frightened. She's frightened out of her wits. I can feel it. And because she's frightened she's put her hooks into me and she won't let go for a minute. Do you know how many times a day she phones?" He shook his head. "Half a dozen. And I see her *every* day. I tried to avoid her for a couple of days, just to give myself time to breathe, or think, and she was round at the apartment, bursting into tears, saying she must have upset me, and didn't I know she couldn't go on unless I was there . . ." Davina paused. He was very quiet, listening to her. "I hate scenes," she said. "I hate people doing an emotional striptease. It's never genuine or they wouldn't drag outsiders in."

"You sound like a Scot," he said. "I think I'd be tempted to give Mrs. Fleming a clip round the ear."

She laughed suddenly. "Do you know, I damned nearly did? That day when she burst in on me, you could have struck a match on her breath, and she was trying to put her arms round me, telling me I was the only friend she had in the world. I had to really hold myself in not to slap her. But there's something else. I think that's what is really getting at me. The first time we went out to lunch she hinted about being scared and in danger . . . pretty broad hints that it was coming from the husband, too. And since then—nothing! Not a word about anything. Just girl talk, and self-pity about being lonely and needing me and if only she could talk to someone—the minute I say, talk to me, she clams up completely. It's just as if she's got what she wants and that's all there is to it. A 'friend' in inverted commas, someone to hang on to like a leech and suck dry."

"You've got to force her out into the open," Lomax said. "Call her bluff; it's the only way!"

"That could frighten her off completely," Davina argued. "All right, suppose I do call her bluff and she runs a mile?"

"You'll be no worse off than you are now. The days are going by and you're getting nothing out of her; she's hanging on to you, taking one step forward and two steps back. You haven't got the time to waste while she makes up her mind to tell you the truth. One thing I have learned." He stared hard at her. "When you're at risk don't hang about. Never mind the deskbound strategists in London; they're not going to be there when the flak hits the fan. Face Liz Fleming and get tough with her." He was leaning forward; he had a way of narrowing his eyes when he was emphasizing a point.

"I'll talk to her if you like," he offered. "She won't play games with me."

"I'm sure she wouldn't," Davina said. "But if that was the way the Chief wanted to handle it, they'd have sent you out here instead of me."

"Pity they didn't," he remarked. "I know that type; men or women, they're much the same. They're bloody leeches, weak as water, looking for someone strong to cling to, someone to carry them. That's why they run to drink when things go wrong. Even when they don't. Take my advice," he said, "tell her you're leaving. Stop Browning taking calls in case she turns back to him. Isolate her, make her feel she's going to be out on her own. Frighten the hell out of her, Davina. Then I think you'll find she'll crack."

"You have a way," Davina said, "of making it sound very ugly. I'm not used to seeing my work through your eyes. I don't like it."

"You didn't like what the KGB did to your husband," he said.

"No," she answered after a pause. "I take your point. Just don't make it again, will you, please?"

"I hope I won't have to," he said. "I'm not trying to hurt you, but you've got to face facts. This isn't a game played by gentlemen in bowler hats; spying is ugly, like you said. There aren't any rules except to get them before they get you. I've fought the Russians before. They've got some set-up here with these Flemings. It's going to be ugly and it's going to be rough. They didn't exactly treat you with kid gloves."

"That doesn't mean I have to be like them," she said. "I don't want to treat Liz as an enemy."

"In this game," Lomax said, "everyone's an enemy till they've proved they're a friend. There's a Chinese restaurant down the block; Peking cooking. It's very good; the food's better than the Unicorn. I'll give you dinner. I can tell you about my promotion."

"Why can't you tell me now?" she said. She didn't want to go to dinner with him. She wasn't even hungry.

"Because there's something else I learned," he said. "Discretion is the better part of valor. You'll take the news better when I've fed you and filled you up with rice wine."

She sat up straight and looked at him. "What news?"

He shook his head, and for the first time there was friendliness in his quirky smile. "After we've eaten," he said.

They walked the block down to the restaurant; he had a long stride that she found difficult to keep up with. She was surprised when he took her arm as they crossed the street. The food was excellent, as he said. And she needed all the wine he provided when she heard of Humphrey Grant's proposal. Lomax was to give her maximum protection. To do this he would have to move into her flat. She faced him across the table.

"No," she said. "Certainly not."

Lomax shrugged. "Contact London then," he said easily. "It wasn't my idea."

"We were right," the brigadier said cheerfully. "It's always gratifying to be right, don't you agree, Humphrey?"

Grant looked glum. "I'd have rather been wrong in this case," he said. "What kind of a mess are we going to find?"

"My dear chap," James White reproved him gently, "don't be such a pessimist. The point is we know there is a mess, and we're going to find out what it is and deal with it. I thought sending Davina out there would activate our little traitor Browning, if there was a KGB connection with the Flemings. And lo and behold, he contacts his controller and alerts Moscow that she's arrived!"

John Kidson was in the office; he and James White were going to lunch before a meeting with the foreign secretary over a delicate operation taking place in Poland. "Chief, now we know it's a Moscow Center operation, is there any need for Davina to stay out there?"

White wagged a finger at him; the smile was still there but the eyes had turned cold. "Now, now," he said. "You mustn't start thinking like a brother-in-law. You know the rules. We don't have any family connections in the service."

"I'm thinking of whether she's in a fit state to cope with a dangerous security mission," Kidson said sharply. "Anything involving a top man like Fleming is going to get pretty rough. She won't stand up to a second interrogation."

"We've taken precautions," the Chief said. "Haven't we, Humphrey?"

"You've sent Lomax out with her, I know," Kidson persisted. "It won't take Borisov's boys long to realize what his job is; they'll simply take him out if they decide to go after Davina."

It was Grant who answered. "A lot of people have tried to 'take him out,' as you put it," he said. "Some of them were Moscow Center trained, too. They didn't succeed and they didn't survive. Davina will be perfectly safe with him."

"In the meantime," James White said, "she's doing very well. She's becoming the odious Mrs. Fleming's indispensable companion and she's made a niche for herself in Washington, where she's become part of the scene—she's in a perfect position to uncover Moscow's little wasps' nest for us. And as Humphrey said, she has Lomax to protect her." He lit his Turkish cigarette; he never offered them to anyone else.

"The person at risk," he said after a moment, "is Mrs. Fleming. If what she says is true, and her husband is a Russian agent, whether willingly or not, then they will want to silence her. The surprising thing is that they haven't already done so. That does intrigue me, doesn't it you?" He looked from one to the other. "And what also intrigues me is that she has stayed on with this husband who she thinks is going to kill her. She could have taken a plane to England instead of running to the embassy . . . It's very puzzling and very original. As I said to you, Humphrey, at the beginning, we may be seeing Borisov's signature for the first time. It certainly isn't going to be the same trademark as the last. Much more subtle, I suspect, than Kaledin. A man who favors slow poison rather than a bullet in the neck. It will take all Davina's skill to unravel this one. But I have perfect confidence in her. You should have too, John, instead of trying to get her brought home." He looked at his watch. "Come along, we'll be late for lunch. We need to fortify ourselves against our foreign secretary's moral indignation. I couldn't possibly eat after I'd seen him; trying to discuss anything sensible with him always gives me indigestion."

"You shouldn't complain," John Kidson said. "There aren't many idealists in politics."

"No, thank God," James White retorted. "Otherwise we'd have been part of Russian-occupied Europe by now! He can afford to have high principles, so long as he has people like us to do the dirty work. Humphrey, I'll see you later. Let me know at once if you get anything from Davina."

They had an excellent lunch at the Garrick Club, and the conversation turned to their mutual interest in the theater. James White invited Kidson and his wife to come to the new production of *King Lear* at the Aldwych, but Kidson said he didn't think it was possible because Charlie was feeding the baby herself. White didn't show his surprise. His impression of the beautiful, much-married Charlotte Graham didn't accord with breast-feeding, but he had ceased to be amazed by anything that woman did.

"Davina. I'm so glad to meet you at last." Edward Fleming had hold of her hand; it was a firm handshake, a little longer-lasting than was customary, but part of the warm way in which he spoke her name. A good-looking man, with friendly brown eyes, hair that was touched with gray, and marvelous white teeth exposed in a generous smile. An after-shave that smelled of lemons. As the ambassador had said, he radiated charm.

She didn't like him. She couldn't find anything to criticize; he was the kind of man that both sexes would find personally attractive, but her dislike was so instant and so strong that she pulled her hand away. "I'm delighted you could come," she said. "Liz tells me how busy you are. Politicians never seem to have any time to themselves."

"Life is hectic," he admitted. "But very exciting. Don't you find Washington is an exciting place? And it's all coming from the

President. It's a new dawn for the States—I feel so privileged to be a part of it. He's a great man, Davina—he brings out the best in everyone because he gives so much himself." He was gazing at her earnestly, and she found herself embarrassed. Suddenly he smiled. "I'm sorry. I get over-enthusiastic. Liz would kill me if she heard me talking to you like that. She says I haven't any conversation anymore; I talk to people like they're in the audience . . . Anyway, I made up my mind that nothing was going to stop me coming to your housewarming. I've heard so much about you from Liz."

Elizabeth Fleming was in the background, talking to a couple Davina had met on the Washington social circuit. Her smile was inattentive; she kept glancing towards her husband and her friend. Her best friend, as she kept telling everyone. She had been delighted when Davina suggested a small party to celebrate the studio flat. What a chance to pin down Eddie—he was always so busy, shut up in the office when he was at home—he'd make a special effort to come because he was curious to meet Davina. He didn't believe she had any real friends. He'd come just to prove that Davina was only an acquaintance from England, that there wasn't any genuine liking between them.

"I'm always a bit apprehensive when somebody says that," Davina said. "Whatever you've heard, I hope it's good. How's your glass?"

"Fine, thanks. I can promise you, Liz has done nothing but sing your praises. What a coincidence, being at school together—"

"Not such a coincidence really," Davina said. "England is such a small place, and people tend to circulate around the same area when they live in the country. If you lived in Wiltshire, you probably went to Highfields."

"And you were such close friends," he prompted. "It's great for Liz to meet up with you again. I'm afraid she's had a lot of time on her hands since I joined the administration. Having you around has been a real tonic for her." And then he said something that caught her right off guard.

"A tonic without the vodka. Believe me, I hope you stay on in Washington as long as possible. Excuse me—there's my old buddy from your embassy. Hi, Peter—Judy." He had gone to the Hicklings, one arm rested on Peter Hickling's shoulder, he was leaning over them a little, enveloping them in his friendship.

Tonic without the vodka. With the skill of a Venetian, he had slipped the dagger into his wife's reputation. Just supposing that her friend from England didn't know she was a drunk, she knew now. Colin Lomax came up behind her. He put his hand on her shoulder.

"Come and talk to a friend of mine. Colonel Kramer, he's at the Pentagon. You might look tenderly on me for a change. We're supposed to be lovers."

"Go to hell," Davina whispered. "Who's Colonel Kramer? This is supposed to be my party."

"He's a Marine," Lomax said. "We had some good times together. You'll like him."

"More than I do Mr. Fleming," she murmured, as they moved through the groups of people. "Go and talk to him. See what you think."

"I will; I'll settle you with Joe first."

The colonel was a small man, neat and taut as a fine steel cable. He had a Southern accent that made treacle of his words. Lomax was right. She did like him. A professional; they all shared a kind of instinctive kinship. Their recognition sign was excellence.

Colin Lomax drifted away after a few minutes. The colonel gazed at her and said, "The boy is looking a lot better, ma'am. That must be due to you."

"I doubt it." She turned the remark aside with a laugh. It didn't make sense.

"I was mighty worried when I heard about it," he went on. "A guy like that couldn't live in a wheelchair—but he was lucky. Luckier than some of my buddies were in Iran."

"You couldn't cripple him," she said. "He's far too tough."

His grin was slow and wide. "He's tough," he said, and it was an accolade.

They talked briefly about Washington; she steered the conversation back to Colin Lomax. She knew very little about his army career; he never talked about himself or mentioned a family. The colonel didn't need encouragement to talk about him; she heard about the mission to Washington to advise on the rescue attempt. "I tell you, ma'am, he had hair down to his collar and he dressed any old how; I admit I said to myself, what's this supposed to be? What kind of a unit are these British running? But I ate my words as soon as he started in on the plan of attack. They know what's it about, those guys. I just wish our boys had had their experience before they went into Iran."

Davina listened, hiding her ignorance. When Kramer mentioned the George Medal she couldn't conceal her surprise. The colonel smiled his wide engaging smile. "He didn't tell you about that? Well, I guess he wouldn't . . . he's a modest type."

"Yes," Davina murmured, "he certainly is. About his medal, certainly." Her ignorance was embarrassing; luckily the colonel didn't seem to notice how little she knew about the man who was posing as her lover. It had taken more than dinner at a Peking restaurant to persuade her that Lomax should spend nights in her flat. It had required a terse telex from the brigadier himself. "Please comply with your instructions or return." She had complied, and surprisingly Lomax had been very tactful. It made sense from the intelligence point of view; if they were openly living together they could operate as a team without exciting comment. And Lomax was able to give her continuous protection. She glanced across to where he stood, locked in conversation with Edward Fleming, and wondered what they had to talk about; they couldn't have been less alike. The urbane political figure and the ex-soldier, prickly as a desert cactus.

Elizabeth Fleming appeared beside her. "Thank you for the party, Mousey darling. It's been such fun—we have to go, Eddie's got some awful dinner party lined up with a senator from some dreary place in the Midwest. I'll be bored out of my mind. When am I going to see you?" She was comparatively sober for a change.

She looked ill at ease, and kept glancing round to where her husband was standing, still talking to Colin Lomax. "He always hurries me away," she whispered to Davina, "just when I'm enjoying myself. Then he keeps me waiting . . . you're free tomorrow, aren't you? We could go round the art galleries if you like. The Smithsonian is out of this world."

I have to do it, Davina reminded herself. It's no good feeling sorry for her just because she's twitchy and trying to cling to you. Lomax is right. You've got to pull the rug out from under her.

"I'll come round in the morning," she said. "I've got bad news, I'm afraid." She saw Elizabeth change color; the artificial pink on her cheeks stood out like blotches.

"Bad news? What do you mean, Mousey, what's happened?"

Davina took her arm and steered her towards Edward Fleming. "I'll tell you tomorrow," she said. She shook hands with Fleming. "Goodbye, thank you for coming."

Elizabeth kissed her on both cheeks. She whispered, "What sort of bad news, Mousey? Please, ring me tonight."

Davina didn't answer. She disengaged herself and walked to the front door with them. "Goodbye, Liz—thanks again for coming round. I'll see you tomorrow."

By nine o'clock everyone had gone. She went round the sitting room collecting dirty glasses and emptying ashtrays. She shook the cushions into shape; she loaded a tray with empty bottles and took it out to the kitchen. The party had been a success. Colin Lomax had gone; he often disappeared without an explanation. It was none of her business where he went. Probably to dinner with the Marine colonel. She didn't feel hungry; she poured herself a drink and sat down. The flat was very quiet. She tried different channels on TV. There was nothing of interest.

She and Sasanov used to give parties in their little house in Perth. Their friends were members of the university, professors and a few students. They gathered together to eat and talk. She had found that Sasanov was gregarious, like all Russians. He loved company and he loved to keep them arguing and drinking into the night. He never wanted anyone to go home. They had been so completely happy together in those three years. As lovers and as friends.

She didn't hear Colin Lomax come in; he crossed the floor and stood watching her. "Instead of crying," he said, "why don't you talk about it?"

"There's nothing to talk about," she said. "It was just very quiet here after the party. I'm quite all right now."

"You don't look all right to me," he remarked. He sat on the sofa beside her instead of his usual chair. "It would help if you didn't bottle everything in so much. And you can't bring back the dead."

"He isn't dead to me," said Davina. "Sometimes I feel as if Ivan was in the room with me. Some mornings I wake up and I think he's just got out of bed. What on earth am I telling you this for? I must be mad!"

"You're not mad," Lomax said. "You're lonely, that's the trouble. You haven't really come to terms with living on your own yet. You're still looking back, and it's no good. I know; I've lost a number of people who mattered to me. I know what you're thinking; they were only friends, there's no comparison. But there is; you get very close to a man who's pulled you out of trouble, even saved your life. And then they get killed. You feel sick and you feel empty, as if a part of yourself had gone. It makes for isolation too, if you're not careful."

"If we're going to talk," Davina said, "then tell me about yourself. I didn't even know you'd been wounded until your friend the colonel told me. And about your medal. What happened?"

"The medal doesn't matter. I only got it because I was lucky and didn't get caught. Better men than I could ever be got nothing. In a way the medal was for them too. That's what makes me value it. Otherwise I wouldn't have accepted any decoration. Not a very interesting story, I'm afraid." He lit a cigarette, then said, "Sorry, do you want one?"

"No, thanks."

"I don't mean to be evasive about that particular incident, but one of my best friends was killed. He got the George too, but it made mine feel rather superfluous."

"I didn't mean to pry," Davina said. There was a short, awkward pause, then suddenly he stubbed out the half smoked cigarette.

"I know," he said. "It must have been embarrassing for you with Kramer tonight. That's my fault, I didn't think he'd mention anything. Sure you don't want a cigarette? I was blown up just at the end of my tour of duty. We were on border patrol in Armagh, I was back in uniform by then. There were four of us, my sergeant and two soldiers. They detonated the bloody mine by remote control from across the fields. My armored car was flattened like an empty beer can. They had to cut us out; my sergeant was dead, the other two died later. Just as well, considering their injuries. I was the lucky one. My spinal cord wasn't damaged but a lot of the stuff made a mess of me inside. They got most of it out; there's a few bits floating around but they're harmless now. I spent a fair old time in hospital, and then I was invalided out. I couldn't pass the medical for active service, although it seemed bloody silly at the time. I didn't want to sit behind a desk and hadn't a clue what to do with myself. Then a chap I knew in the army asked me out to lunch. He suggested I might like civilian intelligence work. I jumped at the chance; I had a couple of interviews in London and they took me on. So here I am."

"I get the feeling," Davina said, "that you're disappointed in it."

"It's a bit soon to tell," he shrugged. "I don't know quite what I expected. Certainly not you. As you probably gathered."

Davina smiled. "How much undercover work did you do?"

"Quite a bit; in Ireland I mixed round in the pubs, picked up information. I had a cover story that stuck, thank God, or I wouldn't be here now. One day I'll do my Cork accent for you—it's not bad. My job was to get people to talk to me; there were quite a lot who didn't like what was happening and would have helped, but it was so bloody dangerous for them. The slightest suspicion and they'd shoot your elbows off, or kneecap you. That was just a warning. Everywhere you went there was the stink of fear; it really smells, do you know that? It's human sweat and there's no smell like it . . . The hell of it was the coutryside was so beautiful—have you ever been to Ireland?" She shook her head. "It's lovely up there; mountainous and wild, like Scotland. It's greener than any place on earth. You can drive for miles and never see a house or a human soul. You know, there were times when I thought, a man could settle here. Other Scotsmen felt the same; it drew them as it drew me, because it reminded them of home. That's where the trouble started. But you'd see the people watching you, three hundred years of blood between them and you, and you knew it wouldn't work. I got to know a lot of families in the area. Funny thing is, I hated those bigoted Unionists as much as the Provos we were fighting. No surrender. Not an inch. So my men get blown up or shot dead. I miss the army but I don't miss Northern Ireland. Have you had anything to eat?"

"I wasn't hungry," she said.

"You must eat," he insisted. "I can't stand a skinny woman. I'll make something while you set the table. We can take our minds off our sorrows by discussing Edward Fleming and that lovely wife of his. What did you say to her? Did you set the scene for tomorrow?"

"I did," Davina answered. "I didn't go into any details, I just said I had bad news for her. She looked worried to death. I had to push her out before she could ask any questions."

"Well done," he said. "She'll sweat all night, wondering what's going to happen. The more I see her, the more she makes my hackles rise. I watched her tonight eyeing herself in every mirror she passed. Even if she wasn't three sheets to the wind most of the time, there's nothing I can find to like about her. By the way, why does she call you 'Mousey'?"

"It was my nickname at school," Davina said. "She gave it to me, now I think of it. She said I looked like a mouse; brownish and always skulking in the corner."

"Stupid cow," Lomax said over his shoulder as he went out.

The new director of the CIA was taking a long weekend fishing in Canada. He and his family were outdoor people who enjoyed skiing and sailing, and played ball games with competitive skill. The director was relaxing with his wife on the banks of one of the inlets of the lake when a voice called to him from the pathway behind. He turned in surprise; the figure walking towards him was that of a well-built man in his late thirties, with fair hair that gleamed in the crisp sunshine and a short, purposeful walk. The director set his rod and went to meet him.

"Jeremy! Hi—this is a surprise."

Jeremy Barr shook hands. His voice had a slight North American inflection but he was obviously an Englishman who was living in the States. "I'm sorry to break in your weekend, sir," he said. "Believe me, I wouldn't have come down unless it was important. Hello there, Mrs. Drew. How are you?"

The director's wife was a handsome woman, noted for her intelligence and strength of character. She had been married to her husband for thirty years, borne him four children, and been the mainstay of his career. She shook hands with Jeremy Barr. Her smile was wide and friendly, but not familiar. She never forgot whose wife she was. "Jerry—lovely to see you. I hope it's a nice surprise that brings you here?"

"That depends," he said. "How are the fish?"

"Biting, aren't they, Bill?" She trilled her cheerful laugh across the scornful Canadian expanse of glittering lake water and thrusting pines.

"Some are," the director agreed. "And then some aren't. Vera, Jeremy and I are going for a walk. Mind my rod, will you?" She smiled her agreement. He wasn't going to catch anything and he wanted to talk to the Englishman alone.

Jeremy Spencer-Barr was his full name. He had been advised very tactfully that Americans didn't like double-barreled names unless they were used by divorced women, in which case they could run to four or five. It had all been handled with humor and Jeremy had understood and become plain Mr. Barr when he took up his job at Langley. Vera didn't know his background exactly, but she understood it was a debt of honor on the CIA's part. They, like the Russians, took pride in looking after their own.

The two men strolled along side by side, hands in pockets, through the pathways that twisted and turned through pine woods as dark as the primeval forests that had once covered the land. It was very quiet and there was no sunlight.

"There's been a development in the Fleming situation," Jeremy said. "I felt I should come down and see you myself, sir. I have first-hand knowledge that I felt you'd want to have. First-hand, so to speak."

"Very thoughtful of you, Jeremy," the director said. "Tell me about it." He was not just the President's nominee, he was in the truest sense the President's man. He was loyal to the country through the man, and the role he saw for himself was to defend and protect both the man and the country against its enemies at any cost.

"It concerns Elizabeth Fleming," Barr said.

The director's exclamation of dislike hung in the dank air under the pine trees like a curse. "That goddamned woman," he said. "Tell me."

"The SIS have sent someone out from London." They walked a few paces more, still side by side, heads a little bent.

"Why should they do that." The director didn't make it a question, it was an observation made to himself. The brown eyes swiveled to Barr. "Why should SIS trouble themselves with her?"

"I don't know," Jeremy said. "I wouldn't have known they had, except for the person concerned. It's a woman. I used to work with her years ago. She arrived out here on a so-called holiday visit. We get notice of everyone who visits the embassy—it's part of my job to go down the list and check them. I saw this one and I knew there was trouble. She turns out to be a great and good friend of Elizabeth Fleming and they're swanning round Washington together. She's a very competent, dedicated, professional operator. I thought I must come down and see you personally."

"I'm glad you did," the director said slowly. "We take this path and it brings us back down to the lake. I don't want the British sticking their noses into our affairs. Edward Fleming is CIA business. He should have gotten a divorce a long time ago. God knows why he puts up with her. You say this woman is a top operator?"

"One of the best," Jeremy Barr said quietly. "I thought she'd retired. I'd like to handle this, sir. I know her. I know how she works. And I'm worried."

"So am I," the director said. They stepped out of the gloom of the pine woods into the crisp air and dazzling sunlight. "We can't have problems so close to the President. You have the assignment, Jeremy. But tread softly, boy. Don't step on any twigs."

"I won't," Jeremy Barr said. "You can rely on me."

Neil Browning's hobby was photography. He spent a lot of his time photographing interiors; the juxtaposition of inanimate objects interested him, distorted by the use of light and unusual camera angles. He had taken some straightforward views of Washington that were much admired; people had suggested that he should get enough material together for an exhibition. He had laughed and denied that he was anything better than an enthusiastic amateur who took snaps for his own amusement. He had a collection of expensive cameras and subscribed to the photographic journals; there were albums of color prints, black-and-white studies, and color transparencies in his flat; he was a regular customer at the smart camera shop on Lexington Street. That afternoon he walked in out of the humid heat and went to the counter. The girl smiled at him. "Hi, Mr. Browning."

"Hello," he said. "Is Mr. Bruckner around?"

"He's in back," she said. "I'll get him."

Curt Bruckner owned the shop. He was a friendly, helpful man who liked to serve good customers himself. He always attended to Neil when he came in. "Afternoon there, Mr. Browning, what can I do for you?" He was a second-generation German, aged forty-three, balding and with a slight paunch about his trouser belt. He was the most expert man on sophisticated cameras in the city. Neil had discovered him soon after he came to the embassy. He was not above printing one or two erotic studies Neil had taken of his girl friend Cathy.

"I've got a roll of film," Neil explained. "I'd like these in a hurry. When could you have them ready?"

"I'm pretty busy right now," Bruckner apologized. "Are you in a big hurry, Mr. Browning?"

"I'm afraid so," Neil said. "I want them urgently. Day after tomorrow at the latest."

Bruckner puckered his full lips and looked doubtful. "Well," he said, "you're one of my regulars, now—I always try to put my regulars up front if I do have a lot of work. Day after tomorrow, they'll be ready."

"Thanks," Neil said. "By the way, I've been thinking about that

Leica forty-two. It's a lot of money but I know someone who's got one and they take better pictures than my Zeiss. You wouldn't have one in stock, would you?"

"No." Bruckner shook his head. "But I could get one for you. I'll make inquiries. How did you find the zoom lens?"

"Great. I used it on some outdoor shots—they're on that roll. I'm very pleased with it. I'll be round for the prints the day after tomorrow. Morning or afternoon?"

"Afternoon," Bruckner said. "Gives me more time."

Neil thanked him and left the shop. Bruckner turned to the salesgirl.

"That son of a bitch," he muttered, "always in a hurry—I'll do these right away."

She shrugged. "Why don't you tell him he has to wait?"

"Because, sweet ass, he's going to buy a fifteen-hundred-dollar Leica forty-two," he said, and hurried with Neil's film to the back of the shop and through the door to the darkroom. He did his own developing and printing of the high-class material. He switched on the red light and started work. It was only half a roll; there were a dozen pictures, all of fine quality; one or two in his opinion were outstanding. He printed the first half dozen, examined them, set them aside. The eighth print was an interior, one of Browning's favorite compositions, taken through a prismatic lens, strong sunlight shattering into rainbow colors over a table by a window, through a low bowl of spring flowers, books, and an ashtray with a cigarette sending a drift of smoke into the fiery light. Bruckner took the print outside into his little office and locked the door. He held a magnifying glass to it, bringing one section up to treble size. The books. One of them was on its side, the spine facing the camera. Its title was clearly visible under the glass. *All the President's Men.* Bruckner put the glass away. He picked up the phone and dialed a New York number.

"This is Bruckner," he said. "Washington Cameras. I have a

client wants a Leica forty-two. Yeah, I need it right away. Day after tomorrow. He'll be in the store that afternoon. Okay? Okay." He hung up and went back to finish the prints.

Whenever Neil Browning filmed an interior with books, the positioning and the title visible conveyed his message to his controller in New York. *All the President's Men* signified Edward Fleming. The book lying on its side meant that it was an emergency. The request for the Leica forty-two was the code Bruckner used with the controller. He had been acting as linkman for the Soviet spy ring in Washington for the past three years. Neil Browning was their newest recruit. He went into the darkroom and printed up the rest of the film.

"Good morning, Comrade General."

"Good morning, Natalie."

"I have the latest report in from Jackdaw."

"Good; let me see it. Thank you."

Igor Borisov had dismissed his predecessor's secretary and employed a young woman from the KGB secretarial pool. She had the highest degrees from the secretarial college run by the service as part of its bureaucracy. She was also feminine to look at; Borisov had old-fashioned tastes in women. He was very pleased with Natalie Alexvievna's efficiency. Although he was a happily married man, he also enjoyed the sight of her bosom bouncing under her green blouse when she walked towards him.

He opened the report from Jackdaw and read it quickly. Jackdaw was a new recruit, one of his own selections in Washington. A greedy young foreign-office official with a taste for good living and expensive photography. Art work, Borisov had heard it described. As far as he was concerned, the pictures Neil Browning took of his girl and himself were just pornography. His stupidity in having them printed resulted in a discreet suggestion of blackmail. The ease with which he succumbed to the threat and the greed with which he accepted payment for his information pointed to a worthless character of short-lived usefulness. Borisov never trusted agents whose motives were either fear or gain, and certainly not both. But unfortunately the true idealists were fewer than they had been. He believed that Soviet action in Hungary and Czechoslovakia had disillusioned many promising recruits in the West, their eyes still full of wartime stars about their allies in the East. A pity, but balanced by the moral decline of the capitalist nations and their people's lack of faith in anything but their own interests. There were many recruits like Neil Browning, and they were very useful while they lasted. He had given him the code name Jackdaw because of his dishonesty.

Borisov had a samovar in his office; it was the same samovar that had served Kaledin. He poured a glass of tea and lit a strong-tasting Balkan cigarette.

Jackdaw's report held a private fascination for him. The wife of Edward Fleming was attracting sufficient British interest to warrant a London expert coming out. Davina Graham. He sipped the tea. She had missed the car bomb. He didn't regret that. There was no need to kill her with the traitor Sasanov. She had served her own country bravely and well. He remembered the drugged and shattered wreck of a woman who had flown back to England. He had never expected to hear of her again. But she had proved to be very strong. He wondered whether she knew who he was and his responsibility for the car bomb. He dismissed the idea as fanciful. But her presence in Washington added a dimension of personal excitement to the operation involving Edward Fleming. Borisov thought of it as a duel; he smoked his cigarette down and rubbed it out. The idea appealed to him. He knew more about Davina Graham than the service she worked for. He had seen her before she was repatriated. The image in his mind was quite clear. A pale, pale face against the white pillows, framed by dark red hair that was streaked with sweat, a mouth that could be sensual but was drawn tight in defense against fear. Eyes too shadowed with drugs to show a clear expression. The windows of the soul, but the blinds were drawn. Very brave, intellectual, gifted, capable of sexual passion. A rare and interesting combination in the cold world of international espionage and terror.

And with one devastating human weakness that he knew could be exploited. A deep capacity for selfless human love. He made notes, attached them to the report, rang for Natalie and told her to file it. Then he composed a memorandum to go before the weekly meeting of his colleagues on the Politburo. One lesson among many had been learned. At this stage in his tenure of power, he had to prove his good faith.

He must confer with the other rulers of Russia about the course of his attack upon the new President and his administration in the United States. It was too important to be kept a secret from them.

"You can't! You can't walk out and leave me!" Elizabeth Fleming faced Davina; both hands were clenched at her sides and there was a strident note of terror in her voice.

"There's no reason for me to stay," Davina said. "I've had a wonderful holiday here but I've decided to go home. And I'm not walking out on you, Liz. There's nothing the matter with you except drink, and not enough to do." She was not enjoying the scene; she found the other woman's fear and confusion distressing. The change of mood caught her unprepared. Liz Fleming's face twisted into an ugly sneer.

"You pompous little smartass," she spat out. " 'Drink and not enough to do.' You go to hell! What do you know about me—what do you care about anybody but yourself? I launched you in this lousy city, I took you everywhere, introduced you to everyone, and that's my thanks, is it? Got yourself a boyfriend and now you don't need me anymore so you're going back?"

Davina picked up her handbag. "Goodbye, Liz," she said. She turned her back and moved towards the door. She was twisting the handle when Elizabeth Fleming said behind her, "Please—for

Christ's sake, wait. Davina—wait!" Davina paused for a moment and then slowly turned back into the room. "I didn't mean that," she said, and her face cracked into soundless weeping. "I didn't mean anything I said. I was just so frightened—don't go, please?"

Davina sat down on the arm of the big sofa. "If you want me to stay," she said, "you've got to tell me the truth. I've spent the past month listening to you, Liz, throwing out hints and being mysterious. I've had enough. Either you come clean with me now, or I walk out of this house and you're on your own. Neil Browning won't be available either. The embassy's closed to you from now on."

"How can you say that? What's Neil got to do with you?"

"He's my subordinate," Davina said calmly. "I've ordered him to cut off from you. As I said, you either tell me the truth now, or you face whatever it is entirely alone. If there's anything to face." She looked at the other woman and said in the same deadly calm way, "If you've been lying just to get attention, I won't blame you. Just admit it, and that's the end of it."

"What are you?" Liz Fleming whispered. "What do you mean, Neil is your subordinate?"

"Never mind what I am," Davina answered. She looked at her watch.

"It's two minutes to eleven. You have two minutes to decide."

"I'm going to have a drink," Liz mumbled.

Davina moved very quickly. She set her back against the trolley. "No," she said. "You're not having anything. You're not going to get drunk and run away this time."

"I need something," the woman quavered. "My nerves—"

"You'll be able to have as much as you like after I've gone."

"He's going to kill me," Elizabeth Fleming said. "The way he killed his first wife."

Davina didn't move. "Why?" she asked.

Liz's hands with their scarlet nails and glittering ring came up to her mouth and partly covered it. They were trembling. "I can't tell you that," she said. "Just get me out of here. Get me somewhere I'll be safe."

"You tell me why," Davina said. "Then I can help you. But not before. Why would your husband want to kill you?"

"Because I found out something." Suddenly Liz Fleming seemed to sag; her body shrank down upon itself until she seemed quite small. Her hands fell to her sides and hung there as if something attaching them had broken.

"Come with me," she said. "Upstairs. I'll show you."

It was a diary; a small brown leather book with the initials RF tooled in gold in the bottom right-hand corner. The leather was scuffed at the edges. It was hidden at the bottom of a box of tissues. Fleming's wife held it out to Davina.

"I change the hiding place," she said. "I hide it somewhere different every day, just in case. He tore the place to pieces looking for it at first. Now he believes what I told him. It's my life insurance." She gave a scared glance behind them at the closed bedroom door. "I've read it over and over," she said, whispering as if they could be overheard. "The last entries—you look at them."

Davina held the little book. "You'd better come back with me. I'll look at this when we get there." One quick glimpse inside showed that the entries were in a woman's writing, and that the diary was two years old. She had a surge of excitement that showed in a flush of color on her cheeks. The thrill of the hunter in sight of his quarry. The spurt of adrenaline into the bloodstream. She had forgotten the sensation. Without knowing it, she smiled.

"Come on," she said. "I'll give you your drink when we get to my flat." She put the little book into her bag; she took Elizabeth Fleming by the arm and hurried her out of the room and out of the house. Lomax had been right. The bluff had indeed worked.

* * *

The studio was very quiet; the single duplex living area was filled with sunshine from the high windows, and double glazing cut out the traffic noise from the street below them. Elizabeth Fleming was crouched on the big green sofa, her legs tucked up under her, both arms hugging herself. Davina had kept her promise and given her one drink to steady her. Elizabeth's eyes were red and her mascara had streaked from crying. Her face was blurred with constant changes of expression, from weeping to anger and back to fear.

Davina had the diary in her hands. The initials RF were for Raffaella Fleming. The entries were varied, some only a line or two marking appointments or social engagements, and then towards the end the writer began to comment. There hadn't been time to read it with close attention. The later entries were the ones that counted, as Elizabeth had said. Davina closed it and put the little book down on the table.

"Where did you find this?"

"I didn't find it," she answered. "I was given it. By the goddamnedest coincidence. You'll never believe it when I tell you."

"Go on," said Davina. "I'll believe you."

"You'll believe me now," Liz accused suddenly. "Now that you've read that other poor bitch's diary and you know what happened to her! But you wouldn't believe me before, would you?" She squeezed out more tears and blew her nose. Don't lose your patience now, Davina told herself. Let her take a swing at you if she feels any better for it . . .

"I'm sorry, Liz," she said. "I misjudged you. Now tell me, where did you get this diary?"

Elizabeth Fleming shifted on the sofa, she brought her legs down and her feet to the floor. "After the wedding we came to Washington. I didn't know the city at all. I like to have regular massages and facials; I asked a senator's wife where to go. She recommended this beauty parlor. She said Eddie's first wife used to go there. She swore by it. So I went. I wanted to see where Raffaella went to keep herself in shape. She was an attractive woman, Davina. Half Mexican, very sexy. And *very* rich. I wasn't bothered by any of that; Eddie was crazy about me and didn't care a damn about her. I was just curious, I suppose. So I went to the beauticians, and as I was paying the bill, a girl came out of the office with a little case. It had a tag tied to it, saying Mrs. Fleming. You know the sort of thing, Davy, people put passports, a paperback in it, things you don't carry in your ordinary bag. She said, 'Oh, Mrs. Fleming, this has got your name on it. I saw it inside in the office safe and got it out when you made your appointment. It's been here ages.' It was Raffaella's; I saw the initials RF on the lid. So I took it. It was locked. I broke it open when I got home. There was a lot of rubbish in it, and the diary. She must have left it behind just before they went to Mexico. Look at the last entry—she burned to death in a fire. A nice accidental fire. Only she thought he might try with the car again. That's what she wrote."

"Yes," Davina said quietly. "That's how it reads. Listen to me, Liz. I've got to have time to study this. I want to check on the facts before I do anything more. It'll take a few days. Do you want to stay here?"

She hesitated. "I'd like to; sweet Jesus, wouldn't I like to hole up here and lock the door on him!" Then slowly she shook her head. "No, Mousey, I'd better not. So long as I stay at home he'll have to behave himself. He thinks I've lodged that diary with an attorney. It sounds like a cheap gangster movie, doesn't it, but that's exactly what I said. You can't touch me, I told him, because your wife's diary will go straight to the police if anything happens to me. Anything. He believed me, after he'd searched the house. He beat me up," she said. "Not where it'd show, of course. I didn't tell him the name of the attorney because I don't have one. I kept the diary all the time."

"Why did you tell him in the first place?" Davina asked her.

Liz Fleming shrugged defensively. "I read it over and over," she said. "I was stunned. I couldn't believe it. Try to understand,

Mousey, I was in shock. I had a drink or two, and when he came home I just couldn't keep it back. I faced him with what she'd written."

"What did he say?" The questions were quiet punctuations in the story; the other woman hardly noticed she was being prompted.

"Say? God, he nearly died. I've never seen a man look so shaken, so bloody scared stiff! And then he got furious. He shouted at me, he denied everything, he said I was drunk. He wanted to see the diary. I remember laughing at him, I was hysterical really, and then he hit me. He ended up saying it was all lies, that I'd made it up to blackmail him."

"Why blackmail?"

"Stop him leaving me," she retorted. "I'd had an affair or two and he was thinking about his reputation. He'd got high on the President's bandwagon and he didn't want me causing a scandal. He had talked about divorce. So he said I'd invented the diary to make him stay with me. I need a drink; just a little one."

"Of course." Davina nodded. "I'll get one for you."

She could imagine the scene. If she hadn't read the little book, she might have accepted Edward Fleming's explanation. Most people would accept his word against the accusations of a woman like Elizabeth Fleming. But not when they read those entries, and the last pathetic words written the day before the fatal trip to Mexico. "I love him enough; I could forgive him for what he is. Maybe I can prove it to him. But I'm so afraid." She shivered, as she gave the whisky to Elizabeth. "Goose walked over my grave," she said.

"It walked over Raffaella's," she answered. She took a long swallow.

"We never spoke of it again. I tried once but he just asked me who I was sleeping with this time. I wasn't, as it happened. I was too scared and too confused. Life went on as usual, except that we were not just strangers but enemies. He hated me, and he showed it. He used to sleep with me, even when we weren't getting on and there was another man. He was completely hung up on me that way. But that stopped. He couldn't bear to touch me. The hell of it is, I used to read that damned diary in secret, just to remind myself that it was really true and I hadn't imagined some of it.

"He was nominated for this post; I remember the evening very well. People kept calling and coming to the house to congratulate him. We opened champagne; he stood beside me and when someone important came up to us, he put his arm round me. It was the creepiest feeling, I can tell you. There we stood, the golden couple, in our lovely Washington house with all the world saying nice things to Eddie and envying me having such a brilliant husband. I made a fool of myself afterwards." She looked at Davina. "You'll think I'm hopeless," she said. "You're a very strong person; you'd never have done it. But I did." She wiped away more tears. The glass was nearly empty.

"I'm not strong at all," Davina said. "What did you do?"

The face looked up at her, wretched with pain and self-contempt. "I tried for a reconciliation," Elizabeth Fleming said. "I nerved myself to go up and tell him I loved him and it didn't matter about anything else. Do you know what he said? He said, Give me Raffaella's diary and then I'll believe you. I'm not a clever woman, not like you. But I'm not a fool either. I know men; I looked into his face and I knew that all he wanted was to get that book, and he'd throw me out in the street. I told him to go to hell. It was very late, into the early morning; the celebration party had been going on all night. Neither of us was sober. I went to bed, and the next thing I knew I was awake and something was choking me. Davina—" she stared into the distance, unaware that for once she had dropped the patronizing nickname, "—Davina, there was a pillow over my face. I couldn't breathe. I kicked out and clawed with my nails, and I felt something, like an arm, in the darkness. Then the pillow fell off and I heard someone moving. I called out, but it was dark and I couldn't see. The movement came again and I knew he'd gone out through the dressing-room door. I got to the bathroom before I was sick. I was sick again and again. It was late morning before I could pull myself together. I had a drink—who wouldn't? I had several drinks. Then I went to the embassy and asked to see Arthur Moore. He was at home; I'd forgotten it was Sunday. I don't know if you heard about that—"

Davina nodded. "Never mind," she said. "You got a bit high, that's all. Nobody blamed you."

"I was terrified," Liz Fleming muttered. "I believed he'd tried to kill me. They didn't believe me, of course. Being pissed didn't help. I wanted to stay in the embassy, not go back to the house. Have you any idea how it felt? It was hopeless! There he was, telling me not to worry, all I needed was a rest—there, there, Mary will look after you, we'll talk about it later. Dreams can be very convincing, you know, it was just a nightmare—Oh, God, talking to Arthur was the nightmare. I didn't try with Mary, I hadn't the strength to go through it all again. I just went up to a room and fell asleep.

"They brought in a young embassy attaché, Neil Browning, Arthur said he would keep in touch with me while they made inquiries. But I must go home. Neil took me back. I liked him, you know. He was very comforting. You don't have to worry, he said. I'm on call day or night if anything bothers you. But it was just a nightmare, you know. He damned nearly convinced me. So I went back, and when I felt lonely or my nerves got out of hand, I used to call him and we'd meet. It became a sort of routine. I relied on him and he kept telling me the embassy were looking into Eddie's past."

"But you didn't tell anybody about the diary?" Davina asked. "Why not, Liz, why didn't you prove it to them?"

"I tried once," Liz mumbled. "I actually brought it with me when I was meeting Neil. I was scared that time; we'd had a bad row and I was jumpy. I was going to show it to Neil . . ." She hesitated. "It sounds crazy, but it was one of those days when he wasn't paying much attention. Do you know what I mean? He was making all the right noises, and his mind was miles away. He treated me like a record, playing the same old tune over and over. And I remember thinking, it's no good. It's no good showing him. He's not taking anything you say seriously; you can't trust him. He'd want to take it away, show it to other people. Without the proof, I'm helpless. Edward can do what he likes . . . It wasn't very logical, I can see you thinking that—but that's how I felt. I didn't tell him about it and I put it away again. Until you came. I knew I could trust you. I knew you were the person to give it to."

"I understand perfectly." God, Davina said to herself. The one day it mattered that idiot Neil switches off . . . "You were quite right to wait. I think I'll have a cup of coffee. Would you like one, Liz?"

"Thanks." Liz Fleming sighed. She leaned her head back. "Oh, God, why did this have to happen to me? Why do I always pick losers? I was so happy with Eddie at first. We had everything. Then it got a bit boring. I thought he was neglecting me for his work—I actually thought he was becoming dull! Dull—my God, if I'd only known what he was really like . . ."

Davina had gone into the kitchen. She hardly heard the monologue of self-pity coming from the sitting room. She went through the routine of making coffee. She closed the kitchen door. She lifted the extension in the kitchen and dialed through to the front hall. The phone was answered instantly by Colin Lomax. "Come up, will you? What—no, of course I'm all right, there's nothing like that—calm down! But come to the flat. Yes, she's here and it's worked." The kettle shrieked and turned itself off. She hung up and made three cups of coffee. She took them into the sitting room. Liz Fleming had helped herself to another glass of whisky. Davina held out the coffee to her.

"No more Scotch for the moment," she said. "Colin is on his way up."

"Your boyfriend?" Liz said. "I don't want to see him, not in this state."

"He's not my boyfriend," Davina said, "we work together. He's here to help you the same as I am. You asked me what I was back at your house. I think you can guess, Liz, can't you? It wasn't a coincidence that I came out to Washington. I was sent out. Especially to look after you. Neil Browning told you the embassy was making inquiries. Well, they were. Colin and I are the result of those inquiries. Put the drink down and have some coffee. You found Neil a great help, Colin is even better. You can trust him. You can tell him everything you've told me."

The telephone rang at eight o'clock. Davina answered it. She recognized the voice at once. "This is Edward Fleming—hallo, Davina, how are you? Sorry to bother you, but is Liz with you?" She covered the mouthpiece and said rapidly, "It's Fleming." Then she spoke into the phone again, "Yes, she is. I'm afraid I've kept her far too late. She says she's on her way home now." "I'll take a cab," Liz called out.

"She'll pick up a taxi," Davina repeated.

"No hurry," his voice said. "So long as I know where she is; I know she's all right if she's with you. Thanks, Davina; see you soon, I hope."

Davina turned to Elizabeth Fleming. "I'm getting through to London. I think the time has come for you to get out of this. I'll call you first thing in the morning. Why not let Colin drive you home?"

"I'll take a cab," Liz said. "If he sees me in a car with a man he'll think I'm up to something. Or he'll pretend to think so." Davina came up to her; she took her arm and held it for a moment. "Don't drink any more tonight," she said. "You've had a long day and you don't want to provoke any trouble. Go home, make an excuse and go to bed. Promise me?"

"All right," she said. She looked wretchedly tired, with deep, dark rings under her eyes. "You'll ring me tomorrow? I know it's silly but I have the feeling that he'll know I've given the diary to you. He can read people's minds. I don't want to stay in America now."

"You won't have to," Davina assured her. "I hope to put you on a flight to London tomorrow. Goodnight, Liz. Do as I said. Don't discuss anything with him. Go to bed and lock the door if you feel safer. Just till tomorrow."

Colin Lomax had opened the door to the street for her; he watched the two women silhouetted against the hall light. Elizabeth Fleming was taller than Davina; he saw the light reflected in Davina's red hair, and then the other woman reached down and kissed her. "You've been such a friend, Mousey—how can I ever thank you?" And Lomax said, "You can stop calling her that bloody silly name, for a start. Here's a cab coming down the street now." He hailed it, and slammed the door when she was inside. He went back into the flat.

"Well done," he said to Davina. "You broke her wide open."

"I see London's reasoning," Davina said slowly. "I can see the Chief and Humphrey sitting together nodding like a couple of Mankin dolls, saying, we'll leave her where she is, because he's bound to try and kill her, if there's any truth in what she says."

"That's a pretty picture," he said. "I don't think I like it." "Neither do I," she said, "but that's the way the service works. They use you and they lose you. Results are all that count."

She sat down, stretched her legs out on the sofa, and kicked off both shoes.

"Sometimes," she said, "I think there's nothing to choose between our lot and the opposition. I can't see why the Russians haven't stopped her already."

"Because of her lie about the diary being sent to the attorney."

She shrugged that aside. "That's nonsense," she said. "If they wanted to find out where she's hidden it, they could have done it easily. It doesn't make sense to me. What time is it?"

"Nearly nine."

"Between four and four thirty London time. I'll have to go to Hickling's house to use the scrambler phone. God, I'm tired!"

"I could make the call for you," he suggested. "Why don't I do that?"

"Because it's not your job," she said gently.

It was after ten o'clock when they came back to the apartment. They were both silent, both depressed. London's reaction had been enthusiastic, congratulatory and absolutely firm. Elizabeth Fleming was to remain in Washington with her husband. It was no concern of Davina's whether she was in actual danger or not. Davina, accompanied by Lomax, was to concentrate on checking the facts in the diary, while London investigated Edward Fleming's early life before his emigration to the States. On the surface, everything must remain the same. The final sting came at the end. London had known for some time that Neil Browning was a Russian agent, and were making full use of that knowledge. Nothing must be done to alert him. That was all. Davina put the telephone down while Sir James was repeating his congratulations to her. They drove home in silence, and came to the apartment door. Lomax went in first, switched on the lights. The phone rang. He strode across and picked it up. Davina stood watching him, listening to the brief exchange, and then moved forward as she saw the look on his face. He turned to her.

"It's Fleming," he said. "He says he's been calling us—he says she didn't come home."

"Oh, my God," Davina said slowly.

Lomax didn't waste time. "We'd better get over there," he said. "She's been gone two hours. I don't like the sound of this. I don't like it at all."

Chapter Four

"I'VE SEARCHED everywhere," Edward Fleming said. "I've called up anyone she might have stopped off to visit, I've been round the places she might go in for a drink. I haven't tried the downtown bars because Elizabeth wouldn't be seen dead in places like that." He turned to Davina, his arms outspread.

"I don't know where the hell she's got to," he said. "And I'm dead worried. She's been gone nearly three hours since she left your apartment."

"Has she ever gone missing before?" Lomax asked the question.

"No," Fleming said, and then he hesitated. "Well—she's been pretty late home, but I always knew where she was."

He went to the trolley and poured himself a drink; watching him, Davina saw that his hand shook. "She spent the day with you," he said, turning round to face her. "How was she? What kind of mood was she in when she left you?"

"Perfectly normal," she answered. "Rather tired. We'd had a long day, shopping and gossiping, and the time just slipped by till you telephoned. She said she was going straight home."

"She'll probably turn up," Lomax remarked. "With a perfectly good explanation. You'd not be offended, Mr. Fleming, if I said she drinks a lot?"

Fleming shook his head. Davina kept her eyes on his hands; they were a better indicator than his face, if the man was a good actor. But he didn't possess a very cool nerve. He had to put his glass down because the ice was rattling.

"She's an alcoholic," he said flatly. "I've done my damnedest to get her to give it up. But she won't. She won't see a doctor; I tried contacting AA but she laughed in my face when I offered to take her to a meeting. It's become a major problem in our lives."

"She could have gone off suddenly on a number one drunk," Lomax said. "But my guess, having seen her when she left, is that she meant to come back here. If you've no other ideas, we'd better contact the police."

He crossed one leg over the other and gave Fleming a hard stare. "You've already left it pretty late."

"It's a last resort," Fleming answered. "The moment I call the police here, it'll make the morning papers. I have a responsibility to the administration. I can't have a scandal. I've got to be certain she's really missing before I have the media camping out here."

"Colin," Davina said, "did you notice anything about the cab she took?" He frowned. "Standard type, yellow cab, colored driver—why don't we call the Yellow Cab Company and ask about the cab? They're all radio-contacted. We can solve this in a few minutes."

Davina got up and went to the trolley. "Do you mind?" she asked Fleming.

"No, no, go ahead, help yourself."

She didn't want a drink. She wanted to see whether the neck of the whisky decanter was wet. Fleming was drinking vodka. She ran her finger over the rim of it. It was dry. She poured a small finger of Scotch for herself. Liz Fleming hadn't had time for a drink if she'd come back to the house.

Fleming was speaking to the cab company. He gave his address and Davina's. There was a long pause. Tension held her and Lomax in taut silence as they watched Fleming. "Oh. Oh, I see. Thanks." He turned back to Lomax. "You got the wrong cab company," he said. "They haven't any cab that might have picked her up around eight."

"It was a yellow cab," Colin said, speaking to Davina. "I don't make mistakes like that."

They saw Fleming shrug the remark aside. "What do we do now?" he asked.

"You haven't searched the house, I suppose?" Davina said suddenly. "She could have slipped in and gone upstairs without you knowing it."

He shook his head. "I can see the hall from here. I didn't leave the room. But I'll look." "I'll come with you," Lomax said. Davina was alone. The house was very quiet; she couldn't sit still, so she got up and moved restlessly about. She paused by the wedding photograph of the Flemings. Elizabeth was beautiful then; they were smiling into the camera, holding hands and looking happy. He must have loved her once.

Fleming, grim-faced, came into the room. Lomax followed and the colored maid was with them.

"Mrs. Fleming hasn't been in the house since she left with you this morning, ma'am," Ellen said. She was sorry for Mr. Fleming. His wife was a no-good. Better for him if she *had* disappeared. She said goodnight to them, and closed the door after her.

Fleming sat down and held his head in his hands. "I'll call the police," he said, "there's nothing else to do."

"Wait till morning. She may come back. Or you may get a message. I think in view of the cab, you've got to consider kidnaping."

He looked up sharply and stared at Davina. "Kidnaping?"

"It's beginning to look like it," Lomax said. "The cab was a phony. Someone has picked up your wife and is holding her.

Davina's right. Do nothing, wait till morning. You'll hear from whoever has got her by then."

"I can't believe it," he said. "Holy God, I can't believe it."

"I think we'd better go now," said Davina. "If you hear anything, call, doesn't matter if it's in the middle of the night. I won't sleep anyway."

Fleming didn't get up; he watched them both and said in a tense voice, "If it's anything political I won't give way. They can have every cent I've got to save Elizabeth, but my duty to the President comes first. I won't be blackmailed."

"Don't tell us," Lomax retorted. "Tell them."

In the car, she said to him, "I don't think Fleming is mixed up in this. He was shaking like a leaf when we got there. Colin—are you thinking the same as me?"

"KGB snatch? It looks like it. Phony cab, they must have the phone or the apartment bugged to know she wasn't being driven back. Kidnapers can grab their victim any time. This was planned well ahead."

"Then why wouldn't Fleming know? They're protecting him!"

"They're not famous for communicating," Lomax said. "And you can bet your bottom dollar his Russian friends don't know we have the diary."

"They do, if our flat is wired up," Davina said. "They've probably been listening in on every word we said today. That explains it. They know Liz has documentary proof that Fleming is a traitor. They also know she gave that proof to us. Oh, Colin, they'll tear her to pieces." She covered her face with her hands. Memories, terrors, came crowding back. She took a very deep breath as she had been taught to do, and fought them off. When Lomax looked at her she was sitting upright again, but her face was terribly white.

He said quietly, "Never mind her. We are the ones they'll come after now, to get the bloody diary back. Let's get the apartment phones checked out straightaway." They called Hickling from the nearest drugstore. He said he'd bring an electronics man within half an hour.

It took the expert ten minutes to find that the main phone and the kitchen extension were being tapped from outside. Then he went through the apartment room by room. He sounded the walls with a detector, the light fittings, every piece of furniture, every crevice that could conceal a microphone. He paid particular attention to the bedrooms. He came back to the sitting room and said to Hickling, "The flat is clear. They didn't have time to do a proper job or they'd have gone into the walls. They just cut in on the two phones." He turned to Davina. "They're OK now. I fixed them so anyone tuning in gets a high-pitched buzz."

"Thanks," Davina said. The man went out to make his own way home. She said to Peter Hickling, "It's very lucky for us they didn't wire up the whole place. Particularly as Elizabeth Fleming gave me classified information. But it's no thanks to the efficiency of your department. I suggest you make it standard procedure to check on any apartment used by British staff *before* they actually move in." She turned her back on him. "Goodnight," she said. He grimaced at Lomax, who didn't respond, and then shrugged slightly. The Scot had changed his attitude towards Miss Almighty God Davina Graham. The fact that she was right, and he'd been negligent, just made it worse. He let himself out of the flat.

Colin gave her a lighted cigarette. "Well done. He deserved that. How about a cup of coffee? You're shaking, woman."

"What bloody incompetence!" She swung round on him. "Fancy not checking on a thing like that, knowing how sensitive this business was with Liz—I've a good mind to make an official complaint—it's time these embassy layabouts woke up."

"Steady on," said Lomax. "Personally I don't think it is a KGB job. They'd have found a way to do the apartment over properly. The phone is easy for anyone with a basic knowledge of electronics. I'm beginning to think this is exactly what it seems. A straightforward kidnaping. Fleming will get a ransom note. Wait and see."

"I don't believe it." She shook her head at him. "I'd like to, because it would ease my conscience. Fleming could buy her back. If the others have got hold of her—I know very well what that means."

"For Christ's sake," he said, "get your priorities straight! The flat's not bugged so nobody knows about the diary. If you were right, they'd have got it out of her, and that would worry me. But nothing's happened, and I don't think anything's going to. You need a good night's sleep. Shut up the imagination. You can't help her by worrying."

"I sent Liz back home," Davina said. "I sent her out to that cab. I don't think I'm going to sleep too well on that." She got up and went to her room.

A few minutes later there was a brisk knock on the door. Lomax came in with a steaming glass. He set it down beside the bed. "Drink that. And no arguments! It's my own toddy—the famous Lomax special. I promise you, you'll sleep!"

"There's no need to be afraid, Mrs. Fleming," Jeremy Barr said. He was shielded from her by a bright light; all she could see was a man in shadow, with other shadows behind him. She squinted against the powerful light; her face was putty-gray with fear.

"Who are you? What do you want?"

Jeremy ignored the repeated question. "We've been watching you for some time," he said. "And we don't like what we've seen. We've brought you here to give you a friendly warning."

"Who are you?" she said again.

"Never mind who we are." His voice was suddenly sharp, bullying. "I'm asking the questions! Shut up and listen!" She cringed, and he changed tactics immediately. It was part of a well-tried technique. "That's better," he said. "I don't want to frighten you.

Just don't interrupt me, OK? I'll ask for an answer when I want one, OK? You understand?"

She nodded miserably.

"Right." Jeremy leaned forward a little; she could see more of his outline but nothing of his face. "You want to know who we are," he said. "Let's just say that we're loyal Americans and good friends of your husband's. We can be very good friends; or very tough enemies with people who cross us. We think you may be doing just that, Mrs. Fleming. We're not very happy with the way you've been treating your husband. You're drinking too much, making people talk. How come you're friendly with Miss Graham? She's hardly your type, is she? She doesn't get pissed. Why do you see so much of her, Mrs. Fleming? What *do* you have in common?"

"We were at school, she came on a visit—who are you, for Christ's sake, stop frightening me, can't you—I feel sick."

"I wouldn't do that," the voice said from behind the light. "We'll only make you clean it up. And you don't need to work yourself up, nobody's going to hurt you. Just answer the questions. Tell me about Miss Graham. Tell me what she says and what you say."

"We talk about school." The voice quivered. "We go shopping. I don't know what you want. I want to go home."

"What do you mean by home?" Jeremy asked her. "Home to Georgetown or home to England? Why don't you go home to England, Mrs. Fleming? What do you and Miss Graham *really* talk about?"

Terror showed in the face of the woman in the circle of light. She made a sudden grimace, and Jeremy Barr thought she was going to vomit. He reached out and switched off the light. "Give Mrs. Fleming a glass of water," he said.

The room was dim, full of shadows that moved. She took the water and sipped it. "Let me go home," she whimpered. "Please, I haven't done anything."

"You've disgraced your husband," Barr snapped at her. The light flared again, blinding her. She dropped the glass and water soaked her skirt.

"The only home you should go to is for alcoholics. There are plenty of places like that. Do you realize, your husband could have you committed and you'd never get out?" She shook her head; tears were running down her cheeks. "I think that's what he should do."

"No—no—please. I won't drink, I won't do anything . . . "

"What does Davina Graham ask you?" The question was shot at her again. "What does she want with a tramp like you?"

"Nothing," she cried out. "I'm unhappy, I'm lonely—I talk about the old days when we were girls." She started to crumple and the man standing behind caught her and held her in the chair. The light went out again. There was no sound except her muffled crying.

"Mrs. Fleming," Jeremy said, and his voice was gentle, "I'm sorry I've upset you. But we have to take care of people living in Washington. We have to keep a watch on them. We even have to call them in and ask them questions sometimes. I can't promise this won't happen again. It wouldn't, if you decided to go back to England. Think about it, won't you?"

He whispered to a man just behind him, "I think that's enough. Get her cleaned up, and get her out of here."

Lomax woke very early; he was a light sleeper by nature, and a man who had to get up once he was awake. It was a beautiful morning, and at five A.M. the Washington streets were deserted. He opened the window. It was cool and fresh at that hour, the humidity held at bay. He went to Davina's bedroom and looked inside. She was asleep, nursing her pillow. He thought she looked vulnerable, almost like a child. He closed the door again very quietly. The disappearance of that worthless woman had shaken her badly. She needed a long healing sleep, before she faced the day.

He dressed, and put the diary in his back pocket. The sooner they could work on it and deposit it in the embassy safe the better. He decided to go for a walk and pick up the early editions of the morning papers.

It was a quiet, tree-lined street. As he strode towards the central avenue bisecting it, a solitary car sped past him. The driver slowed, watched Lomax in the driving mirror, accelerated again. At the end of the street he pulled into the curb. When Lomax disappeared, he put the car into reverse and drove back down the street, slowly this time, coming to a stop twenty yards from the studio apartment door. He checked his watch and got out. There was nobody about. He ran lightly up the shallow steps to the entrance, and jammed his finger on the bell.

Davina heard the persistent buzzing through her sleep; she woke unwillingly, confused by the ringing of the outside entrance bell.

She got up and called out "Colin?" He wasn't in his room and the apartment was empty. "Damn," she said, "must have gone out without the key . . ." She picked up the entry phone and said automatically, "Who is it?" At the front door the man said in a muffled voice, "It's me." She pushed the release knob and downstairs the entrance door clicked open. I'm still half asleep, she thought, and yawned. There was a tap on the apartment door. She slipped the latch and said, "You're an early bird . . ." and started to scream as the man leaped at her.

He was very quick; he knocked the breath out of her with a blow to the stomach that sent her doubled up and reeling, and cut the scream off before it began. She crumpled to the ground. He bent down and pulled her to her feet; she was gasping with pain and shock; he gripped her bare arms and squeezed brutally. Her eyes were full of tears, blurring his face.

"You're going to be quiet," he said. "Or you'll get more." He dragged her to a chair. She was focusing now, seeing him properly for the first time. Young, dark-haired, eyes like a wild animal's in a thin face. He pushed her backwards into the chair. "Don't talk, put your hands behind you." She did as she was told. She had started to shiver. He tied her wrists together and fastened them to the chair rail.

He knelt beside her, and said softly, "Now you can talk. Where's the little book?"

Lomax bought two papers, glanced at the headlines, folded them under his arm, and paused, wondering whether to go home or take some exercise around the park. He had never been able to explain what activated his instinct for danger. It was like a chill, a swift *frisson* of the nerves that was as basic as the warning system of animals in the wild.

Standing there with the newspapers tucked under his left arm, Lomax scented danger. He had never ignored that premonition; it had saved his life on three occasions. He turned for home, and as he came to the top of the street and noticed the distant car parked near Davina's flat, he broke into a run.

"Where is it?" The point of the knife was under Davina's chin. She stared into the eyes and saw the savagery in them. "I don't know," she whispered. "I haven't got it."

"Don't lie to me," he hissed at her. "I'll cut you into little pieces. I'll make a jigsaw out of your face. What have you done with the book? All you have to do is tell me. Then I won't hurt you, see?"

She saw murder in her captor's face, the longing to use that knife on her face and body. "It may be in my friend's room," she whispered. "He kept it." He reached behind and cut her bound hands loose from the chair rail. He said, "I haven't got time to search. You come and tell me where it is." He propelled her forward by the nape of the neck; his fingers were claws digging into her skin.

"Now," he said. "Show me, before I cut a little slice out of you."

Davina's mind was racing. Where was Colin? Had he been hurt?

"It's not on the table, is it? Not in the drawers? You've been stalling, haven't you?" He was holding her bound arms above the elbows, hurting her so that she gasped and almost cried out. She felt the hot, stale breath by her cheek as he brought his face close to hers. "I'm going to cut you," he whispered. "Just a little . . ."

That was when Lomax came through the doorway. Davina saw him standing there, reflected in the mirror, where she had been pinioned to watch her own terrified reflection. The attacker saw him seconds later.

"Hello there," Lomax said, and launched himself into the air. His body struck them both; Davina was hurled out of her assailant's grip. There was a crash and a splinter of glass, as the table and mirror smashed under the impact. Lomax sent the knife spinning with a savage blow to the elbow and followed with an uppercut to the jaw, which poleaxed the man. As he lay half-dazed on the floor the man pulled a gun out of his waistband. He didn't even have time to aim. Lomax kicked him in the throat. There was a cry and a choked gurgle as the windpipe shattered. He died while Lomax was lifting Davina and carrying her out of the room.

He let her cry for some time. When at last she quietened, he said gently, "You'll be all right if I leave you alone now." It wasn't a question. She nodded, shivered once more and then was calm. "Yes. What are you going to do?"

"Get rid of him. I'll drive the car downtown and leave him in it. There's nothing to connect him with us."

"I should have been more careful," she whispered. "What on earth did you put in that toddy?"

Lomax was busy, dragging the dead man across the floor. "He's heavier than he looks," he said grimly.

Davina rose to her feet. "I'll help," she said. "Wait, while I put some clothes on."

Davina went into the street first. It was empty. Washington still slept on a Sunday morning. Lomax pointed out the car, and gave her the keys he had fished out of the dead man's pockets.

She drove the car up to the entrance. Together they supported the body—from a distance he might have looked like a drunk, except for the gruesome way his head lolled—and loaded it into the backseat.

"I'm coming with you," said Davina. "I don't want to be left alone."

Fifteen minutes later they boarded a bus, heading back to the apartment. Once they were inside, Davina started to shake again.

"We were lucky," he said. "He was just a bully boy with a knife. Someone they got hold of in a hurry. If he'd been a Moscow Center man, things might have been very different. But it proves one thing. They've got Liz and they know about the diary." He put his arm round her. "You were great," he said. "A real trouper, helping me get rid of him. I thought you were going to faint when I brought him out."

"I'm not the fainting type," Davina retorted. "Thank God you came back in time."

He reached out a hand to her face, and turned it towards him. "I never thought I'd hear you say anything like that," he said. "I never thought I'd want to do this either."

It was a long forceful kiss. She couldn't have pushed him away if she'd wanted to. There was one flash of guilt and doubt and then her arms went round his neck and her mouth opened.

After some minutes Lomax released her. They looked at each other in silence. Then he grinned and said, "My God, woman, there's nothing 'mousey' about you!"

"This is a mistake. We shouldn't do this. I shouldn't, anyway."

"Because I caught you in a weak moment? Or because of Sasanov?"

"Because we've both got a job to do and it isn't the time or the place to start getting involved."

"There's no such thing as a proper time and place," Lomax answered. "It happens or it doesn't. And if you're not careful I'll start talking about loving you, and then what will you do?"

"Colin, I don't know. I've only been in love once. I don't think I could cope with anything like that again."

"It wouldn't be like that," he said. "He was him and I'm me. It'll never be the same, but there's no reason why it can't be different."

She got up. "I don't know; I'm not ready to start anything serious." He stood with her; he put both hands on her shoulders and looked down at her. "You will be," he said. "And I'll be there. Now, as you nearly got killed for it, let's get down to work on that diary!"

It was the record of a trivial life, devoted to self-indulgence and self-presentation. Trips to the hairdresser in New York, the daily massage, the dressmaker, the lunches with other idle women, the dinners and cocktail parties, and the petulant comments that became more and more frequent as the year advanced. Edward away. Edward in Washington. Edward canceled return. The decline of their relationship marked by underlinings and comments charting furious rows, suspicions of infidelity on his part, and the recurring theme of making up in bed. And then towards the middle of August two sentences inked and underlined. *"Had Edward followed. Certain there is a woman."* Davina leaned over Colin's shoulder. He reached up and caught her hand. "Miserable, isn't it? You find yourself sympathizing with her. She was always alone—no wonder she got suspicious."

"Had him followed," Lomax remarked. "No record of the agency?"

"I haven't found one," Davina said. "I checked through the address section and there wasn't anything that fitted. But there wasn't any woman, as you'll see. There, that's when it comes together; that entry in early September when she gets the agency report—what the hell did she do with that, by the way?"

"God knows," he muttered. "Fleming probably destroyed everything after she died."

"She followed him herself," Davina said in a low voice, "what a crazy thing to do."

The last pages were covered in writing; there were no engagements, just comments and records of Raffaella's shadowing of her husband. She had hired a car and a driver, worn dark glasses and a scarf, and trailed him during the month of September. It was a record of his lies, of appointments that never took place, of meetings with a man at the Lincoln Memorial and visits to a photographic shop. She had written the name down: Washington Cameras. He was not in the least interested in photography and had never owned a camera. She had called in herself once, and found nobody there but a middle-aged man and a girl assistant who couldn't have been the real excuse. The meetings at the Lincoln Memorial were as seemingly pointless as the visits to the camera shop. Having watched from her hired car, once Raffaella had slipped in after him among the crowds. The diary told of her certainty that he was meeting a woman there. Her jealousy had insisted on a woman, even when the private detective reported that he had never been seen with one. And from her place among the wandering crowds of tourists, Raffaella had seen her husband take a seat near the central hall, open a newspaper and sit down. After a few minutes a man sat beside him. He opened a package of sandwiches and began to eat them. Neither spoke; Edward Fleming went on reading his newspaper, the man beside him ate his sandwiches. On this particular day he had told her he was lunching with business clients in New York and would be back on the afternoon shuttle. She watched until he folded his paper, left it on the seat and moved away. From there he returned to his office on Constitution Place. That evening he described in detail his lunch at the Plaza in New York.

The diary didn't offer explanations. It recorded what she had seen and asked the same question over and over without providing any answer—what is he doing? Is he crazy or am I? None of this makes any sense at all. He lies all the time and he sits on a seat in the Lincoln Memorial and goes to a camera shop on a Thursday. The second time she followed him to the Memorial she noticed that the same man came to eat his sandwich lunch on the seat beside him. Again Fleming left his newspaper behind. She hesitated, hiding among a group of tourists. She saw her husband disappear and then looked back at the seat. The man had finished eating. He picked up the newspaper, folded it into his coat pocket and left.

Now the diary described how Raffaella had started searching his briefcase and his desk when he was asleep. The briefcase was always locked. She stole the key one night and opened it. It was the night before he was due to go to the Lincoln Memorial again. Inside she found a folder headed Research Center Wyoming Falls, Appendix D. Highly Confidential was marked on one corner. She hadn't understood what was inside. It was a photocopy of a lot of drawings and technical jargon. She knew that Edward Fleming's company was concerned with the planning and construction of a top-security government project in the Wyoming desert. She put everything back. Next day he went to the Lincoln Memorial, when his secretary had told her he had gone to a Senate committee meeting. Nothing changed in the routine. His discarded newspaper was picked up. That night she opened the briefcase again. The folder was still in it, but empty.

"What a fool I am," the writer scrawled. "What a crazy fool not to know what he was doing from the start—oh, my God, what can I do? Who can I tell?"

She didn't follow him again. She paid off the driver and the hired car, and drove herself to her weekly session at the beauty parlor. Her brakes failed at the first traffic light and she was hit by a truck at the intersection. She was very lucky to escape with bruises and a nasty shock. The truck had been going unusually slowly, but even so the impact wrecked the car.

"He must have found out she was tampering with his keys," Lomax said. "Or following him."

"Or both," Davina countered. Fleming had been tender and considerate: Raffaella noted how he brought her flowers and fussed over her and threatened to sue the garage that had last serviced her car, but her suspicion flared when she called the garage and discovered he hadn't contacted them at all to complain about the brakes. Worst of all, Fleming had made efforts to mend the marriage, which his wife hadn't been able to resist. He had resumed a passionate sex life, which had always been his weapon, and become the loving husband as well as the lover. She loved him and wanted to believe in him; the diary recorded that only too clearly. But she was afraid, and the fear wouldn't be stilled. He was some kind of traitor, a spy. And she had nearly been killed in a car with faulty brakes soon after finding it out. "What can I do?" The cry leaped out of the little brown book. "We are going to my house in Cuernavaca next week—he is so loving to me now, he talks about our second honeymoon in Mexico—I love him so much, I'd forgive him for anything. But I am so afraid, and the fear won't go away . . . "

That was the last entry. Davina closed the diary. "They went to Cuernavaca," she said. "She owned a summer house there. Six weeks later it went up like a torch and she was burned to death. He just happened to be downstairs and escaped. A couple of Mexican servants died with her."

Lomax said slowly, "It ties up now, doesn't it? He's a KGB man all right, and he murdered his wife because she found out. Now this comes into the second wife's possession. He can't find it, and he knows what's in it would hang him masthead-high. He'd like to kill her too, but he daren't because she's got the diary as insurance."

"So in the end he calls in the KGB," Davina suggested. "She tells them she's given it to me."

"By now," Lomax said, "he'll be sweating blood."

"It's nothing to what he'll sweat when our people have finished with him," Davina said. "But that doesn't help Liz. God, Colin, I think we'd better take this over to the embassy and see the ambassador. I don't think we should hang about checking the facts; they can be checked later. The main thing is to get Fleming into the embassy. Then we can present him with this." She picked up the diary. "I'm going to nail that swine if it's the last thing I do!"

"Why should I go to the embassy? What has this got to do with them?" Edward Fleming faced Davina angrily. He looked exhausted, his skin a muddy color, deep circles under his eyes. He couldn't sit still. He kept pushing his hands deep into his trouser pockets and taking them out again.

"And what the hell has it got to do with you two, come to that?" It was the question Davina had been expecting; its vehemence was a splendid piece of acting, she decided.

"I think you know what it has to do with me. I hope it won't involve Mr. Lomax."

"You're supposed to be Elizabeth's friend,". Fleming's voice rose. "She's disappeared—you were the last people to see her—you come here with a veiled threat—what the *hell* are you, Miss Graham?"

"I'm a civil servant," she answered, "and Mr. Lomax is my assistant."

"And I'm not very civil," Lomax remarked. "So I'd accept that invitation, Mr. Fleming, and save yourself a lot of trouble."

He swung round on Lomax, clenching his fists. Lomax raised his head and looked at him. He didn't move. Fleming's hands opened and he turned away. "I see," he muttered. "You'll regret this. So will your government."

Lomax stepped to the door. One hand was hooked into his pocket. "Shall we go, Mr. Fleming? We don't want to keep the ambassador waiting." They drove to Massachusetts Avenue and parked in the forecourt. They went up to an office on the first floor. Outside, Lomax drew back. "You won't be needing me. It's going to be very friendly from now on."

Sir Arthur Moore came from behind his desk to meet Edward Fleming. He held out his hand and said pleasantly, "It's good of you to come, Edward. Do sit down, won't you? Davina will get us a drink."

Humphrey Grant's telephone rang. He was a light sleeper and he had switched on the bedside light and lifted the receiver before it had rung three times. His watch was on the night table, along with a glass of water, his spectacles, and a detective story he was in the middle of reading. It was four A.M. The line from Washington was better than usual. Sir Arthur Moore spoke first. Grant said "Yes" several times and sat bolt upright in bed. Then he heard Davina's voice.

"He's cracked; but not in the way we expected. We need someone to come over and get to grips with him. I can't do any more. He doesn't like me very much at the moment. Also someone got into our apartment and tried to get the diary back this morning. So that clinches the fact that Liz has been snatched and interrogated by the KGB."

"It also authenticates the diary," Grant remarked. Almost as an afterthought he added, "Nobody hurt, I hope?"

"Only the man they sent in," she answered. "Colin dealt with him."

"Good. You've done well. Congratulations. How much has Fleming actually admitted?"

"Embezzlement, as near as dammit murdering his first wife. But nothing else. John Kidson would be the best person to take over."

"He'll be with you tomorrow," Grant's high-pitched voice was crisp. "I mean today. I'll get the Chief to telephone you at eleven o'clock our time."

"I'll be here," she said. "The ambassador asks when you are going to contact the American authorities. Fleming is a U.S. citizen. It could be tricky."

"Tell Sir Arthur," Grant snapped, "that all he has to do is provide Fleming with a bed for the night. The moment Kidson arrives in Washington, Fleming will be off his hands. Goodnight."

He didn't put out the light. He sipped his water, sitting up in bed. Fraud, murder. But not treason, that would come. Elizabeth Fleming had been right after all, and had obviously paid a heavy price for it. This would make Watergate look like a bag snatching. He sighed deeply from relief and from exasperation. The ambassador was right, of course. They would have to disclose their discovery to the CIA. There would be red faces and angry recriminations at Langley. But they weren't going to get their hands on Edward Fleming until John Kidson had finished with him. Fleming was British-born. When and where he was recruited would be very relevant to home security if it had taken place before he went to the States. Grant strapped on his watch. It was now four thirty. Kidson would have to catch the first plane to New York. He decided to wait until six A.M. before he telephoned. That would give Kidson time to pack a bag and get to the airport. He settled down to read his detective story for the rest of the night.

They left the embassy and drove back through the deserted streets to their apartment. It was nearly two A.M. Sir Arthur Moore had insisted on them having coffee and sandwiches after the call to

London. Fleming had agreed to stay the night at the embassy. He'd been given two sleeping pills and collapsed like a rag doll. During the evening Davina had telephoned to Ellen and explained that he was staying with friends and would return home next morning. By that time he would be in Kidson's charge. Inside the flat, she dropped onto the sofa and kicked off her shoes. She covered her face with her hands and yawned.

"God, I'm so tired. I feel completely drained."

"Drink? Cup of coffee?"

She shook her head. "No, thanks. How often did you interrogate people?"

"Once or twice and only superficially. My job was to catch them; other people asked the questions. It's upset you, hasn't it?"

"Yes. He was resisting every inch of the way. He started using filthy language to me, screaming about Liz betraying him giving me the diary. I thought he was going to hit me several times. He would have, if the ambassador hadn't been there."

Lomax was scowling. "Why didn't you send for me?"

"There was no need. He was a trapped animal tonight, snarling at me because I'd caught him. And there was so much hate, Colin. Hate for his first wife, hate for Liz. He was unloading it all on me. When he did cave in it was somehow sickening and pathetic." She hugged herself with both arms and shivered.

Lomax smoked for a while without saying anything. Then he came to the sofa and held out both hands to her. Slowly she took them and let him lift her to her feet. They faced each other for a moment in silence, and then he said, "Woman, you look tired out. Mentally tired. Will you give in and let me give you what you need tonight?"

"And what is that?" She asked the question very quietly.

"This," he said. He held her close and kissed her. She could feel the tremor in his arms as he held her, and knew that he was holding back, being gentle and careful with her. The suppressed passion she sensed in him suddenly lit a quick fuse in her; desire glowed and fizzed in her and exploded before she had time to control it or push him away. She kissed him fiercely and hungrily and he gripped her so tightly that it hurt. His hands began to move over her back, up to her neck and into the thick red hair, rumpling it, the fingers coming round to her throat, moving downwards to her breast. Beside the furious beating of her own heart, Davina felt the thud of his under her hand as she pushed herself free of him.

"Colin—for God's sake—"

"I'm going to say it, whether you like it or not," he said. "I love you."

"You mustn't," she whispered.

"I can't help it. I'll say it again. I love you, Davina. Don't hold back from me."

She came close to him and put her fingers on his mouth to stop him kissing her.

"That's why I am holding back. I want you, Colin, but I don't love you. I'm sorry."

He looked at her, and firmly put her restraining fingertips aside.

"I'll settle for that for the time being," he said.

Davina woke before the dawn broke. He lay beside her, face down, one arm resting heavily over her body. The scars on his back were hidden in the darkness. She had seen them after they had made love, and felt a surge of tenderness as well as passion. He had conjured away the ugliness and the pain of human wickedness for her, and she had taken far more than she had given. He had been right, when he told her it would be different. Ivan had not been a tender or considerate lover; he had swept her along on his own urgent tide of desire. Colin Lomax, surprisingly, was intuitive and loving, and if he had challenged her now about her feelings, she wouldn't have been so sure of her answer. He woke as she got up.

"I've got to get to the embassy for that call," she said. "Go back to sleep."

"Come here a minute before you go." He looked oddly vulnerable sitting up, watching her with quiet expectancy.

"I'm not going to ask you anything, but did I make you happy?"

"Yes," she said gently, "you did."

He held out his arms to her and she came into them. "You loved him very much, didn't you?"

"You knew that."

"And you still do." She didn't deny it; the last thing he would want from her was a lie. "I have to go, or I'll be late for that call."

"Go on then," Lomax told her. "But remember one thing. I'm not giving up."

"I've got a marvelous idea," Charlie said. "Here, darling, don't bundle the jacket up like that, it'll be terribly creased—let me do it!"

John Kidson stood back and let her finish his packing. "Tell me about your marvelous idea," he said. His wife still surprised him after three years of marriage. The one word he would never have used in connection with her was efficient, and yet she could pack far better than he could, and he had lived out of suitcases most of his working life. She never appeared busy, and yet the house was efficiently run. The bills, which had been his chief concern when they married, remained at sensible limits, and when he came home in the evenings there was a drink ready for him and Charlie looking as if she had stepped off the front page of *Vogue*.

Seeing her bend over his case made him sorry he had to catch the early plane. He came up behind her. "Tell me the marvelous idea," he said and kissed the back of her neck. She sighed and giggled with pleasure. "Don't be naughty, darling. We haven't got time. You're going to be in Washington for a week or so, aren't you? And Davina's there too. So why don't I fly out and join you? Wouldn't that be fun?"

He turned her round to him. "It would, darling, but I can't afford it. And the Office doesn't like wives coming along."

"Don't worry about that," she said. "I'll settle Sir James, leave him to me. And you don't have to afford it, John, because I'm going to treat myself. We said we'd have a holiday after Fergie was born, so why not make it Washington? Don't you want me to come?"

He looked into the beautiful eyes and saw them brim with tears. She still cried easily after the baby's birth. He couldn't think of a single argument against having her with him.

"You come," he said, and kissed her. "You won't mind if I'm busy?"

"We'll be together in the evenings," she said. "It's some compensation for being such a rotten milch cow, I suppose. I couldn't have gone away if I'd been feeding Fergie."

"I've got to go," he said. "Let me know when you're arriving. And don't be too long."

Charlie smiled at him and kissed him goodbye. "Two days to get my clothes organized and I'll be on the plane," she said. "Safe journey, darling. Cable me when you've arrived, won't you?"

He promised, and she watched the car turn out of the little drive and disappear down the road. Washington would be great fun; she had paid a brief visit there during her second marriage and loved the city. Not as exciting, as vibrant as New York, but beautiful and historic, with amusing people and lavish hospitality. She examined herself in the mirror, smoothing her dressing gown over her hips, watching for signs of slack muscle or dreaded fat. There was a little fullness, perhaps, but it only added voluptuousness to a perfect figure. John said she was more beautiful since the baby than she had ever been.

John was wonderful. She wandered into the nursery. Their baby lay swaddled in its cot, making the little birdlike noises that signified its own contentment. There was a nice girl engaged to look after the baby; they could both go down to Marchwood under her mother's supervision while she was away in America. The change would do her good. And it would be nice to see Davina. The silly tears welled up again at the thought of her sister.

"I'm going to be especially nice to her in Washington," she told the baby. "I'm going to make a real effort to be kind and take her out and introduce her round. I know she won't have bothered to meet people. I'll see if we can find someone nice for her, shall I, darling? That would be a good idea, wouldn't it—and I won't be away for long and Granny will be thrilled to have you." She bent and kissed the top of the downy head. She smelled the sweet smell of baby powder and picked him up and cuddled him against her shoulder. He was thriving on the bottle; it was silly to mind about not feeding him. He mewed and nestled into her. She forgot all the stern dicta of the baby manuals and took him back to bed with her.

The call from Washington Cameras came through to Neil Browning's office on Monday. "Your films are ready," the girl assistant said. "Could you collect them this afternoon?"

"Thanks," Neil said. "I'll come round just after four." His instructions would be with the films. They must be urgent to require a special call. At five minutes past two he was at the shop door; there was a notice on it saying CLOSED. He rang the side buzzer and after a minute Bruckner came and opened the door.

"Come in." Bruckner held the door for him. He shut it and turned the closed notice over. "I sent the girl out," he said. "You go in back, someone's waiting for you. I'll stay out here and mind the shop."

Browning went through to the little office off the showroom. A man was sitting in Bruckner's chair reading a newspaper. Browning had met him four times in the twelve months he had been working for the KGB. He didn't know his name.

They didn't shake hands; the controller folded his paper and put it aside. He was a middle-aged man, thin, slightly bald and with pebble spectacles that distorted his face. He spoke through his nose with a Bronx accent that was quite genuine. "Things have started moving fast," he said to Browning. "We need some pretty detailed information. You've got to get it for us."

Browning swallowed; his mouth had suddenly gone dry. "What kind of information? I've got to be careful, you know."

"I know," the man said. "You've been well paid for not very much up until now. It's time you earned your money."

"What sort of information?" Browning was becoming more and more alarmed. "I don't have access to anything classified."

"You have access to Hickling and Graham, don't you?"

Neil agreed unhappily. But even so he couldn't be too curious—he'd do his best, of course. The controller's eyes looked froglike behind the thick lenses. "Better than your best," he snapped. "We want to know what the British reaction is to Mrs. Fleming and what she's said about her husband. We want to know what Graham has reported back. Get that information for us, and get it by tonight." He took off his glasses, peered at them and put them back. "You'll pick up ten thousand dollars," he remarked. "That's good money."

"It is," Neil agreed. "But supposing I can't find out today? How do I know Hickling will have anything new or even tell me about it?"

"He'll have something new." The tone was grim. "It's your business to get him to tell you what we want. And don't fail. We wouldn't like that." He picked up his paper and began to read again.

"I'll call this evening," Browning said. He nearly stammered. There was no answer. He went out to the front shop.

As soon as he had gone, the older man threw the newspaper aside. Sometimes his orders didn't make sense. He had been told to send someone in for a diary that incriminated an agent. That someone was to come from the underworld and not to have any KGB affiliations that could be traced if he was caught.

When the controller reported that the attempt had failed, Moscow's reaction had been surprisingly understanding. Use Jackdaw instead to get as much information from the embassy as possible. It was too late to get the diary now; it was in the embassy strongroom, and would soon be on its way to London. All they had to rely on was Neil Browning. The man sighed heavily and picked up the paper again. There was nothing he despised more than a commercially motivated traitor. And a dabbler in dirty photographs who hadn't the guts to face out a threat of blackmail. He was a clean-living family man himself.

"I came here to pick up films," Neil said. "So you'd better give me some."

Bruckner looked at him shrewdly. "You don't look too happy."

"I'm not." Browning took the packet from him. He walked back through the busy streets in the hot sunshine, scowling at his thoughts. The money was tempting, and he hadn't been asked to do too much for it. It was easy enough to pass on items that were within his province in the embassy and report to both sides about Elizabeth Fleming. But to go and prize information out of someone like Peter Hickling was a different matter. Nothing, he decided angrily, would induce him to tackle Davina Graham and try pumping her . . . He was sweating so much by the time he reached the embassy that he had to go downstairs to the washrooms and have a shower.

He took refuge for a while in his own office, saying he wouldn't take any calls. He had to think up an excuse to go to Hickling and start talking. Hickling was antisocial during office hours. His watch showed half past three. He couldn't go on sitting there wasting time. He put a call through to Peter Hickling's secretary. Would she tell her boss that Browning was on his way up?

It was fortunate for Browning that Peter wasn't very busy. He liked Neil, and he put his work aside and offered him a drink or a cup of coffee. Browning couldn't resist the drink. Hickling produced his bottle of gin, and Neil drank it straight with ice cubes from the thermos. It steadied him, and he recovered a measure of confidence.

"I looked in early on," he said. "But you were still at lunch. I wanted the papers on our Peruvian exports."

"Why should I have them?" Hickling said. "I don't deal with bona fide trade; that's your department, old chap."

"Someone said you were looking into the MPs who paid their goodwill visit, and the export figures were included in the file. Anyway I found them. My half-witted secretary had put them in the wrong order."

"She's not half-witted," Hickling retorted. "And even if she were, she's got the biggest boobs in the building!"

Neil laughed. "Had a good lunch?" he asked.

"Lunch, my foot," Hickling said. "I've been closeted up with the Old Man since this morning. Your friend Mrs. Fleming has disappeared."

Browning stared at Hickling. "Christ Almighty!"

"She left Davina's flat on Saturday, took a cab and was apparently going home. She never got there."

"There was nothing in the papers this morning, or on the radio," Browning said. "Haven't the police been told?"

"No," Hickling said. "We're keeping it dead quiet as long as we can. She may have been kidnaped."

She may indeed, Neil said to himself, and I could guess by whom—he felt a lurch of fright in his stomach.

"That's terrible," he said. "I've been out of touch, as you know. She dropped me when Davina came over. I must say, I was bloody glad to get shot of her, but this is awful. Had Davina made any progress with her? Had she got any further than I did?"

"A lot further," Hickling said. "I'm afraid I can't go into details.

It's got a red sticker on the file now. I hope it's not going to be marked 'closed.' "

"You think she's dead?"

"If someone hasn't approached Fleming by tomorrow morning, it looks like it," Hickling answered. "Fortunately for us, Davina broke her open in time. I must say, she's a remarkable operator."

"She must be," Neil muttered. "Is she still dealing with this, or will they send someone out from London?"

"Davina's in charge for the moment," Hickling said. "She and Lomax will be doing the groundwork."

"I wish I was in your section, Pete," Neil said. "The curiosity is killing me! Maybe I ought to transfer?"

"You want more jobs like looking after Mrs. Fleming? You must be crazy. Right now, I'd be only too happy to tot up a lot of figures and go home early."

"You've got to give me one clue," Browning insisted. "After all, I nursed the poor devil along till the star performer came out. Was she telling the truth, or not?"

"That," said Peter Hickling, "is what the star performer and her Scottish friend are finding out. But from what I heard, it looks as if she wasn't lying after all."

Browning stayed on for a few minutes, changing the subject. His memory was like a fly trap, seizing on every word. He might not be able to interpret them but his controller would. Returning to his office, he felt light-headed with relief. When he left the embassy he strolled uptown. He made his call in a public phone booth.

Bruckner answered. "Go ahead," he said. "I'm running it on tape." At the end Browning said, "I can't find out any more."

"OK," Bruckner said. "I guess that will have to satisfy him. You'll be in touch?"

"Yes," Browning said hastily. "If I hear anything." He hung up.

* * *

"Now, comrades, the next item on our agenda is the chairman of State Security's report. Comrade Borisov?"

The head of the Soviet Union directed his flat gaze at Igor Borisov. He had little gray eyes that were as opaque as stones. He was comparatively young for his immense power and responsibility; a man in his early sixties, solid in body, gray-haired and slow in movement. His enemies described him as ponderous, his sycophants called it dignity. He had the measured menace of a rhino whose amble could turn into a thundering charge. He was a supporter of Borisov. Two seats further down the table in the conference room of the Kremlin Arsenal where the Politburo met, the Soviet foreign minister, Rudzenko, fixed the head of the KGB with a stare that was not in the least opaque. It beamed hostility. He was not a supporter of Borisov. His candidate for the vacant seat at the table had been rejected. He was not a man who forgave defeat. Borisov eased his chair back. Blue smoke from cigarettes and a pipe hung like a nimbus in the air above them.

"Comrades, before I make a general report on security, I would like to give you the latest news on our operation in Washington. You have the notes from our previous meeting? Yes—code name Plumed Serpent." He glanced round the ring of faces, beginning with the head of state, the president and general secretary of the Communist party, and made the slightest hint of a bow in his direction. Being a tactful man, he did the same towards his enemy Rudzenko. "I am glad to tell you, comrades, that the plan I outlined to you is progressing as intended. Our agents in Washington are directing the operation with confidence and so far our opponents in London and the CIA have not only failed to penetrate, but are actually helping us."

Rudzenko cleared his throat before attacking. He was known for the habit, and Borisov braced himself. "From my sources of information, comrade," he said sharply, "there has been a great deal of intelligence activity from the British side. London is taking a lot of interest in the wife. And one of their best agents, a woman known to you I believe, is living in Washington in daily contact with the Flemings. Are you saying that this is all part of your plan, or is it possible that attention from a highly skilled intelligence officer like Davina Graham is the last thing we want at this stage?"

Borisov didn't falter; the men watching him from their seats were quick to scent disquiet among their colleagues. Borisov was both young and new to his prestigious job; in the eyes of the old established rulers of the country, he had still to justify himself. Igor Borisov actually smiled slightly at his enemy. "Comrade Rudzenko," he said, "your sources of information are excellent, I'm sure. But while you can certainly rely upon them for facts, you must trust to me and my sources for the right interpretation of them. I am not at all disturbed by the activity from London. In the circumstances, I think that the arrival of Davina Graham and her association with Elizabeth Fleming are exactly what we want to happen. She has gone out to investigate. She will not discover our agent. As you said, this particular woman is known to me. She is an exceptional operator, but all that is needed is to break the code, so to speak. Her code was broken here in Russia; I was a witness to it. I have seen into her mind, comrades, and consequently nothing she can do will ever take me by surprise. In fact," he looked round the ring of faces and paused for effect, "in fact I can predict what she will think and how she will react. If London had asked me to nominate an opponent to our Plumed Serpent operation, I would have asked for her."

The minister for Agriculture nodded, so did the secretary for Industrial Development. There was a murmur, and the note in it was approving. The head of state said to Rudzenko, "I think the General has dispelled my doubts, comrade. Has he satisfied yours?"

"Comrade," the foreign minister answered, "I have doubts about the whole concept of Plumed Serpent. I've never been convinced that it would work in the way that Comrade Borisov thinks it will. The idea was not his originally, and I am always wary of a student altering his master's work. I mean no personal offense to you," he said to Borisov, "but I have always found a simple and original plan to be the best. You have a brilliant record as a young man, but as a subordinate. Again, no personal attack is intended. But this whole scheme is so delicately balanced and so liable to rebound on us if it goes wrong—well . . ." He spread his hands and shook his head. "I don't think that anything will satisfy my doubts, or convince me that we should continue with this. There is still time to draw back. We can remove our agent. By one means or another. That is what I would like to see."

Borisov drew himself up. There was a patch of color in both cheeks. "Comrade Rudzenko is right when he says that the author of the original plan was my predecessor, General Kaledin. I inherited it from him. And I changed it, comrades. With your full knowledge and approval, except for yours, Comrade Rudzenko. I intend no personal slight to you, either, when I say at that stage, you wouldn't have approved of anything I put forward, as I wasn't your candidate for this appointment. However, that was a year ago. I am quite sure you are not allowing your disappointment to color your judgment after such a long time. So far as the student altering the master's work is concerned, it's not a very fortunate comparison. The decision to release Davina Graham, who causes you such alarm, Comrade Rudzenko, was taken by General Kaledin, not by me. We all know the catastrophe our Service suffered as a result of Ivan Sasanov's escape to the West. We need to wipe out that failure by more than just an assassination in Australia that the world has forgotten by now. We need a major intelligence victory, and Plumed Serpent will give it to us. I'm sorry you are not convinced, comrade." He sat down.

An hour and a half later the meeting ended, and the members of Russia's ruling circle dispersed to their offices. Borisov drove to the KGB headquarters on Dzjerzinsky Street. He went into his inner office and slammed the door. His secretary had messages for him, but the scowl on his face deterred her from coming in too quickly. She knew him well by now; he seldom came back from Politburo meetings in a good temper. After an interval she knocked on the door. "I brought you some tea, Comrade General," she said. "And I have a lot of calls and messages. Will you see them now, or later?"

Borisov looked up at her; he had been frowning and slowly the lines smoothed out and he almost smiled.

"I'll drink my tea first," he said. "Come in, Natalie. Sit down. I want to talk to you."

"Yes, Comrade General." She sat demurely, her skirt pulled down over her knees, feet together. She had a gentle personality that he found very soothing. And nothing could disguise the magnificent bosom that gave him such pleasure to look at.

"I want you to forget that you work for me," he said suddenly. "I want you to forget who I am and just be perfectly natural, perfectly at ease. Will you do that?"

She nodded and said, "I'll try, Comrade General."

"Then begin by calling me Igor," he said. "I've had a difficult morning. Very difficult. I need to talk to someone I can trust. I trust you, Natalie."

"Thank you," she said shyly.

He sipped his tea and lit a cigarette. After a moment he apologized and offered one to her. She took it, and he lit it for her. She had large clear gray eyes and thick lashes that needed no make-up to emphasize them. There was a soft, pink blush on her skin when she leaned forward for the match. Borisov looked at her and wanted her. But first he needed to talk and have her listen. And then to answer questions that he couldn't answer for himself, in spite of the boast he had made to the Politburo. It might be that a woman, even a simple woman of average intelligence, could see into the mind of another woman better than the cleverest of men.

Chapter Five

"WHAT YOU'VE GOT to realize," John Kidson said, "is that we're the only people who can protect you. And we are your people; in spite of taking out American citizenship, you're still British, born and bred. That's why I'm here, Fleming. I'm here to advise you and help you if I can."

"Like hell you are," Edward Fleming said. He had found Kidson waiting for him in the embassy when he woke in the late morning. They had been given one of the embassy sitting rooms for their first interview. Kidson had refused to see his quarry in an office. He wanted to create an atmosphere of trust. He wanted his quarry to feel that everything they said was off the record. Fleming looked haggard and jumpy. He immediately declared his intention of walking out of the embassy and dared Kidson or anyone else to stop him. Kidson shrugged.

"You can do what you like," he said. "Nobody is going to try and stop you. There's the door. Go on, open it and walk out."

Fleming hesitated. "You know I can't do that with all this hanging over me! You've got that diary, what more do you want?" He sagged down in his chair and covered his face with his hands. He looked absolutely defeated. Kidson was a kind-hearted man in private life, loyal to his friends and easily roused to sympathy. He regarded Edward Fleming coldly. He had no compassion for the home-bred traitor.

"I want you to talk about it," Kidson said quietly. "I want you to tell me the truth. Then we can see what can be done to save the situation. And it's a very dirty situation, Fleming. Dirty for Britain, because you're British-born, disastrous for the President and his administration."

"I don't believe you." Fleming looked up. "That's a lot of crap about Britain being blamed for what I do. I've been an American citizen for twenty years."

"How long have you been a Russian spy?" Kidson asked softly. "When did they recruit you? In Scotland, in London, before you came out? On a trip home? Or was it recently—it's all very relevant, you know."

"I've told you, I told that bitch last night—I'm not a Russian agent! That is God's truth."

"And your first wife's diary is a lie? You didn't pass papers to a man at the Lincoln Memorial? You didn't frequent a camera shop that we happen to know is a KGB front? Is that what you're telling me, Fleming? Come on, be sensible, man. Nobody is going to believe you. We can check the car hire firm your wife used. We can get a detailed report on where she followed you and when; you must realize that. It'll check out, won't it . . ."

"I don't know," Fleming said wearily. "It's so full of lies mixed in with the truth. She was crazy with jealousy. She'd have said anything to hurt me."

Kidson lit a cigarette. "Why did you let her burn to death?"

"I couldn't have saved her," Fleming protested. "I'd have been killed myself."

"That's not what you told Davina Graham last night," Kidson said.

Fleming sprang up. "I don't know what I said last night!" he shouted. "That hard-faced cow standing over me, asking the same thing over and over again—I couldn't have got to Raffaella if I'd wanted to!"

"And you didn't want to, did you?" Kidson reminded him. "You knew she'd been following you. You knew she'd found out what you were doing and you tried to kill her by fixing the brakes on her car. Isn't that how it happened?"

"No!" Fleming blazed at him. "I never touched the car—I tell you she was paranoid! There was nothing the matter with the brakes, she just rammed into a truck because she was a lousy driver who always jumped the lights! She made it all up—she invented the whole fucking thing. Oh, Jesus God, what's the use?"

"No use at all," Kidson said, "unless you tell me the truth. Where's your wife, Fleming? She found out about you too. What have you done to shut her up?"

"I haven't touched her," Fleming shouted. "The last people to see her alive were Davina bloody Graham and the Scot she's living with! Why don't you ask them?"

"Because you're the most likely suspect," Kidson answered. "She had the diary, and she was holding it over you, wasn't she? Blackmail isn't a bad motive. The story can't be kept hidden much longer. That colored maid of yours will start to talk if she hasn't already. Unless you bought her off. Did you, Fleming—did you pay her to keep quiet and say your wife never came home that night?"

"Why don't you go and ask her?" Fleming snapped back. "Why don't you stop this lousy charade and call the police?"

"Not the police, I'm afraid," Kidson said. "We have no choice except to show the diary to the CIA and let them take it from there. You'll find them much less sympathetic than me. Or Miss Graham."

Fleming looked at him. "That's your threat, isn't it? If I don't say what you want me to say you'll turn me over and let them kill the scandal. And kill is the operative word."

Kidson stared back at him, but didn't answer. He opened his

cigarette case and took out a filter-tip. The case was Charlie's wedding present. It was gold and old-fashioned in the age of modern packaging, but he couldn't bear to disappoint her by not using it. He offered one to Fleming.

"We're not going to tell them unless we've no alternative," he remarked. "We don't want the scandal either. Just stop being a bloody fool, and tell me the truth, so we can work out how to do it. We have a small advantage. We're the only ones who've seen that diary. That gives us a little time. Unless your wife is found dead. Then the whole business will blow up in our faces and we won't be able to do anything but leave you to the tender mercies of the director and his friends at Langley. They won't like you, Fleming, when they find out you've betrayed their country and the trust of the President. I think you know that."

"You want me to say I'm a KGB agent," Fleming said slowly. "Then you can tie up your own end of it, pick over the information for London, and make a deal with Langley to shove it all under the carpet. Dumping me when you're ready. I'm sorry. I can't oblige you." He threw the half smoked cigarette into the grate. "I'm going to my office," he said. "I have an appointment with the President at three o'clock."

"If I gave you a guarantee that we would get you out before we call in the CIA, would that make a difference?" Kidson asked him. "I have the authority to do that."

Fleming hesitated. "What kind of guarantee—what sort of a deal can you make with me when I'm not a bloody Russian agent?"

Kidson didn't answer. There was a moment's silence and at last Fleming moved. He came and sat on the edge of an armchair. There was a strange look of resignation and despair in his eyes.

"You won't believe me," he said slowly. "Even if I tell you the truth. Nobody will believe what really happened."

Kidson was adept at hiding his feelings. His satisfaction didn't appear on his face. "I'm quite prepared to try," he said. "Would you believe me if I told you that I don't sit in judgment on you, whatever you've done? People make mistakes. Some of them are more excusable than others. All I want is to safeguard Britain's interests."

"I'll call through to my office and say I'll be in before lunch. I can't just abdicate and not turn up. That'll cause comment."

"Exactly," Kidson said. "You're keeping your head, I'm glad to see. Let's say we start with—oh, an hour and a half? Then you go to your office and carry on as normal. See the President; say and do nothing out of the ordinary. I'll think over what we've talked about and call you. We can continue this evening."

"All right," Fleming agreed. "Before we start I'd like a drink. Vodka on the rocks."

"Of course." Kidson got up and rang a bell. "You won't mind—I only drink coffee—it's a little early for me." He watched the other man intently. Fleming was either an accomplished actor or he was genuinely giving way. Kidson didn't expect the first version to be the truth. He walked over to Fleming and laid a hand on his shoulder.

"I meant what I said," he said. "I'm not here to pass judgment. Ah, there's your drink. Shall we sit down and you tell me the story in your own way? I'd like to help if I can."

"She's a remarkable woman," Sir James White beamed at Humphrey Grant. He had just finished his telephone call to Davina. "What a blessing I talked her into coming back to work! I think we've broken this open just in time."

"It's going to present problems," Grant said. He was in a gloomy mood through lack of sleep. "How do we prevent a leak? Washington is the worst city in the world for rumors. That dreadful Fleming woman has disappeared—murdered by the KGB to stop her compromising her husband. That can't be kept quiet for much longer—"

"Of course it can." James White was irritated by his colleague's pessimism. He felt particularly buoyant after his conversation with Davina. "If she is a KGB victim, she won't surface again. They never do. Fleming can say his wife has left him and gone to England. When they know the facts, the CIA will back up the story. I don't see what you're worrying about, Humphrey."

"I'm worrying about what we do with Fleming," Grant said. He was irritated in turn by the Chief's airy optimism.

"We'll leave that to the CIA," James White said.

Grant looked up sharply. "Kidson has given a guarantee of safety," he said.

"Oh, my dear chap," the Chief shook his head, "my dear chap, what John agrees inside the embassy is one thing; what happens to Edward Fleming outside that embassy is quite another matter. I'm not interested in the safety of a man like that. Just in his silence. I'm quite sure Langley will take the responsibility away from us. Since we have an ex-colleague high up in their ranks, it won't be too difficult to arrange."

"The odious Mr. Barr, as he now calls himself." Humphrey Grant grimaced. "He wears button-down shirts and tries to cultivate an American accent. I wouldn't trust him an inch."

"I'd trust him to get rid of an embarrassment like Edward Fleming, though," James White remarked. "Wouldn't you?"

There was nothing Grant could do but agree with that.

"He wants us to go down to Mexico," Davina said. "To Cuernavaca, to check on the fire and Raffaella's death."

"I've never been to Mexico," Lomax said. He reached across the table and took her hand. "Aside from playing detectives, it might be nice for us, too. You could do with a break, my love." He twined her fingers through his. "You are my love, you know. I don't expect you to say anything. I just wanted to tell you."

They held hands in silence for a moment. "I'm glad," she said at last. There was nothing more she could say, without dishonesty. "It won't be much of a break, going through police records and newspaper reports. How's your Spanish?"

"Nonexistent," he answered. "What about yours?"

"It's adequate. Enough to find out the facts. If it gets complicated there's a contact in Mexico City who'll come out and interpret. I don't think we'll need him. The Chief was brimming over with congratulations, lots of praise for you too. He said we weren't to worry about expenses."

"That's good," Lomax grinned. "What's the best hotel in Cuernavaca?"

"He also said I could stay on here afterwards for a time. I didn't expect that. He must have some ulterior motive for all this human kindness."

"You don't trust him an inch, do you?"

"No," she answered quietly. "I learned the hard way not to rely on his promises. Or his feelings, because he hasn't got any. It's funny, Colin. Here I am working against a man in Moscow, and the one I really hate is my chief in London."

"I don't understand that. The man in Moscow killed Sasanov. How could you hate anybody more than him?"

"It was his job to kill my husband. It was the Chief's job to protect him. I hate Borisov, Colin, but it's one professional hating another. I'll work for the Chief because I'm working against Borisov. But I'll never ever forgive him. You know that saying in the Bible, 'Naked to mine enemies.' That's how he left Ivan. And me, incidentally. One day, somehow, I'll pay him back."

"I don't see how," he remarked quietly.

"I don't either. But there'll be an opportunity. I'll wait. Anyway, don't let's talk about it. We'll have a little time to ourselves in Mexico. He said not to worry about expenses and we'll damn well take him at his word. Do you like sightseeing?"

"Not much, but I can try. When do we leave?"

"As soon as possible." She frowned. "We need to book into a

hotel and get on a flight in the morning. I really want to find out how Kidson's getting on. And I want to go over to the house and talk to that housekeeper Ellen. I had the feeling she was holding something back."

"All right," Lomax said. "Why don't I fix the hotel and the flight while you do that? One thing I've learned about you is not to go against that damned sixth sense of yours."

"If you'd called it intuition," she smiled at him, "I'd have been furious."

"Same thing," he retorted. "I've an idea; why don't we take the morning off? Take a walk through the city, I'll give you a special lunch. At the Unicorn. How about that?"

"Shoe-leather steaks?" she teased him. "Just leave your right eyeball for the tip—no, Colin love, not the Unicorn. Let's find somewhere simple and nice near the river. It's a lovely day and we can pretend we're plain tourists like everyone else." She got up and came beside him. She slipped her arm round him and bent down and kissed him. "I know one thing," she said. "I'm very, very lucky to have you."

Jeremy Barr stared at each of the men in front of him; he had cold eyes that never warmed, even when he was being friendly. He was feared by his subordinates.

"Are you telling me," he said, "that you've lost her?"

The senior CIA operative nodded. "Yes, sir," he said flatly. "That's what I'm telling you."

"Tell me again," Barr snapped at him. "Tell me how the fucking hell you lose a woman we've been tailing night and day for months, and had right here in this office only two nights ago? Tell it to me again, Frank."

Frank had a line of red creeping up under his collar; he felt it spread up his neck at the back. His assistant kept shifting his feet, from the left foot to the right, and back from the right to the left.

They were both going to lose their jobs and go down the line for having mislaid Elizabeth Fleming.

"We took her home that night," Frank repeated. "Joe drove the yellow cab and we followed. We set her down by the house; Joe drove off and we waited till she went in. Then we drove up the street, turned round and took up our positions for the night surveillance. Nobody came or went out of the house till the English dame and her sidekick drove up. They stayed around an hour, and left after twelve. There was nobody else in the car with them."

"Where did they park?" Jeremy snapped at them.

"Right in front of the house," the second man muttered. "Frank and I never took our eyes off. Just the two came out. She couldn't have gotten in without us seeing."

"My guess is," the Englishman said, "she not only could but did. She slipped out some time while the others were inside. You weren't watching that automobile, not till the front door opened and they came out. You wouldn't have been expecting anyone to open a door and get in the back and just lie down out of sight. There's no other way Mrs. Fleming could have disappeared, without those two British helping her. Right under your goddamned noses. I want a full report by midday." After they had gone, he sat motionless at his desk, scowling at the telephones and the recording apparatus, and the minicomputer that could supply data at the touch of a button. Elizabeth Fleming had disappeared. How? He answered his own question with a string of four-letter words. Because British intelligence had taken the initiative and got the woman out of his reach. He believed he had laid the ground for a separation between her and Edward Fleming that could be tactfully managed without too much fuss. Instead there was a British-assisted flight out of the country. His director would not be pleased.

Jeremy sat on for some time; he refused to take calls until he had made his decision. He had to see Edward Fleming and find out exactly what had happened. It would help if he could assure the director that a natural explanation for the disappearance would come from the politician himself. If he were really clever, and banished the two witnesses of his failure far enough from the center at Langley, he might even turn his disaster into a triumph. He snapped on his intercom and said to his secretary, "Get me Edward Fleming at the White House." When the light showed on his personal telephone link with the White House switchboard, he picked it up and said, "Mr. Fleming? My name is Jeremy Barr. I'm an associate of General Hutchins. It's important I meet with you right away. What time can you give me today? Around four thirty. Fine. I'll be there."

Davina stepped out of the car. Lomax leaned forward out of the window and said, "I'll call back in an hour, unless you telephone the flat. All right?"

"Fine," she said. "Book us the royal suite, and we'll fly first class!"

"Don't run away with yourself, woman," he mocked her in a Scottish accent. "Just because we've been treating ourselves to lunch—" She smiled and waved back at him; the car moved off and she went to the front door of the Flemings' house and rang the bell. After a pause Ellen opened it. Her handsome dark face showed no surprise.

"Mr. Fleming is out, ma'am," she said. "And Mrs. Fleming hasn't come home."

"I know," Davina said. There was something about her that prevented the maid from closing the front door. "I want to talk to you, Ellen. May I come in?" She walked into the hallway and Ellen slowly closed the door.

"Will you come to the kitchen, please?" she said. "I don't like using the rooms when Mr. Fleming's not here." Suddenly, the stern face softened. "I'd feel easier in the kitchen if I'm going to talk to you." She offered Davina coffee or tea; she filled a glass with iced Coke for herself and sat down at Davina's suggestion in the dinette off the kitchen area.

"There's still no news of Mrs. Fleming," Davina told her. "Mr. Fleming spent all morning calling people who knew her, trying to trace her through the airlines and the travel agencies in the city. He found nothing. You know I'm a friend of hers from England?"

"I heard her say something about it," Ellen answered. "You went to the same school. That's what she said."

Davina lit a cigarette; the hostility was in that one word, "she." It was like an insult. "You don't like Mrs. Fleming, do you, Ellen?"

Ellen's face closed. "I don't talk about my employers, ma'am."

"You may have to," Davina said shortly. "When we call in the police."

The black eyes gleamed at her. "There's no need for that. There's no harm come to her."

"How do you know? How can you say that, Ellen?"

"Because bringing the police in is just going to make a mighty big fuss for Mr. Fleming and then she'll come home anyway."

"Has she ever done this before—is that what you mean when you say she'll come home anyway?"

Ellen lifted her shoulders a little. "Sometimes," she said. "She goes away and she comes back. He's going round fretting himself, thinking she's been snatched or something bad's come to her. She'll come back when she's good and ready. Like the other times."

"Then why is he so worried," Davina countered, "if she'd done this before?"

"Because he don't know about the other times," came the answer. "Mostly he was away when she took off. I can't tell him that. Maybe—" there was a hesitation, "—maybe you could."

"Maybe," Davina agreed. "If I knew what to say. You'll have to tell me, Ellen. Then perhaps I can stop him worrying. Where did Mrs. Fleming go when she took off?"

The look of contempt on Ellen's face was chilling. "With a man," she said. "There were a lot of men. Senators, a general in the Air Force. They used to call her; sometimes she had them here when he was out of town. I'd find things that told me what she'd been doing. When I cleaned up next day. Mr. Fleming, he found out about one of them. Right after they were married too. She talked her way out of it that time; I guess it made her careful."

"How do you know this, Ellen?" Davina said slowly. She couldn't believe it . . .

"I heard, Miss Graham," came the answer. "When they had a fight I didn't need to listen at the keyhole. All of Washington could hear her when she was mad at something. But he was the one who got mad that time. She did the crying and the end was he blamed himself for being busy and not paying her attention." She gave a little snort. "Some men don't have any sense. I wish I could tell him not to worry; it's a man, that's all it is. She's gone off like a she-cat in the night. She'll be back when she's had enough."

Davina didn't say anything for a few minutes. She didn't know what to say. There was a sick feeling in her stomach, as if she had lifted a stone and found a nest of maggots wriggling underneath it.

"Is that why you hated her? Because she made a fool of her husband?"

Ellen didn't deny it. She looked directly at Davina and said, "He's a good man, and she's trash. But that's their business, Miss Graham, not mine. I don't poke my nose into what white people do. You ask why I hated her? I'll tell you why. My husband died, my children are all gone, I had a little dog. Mr. Fleming didn't mind it. She made me get rid of it. She said he smelled bad. It was a lie, she just did it to show me who was boss when they got married. When she came first she was all sweetness, but just as soon as he puts on the ring, it all changed. She treated me like nigger dirt. I said to her once, I said 'I'm not staying here to be talked to like I was on a cotton plantation, Mrs. Fleming. Those days are long gone. You find yourself another maid.' She got all worked up then; thought she might have to do her own dishes for a change. She squeezed out some tears and said how sorry she was and how they couldn't do without me, now that Mr. Fleming had this important job. Wouldn't I please stay? I said, 'No, ma'am, I won't.' Then Mr. Fleming comes and talks to me and says she's not been too well lately, and won't I please stay for his sake? I refill the liquor supply, Miss Graham, every morning I check the decanters and the bottles, and I knew what he meant by 'not too well.' Times she's been drunk when I brought up her breakfast tray. So I stay, for his sake only. I don't get myself too close to white folks, Miss Graham. It's not so long since they stepped all over colored people. But Mr. Fleming doesn't come from here. Maybe that's why I stayed with him. In spite of her. But she learned her lesson. She treated me right from then on. That's all I ask when I work for someone."

"Ellen," Davina said at last. "Did anything happen to change Mrs. Fleming? You said she was all sweetness before they married. How long before she started to drink and play around?"

"A few months, maybe. Not long, that's for sure. Just like she was waiting till she got a hold of him."

"Who was the last man she was with?" Davina asked her.

"Some man from the British embassy. Browning, his name was. She was always calling him. Then you came and she stopped. I guess she was ashamed to let you see what she was doing. But it didn't last. She couldn't keep her pants on for that long. She's found some other guy if she's not back with this Browning."

"No," Davina said slowly. "She's not with him. Ellen, I'm sorry to hear this. I can't understand how she sank so low. Thank you for talking to me. I'll see Mr. Fleming this evening and try to calm him down. If you're right, there's nothing to worry about. She'll come home with some excuse."

Ellen got up. "That's the doorbell," she said. "Excuse me."

"It's Mr. Lomax come to fetch me," Davina said. She held out her hand. "Goodbye, Ellen. If you think of anything, would you call me. I'm at 834-6022."

"I'll write that down," she answered. She shook hands briefly as if she didn't like the contact.

"Give me a cigarette," Davina said, and Colin passed her one.

"Well," he asked, "was the sixth sense right? You don't look very pleased—didn't she want to talk?"

"No, she did not. But she did when I mentioned the police. And now I almost wish she hadn't!"

"Why?"

"Because I can't make sense of it. Ellen hated her. She said she'd been sleeping with men behind Fleming's back soon after they were married. I grew up with Elizabeth. She was shallow and selfish—but not rotten."

She turned to him in the car and laid her hand on his knee. "Even if it *is* true, she's certainly paid for it."

"I think you'd better stop identifying with her," Lomax said quietly. "That's what you're doing. You're seeing yourself in KGB hands again. Living it over through her. You mustn't. Listen, I've booked into the Alameda Hotel in Mexico City. It's only an hour's drive away from Cuernavaca. There are some Aztec temples close by too. Name like a Welsh railway station, I couldn't start to pronounce it—pyramids to the Sun and Moon—I've done a lot of homework this afternoon. And we fly first class at nine o'clock tomorrow." She looked white and drawn. She was biting her lip. He had never seen her do that before.

"The investigation shouldn't take too long. We can spend a bit of time there and enjoy ourselves, if we like it. I'm going to make it happy for you."

She looked at him and smiled. "All right. And you've hit the nail square on the head about Liz. I have been identifying—reliving certain things—I'll stop. Thanks, Colin love. Look, I must see Kidson tonight, before we go. Maybe he's got more out of Fleming." She turned and stared out of the window.

"There's something about this that isn't adding up. I don't know what it is, but it's not right and it's driving me mad. What time is it?"

"Just on six."

"Take me to the embassy. Don't wait for me—I'll get home when I can."

"OK. I can amuse myself. I'll call in on the Hicklings. She's a nice girl. She'll give me dinner."

Igor Borisov's wife and children went to their *dacha* at Zhukova on the weekends. It was not unusual for Borisov to remain in Moscow on Friday and sometimes Saturday when he was very busy. He then drove out and joined them on Sunday. That Friday night he was in bed with his secretary, Natalie. He had invited her back after their second private supper, and he no longer even wanted to go to the *dacha* on a Sunday.

He found her a satisfying lover and a girl of natural sweetness who charmed him as a companion. Most of all, she possessed an extraordinary unconventional intelligence. He had hoped in his uncertainty, haunted by the boast made before the other Politburo members, that she could help broaden his understanding of women and their motives. It was a gamble, and he didn't expect it to win him anything but an audience and a few platitudes that might contain some undiscovered truth. Instead her replies had been trenchant and clear. And not just about women. Her judgment of men was equally perceptive, and her comments on some whose names made the world apprehensive amazed him by their accurate assessment of human weakness. She didn't mock or criticize. She merely stated that one was vain, another greedy, and a third was hiding something. He made love to her with unrestrained sensuality and talked to her long into the night about the dangerous, twisting route that operation Plumed Serpent was taking. Most of all he talked to her about the woman who was in the center of the sticky web of lies and treachery that he had spun since he had taken Kaledin's place.

"It's a matter of timing, now," he said. She nestled warmly into his arm.

"It's got to draw together, Natalie; all the different elements must magnetize on one spot at one moment and then I make the move. A day too soon and the whole thing will fail." Strangely he didn't mind showing weakness or indecision to her. He had discovered how lonely it was to live on the peaks of power. "Perhaps I should have stayed with Kaledin's original plan," he said. "But this seemed such a good opportunity to turn the whole thing round and strike a shattering blow at the Americans. The kind of blow that would crack and undermine one structure of their administration after another! I couldn't resist it. But if it fails—"

"It won't," she said. "The only danger is if this English woman is as clever as you are. And she isn't, my beloved love. But one thing puzzles me—" He raised his eyebrows. "Why did you call it by that strange name? Plumed Serpent. What does it mean?"

Borisov smiled. "General Kaledin used the code name Fallen Eagle," he said. "That suited his concept very well. But not mine. The emphasis is not the same. The eagle is a noble bird of prey; it was our own emblem, after all, before the Revolution. The eagle is the symbol of majesty and power. Imperial power. Rome, Russia, Austria, and Napoleonic France. Mexico, too, when it was ruled by a Hapsburg. It signifies our great enemy America. There was a legend, thousands of years ago, that only the serpent could kill the eagle. I found my serpent in Mexico, at the City of the Gods. She's a thousand years old, Natalie, and she demanded human sacrifice. She has eyes of jade and her fangs are pure gold. On her head she wears the plumes of divinity. She has a long Indian name and her temple is guarded by stone jaguars. The Sun and the Moon were worshiped from the top of great pyramids, but the Serpent God's temple is closer to the earth, and the Indians built it at the end of a long road they called the Avenue of the Dead. The serpent destroys by stealth; the approach is silent and the bite is instant death. My serpent will prove that the old legend is true. It will sink its teeth deep into the American eagle." He saw her gazing up at him, and the admiration in her eyes was childlike. "I have a picture of the carving," he whispered, holding her closer. "I'll show it to you. A little later on. It's beautiful in a cruel way. But not as beautiful as you." He drew her to him and she put her lips to his mouth.

"I like your house," Kidson said. "Is this all your wife's design?"

"Yes," Fleming said sullenly. He slouched in an armchair, grasping a glass of vodka in both hands.

Kidson moved close to him. "Look," he said. "Don't worry about that fellow Barr coming to see you. There'd been rumors about your wife's drinking. It was bound to happen. He was checking up, that's all."

"He suggested it might be better if she took a trip to England," Fleming muttered. "Why would he say that if he didn't suspect something? Suppose *they've* grabbed her . . . Jesus," he groaned, "she'll tell them everything. She'll lie her head off, the way she did to Davina and Arthur Moore."

"If the CIA had taken her in," Kidson remarked quietly, "they wouldn't be asking questions. You parried very well, saying she'd left on a trip to New York. He'll believe that, for the moment anyway. I think you've got to admit that your friends the Russians have stepped in to stop her talking to us. I think you know that, don't you?"

"They're not my friends!" Fleming roused himself and shouted. Kidson shrugged. "I keep telling you, I didn't give way to them!

They dropped the whole attempt when I said I'd go to the CIA director himself. It's no use, is it? You don't think anyone ever resisted blackmail, do you? You think they caught me out and I just gave in and sold out my country and the President and tried to fix my wife's car to get her killed!"

"You were embezzling her money," Kidson pointed out. "And when the fire started, you said yourself you walked away and let it burn, knowing she was inside. Just because she'd discovered the fraud? A man who'd do that wouldn't stand up to blackmail from the KGB."

Fleming surprised him then. He got up from the chair, put the glass down and visibly straightened. "I let her die. I didn't kill her. I didn't fix her car brakes, I just didn't risk my own life trying to get her out when the place was blazing like a torch. She'd found out about the money and she was making my life a living hell. I hated her and I was glad she was dead. You'd call me a murderer, wouldn't you?"

"By default, if nothing more," Kidson answered.

Fleming nodded. "All right. But I didn't betray anything to the Russians. They tried blackmail and they dropped out when they knew it wouldn't work. I may be every kind of a bastard in your book, but I'm not a traitor."

He looked at John Kidson, and for the first time Kidson began to believe him.

"I love this country," he said. "I also think the President is a great man. I'd see Raffaella burn all over again and I wouldn't lose a night's sleep. But nothing would make me harm America."

Kidson got up and mixed himself a drink. "This morning you said the diary was lies," he said quietly. "Now you admit you had meetings at the Lincoln Memorial and went to the camera shop. Raffaella wasn't lying when she wrote that down. She said she saw you passing something to the man on the seat."

"She didn't," Fleming answered. "That was a lie; seeing me at the Memorial was the truth. They were meeting me to put pressure on. The same thing at the camera shop. I told you, I didn't know who they were the first few times. I thought it was criminal; I thought maybe I could buy them off somehow. Then I found out it was the KGB and I told the guy to stuff himself. That was the end of it. The diary is full of distortions, full of lies mixed in with things that really happened. Raffaella was neurotic. Christ knows what was in her mind. But there's enough truth amongst the fantasy to hang me." He went back to his chair and sat down. "She must have hated me as much as I hated her."

"Well, we have the diary now," Kidson said. "We could destroy it, if we thought you were really innocent."

Fleming raised his head. "You couldn't do that; you couldn't take the chance."

"I can do whatever I like," Kidson replied. "I have authority from London to take any action I think fit. But I've got to have a full confession from you first."

Davina and Lomax played the taped interview that followed that ultimatum. The little machine was no bigger than a pocket calculator but the voices of Fleming and John Kidson rang clearly through the hotel room.

"I met Liz in Mexico, you know. Before Raffaella died. She was the loveliest woman imaginable. All I could do was contrast her with my screaming bitch of a wife."

Kidson's voice was casual. "Really. I didn't know you met while Raffaella was still alive. Tell me about it."

"We met at a recital in the Cortes Museum," Edward Fleming's voice said. "Raffaella was crazy about the classical guitar and there was some Englishman giving a concert she wanted to go to."

"John Williams?" Kidson suggested. The tape registered a grunt.

"I think so. I'm not musical and I didn't really take it in. I saw Elizabeth in the audience and I remember thinking, Jesus, what a gorgeous-looking girl. She seemed like a girl, anyway, with all the

Mexicans round her. I never realized how quickly they get old. That was one of my wife's obsessive fears. Losing her figure, getting wrinkles on her face. She drove me crazy talking about it. She spent a fortune on beauty treatments and massage." There was a short, bitter laugh. "How was I to know Elizabeth would be the same?"

"Did you meet at the concert?"

"Friends of Raffaella's gave a supper party afterwards. Barbecue in the garden, swimming in the pool—the usual form. I was introduced to Liz. You know, I could feel my wife watching me. She had another obsession, apart from her own looks, and that was other women. You know something funny—she was wrong up until then; I'd never thought of anyone before. But Elizabeth was different. She had this lovely smile; we talked about London and all the things I'd left behind when I came to the States. I remember Raffaella coming over and I could see I was going to have the grand opera played out when we got home.

"She was rude to Elizabeth. I could have punched her right in the mouth. We went back to her house and the scene started. It went on most of the night, till I locked her out of the bedroom to get some sleep. Next day I sent Elizabeth some flowers and asked her to meet me for lunch. We arranged to drive to Mexico City. I told Raffaella it was business. She didn't argue; she got lazy when she went to Cuernavaca. She spent her time lying out in the garden. She didn't like going to Mexico City because the altitude made her tired. I had a wonderful day."

"Did you fall in love with her then?" Kidson's cool voice sounded slightly thin on the tape.

"No, not till we'd met a few more times. She told me she was divorced, taking a trip to get over it. The husband sounded quite a bastard. She said he'd had an affair with a great friend of hers. That broke up the marriage."

"When did you first sleep with her?"

"I didn't."

In the shaded hotel room, Davina and Colin looked at each other. She put her finger to her lips. The tape wound on.

"She wasn't cheap," Fleming explained. "She wasn't the kind of woman you met and laid in a week or so. She meant more to me than that. I wanted her to come to New York. I didn't know what the hell was going to happen, but I didn't want to lose her."

"Your wife never suspected?"

"No. I suggested staying longer than we'd planned. That pleased her. We extended the stay there for almost six weeks. Elizabeth didn't go on to New York either. Raffaella and I were to fly back at the end of the month. A week before, the house caught fire."

There was a pause, and the click of a lighter snapping once or twice before it caught alight.

"Did you start the fire, Fleming?"

There was another pause. "No." The voice didn't hesitate. "No, I didn't. But I would have if I'd had any guts. I just let it burn."

"How did it start? There must have been an insurance investigation—the police, fire department . . ."

"It wasn't insured. She didn't think it was necessary. It was just a holiday house—nothing of value in it. The Mexican police and fire department thought it was caused by one of the maids knocking over an oil stove in the back. The servants cooked on their own stoves. They weren't allowed near the kitchen. My wife was no democrat so far as Mexicans were concerned. The oil tank caught and that was it. The place was full of beams. It went up like a torch."

"Where were you at the time?"

"I told you—I'd been with Elizabeth. I'd told my wife some lie about going to Mexico City and the two of us had taken off in the car and toured round. I dropped her at her hotel and came home. I saw the fire from the garden. There were flames pouring out of the upstairs windows. Why do you keep asking this—over and over again? What do you care about it anyway—all you want to know is whether I worked for the Russians?"

"He's got a point there," Lomax muttered.

"Ssh." Davina shook her head at him. "I missed that. Damn—" She pressed the button and rewound. The last sentences were repeated and then Kidson answered Fleming's question.

"That's right. But your wife's diary states that you did. You admit they were trying to blackmail you at the time she followed you in Washington. When exactly did you tell their contact to stuff himself? Before you went to Mexico or after Raffaella died?"

"Before we went," Fleming answered. "I went to the camera shop and this little bastard was sitting there. He asked me if I'd made up my mind to cooperate. Cooperate with whom? I wouldn't say anything till he answered that. He hedged and circled but I kept on. Who was he working for and what the hell did he mean by cooperation? Then he told me. He wanted a copy of the plan of the nuclear plant we were building in Wyoming. I said, you want me to show you classified information? That's right, he said. He came from the Bronx. The only people who'd have wanted to see that were the Russians. I said so. He just sat there; he didn't deny it. He said to me, 'You've been stealing your wife's money. You only have to show me this one thing. That's all.' "

"And you're theirs for life," said Kidson.

"What sort of a fool do you think I am?" Fleming sounded angry. "I've been in business and politics for twenty years. I know what the score is. I told him I'd go direct to General Hutchins and confess the whole thing. He didn't seem to give a damn. He just shrugged; he reminded me of Rod Steiger in *The Pawnbroker.* He said, 'Think about it. I'll call you tomorrow.' " He never did call. I never heard from them again.

"Not a word?"

"I told you, nothing. He knew I meant it."

"It's unlike them to give up so easily," Kidson remarked. There was another pause. The lighter clicked and someone put ice in a glass, which tinkled faintly in the background. "What about your wife? She doesn't sound the kind of woman who could keep her suspicions to herself. What did she say about those meetings at the Lincoln Memorial?"

"She never mentioned them," Fleming said flatly. "She talked about the money and said I'd robbed her; that was brought up in every row. She must have been keeping that diary to throw in my face at a really awkward moment. She knew the President would offer me a job if he was elected. I guess she was going to throw the switch on my career when it would hurt most!"

"No wonder you fell in love with Elizabeth," Kidson murmured. "But it does seem a little out of character for your wife to have kept this knowledge to herself. Let alone leaving that diary in a beauty parlor."

"They used to post parcels for her, collect goods and drop them by the apartment. She practically owned the place, she spent so much money there. 'Manuel *querido,* take good care of this, will you? I'll pick it up next time I'm in for a treatment . . .' I heard her say it dozens of times when I collected her. She knew it riled me; Manuel was a Pag who put on a phony accent. She used to speak Spanish to try and embarrass him. She knew he was a fake and it amused her."

"She sounds a very unattractive woman," Kidson said.

"Not at first. She was full of life, very Spanish-looking, with big dark eyes. And rich. I needed the money to get started properly; but I was in love with her too. It was great to start with, just like Elizabeth. Only it took Raffaella longer to change."

"Perhaps you didn't give yourself a chance to know Elizabeth," Kidson suggested. "You married very quickly after you came back from Mexico, didn't you?"

"She was going back to England," Fleming said. "I couldn't lose her, not then. We'd been separated for nearly two months. She stayed on in Mexico at a health farm in Tula. She wrote she wanted me to have time to think. I missed her like hell. When she came to New York, I was in San Francisco. I flew straight back and saw her. She talked about going back to England and I knew I couldn't let it happen. We got a special license."

"You must have been relieved not to hear from your Bronx friend again." Kidson changed the subject suddenly.

The tape registered Fleming's momentary loss of concentration. "Oh—oh, yes, I was relieved all right. But not surprised. That guy knew he'd picked the wrong man. He knew I wouldn't give him anything and I'd go to the CIA if I had to. He dropped it. I was expecting one more try, in Mexico maybe, but nothing happened. After Raffaella died I inherited everything; she hadn't changed her will from the time we married. I paid the money back and covered the whole thing up. I was safe. They probably knew that too. I never understood how they found out about the money in the first place."

"Perhaps they heard about it through your wife. Maybe she told someone. A man like you, close to the Republican candidate, working on secret government projects, is bound to attract Soviet attention. On a minor scale, of course. But someone somewhere picked up a hint and then they were on your tail. I think we've done enough for tonight. I think we'd better meet at the embassy tomorrow. I'll get Arthur Moore to ring your office and invite you to dinner, if he's not engaged. Otherwise we'll think of something. Does that suit you?"

"What happens if I say no?" Fleming's voice was sarcastic.

"Nothing at all," came Kidson's answer. "You needn't see me again if you don't want to. But London is pressing for a look at that diary. I can't hold them off for too long."

A single crude expletive followed from Fleming and then the tape ended. There was a second smaller one. Lomax slotted it into place.

"Davina," Kidson spoke to them. "You've listened in to this, and I expect you'll have some thinking to do. I've a few ideas of my own. But we'll discuss them when you get back. I want you and Lomax to find out everything you can about the fire that killed the first Mrs. Fleming. And I want you, Davina, to concentrate on Mrs. Fleming number two. Where she stayed, whether Fleming was telling the truth about meeting her secretly, how long she spent at this health farm place at Tula and when she went to New York."

"What the hell does he mean by that?" Lomax demanded as the tape finished.

"It means he thinks Fleming is still lying," Davina answered. "On the face of it I'd say the whole thing is a pack of lies. He did pass secrets to the Russians, and he got rid of his wife to inherit her money and marry Elizabeth. That's what Kidson wants us to prove. Then he'll blow Fleming's story sky-high. I don't much feel like a siesta, do you? Not after this."

"It doesn't matter what I feel," Lomax said. He perched on the arm of her chair and slipped his arm round her. She had soft, shining hair and he liked the red lights that gleamed in it. He kissed the top of her head.

"You'll have to retire," he murmured, "if we're going to have a proper sex life. Don't worry. We'll have dinner and tequila and I'll carry you to bed."

She reached up to him. "Not too much tequila, love, or all you'll do *is* carry me to bed . . . I don't like this at all. I've got this nag, nag inside, telling me it's all too glib. Every move we make has been thought out beforehand. It's like playing follow-my-leader with Borisov." She stood up quickly and turned round to face him. "Colin," she said, "you go to Cuernavaca. I don't know the first thing about arson. That's your department. I'm going to the health farm at Tula."

He didn't argue with her. He just said flatly, "You're not going anywhere without me. Those are my orders, Davina, and I'm sticking to them. We go to Cuernavaca together and we go to Tula afterwards."

It took just over an hour to reach Cuernavaca. The town had been the headquarters of the Spanish conquistadores, led by Cortes, who had built a castle there. There was a lovely square, surrounded by fine seventeenth-century houses. The castle had been turned into a museum, and a crowd of Mexican schoolchildren in summer dress trooped through the dark portico shepherded by nuns. Lomax parked the car in the square. A yellow dog slunk toward them, tail wagging apprehensively. Davina stopped to stroke it and it cringed, watching her with hungry eyes. Lomax caught her arm. "Don't touch it," he warned. "They haven't stamped out rabies here." He had a small street map, bought at the hotel. Lomax pointed to the residential area just outside the castle. "That's where the Flemings' house was. Near the Borda Gardens. We can drive there."

The property was surrounded by a white crumbling wall covered in creeper. The gate was padlocked, but it hung askew on one hinge. It had once been a well-kept garden; there were fine trees and bushes, and the remains of a tarmacked drive, now cracked and invaded everywhere by weeds. A fallen tree blocked their path to what was left of Raffaella's summer house. Two of the outer walls were standing; they were blackened, with deep cracks driven through them by the fire. There was a coating of black ash mixed into the earth where they stood.

"Stay here a minute," Colin said. "You'll only get filthy. I'm going to poke around inside."

Davina watched him pick his way carefully through undergrowth, charred timber, and rubble that had crashed through to the ground. There was a big round stone nearby; she guessed it had once been a mounting block. She sat down on it to wait and lit a cigarette. A bird whooped from the trees, making her jump. The air was very still. She felt uncomfortable and frightened, as if there were a watcher in the dense bushes. Was it her imagination that she could still smell the fire? The silence and the shadows, growing as the sun dipped, were beginning to get on her nerves. She had just got up to go and find Colin when she saw him coming back. He was brushing the dust and the ash off his clothes. There was a broad dark smear on his face. She felt foolishly pleased to see him.

"Did you find anything?"

"No. But that was one hell of a blaze. I wouldn't think an oil lamp could generate that kind of a fire. Phah, the ash gets everywhere—I wish I had some kind of a ground plan."

"Whoever built it might have one," Davina suggested. "Why don't we go back and call into the police station? They might be able to tell us if it was a local builder. And who came out to fight the fire." She came up to him, took a handkerchief out of her pocket and wiped the dirty mark off his face. "I'll be glad to get away from here," she said.

He looked round and nodded. "There's something about violent death that lingers in a place. We'll go to the hotel where Elizabeth stayed and clean up. You can ask about her at the same time. Then we'll call on the local gendarmerie."

The hotel was close to Cortes Castle; it was an unpretentious building with a dozen rooms and a large Mexican proprietress who was only too pleased to talk to the strangers. Señora Veranez spoke good English and when Davina asked about a friend of hers, a blonde English lady who had stayed there just over a year ago, she thought for a moment, and with a beaming smile said yes, she remembered her. How could one forget such a lovely lady? And with such a disposition: so sweet always, so polite to everyone. Every man in the hotel was in love with her, Señora Veranez declared, including her own husband.

Everyone, she said, wanted to do things for her. She soon made friends, and instead of staying for a week or so, she stayed for a long time. There was one man, an American with a wife—they lived part of the year in the town—the Señora lifted her plump shoulders. He was always with the lovely English lady. And then his wife died in a terrible fire, and the English lady left the hotel.

"What time was this fire?" Davina asked.

"In early evening. I remember, it was getting a little dark and the sky was like a sunrise. All the town went to watch it burn. We had a fire engine and some men, but it was useless. They couldn't get near to put the water on. Everybody inside was burned. It was terrible."

"You say it was like the sunrise?" Colin asked her. "You wouldn't remember the color of the fire, would you? Was there a lot of smoke—black smoke?"

She paused, trying to think. "No," she said. "No black smoke. Just yellow fire. And some blue. Big blue streaks in the middle of the fire. Somebody said it was like salt burning. It was terrible," she repeated.

"Yes," Lomax muttered to himself. "I'll bet it was."

They ordered drinks. Davina said, "I think I'll try tequila."

The proprietress recommended a dish of salt and limes to be taken with it. "The Americanos get drunk," she said. "They don't like to drink and take the salt. But it's the way it's done in Mexico."

"Did my friend the English lady drink it like that?" Davina asked casually.

Señora Veranez shook her head. "Oh, no. The Señora never drank tequila. She didn't drink anything at all. Sometimes a little wine, that's all."

Davina smiled and picked up the glass. She dipped a finger in the salt, tasted it, and sipped the tequila. It was a raw spirit and the salt burned. "Very good," she said. "Thank you."

The woman went away back to her desk. A few people drifted in and a boy came out to serve from the bar. Lomax looked at Davina.

"Just a little wine," he said.

"I know," Davina said quietly. "Within a year she's an alcoholic. Why did you ask about the fire—what difference would black smoke make?"

"It would point to oil being the agent," he replied. "There would have been a pall of black smoke over the flames. Instead—" he finished his tequila and grimaced. "Instead she sees blue. Which means that fire began with a potassium hydrate substance. It burns blue like salt."

"Meaning it was deliberately started," Davina said.

"And not by an amateur fiddling around with petrol and rags. Potassium hydrate acts a bit like gunpowder. It ignites with a bang. It also generates intense heat. I saw six-foot beams that had been turned into charcoal in those ruins today. If he was outside when it happened, there was no way he could have got in to save Raffaella or anyone else. She was murdered all right, but not by him."

"Moscow Center," she said it very low. "But why?"

"I wish to God I knew," he answered.

"Why don't we see the police now?" Davina said. "It's getting near seven o'clock."

"If they had an autopsy report on the bodies," he mused, "it would probably bear this out. You wouldn't expect an ordinary coroner in a place like Cuernavaca to know the difference between a corpse burned in an ordinary fire and one that was subjected to the heat intensity of KOH. But we can try. Do you want to finish this stuff? I think it's filthy."

"So do I. Let's go."

There was a duty sergeant in the police station. A young, alert man with the broad cheekbones and brown skin of Indian ancestry. No, he had not been on duty the night the Flemings' house was burned down. He couldn't give information without authority. Lomax nodded and produced a little card with a cellophane window and his photograph in it; the sergeant studied it, studied him and then said, "Excuse me. Come into the office. I will see what we have on our files here."

There wasn't much data, just the time, date, and the identity of three people who had lost their lives and whose bodies had been identified. One was so badly burned that the relatives couldn't find anything recognizable, but the remains corresponded to the maid working in the house who had not returned home. Her husband had identified the owner of the house by the remains of a medallion found inside the charred corpse. The cause of the fire was stated to be accidental. The firemen believed it was caused by a small fire reaching the oil tank at the back.

Lomax thanked him, refused a glass of beer, and guided Davina out into the square. The sun was almost set and the sky flamed pink and red behind the silhouette of the castle; children played on the cobblestones and another yellow dog scrounged nervously round the perimeter of the two open cafés where people drank tequila or cold beer.

"I saw the tank, or what was left of it," Lomax said. It wasn't a big one, and it certainly hadn't exploded. My guess is there wasn't anything but a dribble of oil in it. The so-called fire brigade couldn't think of any other reason why the house should catch alight, so they just said accident, and oil tank, like that. Someone banged a rubber stamp, sent the report to the local coroner, who banged another stamp down, and that was that. Fleming got a death certificate and the will was probated. I don't think we need to come back here again, do you?"

"Once more," Davina said. "There's just one more thing I'd like to check, before we go to Tula. I want to meet someone else who knew Liz and saw her with Fleming."

"Ten out of ten for persistence." Lomax grinned at her as he drove. "We'll come back tomorrow. Now I'm looking forward to taking you to dinner and forgetting all about the Flemings for tonight. Do you think you can manage that?"

"I think so," she smiled back at him. "I think I'd like that very much."

* * *

She woke at the hour when the body is at its lowest ebb. Her watch face showed four A.M. on its luminous dial. She listened to Lomax breathing deeply beside her. She got out of bed and slipped through into the sitting room, closing the door so she could turn on the light. She found a cigarette and lit it; she lay on the sofa and smoked and let her mind range backwards and forwards over the day's events like a tiger pacing a cage, only to come up against its bars.

Next morning they reached Cuernavaca early. The same soft haze hung in the air, the yellow dog or its twin slunk flat-bellied along in search of scraps, and Señora Veranez was perched like a plump parrot behind the reception counter.

They exchanged civilities in Spanish, and then she talked English, glad to show off. She answered Davina's careful questions with disarming eagerness.

The English lady, her friend, yes, she used to visit the Herrendos family. They were very rich, important landowners. They were Germans with a name nobody could pronounce. Everyone called them Herrendos. She told Davina and Lomax how to get there. As they thanked her and turned to leave, she called out softly after them. "If you are from the government, Señora, be careful. Señor Herrendos doesn't like to answer questions. People say he came to Mexico to hide." She smiled a brilliant smile at them and waved.

They drove fifteen miles outside of Cuernavaca till they came to the tall white gates of a handsome estancia. The drive was free of weeds, its tarmac glinting in the sun. The low-built house was shaded by a long veranda, the porch colorful with flowers. Everything was neat and well-maintained. It seemed like an alien settlement in the wild Mexican landscape. They stepped under the shelter of the porch and rang a bell that hung on a brightly polished brass chain. After a short pause the front door opened and a woman in her late forties, dressed in an embroidered skirt and white blouse, looked at them and said in Spanish, "Good day. Can I help you?"

She had fair hair that had faded in the sun and blue eyes fanned by wrinkles that gave her a good-humored expression.

"Are you Mrs. Herrendos?" Davina spoke in English. A few moments later they were seated in the cool, white-painted sitting room. A Mexican girl brought a tray of glasses and fresh iced lemonade. Señora Herrendos sat opposite them. Davina explained that she was trying to trace a friend of hers who had spent some time in Cuernavaca. When she heard Elizabeth's name, the German woman smiled. She had a charming manner totally without stiffness.

"Of course I remember her! You say you've lost trace of her? She went to New York—we were great friends, she and my husband and I. I was surprised she didn't write to us after she left. She promised to come back and stay." She shrugged lightly. "To be truthful, we were rather hurt. But, I suppose it was an interlude for her. For us, it was more important. We don't see that many Europeans here—only American tourists. My husband misses Europe. How did you know about us?"

When she heard about the hotel proprietress, her blue eyes twinkled mischievously. "A splendid gossip—but she keeps a good hotel. She was very fond of our dear Elizabeth; she made her very comfortable. Did she tell you my husband Hans was a war criminal? Oh, please—" she laughed aloud at her guests' discomfiture. "—don't be embarrassed. We know all about it. My husband will be back at any moment. I think you'll see why we think it's amusing. The war has been over for forty years. My husband was eleven when it finished. Both our families lost estates to the Russians. We didn't want to stay in West Germany, so we decided to make a new life here. And here he is—Hans, these are friends of Elizabeth's. They are trying to find her."

He was a short, stocky man, dark-haired and very tanned. He shook hands with Colin and bowed to Davina. In the middle of

Mexico, he still retained the manners of his Junker background. "You have lost Elizabeth? She would be difficult to lose—even the dogs followed her, apart from all the Mexicans! Where is her husband?"

"He's in Washington," Davina explained. "But when we arrived there he was away on some fact-finding tour in Central America. His office couldn't contact him, and all anybody knew was that Elizabeth had gone down to Mexico for a short holiday. We're not staying long in the States and we did want to see her. Someone thought she might be here, so we flew down." She smiled at him; the story sounded most unlikely, but he seemed to accept it. She was grateful when Colin added, "I wanted an excuse to come to Mexico. It coincided very well. Your wife says you last heard of her a year ago, so it seems we've drawn a blank."

"I'm afraid so," Hans Herrendos said. "It's a pity. We spent a lot of time together, didn't we, Ilse?"

His wife gave her warm smile. "Yes—she was not just beautiful, but so sweet you felt you had to run and take care of her. Even women felt like that. As you know, of course."

"Of course," Davina murmured.

"We were very sad when she left," Herrendos said. "And very surprised when we read about the marriage."

Davina saw Lomax look up, and the narrowed eyes flashed a warning at her. "Surprised? We thought it sounded like a real love match," he said. "Didn't we, darling?"

"Yes," Davina was emphatic. "But of course you had seen them together."

"We knew the Flemings slightly," Ilse Herrendos said. "Señora Fleming was a very difficult woman; he didn't come here very often. But when he met Elizabeth it was obvious that he had fallen madly in love, wasn't it, Hans? Of course she must have been used to it. She was a little lonely too. I think she encouraged him because of that. Then his wife was burned in a terrible fire at their house, and Elizabeth was very upset. She talked to both of us about it. She said that Señor Fleming was pressing her to come to America. She wasn't sure at all. He was the one who was crazy in love, you see. She was glad when he left after the fire; that's what she told us. We were so surprised to see the report of the marriage in the American papers afterwards." The fine gray eyes shaded for a second.

"And we were hurt, too. We had been her best friends here. She never wrote or contacted us after she left. Hans wrote congratulating her on the marriage and she didn't answer. It seemed very rude, to drop us without a word."

"My wife was upset," Herrendos explained. He looked at her with affection. "She hasn't learned that people mean different things by friendship. Elizabeth was a lovely person, but she was not what I would call—deep? Ilse gets too involved with people. Then they hurt you. I am more philosophical; I learned very early not to expect too much."

There was a pause, and Davina got up. "You've been very kind." And because she liked them both, she said, "And don't let it worry you about Elizabeth, Señora Herrendos. I knew her from childhood. Your husband is quite right. There wasn't much depth of character there, I'm afraid. We mustn't keep you any longer. I think we'll drive back to Mexico City and enjoy ourselves." Herrendos had slipped an arm round his wife's shoulders.

"You could telephone the hotels in Acapulco," he suggested. "When Americans say Mexico, they usually mean Acapulco. Perhaps she has gone there."

"That's an idea," Colin agreed. "Maybe she went back to that beauty clinic she told you about," he said to Davina. "The one at Tula, wasn't it?"

"Yes, that's right. Especially if she liked it there the first time. Have you heard of it, Señora Herrendos?"

"Oh, yes; it's become a very fashionable place. Clinica Quetzalcoatl." She shook her head at them. "But Elizabeth never went there. When she left Cuernavaca she went straight to the airport.

We drove her there; she was flying to New York and then back to England."

"More lies," John Kidson said when Davina telephoned that night. "No doubt she was tucked away in New York till he could marry her after a decent interval. Never mind, it gives me something fresh to hit him with. It's typical of the way he tries to put the whole sordid thing in a good light. The love of his life, et cetera. Yes, he's putting up a strong resistance, but he'll give way in the end. He certainly doesn't want us to let the Americans know about the diary. He knows they won't sit him down for a friendly chat with cups of coffee. You take a couple of days' break if you like—by the way, Charlie's arriving on Thursday. Yes, isn't it—baby's fine, everything's grand. Keep Thursday night for dinner." He paused and listened while Davina spoke.

"Lomax too? Yes, of course."

When he put the phone down he tilted his head a little and said to himself, "Good Lord, don't tell me those two are getting on!"

Chapter Six

"WE ARE GOING," Lomax told her, "to the city of the gods this morning." They were breakfasting together in their room. Their mood was happy as they planned their two days of holiday. Lomax had been very firm with her after they spoke to Kidson. "Not a word about the Flemings," he said. "I can see your mind starting to whirl round like a bloody windmill again, and I'm not going to have it. We've got two whole days to spend London's money and enjoy ourselves, and that's what we're going to do. Starting this minute!" He had taken her into his arms and kissed her till she was breathless. And he did it again until she stopped trying to push him off and argue.

They spent the evening wandering round Mexico City; it was an enchanted place by night, dominated by the magnificent soaring cathedral in the Zocalo, the splendid square, its towers and façades floodlit against the darkness. They idled down the Paseo de la Reforma, lined with smart shops and restaurants. They drank fruity red wine at a little café under a canopy of vines, and watched the crowds pass by. He reached out and held her hand and she twisted her fingers through his. They avoided the elegant restaurants and found a little place two blocks down from the Alameda Gardens, where they burned their mouths with chili and ate tortillas. Lomax tried tequila again and decided he quite liked it. When they came back to their hotel on the Avenida Juares, they were exhausted and slept immediately in each other's arms.

Davina laughed at him with her mouth full of grapefruit at their breakfast the next morning.

He looked very boyish, with a pleasant tan and the casual open-necked shirt in bright denim. Not strictly handsome, she thought, savoring the luscious fruit, but carefree and attractive. Very attractive indeed, when he really smiled, with white teeth and a small cleft that appeared at one side of his mouth. A dimple; she giggled. She would tease him to frenzy about the dimple . . . "What city of what gods? The altitude in this place is making you light-headed!"

"Teotihuacán," he pronounced it very slowly and carefully. "And if that doesn't sound like a Welsh railway station, I don't know what does. It's about thirty miles away. The greatest pre-Columbian excavated city in the Americas. It has everything, according to the booklet I was given. A pyramid to the Sun, and a pyramid to the Moon, a royal palace, frescoes, carvings, and a temple dedicated to something that I'm not even going to try and spell! There you are—the Plumed Serpent." He passed her the booklet. "You said you wanted to go sightseeing and you're going to get your wish. There's also a place not too far away where they make and sell native silver. We might drop by and see what we can find. What are you laughing at?"

"Nothing," she said. "I'll tell you later." She hummed as she put on a little lipstick and brushed her hair in front of the bathroom mirror. He didn't hustle or fuss; he had a Celtic disregard for time when there was nothing urgent to be done. He made jokes that were silly and funny and sometimes even annoying, but she spent a lot of time laughing when they were together. A superficial affair—two professionals who were lovers in their free time—she shook her head slightly at her reflection as the thought came and was dismissed. No. Not the aching love of her first experience; he was not a complex, somber man like Ivan Sasanov. But not simple either; a personality that was full of contradictions of a different kind. The ruthlessness of the Celtic race, the pride and the flash-point temper if provoked—these were combined in the romantic who bought her roses after they had made love. And who was trying very hard to make her fall in love with him.

Teotihuacán was a breathtaking panorama of ruins, dominated by the two vast pyramids built in honor of the Sun and the Moon. As Davina and Colin walked along the pavements, the symmetry and splendor of the vanished city unfolded before them. The power and wealth of the Toltecs had created a complex of temples and palaces, bisected by great avenues. The Aztecs who followed them adopted the city and its gods. There were complex carvings everywhere, angular and fierce in concept and design; an eyeless death's head grinned at them from the ruins, and savage animal heads snarled with bared stone teeth from the roofless walls. The air was pure and very thin on the high plateau; the sky was like a bowl of pure blue inverted over their heads. There was a silence that discouraged talking. They wandered down the Avenue of the Dead, hand in hand, not saying anything. On all sides the symbol of the Aztec religion grinned at them, carved into the massive walls, enshrined in the houses of the vanished race of Indian people. The skull, reminder of mortality and the tribute exacted by their god the Sun, and by his satellite the Moon Goddess and the hierarchy of the gods, was presided over by the pitiless Quetzalcoatl, the Plumed Serpent, whose temple pyramid brooded at the end of the Avenue of the Dead. There the stone jaguars crouched on guard, jaws gaping in menace, and the image of the Serpent God, plumed with feathers, was worshiped and offered human blood as homage.

They paused in the place; other tourists drifted past them, but even the children's voices were muted. Davina slipped her arm through his; he felt a tiny tremor pass through her, as if she were in a cold draft of air.

"Death," she said in a low voice. "The place is dedicated to death. It's all so cruel, so merciless. What sort of people were they, to live like this? All this splendor and so much terror—everywhere you look there's a reminder of their horrible gods and that grinning skull."

" 'Man is born but to die,' " Lomax quoted. "We see death as an enemy; maybe they saw it as a friend."

"I'll never see it as a friend. It took everything away from me. Let's look at the pyramids."

Lomax walked beside her, her arm linked with his; she saw the expression on his face.

"I'm sorry I said that. It just slipped out. Forgive me, Colin?"

"Only if you climb to the top of the Temple of the Moon with me," he said, and she was not deceived by his smile.

"I'll try," she promised. "But it looks like a difficult climb."

They rested several times on their way to the summit. The steps were massive, broad, and high, and they grew dizzy looking upward as they climbed. Once Davina paused and glanced down to the ground. The ruins below looked like a jigsaw puzzle waiting to be finished. And still the peak towered overhead. She leaned more and more on Lomax; the altitude of seven thousand feet was starving them of oxygen. Lomax pulled her to the final step and she sank down gasping for breath. For some moments she couldn't speak, and even Colin was obliged to find his breath. He put his arm round her. "Look at that," he said. "It was worth it, just to see this!" The view was endless; from the top of the incredible human tribute to the Goddess of the Moon, they saw the Mexican landscape for infinity, running into the horizon. The arid plateau, the dense green forests, the gray-blue snake of man-made highways, the distant blur of Mexico City. And then there was the towering

Temple of the Sun, an errant cloud pinned momentarily at its peak.

Below them, a middle-aged couple, burdened with cameras, were debating whether to struggle up any further; otherwise they were alone.

"Have you got your breath back?"

"Just about," Davina nodded.

"Then it's time I took it away again," he said and kissed her. Later he said, "We could make love up here."

She had been lying in his arms, her eyes closed, her body disengaged from reality. Dizzy from the thin air and the powerful stimulus of his hands and his mouth, wanting to lose herself in him, she could so easily have complied, and stretched out in the sun upon the gleaming stones. But she didn't. She opened her eyes and sat up, pushing her hair back from her face, buttoning the shirt, which he had opened to her waist.

"What's the matter?" he asked. "What's wrong, my darling?"

"Nothing, nothing's wrong." She gave a nervous little laugh. "I suppose I'm not used to making love al fresco. You forget, I've led a very sheltered sex life."

He slipped his arm round her. "Let me do that," he said and buttoned the last three buttons on her shirt. "You've never made love in the open, under the stars?"

"No," she said.

"Thank God for that," Lomax remarked. "That's one thing you haven't done with him that I can show you."

"Don't say that, Colin. Don't spoil everything by saying things like that."

He helped her to her feet. "I'm sorry. I knew you wouldn't like it, but for once I said what I thought. I have feelings too, you know. Loving you so much isn't easy when there's a third person in the background all the time."

"You don't have to be jealous of Ivan," Davina said.

"I don't have to be," he answered, "but I am."

"That was a slip of the tongue," she said. "When I said death had taken everything from me. That's what upset you, isn't it?"

"It didn't make me particularly happy," he admitted.

"I'm sorry, Colin. I didn't mean it like it sounded. Forgive me."

He looked down at her and the brief quirky smile came and went. "Forget it, sweetheart. There'll be another time and a better place than here. I was a bloody fool; I was shaken and I wanted to reassure myself by making love to you."

She smiled and said over her shoulder, "Well, you damned nearly succeeded—let's go back down to earth, shall we?"

He took her hand and squeezed it hard, then in silence they began the long, slow descent.

Twelve miles south of Teotihuacán they stopped at a town that had a picture-postcard square of adobe-walled buildings, a little church, and a restaurant with a couple of tables outside.

They sat down in the sun, and Davina closed her eyes. The intense heat of the day had been replaced by a soothing warmth.

"How about ham and eggs?" said Colin, surveying the menu. "Apparently it's their specialty. It'd make a change from refried beans."

The portions were vast, the ham cut thick and the eggs rich with big yellow yolks.

A black dog, low-bellied and cowed, sniffed at them from a distance. Davina threw it a few fatty bits, and soon it was crouching under their table, wagging its ratty tail in gratitude.

"If you go on doing that," Colin said, "we'll have every rabid mutt in Mexico after us."

Davina looked up at him. "You remember what Herrendos said. Even the dogs followed Elizabeth—" she paused, frowning. "She loved dogs. She had a Jack Russell, a fierce little devil, it used to fly at everyone. She had a snap of it at school; she stuck in on the wall over her bed. Rusty—that was it . . . Now why does that bother me?"

Later they walked round the little town and stepped into the church; the interior was lit by small windows set high up, and there were little gleaming pinpoints of votive candles in front of the altar and the side altars where the Virgin and the saints were enshrined. A group of women knelt saying the rosary in a soft murmur before a statue of the Mother of God. She was dressed in stiff brocade, paste jewels winking from her blue mantle and the elaborate gold wire crown and halo round her head. She had a china face and black eyes and she was a Mexican Indian Madonna, her china hands outstretched to bless her people. Lomax whispered to Davina, "Now that would have given my grandfather a heart attack! Popish idolatry—"

"Mine wouldn't have been too keen either," she whispered back. "But if that's what makes people happy, and brings them nearer God, why shouldn't they have it? I think she has a sweet face—I saw some marvelous Japanese Christian paintings once; Christ, the Virgin Mary, God the Father—they were all slit-eyed Japanese. Mary was dressed in a kimono! What would your grandfather have made of that?"

He shrugged. "I'm not sure what I make of it myself. Let's get back into the sunshine."

They spent the rest of the afternoon driving back to Mexico City at a leisurely pace. Lomax surprised her by suggesting they tour the superb modern university complex. He had had enough, he said, of ancient Mexico. He wanted to get back to the twentieth century.

Soon after she went to work for Edward Fleming, Ellen learned to drive a car. Before he remarried, she did all the shopping and supervised the food if he had guests. Her fear that this would be taken over by Elizabeth was quickly dispelled. Mrs. Fleming liked food in the house and good dishes on the table; she didn't want to be bothered with how any of it got there. Ever since she walked out on them, as Ellen described it to herself, Mr. Fleming had been in and out at erratic times, and every evening he had the same friend round at the house. They spent their time shut up in the little study, and Ellen served them supper on trays. She was distressed to see how little Mr. Fleming ate. She got ready to go out to the best supermarket that morning, determined to find something to tempt his appetite. He looked so gray and drawn, and seemed so jumpy. His friend Mr. Kidson seemed a kind, reassuring man to have around. He treated Ellen with impeccable courtesy.

She went down to the garage through the kitchen entrance. Mrs. Fleming's big white Mercedes was parked in its normal berth at the back. Ellen carried a big basket for groceries; she set it on the ground while she unlocked the trunk with the duplicate keys now always kept in the kitchen. Whenever Mrs. Fleming wanted something, she would send Ellen out to get it. "Take my car, Ellen, and buy me some . . . I've got such a terrible headache today." She thought of her, as she turned the key. Not a word for five days. Maybe she would never come back again. She had long lost her belief in miracles.

The trunk lid clicked open and raised itself automatically. Ellen reached down for the empty basket to put it inside. As she bent down she stared straight into a blackened human face.

There was no one in the house to hear her screaming. She only stopped when her breath choked and she doubled up beside the car and retched at the fetid smell of the decomposing body. She knew by the blonde hair that the hideous face and the limbs cramped up in the narrow space belonged to Elizabeth Fleming. She slammed the lid down on the horror. The tongue was protruding, and the eyes were out of their sockets . . . Head swimming, she stumbled across to the kitchen door for the telephone. The vile smell drifted after her.

* * *

They didn't go back to the Alameda. They had an early dinner, listened to the mariachi musicians who played outside in the evenings and joined the cheerful crowd who danced in the square. At one moment Lomax asked her if she was happy.

"Very happy."

"Good," he said and pulled her closer.

The reception clerk came quickly to meet them as they walked into the hotel.

"An urgent message for you, señora."

She read it quickly and turned in alarm to Lomax. "Kidson's called three times."

They got a connection immediately.

"Davina—the worst possible news, I'm afraid. The whole bloody thing has blown sky high. Elizabeth Fleming was found dead this afternoon. Yes, yes, that's what I said! Strangled, hidden in the trunk of her car in their garage—I've spoken to the Chief, and Humphrey's flying out."

He went on talking for a few minutes and then Davina put down the phone. She had repeated the news as Kidson gave it.

"We should get back tonight if we can. They've called in the CIA and they're keeping it quiet for the next forty-eight hours anyway. My God—what do we do now?"

"Pack," Lomax said tersely. "Try reception and see if there's a flight tonight. If there is, we've got to be on it."

He was throwing their clothes into the cases when she came back and stood in the bedroom door. "We're in luck. We've got two reservations on the last plane. Eleven fifteen. You realize, don't you, Colin—I've failed."

He snapped the cases shut and heaved them off the bed.

"Like hell you have," he said. "Let's get that flight!"

"They're doing the post mortem tonight," Kidson said. "She'd certainly been dead for some days. Fleming collapsed after he'd identified her."

"Where is he now?" Davina asked.

"Under sedation at home. Thank God the housekeeper kept her head and called Fleming at his office instead of the police; he called me, and I thought it best to go direct to the CIA. And guess who was in charge. Our old friend Spencer-Barr!"

"They put a security stop on it," Lomax remarked. "It won't hold for long."

"No, it bloody well won't," Kidson snapped back. He very seldom swore; he looked tense and exhausted. "I need a drink!"

"Give me one too, Colin, please," said Davina. "Has Fleming admitted anything?"

"No. I couldn't get him to budge. He insisted he was telling the truth about everything. When I got to the house he was in a state of collapse; the maid Ellen was like a zombie. She'd been strangled so hard her eyes were out of their sockets. But I did try to get a confession out of Fleming as soon as I'd pulled myself together. He went to pieces, but he didn't change his story. He hadn't killed her. By that time Spencer-Barr had arrived, and they got a doctor to give Fleming and the maid sedatives to put them out for the night. Then that creep Jeremy started on me and I told him to put the house under close guard before he started throwing accusations about. I really lost my temper with him!"

"What sort of accusations?" Davina asked. "You notified him, what was wrong with that? You acted perfectly properly."

"That's what I said," Kidson answered. "He seemed to be beside himself, almost hysterical. He'd accepted Fleming's explanation that his wife had gone to New York. All right, that made a fool of him when she's lying dead in the garage, but he was shouting and threatening me with God knows what, saying we'd interfered in United States affairs with a U.S. citizen—he knew a lot more about our involvement with Fleming and Elizabeth than he admitted."

"It sounds like he's afraid of something," Lomax suggested. "If he's the cold-blooded type, the only thing that gets under their skin is a threat to themselves. You know something, Davina?

We've assumed Elizabeth was kidnaped by the KGB and murdered to shut her up and protect Fleming. Did Hickling ever try and track down that cab? I gave him the registration number."

"No," Davina said. "No, he didn't. What are you getting at?"

"Just a thought," he muttered. "I'm not in your league, or yours, John. I've only hunted small fry. But I don't think there's anything more we can do tonight; it's nearly four in the morning."

"Oh, God Almighty, so it is," Kidson groaned. "Poor Charlie; she arrived this morning. I was supposed to ring her this evening after she got in. You two go off and get some sleep. Tomorrow is going to be a bloody day for all of us. Davina, Charlie asked about you as soon as we talked. You couldn't spare a few minutes tomorrow morning and call her at the Hay-Adams, could you? This is going to be a wretched holiday for her."

"Of course I will," Davina said. "Get some sleep yourself; you look dead beat, John. Don't worry about Charlie. She'll understand."

They didn't go to bed. Davina made coffee, Lomax had a shower. They sat through what was left of the night, smoking cigarettes and emptying the percolator, and they saw the dawn break over Washington together.

"If Igor Borisov had written the scenario himself," said Davina, "it couldn't be worse for us or better for him. And he did write it, Colin, I know that."

They were standing together by the big window, with the sunlight turning yellow above the rooftops and the last pink streaks fading from the morning sky.

She leaned her head against him, and with one hand pushed the straying hair from her forehead. "How did he do it?"

"We've got forty-eight hours to find out," he said.

Neil Browning couldn't get Hickling alone. He had used up his store of excuses to hang around the office, and the atmosphere was growing unfriendly. Hickling seemed typical of the intelligence section that morning; Browning had been alerted by the rush of phone calls coming through to Hickling's people, and a hurrying secretary had committed the unpardonable sin of saying, as he tried to stop her, "I can't, Neil, there's a panic on upstairs." That was enough for him. He knew that his instructions from the controller hadn't been suspended; find out anything you can and pass it through immediately. A panic meant one thing. Something had broken about the Flemings. He brazened it out with Hickling until Peter actually told him to leave the office. He looked tense and irritable; he was waiting for a phone call and he kept glancing at his watch and then at the telephone.

"Look," he said, "can't you see I'm bloody busy? I know you've got nothing much to do, but I'm up to my balls in it this morning." Hickling's ears were still hot from John Kidson's reprimand. And now the Sea Green Incorruptible himself was on his way from London. Heads would certainly fall and Peter Hickling's seemed likely to be the first.

"I'm sorry," Neil repeated. "But what's the flap? What's everyone running round like blue-assed flies for? Has Mrs. Fleming been found?"

Hickling's nerves were ragged. "Yes," he snapped. "She has—in the trunk of her car! Will you shove off, for Christ's sake, Neil?"

"Sorry, sorry," he said hastily. "I'm on my way—she's dead?"

Hickling only nodded and then his phone buzzed and he grabbed it.

Neil hurried back to his own office. His work would have to wait. He called through to his secretary.

"Jean—I've got to go uptown. Refer all calls for an hour, will you? Thanks." He made his way to the nearest outside phone booth and dialed Bruckner's number. The girl assistant answered. No, Mr. Bruckner was not in the shop that day; he'd taken the shuttle to New York to go to a demonstration and lecture on some new telephoto equipment. She hadn't any idea where it was, and he didn't expect to be back before tomorrow. No, she didn't know where he was staying.

Reluctantly, she offered to call his home. Browning waited in the phone booth, picking anxiously at the skin on his forefinger. It was raw with a tiny rim of blood round the nail by the time the girl rang back on the booth number. There was no reply from Bruckner's home. His wife must have taken the trip with him. She hung up.

Browning swore with frustration. Bloody marvelous, weren't they, walking off without leaving any means of contact—he paused, and shrugged off a sudden qualm of fear. It had never happened before. If Bruckner wasn't in the shop he always left a number where he could be reached. Well, they couldn't blame him if they got his information a day late. He returned to the office and settled down to work. At the back of his mind he had made a decision. He had had enough of Washington. Enough of Bruckner and the man with the pebble glasses. To hell with the money. He'd apply for a transfer. Somewhere unimportant, where they wouldn't bother following him up. It would be dull and a setback to his career, but it would be worth it to get off the hook.

Peter Hickling had arranged to meet his caller. He left the office and the embassy by eleven fifteen and drove to a small singles bar in Georgetown. His contact was waiting at a table in the corner; he was a small man in his early forties; he wore a linen suit and a short-brimmed homburg made of straw.

They didn't shake hands. Peter Hickling ordered beer. He leaned nearer the American. "I need your help, Sam. I've done you favors, now I need one."

"Such as?" Sam sipped his beer. They had worked together a lot since Hickling got the Washington appointment, but unofficially, in the private way of rivals in rival services who are supposed to be allies against a common foe. Sam was an old CIA operator. He was beyond cynicism and he said himself he'd forgotten how to spell scruple. He had taken favors from Hickling, and he knew that the time would come when he'd have to pay them back. The system of mutual exchange worked very well between individuals. Nobody broke security because the penalty was noncooperation, and neither the men from Langley nor those from British SIS could work effectively without the clandestine leaks between the two. "I want to know about this," Hickling said. "A yellow cab, this registration number. It's a fake, we checked with the cab company. Does it mean anything to you? Can you check on it for me?"

Sam pushed his ugly little hat further back from his forehead. He had begun to go bald very early. He squinted at the number. "I don't need to check," he said. "It's one of ours. We use those last three letters plus the *Z* registration on all our decoy autos."

"Jesus," Hickling hissed under his breath. "You mean it's a CIA decoy number?"

"That's what I said," Sam agreed. "And that's all I can tell you, buddy boy. I hope it's helped."

"Yes, yes, it certainly has." Hickling pulled himself together and managed to grin. The CIA had picked up Elizabeth Fleming. He felt the sweat break out and trickle down the side of his face. They had all been completely off course . . . He finished his beer, exchanged a little inside gossip with Sam, and hurried out of the bar. He couldn't wait to slap John Kidson in the face with this.

The girl assistant in Bruckner's camera shop went on dusting the shelves. The note with his number in New York was safely filed away in a drawer with some order slips. Her instructions had been emphatic. Nobody was to contact her boss while he was out of town. Especially Neil Browning. She didn't say much; she was used to taking short, unexplained instructions over the two years she had been in place in the camera shop. They didn't come from Peter Hickling, nominal head of the intelligence section at the British embassy. They were issued by a quiet-spoken Englishwoman who had lived in Washington for years, the widow of an American political journalist who was persona grata with everyone of consequence. She had no contact with Hickling or his department, or with any member of the embassy. Her orders came direct from Humphrey Grant in London.

Bruckner's assistant didn't know her; she only knew that the monthly check paid into a separate account in a New York bank was generous. For two years she had been keeping a watch on the customers at the shop, and it was her observation of Neil Browning's visits that alerted London. She had sent copies of the films he took for development, and the recurring presence of the book, *All the President's Men*, tied in with the other visitor, the photographic salesman with the Bronx accent and the twenty-twelve vision. Bruckner was to be kept cut off till he came back from Washington. She hummed as she dusted. He thought she was stupid, and when he wasn't squeezing her bottom, he shouted at her. She didn't mind. She had a big bank balance and she was saving up to get married. She'd think of Mr. Big Mouth Bruckner when she was on her honeymoon in Tahiti and her husband had set up his own photographic shop . . .

Charlie Kidson was asleep when the telephone rang in her hotel bedroom. She heard it shrilling through her dream and didn't move. It would stop and she could sink back to a deep sleep. But it didn't; it went on and on until she was fully awake, and she reached out and picked it up. "Davina? Oh, hello—I'm sorry, I was still dead to the world—no, no, of course you didn't, how are you? Where are you?"

She was sitting up now, holding the receiver in both hands, laughing with excitement. "Come on over! Oh, why? Why not—poor darling John is up to his eyes in some crisis and I've nothing to do all day—you are too? The same one. Listen, I'm coming over to you! No, Davy, I won't be put off. Give me the address; I'll be over in half an hour. No, I promise. Half an hour!" She sprang out of bed; her jet lag had vanished. She rushed through her shower, checked her watch as she made up, and decided she'd rather see her sister than put the final gloss on her appearance. She knew by the heads turning in the hotel foyer that she looked as beautiful as ever. She arrived at the studio apartment only ten minutes late, and the person who opened the door to her was Colin Lomax.

He stared at her. She stared back, and then her lovely smile appeared. "I hope I haven't got the wrong address. Does Miss Graham live here?"

"Yes, she does." He had a faint Scots accent, just the merest inflection. It was very attractive.

"I'm her sister, Charlie."

"I'm Colin Lomax. Come in, won't you?" He didn't shake hands with her; she smiled at him, and she thought with amusement that he looked rather embarrassed.

"Do you live here too?" He stiffened and his mouth snapped into a thin line. She didn't think he was quite as attractive as she'd thought. "I do, Mrs. Kidson. Davina's upstairs."

She followed him up the narrow stair to the big open-plan living room. Davina was sitting with her back to the window; she got up and came quickly towards her. They embraced, and Charlie held her at arm's length and said, "Davy, darling, you're looking marvelous!"

"I'm surprised to hear it," Davina said. "I've been up all night, and I feel like death on a plate." She caught a glimpse of Colin; he was standing by the door, his hands in his pockets, a scowl on his face. He looked just like that when I first met him, she remembered. All tight with quills on end like a porcupine. Charlie must have upset him. What a change from most men . . .

"I'm sorry I woke you up, Charlie," she said. "But poor John was so worried about leaving you on your own like this, he asked me to call you and explain. You're looking just as good as ever. Better, even."

Charlie laughed. She threw her bag on a chair and dropped gracefully onto the sofa. She held out her hand to her sister. "Come and tell me what's been happening," she said. "As much as you can, anyway. Mr. Lomax?" Her voice was sweetly innocent. "Are you working with my sister?"

He came towards her stiffly, unwillingly. "Yes, Mrs. Kidson, I am. I'm here to protect her, as a matter of fact. That's my job."

"I see; well, please don't look so cross with me. I'm not going to hit her over the head or anything. Won't you come and talk to us too?"

Davina saw him turn slightly red. Damn you, Charlie, she thought, and then she started to smile. She's not trying to pinch him, she's poking fun at him. And she knows men; he won't take kindly to being teased by a stranger. Oh, my sister, how you've changed since you got married. How we've both changed. And she saw the gleam in Charlie's enormous gray eyes and understood its meaning. He's yours, it said. Good for you, Davy. Good for you.

"I'll make coffee," Colin said abruptly.

"No, you won't." Davina got up quickly. "I'll make it," she said firmly and went out leaving them together. Lomax crossed one leg over the other and looked at his foot. He looked at it and it began to swing back and forth.

Charlie was the most beautiful woman he'd ever seen. Everything about her was an exaggeration: taller than average, exquisitely slim, hair like a red cloud, a perfect face almost devoid of make-up, eyes that overpowered her other features until she smiled, and then all you saw was the delicious curve of her mouth. She had a strong scent that wafted at him when she moved; she used her hands in little graceful gestures to emphasize what she was saying. They were white with long silver polished nails and gold rings. This was Davina's sister. This natural freak of perfect beauty.

"Do you have a cigarette?" she asked. He grunted, and gave her the crumpled packet out of his pocket. She took one and he had to fish out his lighter.

"Thank you. Can you tell me what's going on?"

"No, I'm afraid not."

She ignored the curtness of his answer. He couldn't go on avoiding her, and when he reluctantly faced her, there was no trace of the mocking amusement in her eyes. There was a serious, determined expression in them that reminded him suddenly of Davina. "I know Liz is dead," she said. "John told me. But that's all. I don't really care, you know; I just want to be sure there's nothing dangerous in it for my sister. She's been through quite enough."

Lomax found an ashtray for her. "You don't have to worry about that," he said. "That's my department. I'll take damned good care of her."

"I'm sure you will," Charlie said, "if she'll let you. She's a very determined person."

"So I've noticed." He wished Davina would come back. He felt certain that this amazingly self-possessed woman was going to say something personal and embarrassing at any moment. After a couple of puffs, Charlie stubbed out her cigarette.

"I think you're fond of Davy, aren't you? You don't mind me saying so, I hope."

"Not at all," Lomax said. "I am fond of her. You're right."

"I'm glad. She needs someone to love her. You seem the right sort of person for her. She's got to have a strong man, because she's so strong herself."

He couldn't help it, he had to ask the question, one eye on the door in case Davina came through it.

"Did you know her husband?"

"Slightly," Charlie said.

"What was he like?"

"Very strong," she answered. "He adored Davy; they adored each other." Then she answered the question he wouldn't have asked for himself. "Not like you to look at. Not at all good-looking, very Slavic. Much more friendly, actually," and he saw her smile.

It didn't come easily to him but he smiled faintly back at her.

His instinct counted her as an ally; a most unlikely ally, but somehow she was on his side. He felt and looked rather sheepish. "Would you like another cigarette?"

"No, I only half smoke them anyway. John says it's an awful waste. Don't tell Davy I talked to you about Sasanov, will you? She'd be very cross. She hates being discussed."

For the first time Colin looked directly into her beautiful eyes and said simply, "I'll ask the same of you, Mrs. Kidson. She'd be cross as hell with me too." He got up as the door opened and took the tray of coffee from Davina.

"How awful," Charlie said a little later. Davina had been surprised to discover how much John Kidson discussed his work with his wife. "But if Edward Fleming didn't murder her, then who did?"

"That's the question we'd all like answered," Davina said.

"And it's not the only one. How well did you know her, Charlie? There was quite an age gap between you, she was my contemporary."

"I know, but it didn't seem to matter. I was married to Peter first—" She hesitated and Davina nodded.

"Go on."

"We were living in London and I met her at some lunch party. I can't remember. She was very sweet, and suggested we might have dinner. She was getting married herself quite soon, so we all met and got on together and we used to go out as a foursome, and sometimes she and I would have lunch or go to the cinema. She always looked immaculate and wildly attractive; she wasn't bothered about men particularly, she liked having them around. But she didn't hurry to get married, and I never heard any gossip about her. I mean, that's really all I can tell you, Davy. She was not a very close friend." There was a wide, disarming smile. "She was even more selfish than me, and there's a limit to friendships like that. She was terribly sweet-natured on the surface. Everybody raved about how nice she was; just like when we were all at school."

"She certainly changed," Lomax said. "Sweet and nice she wasn't."

"If she took to drink," Charlie suggested, "maybe her real self came to the surface. But I must say, I find it hard to imagine Liz doing anything to spoil her looks. She told me she wouldn't have children because it'd ruin her figure. I don't think the husband was too pleased about that. She had two frightful little yappy dachshunds that went everywhere with her."

Davina put the coffee cup down. "Two dogs?"

"Yes; you know I'm fond of animals, but I couldn't stand them. Why?"

Davina shook her head; she was frowning. "Oh, nothing . . . Look, Charlie, I think I should go over to the Flemings' house. He's under sedation, but I might be able to talk to him for a few minutes. You don't mind, do you?"

"Why don't I come too?" Charlie suggested. She got up and slung her handbag over her shoulder. "I've got nothing to do. I won't be in the way. Please, Davy; John won't mind."

It was Colin Lomax who said, "Why not? Your sister can wait with me."

Humphrey Grant arrived at Dulles airport just after eleven A.M. He had slept during the flight, his ears plugged and his gaunt face half covered by a black sleep mask. He disliked flying and detested the prepacked food and rattling carts full of drink he didn't want. Worst of all was the hazard of a talkative neighbor. He repulsed the stewardess and his fellow travelers with his sleeping mask and earplugs, and woke up exactly fifteen minutes before they came in to land.

Kidson was waiting for him at the airport. He looked as gray-faced as Humphrey Grant. They collected his small bag, went through customs and immigration and out into the hot sunshine. Kidson drove him through Washington; Grant stared gloomily out of the window. They didn't speak, except for Kidson's inquiry about Sir James White. "How's the Chief?"

Grant's little hooded eyes flickered at him and then away. "Not best pleased," was all he said. They drove to the embassy and went in through a side entrance. Kidson took him straight to Hickling's office. The secretary informed them that Peter Hickling had gone out. Grant lowered his long body into a chair; the movement reminded Kidson of a grasshopper disposing itself on a twig.

"We may as well go over the facts," he announced to Kidson, "since apparently our principal intelligence officer has gone out on some errand or other. Didn't he know I was coming?"

"Yes, of course he knew," John Kidson answered irritably. "If he's out, there's a good reason for it. But before he does come back, I'll say this to you privately, Humphrey. He needs a good sharp kick up the backside. He's got slack over here."

"That's obvious," Grant muttered. "I shall be doing the kicking. He's being replaced. Where is Davina?"

"She's over with Fleming." Kidson said. "She's going to ask him a few questions while he's still woolly from the dope they gave him. It's possible she might catch him out."

"If she does," Grant said, "it's still too late. He obviously panicked and killed his wife. There won't be any hiding that away. It hasn't gone according to plan, has it, John?"

"No," Kidson said. "It hasn't. Not that I quite knew what the Chief's plan was. Elizabeth Fleming was always in danger from the KGB."

"Naturally; if they acted against her that reinforced our case against the husband. We were waiting to see if that happened. Had it done, she'd have either vanished or been the victim of a very convincing accident. Not murdered and hidden in her own car in her own garage. That, my dear John, is not the way the opposition protect their agents! Which makes Fleming the killer. And a clumsy one, unfortunately for us. It's going to be difficult convincing the Chief that there hasn't been all-round imcompetence."

"I expect it is," Kidson said sharply. "Here's Hickling now. Peter? Where the hell have you been? Mr. Grant's been waiting nearly half an hour."

"I'm sorry," Peter Hickling said. He offered his hand to Humphrey, who shook it reluctantly and briefly. "Did you have a good flight?"

"I don't know. I slept."

"Sorry I was out," Hickling went on. He gave Kidson a quick glance; it wasn't at all friendly. "I went out to meet a contact from the CIA. We've done deals before, exchanging information. I asked him to check the registration number on the cab that picked up Mrs. Fleming. And I struck lucky."

He paused; both his seniors were watching him intently. "The cab that abducted her was one of their own decoys," he said. "She was picked up that night by the CIA and taken in. I think that alters the picture quite considerably."

There was a silence that seemed to Hickling to go on too long. Then Humphrey spoke to Kidson. "It does indeed," he said. He let out a long slow sigh.

"What a tiresome, brutal lot of bunglers they are," he said. "I think we are in a position now to ask for an urgent meeting with our erstwhile colleague Mr. Spencer-Barr. I want to hear his explanation for covering up a CIA murder by framing a personal advisor to their own President. Get him on the phone, will you, Hickling? Thank you."

Lomax's ID card got him and Davina and Charlie past the CIA man sitting inside Fleming's front door. He stared after the younger woman as she walked past him, and puckered his mouth in a whistle. He knew the British were an odd lot, but if that woman was a cop . . .

Davina said, "Charlie, you and Colin better wait downstairs. I'll go and see if Fleming is able to talk."

He was in a spare bedroom; the guard on the upper landing

opened the door to her. He was sitting up against the pillows: his eyes were dull, the pupils enlarged. Davina sat down on the edge of the bed. Fleming looked at her. "Get to hell out of here!" he said.

"I came to see how you were. And to say I'm sorry about Elizabeth."

"You're not sorry about anything," he muttered. He lolled sideways on the pillow and for a moment his eyelids closed. "She's dead, I did it. That's all there is. I give up; now go away, will you?"

"No, I won't," Davina said. "Because I don't accept what you've just said. I don't believe for a minute that you killed your wife."

He turned back and opened his eyes. "You must be the only one," he said. "The CIA, John Kidson—they were all here yesterday, and they know I'm guilty. They just haven't made up their minds how to hush up the scandal."

"They can't," she said. "We've got less than two days to prove you're innocent. It was a plant, Edward."

He sneered at her, his mouth twisted into a grimace. "You know I'm a Russian agent, don't you? You know I stood back and let one woman burn to death. How come you're so sure I didn't choke the next one . . ."

"Because I'm not a bloody fool," Davina snapped. "You had that diary hanging over your head—you couldn't have hurt her if you'd wanted to. You don't take risks like that; you're not the reckless type. You listen to me. I don't care a tinker's damn about you, Edward Fleming. You turned Elizabeth into a drunk and a slut; you ruined her. She wasn't much to start with, but by the time she'd been married to you for a few months, she was drinking heavily and sleeping around."

"That's not true," he summoned enough breath to shout, and heaved himself upright. "She drank, but my guess is she'd been doing it all the time; she hid it from me before we got married—but she didn't sleep around."

"She never had a lover?" Davina insisted. "Not even one? That's not what Ellen told me. There was one, wasn't there?"

"Oh, yes, one. One guy I found out about—she admitted it. She was drunk when it happened. Ellen hated her; she'd say anything, she hated her so much." He sighed, the effort had exhausted him. "She made Ellen get rid of her dog," he muttered. "That started it."

"You hated her too, didn't you?"

"Yes, I hated her. I hated the very sight of her. As much as I loved her, and that is one hell of a lot."

"Why?" She shook his arm. "Tell me. Why did you hate her so much? Because of the man, the drink—why?"

"I forgave the man," he said slowly. "I had to; I had to find an excuse. I tried to live with the drink." He stared at Davina without focusing on her. "It wasn't easy, but I tried. I did love her very much. I kept reminding myself of how she was when I first met her. She was beautiful, but it was more than that. Beautiful women grow on trees here; every sidewalk is crammed with beautiful girls. She had a beautiful nature; there wasn't a lousy thought in her head or a mean word about anybody. And she was no tramp, whatever you say—she never slept with me in Mexico, and Jesus, I tried hard enough at first . . . then I realized she wasn't that kind of woman. I respected her, doesn't that sound funny to a liberated little hard-nose like you? Sure it does, but it's true. I wanted to marry her, take care of her. I closed my eyes to it all at first. She was such a liar, that was the first shock; she sneaked about the place, drinking on the side, sidling up to me one minute wanting to go to bed, yelling at me the next; she picked on Ellen, she started touting for clients to do up their houses for them, and she wouldn't accept that it jeopardized my position in Washington. There was a row that I'll never forget. She used language . . . I couldn't believe it."

"I want to ask you one thing," said Davina. "It's very important you tell me the truth. Was there anything that happened to make Elizabeth go to pieces like that? Anything between you after you got married? Your sex life? Did you put pressures on her?"

He said dully, "Nothing happened. No traumas, nothing. So far as sex is concerned, all I wanted was a lot of it. She did too. I don't have any kinks, if that's what you're getting at."

"You said," she continued after a pause, "that she wasn't very keen on sex. Before you married, anyway. Now you say she liked it. Did that happen quickly?"

"I'm good in bed," he answered. "I made sure she liked it. You must be quite a kinky lady, asking all these questions. She hated you, did you know that?"

"No," Davina said quietly, "I didn't. We weren't friends at school, but she was always telling me she was fond of me. She was on the phone every minute if I didn't see her. Why do you say she hated me?"

"Because she did," he answered. "Miss Smartass, she used to call you. I heard her say it, when she hung up after talking to you. She thought she was alone. I didn't ask about it; she was being nice to your face, making use of you. That was Elizabeth."

"Yes," Davina said. "You identified her, didn't you?"

He nodded. "Ellen found her. I identified her. I cracked, but it was just shock. Shock and the strain and your bloodhound Kidson on my back. It wasn't grief."

"I'm not surprised," Davina said. "I'm going now." He glanced at her from the pillow; his face was gray and the cheeks had sunk.

"And you still think I didn't kill her?"

"I'm perfectly certain you didn't."

"I'm not a Soviet agent either. Not that anyone believes me."

"I believe you," Davina Graham said. She opened the door and went out.

* * *

"How do you account for this, Jerry?" The director asked the question very quietly. Spencer-Barr was standing in front of his desk; he hadn't been invited to sit down.

The pick-up team were being assembled; the two responsible for Elizabeth Fleming's surveillance were on their way back from the East Coast where Jeremy had exiled them. Messages hummed from the director's office. One message was still to be delivered. He hadn't decided when to inform the President of what had happened. It had to be timed exactly, so that the President heard from the director before there was any leak to the media, or an echo from the giant sounding board of Washington rumor. The police were pledged to secrecy; the Fleming household was being guarded without any outward sign of a police presence, the telephone was monitored and calls referred to Fleming's secretary. Fleming himself had recorded a message saying he was going out of town for two days, and this had been played over to the unsuspecting staff in his office when his secretary checked the recording machine for late messages. It was sewn up and sealed tight like a plastic bag full of poison gas.

"How did you let it happen?" the director said.

"I don't understand your question, sir," Jeremy fenced with outward coolness. "Nothing happened to Mrs. Fleming as a result of her interview with me. She was questioned, warned, and then driven back to her home. You've had the tapes and the transcript. My people set her down and she went into the house. That was the last time anyone saw her."

"You mean your team lost sight of her until her body was discovered? And you didn't report to me? You took no action? Explain this; explain why you bawled out your operators and sent them to a low-grade posting. Wasn't that a punishment, a punishment for fouling up the job?"

"Yes, it was." He squared his shoulders and looked as if he were going to admit something unpleasant. "I believed the British had got her out of the country," Jeremy said. "Two of their people, the woman Graham and a man, came to Fleming's house some time later. They stayed quite a while and then left. My operatives said they were certain Mrs. Fleming wasn't with them. I thought they'd relaxed their surveillance at some point and she'd slipped out to Graham's car. That's why I reassigned them. They'll confirm this. I was disturbed, sir, very much so. But I decided to wait it out and see if my contacts in England picked her up. In a way I thought I'd achieved my object. She'd left the country and there'd be no more chance of a scandal. I was wrong."

"You were," the director repeated. "I told you not to step on any twigs, Jerry, remember? You asked to handle this; I said OK, but I told you, be careful. So what do you do? You take in this woman for an unauthorized interrogation, you frighten the shit out of her—oh, yes, that came across in the tapes to me—how much did you edit out, by the way? Then you send her home to her husband. You send an alcoholic back in a state of panic? Hysteria? That was a fool thing to do—suppose he'd just gone to the President and raised hell, that would have been bad for all of us. Especially you. But he killed her instead. And he's going to stand trial for it, and he's going to testify that she'd been held by the CIA. If he gets the right kind of lawyer—and he will, Jerry, he will—he'll say he found her dead and he panicked. He panicked and hid the body. He knew she took a cab. The two limeys knew she took one. That cab can be traced if anyone saw the registration. That lands the agency right in the shit. That's where you've put us, Jerry. In the shit."

Spencer-Barr opened his mouth but the big square hand came up to silence him.

"And that's where I'm going to put you," the director said. "Right in it, Jerry, up to here." The hand rose to the level of the director's eyes. "You're going to carry the can for the agency and I'm going to see to it in person that you do. You can walk out of here right now. And you're suspended."

There was nothing Spencer-Barr could answer. His face had

flushed a deep red. He turned and left the office. He had been working at Langley long enough to know that the director could do exactly what he threatened.

Unless he could get the agency off the hook first. Suspended or not, he went back to his own office and there he found Humphrey Grant's message. He left the building and within an hour he was at the British embassy, taking the same side entrance that Kidson and Grant had taken earlier that morning.

"There's a funny feel to this house," Charlie said.

"That's hardly surprising," Lomax answered.

"I mean it doesn't feel like a proper home," Charlie retorted. "Look at this room, for instance, this is the study or whatever Americans call it, the den, that's right. We have a room like this at home, John and I, and my parents always use a small room for relaxing and watching TV. It's supposed to be casual and untidy, somewhere you can put your feet up, pile magazines and papers, generally make a cozy mess. Have you ever seen anything more formal, in a funny way?"

Lomax looked round. "I suppose not. We only had the one sitting room. I'm not too sure what a study ought to look like."

"Not like this," she said firmly. "There's only one photograph in the room—that picture of their wedding. It's so impersonal, all perfectly color-matched and terribly *Homes and Garden*, but you can't imagine anyone actually spent an evening here. I wonder what the rest of the house is like. Her flat in London wasn't like this. She was very keen on blue . . . I'd like to wander round, do you think it'd be all right?"

"If I come with you," Lomax said. "Those gentlemen outside won't let you go anywhere without an ID. Where do you want to go?"

"To the bathroom for a start," Charlie said. "Upstairs; I'd love to see her bedroom. Why are you looking at me like that, Mr. Lomax?"

"She's dead," Colin said flatly. "Doesn't it bother you?"

"No," she said calmly. "It doesn't. I was shocked when I heard, but now I'm frankly curious. Shall we go upstairs?"

He nodded, not sure what to say. Under all the fluffy femininity there was a very cool streak. She had more in common with her sister Davina than people might imagine. He led the way upstairs; he knew which was the Flemings' bedroom because he'd searched the house with Fleming the night Elizabeth disappeared.

"This is pretty," Charlie remarked, standing in the middle of the bedroom. "Much more Elizabeth's style than downstairs. That's her sleep pillow."

"Her what?" Lomax asked.

"Her sleep pillow, there on the bed." She picked up the little lace-covered satin cushion shaped like a neck rest. "She always had one, she said she couldn't sleep without it. That must be the bathroom. I won't be a minute."

Lomax glanced round the room; he remembered the frantic search that night, with Fleming opening and shutting doors and calling her name. The post mortem had revealed that she must have been lying in the trunk of the car in the garage while they were looking for her. He went over to the bed and picked up the wedge-shaped cushion by its lace edge.

There was a knock on the bedroom door and Ellen came in. Her dark face was pinched and the skin had a grayish tinge. She had some clothes over one arm and a pair of high-heeled shoes. "These came back from the cleaners yesterday and her shoes from the shoe man. I don't know what to do with her things."

"Put them away, Ellen," Lomax said. "You had a very nasty shock. Are you feeling all right now?"

"Not too bad, thank you. They gave me something last night and I slept through. They won't let me go out of the house, or call home." The dark eyes filled with tears; she blinked them back. "I can't believe it," she said. "I can't believe he did it." She turned quickly as the bathroom door opened and Charlie came out.

"This is Miss Graham's sister, Mrs. Kidson," Lomax said. "It's all right, Ellen. We'll put Mrs. Fleming's clothes away. Maybe you could make us some coffee." Ellen nodded and quickly left the room.

Charlie opened one of the closets. "Christ," Lomax exclaimed. "She had enough clothes! And shoes—there must be sixty pairs!" Charlie took the dresses from him and hung them up. He held out the shoes and she hesitated.

"They can't be Elizabeth's," she said. "They're far too small. Never mind, we'll put them with the others . . . She did buy a lot of shoes, didn't she? And I thought I was extravagant!"

There were shoes in dark shades and pastels, rows of evening shoes; gold, silver, shoes dyed to match dresses, glittering with diamonds, country shoes and flimsy sandals, elegant courts with high heels. Charlie stooped and picked out one after another.

"I don't understand this," she said to Lomax. "Elizabeth had enormous feet. These are size five, they can't possibly be hers."

Lomax didn't answer. He picked up a shoe and turned it over; the size was on the sole, 5AA. A tiny, narrow foot. "Mrs. Kidson," he said slowly. "I think we'd better check."

"She was terribly self-conscious about her feet," said Charlie. "They were the only thing that spoiled her. She couldn't have worn these in a million years."

Lomax took her by the arm. "Let's find Davina."

Ellen came back to the bedroom with them. She opened the closets for Davina. She took out dresses, a mink coat; Charlie nodded. "They're the right size," she said.

"And all these shoes belonged to Mrs. Fleming?" Davina asked.

"Yes, Miss Graham. They're all hers. She was forever buying more; she was mighty proud of her feet."

"Thank you, Ellen," Davina said. "You've been a great help."

They went back down the elegant staircase in silence. Lomax closed the study door behind them. Davina had a shoe in her left hand; it hung from her fingers by an ankle strap. "You realize what this means? Don't you see what it means? Whoever Edward Fleming married, it wasn't the Elizabeth Carlton we knew! Oh, God, it's so obvious when you think of it—why, why didn't I see it before?"

"Wait a minute," Lomax interrupted. "We've got to be sure."

"I am sure," Davina said. "It looked so convincing on the surface. But there was always something wrong. Now all the inconsistencies make sense. Give me a cigarette, love, will you?"

"Me too," Charlie said. "I can't believe it's possible. But Davy's right. Feet get bigger; there's no way you can come down two sizes in shoes . . . What about fingerprints? Wouldn't they prove it?"

"They'll check with the body," Lomax said. "They'll be all over the house here."

Davina wasn't listening; she was almost talking to herself.

"She was a plant," she said. "God knows how they worked it, but they switched a double for the real Elizabeth . . . don't you see, it all makes sense now? The personality change, the drinking—and the dog! God, how could I have missed out on that? Liz adored dogs, you reminded me this morning, Charlie, and I still couldn't pin it down—she had that awful terrier Rusty when we were at school—two dachshunds in London. She had dogs instead of children. You remember what that German said in Mexico? Even the dogs followed her? Of course they did—that was the real Elizabeth. The one in Washington wouldn't let Ellen keep her dog. Fleming fell in love with Elizabeth Carlton; sweet-natured, placid, didn't sleep around, hardly touched a drink—what did the old Señora Veranez say? Sometimes a glass of wine. All that is typical. The one in Washington was drunk at eleven in the morning! The woman who came to New York and married Fleming was another person. What did Ellen say? 'She changed mighty quick after they got married. She treated me like nigger dirt.' Colin, I said to you at the time that wasn't the Elizabeth I knew—she'd *never* have behaved to a colored person like that!" She began to pace up and down the room. "The double slept with men behind Fleming's back. That wasn't Elizabeth either. She used filthy language when they quarreled. Liz never said more than 'damn' in her life. Why didn't I think of that before? The one here swore like a trooper. My God, I'm beginning to see it now. We've got to get back and see Humphrey right away! Wait, what have I done with that bloody shoe . . . Charlie, you'll have to come with me. You're my star witness."

In the car Charlie touched Davina on the shoulder; she looked back at her. "If you're right, and it looks like it," she said, "what happened to the real Elizabeth?"

It was Colin Lomax who answered as he drove. "She never left Mexico alive."

Chapter Seven

BORISOV TOOK his place at the long table in the Kremlin conference room. The other members of the Politburo were all seated; only the chair reserved for the head of Soviet Russia was still empty. When he came into the room there was a shuffling movement and his colleagues stood up. They exchanged greetings and he moved at his slow pace to the vacant seat. There was an atmosphere of expectancy in the room. Secretive, enclosed as it was, the Politburo had its own source of internal rumors; the spies spied upon each other. Every member of the ruling council had contacts who kept them informed of what the others were doing. They knew by report that Igor Borisov had something important to tell them, and it was obvious by the confidence in his manner that it signified a major intelligence success. His business came midway through the meeting. The general secretary raised his heavy head and nodded towards Borisov, who stood up. He had spoken to his enemy Rudzenko in a pleasant exchange before the meeting started. He was aware of the eyes focused upon him and knew which were friendly, hostile or still neutral.

"I am glad to tell you, Comrade Secretary, comrades, that our operation Plumed Serpent has reached its final stage. A full report is in front of you, but before we discuss it, I wish to say this. We are about to activate a certain political journalist in New York. He is not one of our official agents; rather I'd describe him as an unwitting ally. He is one of those phenomena produced by the decadence of capitalist society. He sees nothing but corruption and evil on the part of his own people; he seems to take pleasure in attacking his country and the society he lives in on the assumption that anything it does must be wrong and its opponents right." He glanced around at them and smiled gently. "It's a sickness we wouldn't permit here, although we've seen some symptoms in the attitude of our dissidents. This particular man prides himself on exposing scandals in his own government. Considerations like loyalty or benefit to his country's enemies don't influence him. I expect the scandal to be publicly exposed within the next few weeks. Beginning with the accusation of murder against a personal advisor to the President, Edward Fleming.

"Our journalist friend will be followed by a pack of fellow investigators, sensing a nationwide media story. They will uncover the trail of lies, deception and treason we have carefully laid for them. Each disclosure will be more sensational than the last. The British have involved themselves as deeply as I hoped, concealing vital information from their allies the Americans, allowing a man accused of betraying secrets to us to stay in office and close to the President. That should damage Anglo-U.S. relations for a long time to come. And the CIA—" he shook his head slightly "—better than we could have hoped; they've done everything wrong. Their interrogation of Edward Fleming's wife will be exposed; many will be convinced that they murdered her to frame him because he was a Russian agent. The possibilities are endless; the more the world speculates the greater the harm will be.

"The President himself will be called into question. How could he make a friend of a man who was a Soviet agent, put him into one of the most sensitive positions in the government—what kind of security check did they run on Fleming if he was able to slip through it? How many more people close to the White House have escaped detection? Comrades—we all remember Watergate. The United States has elected two men to lead them since Nixon. Both have a reputation for honesty. For straight dealing, as they like to call it. No lies, no corruption, no cover-ups. The country will tear itself to pieces over a political scandal like this. It will undermine the new administration and shake the American people's confidence. And as we know, a country that examines its conscience and doubts its institutions is a vulnerable country. Now, comrades, if you would like to read through your reports, I can answer any questions."

It was Rudzenko who hoped he had found a loophole.

"The diary," he said. "They can prove that a forgery."

"If Fleming is charged with treason, yes," Borisov said. "But the charge will be murder. Of course SIS will know the diary was forged when they check against the first wife's handwriting, but what good will that do them? It was very skillfully composed; genuine items copied from her real diary and our additions. The British won't produce it because it would only point out their incompetence in believing it to start with. It will vanish, Comrade Rudzenko, especially when they know we manufactured it and our agent planted it on them."

"The agent herself? She must be an exceptionally gifted operator to have deceived Davina Graham," Rudzenko remarked. "Her record doesn't indicate anything outstanding. A failed actress, supplementing her income by passing information on to us from the men she slept with. Not a very reliable type, surely? Not an obvious choice to cross swords with a woman like Graham."

He leaned forward, his elbows on the table, his head poking out like a turtle's from the shell of his collar. "You took a great risk, Comrade Borisov. You tell us that your Plumed Serpent has succeeded, but I think it's premature to celebrate. Until we see and hear evidence from the United States that the scandal had broken in the way you expect. Personally I reserve my congratulations until then."

"I hope to hear them at our next meeting," Borisov said smoothly. There were a few questions from other colleagues; the general secretary himself made one comment and then the subject changed to the next item on their agenda.

"If Comrade Borisov's plan succeeds," he said, "and there is a loss of confidence and morale in the United States, we might consider a stronger attitude to Poland. We will consider item twelve, comrades."

Papers rustled and heads lowered over them. Borisov had received the support of the one man among them who really counted. As he continued in the meeting the thought flitted through his mind that he might well be strong enough to set a snare for Comrade Yuri Rudzenko before very long.

"Your people were the last to see Mrs. Fleming alive," Humphrey Grant stated. "You never disclosed the fact that you had abducted her when her body was discovered. I believe you accused John Kidson of acting behind the agency's back and made yourself very unpleasant. What happened, Spencer-Barr? Did the wretched woman die on you?"

"She was dropped back at her own front door," Jeremy shouted. "My men can swear to it. She went inside and she never appeared again. They reported to me and I sent both of them away for dereliction of duty. I went to Fleming's office the minute I heard about it and he said his wife had gone on a trip to New York. You're wasting your time, Grant; you can't pin anything on the agency."

"Only abduction," Grant remarked. "It wouldn't look very good. Especially since your concealment has hampered our investigations."

"Your investigations," Jeremy snarled at him. "Who gave SIS

the right to investigate an American citizen, especially one with close personal ties to the President himself? How do you explain that?"

"It seems to me," Humphrey Grant said acidly, "that we are all going to be doing a lot of explaining very soon. It won't benefit us or the agency. We have a murder and a security scandal on our hands. Why don't you stop shouting, Spencer-Barr? There's more at stake than your grubby career."

"Why did you pick up Elizabeth Fleming?" Kidson asked. "Look, for Christ's sake, we're all in this together—there's no time for rivalry or personal vendettas. What alerted you?"

"Davina Graham." It pleased Jeremy to see the shock it gave them. "I take a personal interest in all UK personnel and visitors to Washington. I get all the lists. The minute I saw her name I knew there was a security problem. Our people had been keeping a watch on Fleming's wife for some time. She'd been sleeping around with some pretty important people in the early days; she was known to drink too much and the marriage was shaky. We had her under routine surveillance and when Davina started seeing her, I alerted the director. I pulled her in and questioned her myself. I wanted to know what our loyal allies in SIS were cooking up behind our backs."

"And what did she tell you?"

"Nothing," Spencer-Barr said flatly. "She denied talking about Fleming; I knew she was lying but it didn't seem worth pressing any further. I suggested she'd be better off going back to England." He lit a cigarette, and flicked ash upon the floor deliberately. He remembered how much Grant hated smoking.

"It would seem that she and Fleming quarreled, if what you say is true. He killed her; she was brutally strangled, I'm told. He rang Davina and her colleague to cover himself, pretending she hadn't returned. That is the theory, isn't it?" Grant ignored the cigarette and the dropped ash.

"Suggest another one," said Spencer-Barr. "I'm listening."

The telephone rang; Kidson picked it up. "Yes, of course, send her up. My wife? Well, yes, right away." He said to Humphrey Grant, "Davina and Lomax are on their way up. I'm afraid Charlie's with them, they're insisting on bringing her in to see us."

"I hope," Grant said in a tone like a cold tap dripping, "that it isn't a social visit."

Ten minutes later there was silence in the room. Humphrey Grant was standing balancing against the paneled wall. Kidson, Lomax, and Charlie were sitting down, Spencer-Barr was leaning on the back of one of the embassy Chippendale chairs, supporting his weight on his wrists, his legs braced as if he was going to spring. They were staring at Davina. In the middle of the polished table, one of Elizabeth Fleming's gold evening shoes gleamed in the sunlight. Kidson was the first to speak.

"We'll never prove it," he said. "That's where Moscow's been so diabolically clever. She's dead, and by the time we get any kind of evidence together, the scandal will have brought the roof down on the lot of us."

"I don't believe it," Spencer-Barr said. "It's fantasy. I'm sure Mrs. Kidson thinks she's right, but it would take more than a difference in shoes to convince me."

"I knew her," Charlie said firmly. "You didn't."

"You don't have to believe it," Davina said. "You've made such a bloody mess of things already, I'd rather you kept out of it!" She turned to Grant. "The Chief said this was a Moscow Center operation. He said it from the start and he was right. They had it all set up for us, and for the agency too. Edward Fleming told the truth; they did try to blackmail him because they'd found out he'd been stealing his wife's money to finance his business." She heard Spencer-Barr mutter "Jesus," but she ignored him. "He wouldn't give in to them. In the meantime he went to Mexico, where you can be sure they had him watched, and fell in love with Elizabeth Carlton. That's when the idea came to Borisov; Kaledin had retired and he was in the top job by then. That's where his style shows; he likes to do things his own way. He has changed other people's plans before, in Egypt and in Canada. He did the same with the plan to recruit Edward Fleming. Colin gave you his report on the fire that killed Raffaella Fleming and the two Mexicans. It was professional arson, using highly sophisticated chemical agents. That cleared the way for Fleming's romance. And between the time he left and what appeared to be the same woman joined him in New York and married him, they made the switch. Elizabeth Fleming was a Russian look-alike; everything she did and said was programed to throw suspicion on Fleming, involve London, and appear to expose him as a Soviet spy. They didn't mind me coming to investigate; that's what they wanted. They wanted a means of producing the diary, faked up with a mixture of lies and truth. And then they killed the woman to stop any chance of her being discovered when the scandal exploded. The neatest way to do it was to stage a murder. That meant the police, the civil authorities. There was no chance of an intelligence cover-up either by our service or yours, Spencer-Barr."

"If you're right," Jeremy spoke suddenly, "they won't leave the exposure of the security aspect to chance. There are people in the media who would jump at the first hint of irregularity in this administration. Somebody like that will be set on the trail. We all know how effective these newspaper bloodhounds can be. We've got to think of something—I'd better contact the director right away. He'll want a meeting."

"We can take the copter to Langley," Grant said. "But how much longer can you keep this quiet?"

Jeremy gestured impatiently. "Let me talk to the director. Our men are on duty at the house and the morgue; nothing will leak out from there. But what about Fleming? How long can he play sick without someone beginning to ask questions? And there's that damned colored woman who works there."

"She'll be more discreet than some people I can think of," Davina interrupted.

"One moment," Grant's voice broke in upon the threatened argument. "Fleming identified the body. There's no point in getting him to look at it again. But I think we should ask for a positive identification of the woman calling herself Elizabeth Fleming, whoever she was. Can you arrange that, Spencer-Barr—before we leave for Langley? Fingerprints, of course. They'll match the ones in the house." He cleared his throat slightly. His little gray eyes flickered towards the gold shoe in its little pool of sunlight.

"And check the size of her feet," he added.

"Why? Can I ask that question?"

"Because in my experience the KGB don't murder their agents unless they've betrayed them. If this is a new pattern of behavior, I'd like to know about it. I suggest we meet here in two hours. After I've had some lunch. Goodbye, Mrs. Kidson. I hope you enjoy your stay in Washington."

"Thank you," Charlie murmured.

John Kidson came over to her and whispered, "I'm sorry, sweetheart, you'll have to go with Davina. I can't leave the SGI to himself."

"Don't worry," she whispered back. "I've never had such an exciting morning in my life."

They went to a downtown drugstore and tucked themselves away in a booth. Lomax bought them sandwiches and coffee and Charlie asked for salad. There had been a sudden lull in the noise of customers talking and eating when she walked in. Lomax leaned over and took Davina's hand. "My God," he said, "but you're a clever lassie!"

"I didn't see it," she answered impatiently. "If it wasn't for Charlie noticing the shoe sizes I never would have seen it! Now it's too damned late to be any use!" She pushed the food aside. "It fits, the more you think of it," she said. "Fleming married her as soon as he could get a license in New York. All he saw was someone who *looked* like Elizabeth, and she certainly did. She fooled him, so it's not surprising she fooled me. He hadn't slept with her, so there was nothing to alert him there. Besides, it's so fantastic, so incredible, that whether she was different in some ways or not, he wouldn't have imagined the real reason. Nobody would. Who was she? What sort of a woman was she? I know she was English, she couldn't have faked that accent. But now I think of it—it was a bit funny. Some of the expressions she used. American slang in that Mayfair voice. Smartass, that's what she called me once. It sounded so incongruous, coming from her. But all I could see was the face, so I accepted it. That's the beauty of what Borisov did. Oh, God, if only I'd thought it through . . . I felt it in Mexico at Teotihuacán. Something didn't add up. It was nagging at me, all the discrepancies, the things she did and said that were completely out of character with the girl I knew. I made excuses; I said it was drink that changed her . . ."

"I said that," Lomax interrupted. "I said it, not you. Stop blaming yourself. For God's sake, woman, don't you realize that you were the only one who *did* see through it in the end? Thanks to you they'll try and do something about it!"

"There's nothing they can do, and they know it," Davina answered. "It's Borisov's finger on the button. All he has to do is press it. They can't muzzle the police, the media; they can't stop people talking in Washington. Fleming is too important to lie low; he's got to show himself and I don't believe he's got the nerve to carry this through without cracking wide open. The best thing to do is lay the whole thing out for the President himself. At least our service won't be party to any cover-up that could embarrass him."

She remembered her sister sitting with them and said, "I'm sorry, Charlie, this must be a lot of double Dutch to you."

"Don't be silly," Charlie said. "I'm fascinated, I've heard snippets from John about the work you both do, but I'd no idea it was so exciting. What did he mean, they never murder their agents?"

"They never did," Davina explained. "That's what he meant. People who worked for the KGB had a guarantee that if they were caught, Moscow would do everything possible to get them out or exchanged. Remember Blake, Lonsdale, and that rotten trio—Burgess, Philby, and Maclean? We connived at it in those days; you wouldn't find James White letting them slip away to their reward in Russia. And there's a new KGB man in the job now; he may set a new style altogether. They needed a dead Mrs. Fleming to bring the operation to its climax, and she was it. It's just a precaution to check the fingerprints and the shoes. Humphrey likes to tie everything up into neat little parcels with proper labels on them. One Soviet agent, dead. We'll make use of it, too."

"How?" Charlie asked.

"By making certain the word gets out that the KGB doesn't protect its people any longer."

"One thing bothers me," Lomax said. "I didn't like to ask back there with all the experts. Why would Moscow employ a woman who was a drunk? That's the kiss of death to an agent. In our set-up the minute a man went on the bottle he was written off. Sent back to the nearest desk."

"That's a good question." Davina nodded. "She could have blown it at any minute. But there wasn't much Borisov could do about it if she began drinking heavily, because she *was* the operation. Without her, all they had was Edward Fleming, who had refused to be blackmailed. I should think our friend in the Kremlin had some sleepless nights over the past year. He must be crowing now. Damn him." She looked at her watch. "It's time to get back. Charlie, I don't know whether we'll go to Langley or what will happen. I'll ring you, will you be at the hotel?"

"I'll go and wander round the shops," Charlie said. "I'll be back about four, I expect. Anyway, leave a message. And don't worry about me, I can amuse myself."

"The answer to your telex has come in, Comrade General," Natalie said. She used his proper title during working hours. There was no familiarity between them in the office. Now that they were lovers, Borisov treated her with extra formality in front of others. She played her part so well that she cultivated a younger officer on the staff and went out with him regularly. She was perfect, in Borisov's opinion; a perfect secretary, discreet and respectful in public, passionate and loving in their private hours. And with this subtle intuition that he used to clarify his own ideas.

"Thank you," Borisov took it from her, and placed it in his Urgent tray.

Everything had gone according to plan. The dead woman's body was in place, there had been an attempt to seize the diary, which had failed, but even that had worked to his advantage. His agent in New York, one of the subtlest disseminators of misinformation in the American media, had already contacted the chosen journalist and primed him with hints of a massive scandal involving a top man in the administration.

Borisov picked up the decoded telex. KGB surveillance on the Fleming household indicated security activity from Tuesday afternoon, soon after Fleming returned early from his office. London's representative John Kidson had joined him there. CIA security men had taken up positions in the house and its environment, and the Russian surveillance team had been forced to withdraw outside the area. Borisov smiled. The body had been found. He could imagine the panic among his adversaries. There had been no confirmation from the despicable Jackdaw, Neil Browning; the British embassy would know of its discovery even before the CIA. But their agent Bruckner had not heard anything from him. Borisov hesitated. He wanted to send the journalist speeding down to Washington like the angel with a flaming sword. But he had to be certain that the timing was exactly right. He buzzed for his secretary. Natalie came in and he said, "I want to send another telex." She sat down and wrote as he dictated. " 'Imperative Jackdaw be contacted and final phase of Plumed Serpent be confirmed, with utmost urgency. Report immediately information received.' And go to the apartment this evening. Wait for me."

She paused by the door and said softly, "I'll be there."

"There are the reports," Jeremy Spencer-Barr said. "There's not a fingerprint in the house that matches the dead woman's and she has a size seven foot."

"I see," Humphrey Grant said. "I think we all see, don't we, gentlemen—Davina?" He didn't wait for the silent group to answer him. He faced them like a schoolmaster, his hands behind his back, his skull of a head thrust forward. "Borisov didn't murder his agent. The unfortunate Elizabeth Carlton was kept in readiness for this moment, and then murdered while her substitute escaped. I think we have a man in Moscow who is just as merciless as his predecessor but a good deal cleverer. And what are the weapons at our disposal? Sixty pairs of women's shoes that don't fit. I think we had better take that copter to Langley, Spencer-Barr, and see if your director can think of a solution. Any suggestions?"

He glanced round; Kidson shook his head. Spencer-Barr said viciously, "I can think of one. Just keep your nose out of CIA business in future. If you had come to us with that woman's accusations against Fleming, instead of playing your own double game behind our backs, none of this would have happened. We'd have broken her."

"Then why the hell didn't you?" Kidson rounded on him. "You questioned her, but you didn't get anywhere near the truth. You knew there was a security check going on from our side and you ballsed it up yourself! You had her in your hands, and you let her walk away. And the KGB pulled her out from under your bloody noses."

"One minute," Davina interrupted. "Fighting each other isn't going to help. That's part of what Borisov wants us to do. Humphrey, you said just now that he was cleverer than Kaledin. Keeping the real Elizabeth alive all this time and then substituting her body for his agent. Well, I don't agree with you. I think that was his one mistake."

The three men stared at her.

"The KGB have never murdered their agents unless they turned double. Borisov's mistake was to follow the tradition and get the woman out. He should have killed her as well as the other poor creature. Then we'd have never known the truth. I believe this one mistake has given us a chance. A chance in a million, but it's the only one we have."

"Go on," Humphrey Grant murmured. The atmosphere in the room was charged with tension. There was a taut excitement in her voice and in the abrupt movement of her hands as Davina began to speak.

"I've been thinking all the time, how did they do it? How did they find someone so like Elizabeth Carlton that they could deceive Fleming—never mind me? The answer is they couldn't; what they did was pick a woman who was very similar and then they made her into a double. And I'm damned sure where they did it, and you'll find that they held poor Liz there too, modeling from life. Fleming said when he left Mexico, Elizabeth went to a clinic at Tula. For two months. You remember, John? Yet my inquiries showed she was going straight back to New York. She must have been kidnaped at the airport and taken to the clinic. And that's where they did the plastic surgery on the other one. The Quetzalcoatl Clinic at Tula."

"That makes sense," Humphrey said slowly. "That's very clever, Davina."

"I'm waiting for the million-to-one chance," Spencer-Barr snapped.

Davina didn't look at him. "The only way we can wreck this for Borisov is to produce the double," she said. "They'd have to change her again; she couldn't risk being seen anywhere until they'd operated. My guess is, she's at the same clinic in Mexico." She turned to Spencer-Barr. "I want a plane to take me there," she said. "I'm going to book myself in for treatment. If she's there, I'll find her and I'll bring her back. But I want Colin as back-up, and I want your director's assurance that there'll be a complete security clamp-down on the whole business."

"For how long?" he demanded. "It won't keep more than a few days; there's talk already that Fleming's illness is a fake-up for a nervous breakdown or a bust-up in the marriage. It's like keeping the lid on a powder keg."

"Then I suggest you sit on top of it," Davina said. "I want to fly down this afternoon. Can you arrange that?"

He looked sullen and then said, "I'll have to check with my director."

"There's the telephone."

He gave her a look of real hatred; then he went over and picked up the receiver. Forty minutes later it was all arranged. She said goodbye to Humphrey Grant and Kidson alone. They were on their way to Langley by helicopter. A private executive jet ostensibly owned by an electronics company would fly her and Lomax to Mexico later that day. She had booked in for a week's slimming course under the name of Mrs. Maxwell. Grant shook hands with her. "Be careful," he advised. "You are going into a hornets' nest, you know. This place must be Russian run and controlled."

"More like a snake pit," she countered. "Tula is the city of the Aztec god Quetzalcoatl, the Plumed Serpent. That's why they named the clinic after it. Don't worry, Humphrey. I know what I'm up against. I shall be very, very careful, and I'll have Colin near at hand."

"Bring her back," Humphrey murmured in his flat little voice. "Just bring her back."

Kidson put his arm around her. "For God's sake," he said, "don't risk yourself in a place like that . . ."

She knew what he was thinking. "They'll never get their hands on me like that again," she said. "Wish me luck, John, and don't worry. I owe it to Liz Carlton, too."

* * *

"She has to have time," Humphrey explained to the head of Chancery. "We have a leak here in the embassy—no, no, don't get fussed, we know all about it in London; it suited us to leave it unplugged for the time being. Hickling isn't aware of it; he's going anyway, as you know. Neil Browning is the chap." He gave a sepulchral smile at the other's exclamation. "Browning? But he's such a pleasant fellow—he hasn't any classified information to pass on!"

"You can deduce more from embassy gossip than from a lot of files," Grant said acidly. "I want you to send him home immediately. Tell him it's an interview for a new post. Get him on the plane as soon as possible and don't let him communicate with anyone outside."

"I'll see to it," the head of Chancery said. He paused for a moment. "It would help all of us," he said, "if you people in London didn't keep us in the dark about this kind of thing."

"I do apologize," Grant said. "But keeping people in the dark is what our service is all about, isn't it? I must hurry now, I'm afraid. If you need to contact me, I'm with our friends at Langley." He hurried away, and the head of Chancery said something very undiplomatic under his breath.

There was nothing faked about Browning's enthusiasm when he heard the news.

"A new posting? Well, that's very exciting, sir. Can I ask where it's likely to be?"

"I'm sorry, but I can't discuss it with you. London wants you to return immediately, so it must be something fairly important." He made himself smile and sound congratulatory. "If you rise to this, you could do your career a power of good. It's a bit sudden, but we can get you on to the five o'clock from Kennedy if you catch the shuttle. Actually there's a queen's messenger going too, so you might as well travel together."

"Yes, fine," Browning agreed. "I'll go and pack a bag. I'll be sorry to leave Washington, of course—everyone's been very good to me here."

"I'm glad you feel that."

"I do indeed," Neil said heartily. "But I'm about ready for a change. Thank you, sir, and—er, goodbye!"

"Goodbye. Good luck in your new job." He looked at the door that had closed behind Neil Browning. "I can't believe it," he said under his breath. "A young man like that—good God. Who can you trust . . ."

Neil went off down the corridor. A new appointment; a summons back to London. He couldn't believe his luck. Sorry to say goodbye to Washington? Like bloody hell. He'd thought he'd never get out and leave Bruckner and his four-eyed friend as far behind as possible. They wouldn't follow him; it wasn't worth their while. He comforted himself with this, stilling the nasty little doubt that said, Once you've given in they've got you for life. . . . He packed enough to get him to London; he had very little time to catch the shuttle. He wouldn't even have a chance to tidy up his office. He poked his head through the door and his secretary said, "Oh, Mr. Browning, somebody called Bruckner telephoned about some films." The happy grin faded quickly. "I can't get a line at the moment," the girl said. "Our outside line seems to be on the blink for some reason and the switchboard keeps saying they're busy."

He looked at his watch. There wasn't time to hang about or he'd miss the shuttle and the connection. He'd tried to pass the information but Bruckner hadn't left a number in New York. Let him carry the hot potato. "I've got to catch a plane," he said. "I'm going on a quick trip to London. If he calls again tell him I'll pick up the films when I get back. 'Bye, Jane. See you."

There was a car waiting outside; he got into the back and the queen's messenger grinned at him and said, "Hello. We're traveling together, I hear."

Browning settled back; he felt suddenly weak with relief. With luck he'd never come back to Washington. "Yes," he said. "It'll be great to see England again."

In his office behind the shop, Bruckner dialed Browning's office number for the third time. He swore repeatedly in German as he punched the buttons on the dial. First the bastard was out; then he couldn't get the right connection when he asked for the extension. Finally he got Browning's secretary. His face turned a deep red when he got the message. No, she said firmly, she didn't know when Mr. Browning would be back. He'd collect the films when he returned, that was all she knew. Bruckner rammed the telephone down so hard it jangled in protest.

His New York contact had snarled at him like a tiger with adenoids. Find Browning; get the answer from him! But Browning hadn't tried to reach him; the dumbbell in the shop was sure about it. And she got surly when he started yelling, and gave in her notice. That was all he needed. New York breathing down his neck and having to find a new assistant. He pulled a bottle of bourbon out of his desk drawer and swigged from it. His temper rose as the whisky took effect. He thought of the girl outside, and her stupid little face pouting at him swam before his eyes. He needed to take it out on someone before that short-sighted kike started ripping pieces off him. He pushed back his chair. He'd kick her ass right out of the front door. He knocked his chair over and swung round, blaspheming. His arm hit the telephone and sent it crashing to the floor. There was another loud mechanical squawk from it. He bent down and picked it up. The base was broken. He stared at it, and put the receiver to his ear. It was dead. He roared an obscenity and started for the shop.

The girl had heard the noise of his chair falling. She followed instinct and the instructions she had received only that morning. If anything happens, don't wait around. Don't even pick up your handbag. Run. She ran.

Bruckner's shop was empty. The nearest public phone booth was two and a half blocks away. He slammed the door shut and switched the OPEN sign to CLOSED. The bottle of bourbon waited for him in the back room.

It was well past five when he had finished half the bottle and made his way to the parking lot. He was driving along Pennsylvania Avenue when a car cut across him. Bruckner rammed the accelerator down and drew up alongside at the traffic lights. He leaned out of the window and yelled a string of abuse at the driver. It was part of the ill luck that had dogged his day that the car should be driven by an off-duty policeman who booked him for drunken driving. He spent the night in the cells at the Central Police Station and the only person they allowed him to telephone was his lawyer. Due to the time difference between Moscow and the United States, it was an extra day before Igor Borisov knew that his Washington connection had broken down.

But the night before he spent part of the evening with Natalie in the discreet little two-room flat in the suburbs of Moscow. They had made love, and as usual they were sitting together in the late sunlight, talking. He talked while she watched and listened, and sometimes asked one of her preternaturally shrewd questions.

"I can confess to you now," he said, "there were many times in the past year when I thought it would all end in disaster. Think of it, Natalie—an intelligence operation of this importance at the mercy of a drunken slut! If I had known she would start drinking, I would never have gone through with it."

"And think what a loss that would have been," she reminded him. "You took the risk, my love, and it succeeded."

"No, I took other risks, but not that one. That's something I hope I have learned. The only risk worth taking is a calculated one. I calculated all of them. The woman's past record, her basic stupidity, the chance that someone somewhere would catch her out. I made an absolute analysis of everything against it, and then I set down the things in favor.

"Her cunning; she was always cunning like an animal. Predators develop cunning to protect themselves. She was asked to impersonate another person, to memorize her gestures, accent, past connections; to study Elizabeth Carlton as if she was rehearsing for a play. She could learn lines, we knew that because of her time in Hollywood. Acting is deception; she had learned to assume other personalities and believe in them. And then there was the basic resemblance. The Hollywood blonde; one would think they poured them out of plastic molds. The hair, the featureless little cheap faces, the teeth created in the dental surgeries, the breasts pumped full of cellulose! She was nothing like the English woman except for her figure and the color of her eyes. But all the surgeon needed when he saw her was to change the nose and open out the eyelids. I saw the finished photographs. It was incredible; they were identical. And it appealed to her vanity. Do you know, my Natalie, what decided it for me? The woman had one ambition; to be a famous actress. She went to acting school, she studied, she paid for elocution lessons and dance lessons by sleeping with men; but she didn't get anywhere. She was a better actress than many of the ones that did become world-famous. That made her bitter. She was ready for anything when we recruited her. She wasn't getting work. And then this role was offered to her. That was the sum of my risks and the gains. But I didn't foresee that she would go to pieces under the strain of living her life with Fleming. When I first heard she was drinking, I thought of having her removed. The one person I really feared was Davina Graham. But you helped me, sweetheart. You saw into the mind of a woman who meets someone she hasn't really known since they were at school, and you reassured me. She will accept her because she didn't like her, and she won't be surprised to find that she has become even less likable. All she will see, you said to me, is what she is expecting to see. And now, at last, it's nearly over."

"What will happen to her now?"

"She will stay in the clinic till they have remade the face again.

Then she has been promised a place in the State Theater in Prague. They perform English plays there. But she will have to stop drinking."

Natalie reached across and took his hand. He had never told her what happened to the real Elizabeth Carlton and she had never asked. She didn't want to hear anything that would diminish that love. "You look tired," she whispered.

"I am," he admitted. "But the worrying is over and the fun begins. I shall sit here in Moscow and watch the Americans and the British at each other's throats and the American media tearing the country to pieces. And I shall start making other plans."

"Can you tell me about them?"

He squeezed her hand and glanced down at her fondly. "Not yet, my Natalie. But I will. I shall tell you everything in time. And now," he released himself from her clasp and stretched his arms and yawned. "Now I must go home. I don't want to leave you, do you understand that? But I have to go home to my family now."

"I understand, Igor Igorovitch. I will see you tomorrow." She smiled in her sweet way. "After all, it isn't very long to wait, is it?"

He kissed her long and tenderly before he left.

They arrived in Mexico City just after eight o'clock. Lomax was very silent during the flight. Davina had briefed him in the studio apartment while she packed. Neither of them had recovered from the row that followed.

He had refused outright to let her go to Tula and book into the clinic. It was the worst approach he could have made. Davina said quietly, "We're lovers, Colin, but that doesn't give you any rights over me. Never say anything like that to me again. This is my work and I'm going to Mexico, with or without you." And she had walked away into the bedroom and finished packing. She heard him pick up the telephone and ask to speak to John Kidson. She came to the doorway and spoke to his back. "He's at Langley. You're wasting your time, he wouldn't listen to you, anyway. Don't do this, Colin, don't react like this. We're finished if you do."

"I'd rather I never saw you again," Lomax said, "if that's the way to stop you risking your life in a damned crazy thing like this. Kidson's your brother-in-law! You mean to tell me he sanctioned you going to this clinic?"

"John is in the service, so am I. And so are you. You can't let personalities or relationships influence you in this kind of work. If you do, you shouldn't be in it! You know this, Colin, you know you have had to risk people's lives, however much you liked them, whatever the ties you had!"

"They were men," he said. "They were soldiers. I wouldn't send any woman into a place like that clinic, and if that makes me unsuitable for your bloody service, then I'll resign as of now!"

"All right," Davina said. "I'll go alone."

He came to her and tried to put his arms round her. "I love you," he said. "I don't give a damn about anything else."

"I know," she answered. "But I give more than a damn. I'm surprised I have to spell it out for you. Borisov had my husband murdered. He's not going to get away with this if I can stop him. That, my dear Colin, is why I came back to the service in the first place. Now, please—I'm going to be late."

He turned away from her; she couldn't see his face. "Give me five minutes to pack my stuff," was all he said.

They hired a car at Mexico airport. Tula was some fifty miles to the north. It was a beautiful, cool evening and they reached the town itself just after nine thirty. They booked into a modest hotel for the night, left their luggage and went out. The clinic, the proprietor told them, was about eight miles further north. They drove in the moonlight along the highway, and turned off at the signpost that said Clinica Quetzalcoatl. The approach was a good driveway behind a pair of elaborate wrought iron gates. The symbol of the

Plumed Serpent was carved into the archway. The gates were open, there was no sign of security.

It was a big, modern complex of single-story buildings in the style of the Spanish hacienda, centered round a courtyard. It shone white as a sepulcher in the moonlight. There were lights in the windows and the sound of guitar music from someone's radio drifted to them on the light breeze.

"It doesn't look difficult to get in or out," Lomax remarked. "Let's drive right round; all I can see is open fencing."

"It's a very well-known health and beauty center," Davina reminded him. "For the one KGB client, there'll be a hundred genuine customers. Women come here from all over Mexico. Apparently the plastic surgeon is one of the best in the world."

"You've done your homework, haven't you?" he said. "How long have you known you were going to come here?"

She looked straight ahead. "Since I knew she was a double; I had an instinct there'd be an answer here, and I'd be the one to find it."

"You could have told me."

"I didn't want to be stopped."

"Did you really expect anything else? Did you think any man who loved you wouldn't try to stop you?"

"I told you, Colin, there's no place for personal feelings in the service." They didn't speak for the rest of the drive. She thought suddenly that she had never seen him look so unhappy.

Later that evening, at a little restaurant that served the most delicious venison, she reached out to him across the table.

"Colin, I'm sorry. Won't you please cheer up? It's going to be all right. I know it is. But it won't help if we quarrel about it. We've got to work as a team, we've got to forget about our private lives. Please try."

He gripped her hand in his.

"I find it very difficult," he admitted. "For the first time in my life I can't see the wood for the trees. Ever been called a tree before?"

She shook her head. "No, I haven't. Trust you to be original."

"Copper beech," Lomax said. "Christ, I love you so much I don't know what to do. I don't know how to cope with you, either. You won't let me protect you, you make me feel a fool if I try. You want me to go marching into battle with you, shoulder to shoulder—isn't that it? Highland Bull to Copper Beech, are you reading me? Over! I can't do it. I feel like busting into that bloody clinic tonight and pulling her out myself!"

"Just promise me you won't try," Davina said. "Highland Bull suits you; we'd better adopt it as a code. I'll tell you one thing; I can't stand seeing you look miserable. It makes me feel miserable. That must prove something, surely?"

"It proves you've a kind heart," he said gently.

Davina looked at him and said, "It proves a lot more than that. But we won't talk about it now. Let's go to bed, shall we?"

"I can't think of a better idea." He paid the bill and they walked back to their hotel. The bedroom was small, and the bed narrow and hard.

"One thing," she whispered as she nestled into his arms. "You've got to admit I learned one thing from my husband. How to say I was sorry when I was in the wrong."

"If he taught you that," Lomax murmured, "he was one hell of a strong man."

They woke early; she was glad to see he was cheerful and brisk, as if the conflict had been resolved between them in the night. Resolved or shelved; she didn't dwell on which. The sun was bright and the air delightfully crisp and cool. She was booking into the clinic just after ten. Lomax would stay in the hotel and they would wait till she contacted him.

As they drove through the gates to the clinic, a group of joggers passed them in track suits. Davina was surprised to see that there were men as well as women. They parked in the forecourt and Davina went up the three steps and through an open archway to the reception center. Lomax was behind her. A beautiful Mexican girl in a white uniform came forward, smiling, to greet them.

"Mrs. Maxwell," Davina introduced herself. "I booked for a week."

"Of course, Señora Maxwell. Will you please sign in here? I'll show you to your room, and Doctor Felipe will see you in half an hour. You have been to a health course before? No—well, it is very simple. You have a thorough medical check to make sure you are in good physical shape, and then Doctor Felipe works out a treatment program for you. You have thermal bath treatments, special diets, a program of exercises and a lecture at ten forty-five every morning. You can play tennis, we have an indoor court for squash, and of course a very nice swimming pool. There is TV in your room if you like to rest in the evening, and we have common rooms where you can meet other guests. The restaurant serves only health foods. Doctor Felipe won't allow anything artificial in the diets. He discourages smoking, so if you want to smoke I'm afraid it's restricted to your own rooms. And of course, there is no alcohol."

"That's the only thing I'm going to quarrel with," Lomax said cheerfully. Before Davina could say anything he joined her at the desk and said, "I've decided to book in with my wife. I want to keep her company. I hope you can fit me in?"

She gave him her most brilliant smile. "I'm sure we can; but I can't guarantee adjoining rooms, and all our double suites are full."

"Never mind," he said. "We'll manage. Won't we, darling? Don't you think it's a good idea if I come too? After all, it looks such a nice place to spend a week doing yourself good." He leaned towards the Mexican girl. "The hotels in Tula aren't exactly three-star." He turned and took Davina's arm. He felt her go rigid and he grinned and tapped her playfully on the bottom. "Do I see Doctor Felipe too?"

"No, Señor Maxwell. Doctor Mendoza looks after our gentlemen guests. He will call on you at about ten forty-five and he will give you . . ."

"A thorough physical check," Lomax repeated for her. "Don't worry, señorita, you don't need to go through it again. Actually I'm pretty fit. All I want is a nice room and access to my wife!"

This time the smile was cheeky. "Thank you, señor," she said. "I get sick of hearing it myself. I find a nice room for you, not too far from your wife's. Please follow me; I'll have your bags sent up." It was then that Davina noticed he had brought his own case as well as hers. They followed the girl down a long white corridor, lined with exotic house plants.

"Colin," she hissed at him under her breath, "I'll never trust you . . ."

"Ssh," he said. "It's about time I was one jump ahead of you, sweetheart. Look at that lovely little bottom in front of us, and doesn't she know how to swing from the hips? You didn't really think I'd sit in the hotel like a good boy and wait for you to whistle? You've got a lot to learn about Scotsmen, if you fell for that."

They were at opposite ends of a corridor; one wall was plate glass, looking out over the gardens, which were beautifully laid out round a central fountain, copied from the traditional Moorish fountains in the courts of the Alhambra. People were lying on sunbeds; one group was playing cards. It was a scene of idyllic calm and luxury. White-coated attendants wandered about, adjusting chairs or sunshades, bringing trays of fruit juice. Most of the clients were in middle age, and some were very overweight.

Davina's bedroom was a large airy room, with the same expanse of plate glass down one wall. There was a clever blend of modern and Spanish traditional in the brilliant Indian rugs and the handsomely carved bed. Hothouse plants towered in a tier of elaborate ironwork. There was a green-and-white tiled bathroom leading off the room.

"This is lovely," she said. "Thank you."

"The doctor will be along soon," the Mexican girl said. "You'll have time to unpack. This way, please, Señor Maxwell." She gave Lomax a bold flirtatious glance and swayed out of the door ahead of him. He countered Davina's angry look with an infuriating wink.

She put her few clothes away, looked at her watch, and decided that she didn't have time to explore before the arrival of Doctor Felipe. As she waited, all her annoyance with Colin drained away, and she was unaccountably glad that he had snapped his fingers at her instructions. In the charming sunny room she sat on the bed under the baroque Spanish cupids and felt suddenly very much afraid.

"You're worried, aren't you, John?" Charlie reached up and stroked his cheek with one finger. "What haven't you told me?"

"Nothing." Kidson looked down at her head on the pillow and smiled. I'm not going to tell her about Davina because it'll worry her sick, he thought. She's seen and heard too much of this business already. "We had a less than friendly meeting with the people at Langley. I wish the Chief had come out himself. He's so good at dealing with awkward situations; Humphrey just looked greener and stiffer and started being thoroughly sarcastic. Anyway, I'm not going to bore you with it, darling. I was just dying to get into that chopper and get back. What did you do with yourself? I never even asked you."

"Davy, Colin and I had lunch," she said. "Then I went round the shops and bought you a present. He's madly in love with her, isn't he?"

"What?"

She burst out laughing at his expression of amazement.

"Darling! Don't tell me you haven't noticed? You've been here for ages and I only saw them together for five minutes and it was obvious . . . Really, aren't men funny? They never see anything, even when it's right under their noses! Tell me about him; he's rather an odd type."

"Just because they're sharing the flat that doesn't mean anything—it's a cover so he can be on hand to look after her, that's all."

"My darling John," she said, "you may be able to catch spies, but I know a man head over heels in love when I see one. Your big tough major was gazing at my sister just the way you used to look at me."

"What do you mean, used to look at you?" he demanded, and saw the twinkle in the beautiful eyes.

"Still do, thank heavens," she admitted. "It's strange that Davy should find someone else so soon. But however dotty he is about her, I don't think she feels the same. I watched her; she's quite independent, although you can bet your boots they're having an affair—yes, they are, John, so don't argue—but I don't think she's in love with him because she's still in love with Ivan Sasanov. Which is a pity, isn't it?"

"I don't know," Kidson said slowly. "I should think Lomax is the kind of man who'll get what he wants in the end. If you're right about them."

"I'm right," Charlie said. "She promised to phone the hotel, but she never did. Where are they, John?" And then she saw the flicker of hesitation in his eyes, and she sat up quickly and made him look at her.

"John? What are you hiding from me? Where's Davina gone?"

He knew her too well to try and lie his way out. There was no stopping his wife when she was determined about something. She had that much in common with her sister. "She's gone to Mexico," he said. "She thinks the Russian agent who doubled for Liz is hiding out there. She and Lomax have gone down to try and flush her out."

Charlie leaned back against the pillows. "I needn't ask if she's in danger. Oh, God, darling, why does she keep on with this sort of thing?"

"Because she lost Ivan and the baby," he said gently. "She has to wipe that out. With luck, this may do it."

"It won't," Charlie said. She threw back the bedclothes and pulled on one of the expensive flimsy negligees she had bought specially for the trip. She went to the dressing table, sat down and began to brush her hair. "She won't stop because she's just like you, John. And Grant and Sir James and all of you. She loves it. That's the truth. If poor Major Lomax thinks he can compete against your bloody service, he hasn't got a hope in hell. Now I'm going to get dressed and you can take me out to dinner."

"That's very satisfactory, Mrs. Maxwell. Your heart and blood pressure are excellent. In fact you are in very good shape." Doctor Felipe looked down at his notes. He was a tall, slim man in his mid-thirties, almost theatrically handsome, with big black eyes and flashing teeth. He had a charming manner that didn't detract from his efficiency. "You have no record of illness beyond the usual, appendix and tonsillectomy. And you are just a pound or two over the perfect weight for your height."

He looked at her, and she could imagine the damage he would do to susceptible middle-aged women who were worried about losing their looks. "You can do that very easily here, without too rigid a regime. I think a medium diet, say two thousand five hundred calories a day, and a program of exercises and some massage. You don't need steam treatments, they're too drastic for what you want to lose. And perhaps a relaxing stay with afternoon rests and early bedtimes for the first three days. If I could diagnose anything, I would say you were a little tired. Would that be right?"

"Absolutely," she agreed. "We've had a hectic time since we came to America."

He put his notes aside and said, "And why did you come all the way to Mexico? There are plenty of health farms in the States."

"We're planning to tour the country after we leave here," Davina said. "It seemed a good way of doing everything on the spot. Besides . . ." she hesitated.

He waited a moment and then said encouragingly, "Yes?"

She gave the impression she was embarrassed, and then squared her jaw and said in a lower voice, "I've heard you have a marvelous plastic surgeon here. That's one of the reasons I came."

"We do indeed," he agreed. "There's no reason to be shy about it; we have clients from all over the American continent. If you are thinking of a breast implant, or buttock reduction—I can't say I see the need for either, but if you would like to see our surgeon, Doctor O'Farrell, it can be arranged."

"It's my nose," Davina said. "I'd like something done about it. Without ayone knowing, of course."

He raised his eyebrows and smiled. "Mrs. Maxwell, I don't see anything wrong with your nose. It's in very good proportion to your face. Your jaw, now—that is a little square. Why do you want to change your nose?"

"Doctor Felipe," Davina said, "you're not a very good salesman, are you?"

The smile faded. "I'm not a salesman, I'm a physician. The fact that I have to check on the health of a number of people who would benefit from a hard day's work doesn't change that. I prescribe our treatments as I would prescribe medicine in my own surgery. You don't really need to lose weight; you do need a rest. In my opinion, both as a man and as a trained psychologist, you should not interfere with your face by altering any of the features.

It will not be satisfactory and you could suffer trauma afterwards."

"I'm very sorry," Davina said quietly. "I didn't mean to be offensive. I was just surprised; I suppose I expected a hard sell and I didn't get one."

He had stood up, his notes on her gathered in one hand; the other was in the pocket of his white overall. She had the impression that it was clenched into a tight fist. "There are doctors in this clinic who will persuade you to have everything from a pedicure to an implant of unborn lambs' testes to stave off the natural aging process. I am not one of them. If I was hasty tempered, I apologize."

"But I would like to discuss this with Doctor O'Farrell," she said. "He'll probably say the same as you."

He opened the door. "I hope so, Mrs. Maxwell. I'll make an appointment for you today. Have a pleasant stay, and I'll see you again before you go. If you have any problems, I'm in residence here, just call me any time."

She went along the corridor to Lomax's room. He had changed into a track suit; she thought suddenly, he looks all wrong for a place like this. He's superbly fit and it shows.

"You know what you remind me of," she said.

"Tell me." He gave a wry little grin. "I know it's going to pay me out for coming here, but go ahead."

"You look like a member of the SAS in training."

He came towards her and pushed the door shut. He held her by the shoulders at arms' length. "And you look like a beautiful spy. Have you seen anyone yet?"

"Yes, have you?"

"No, not till this afternoon. I was issued this and some swimming trunks and shorts, and I thought I'd have a quiet jog and check the layout of the place. What's your program?"

"Medium diet, mostly rest for the first three days. I'm seeing the plastic surgeon today. The doctor is an odd type; there's more to him than meets the eye."

"Oh?" Lomax let her go. "In what way?"

"It's difficult to explain," Davina said. She sat on the bed; it was antique and crowned with fat little Spanish cherubs. "At first sight he seemed the typical smooth quack; good-looking, full of charm, and I expected to get the full sales treatment when I asked about plastic surgery. It's one of their biggest money-spinners here; clients pay thousands for a simple nose job. Instead, he told me I didn't need it. I put my foot in it by making a joke and, my God, he got furious! I could have kicked myself for making the crack at him. I got the feeling that he hates what he's doing here. He doesn't fit, Colin. Not under the surface, and the surface is pretty thin."

"I think," Lomax said, "that we should rethink our strategy."

"You've already done that by coming with me," she pointed out. "There aren't going to be any more changes."

He looked at her and said simply, "Let me find her and get her out. I'm trained for this kind of thing, you're not. And if you're right about Felipe you've drawn the joker. See the surgeon, talk to him, find out what you can, and then please, my darling, leave it to me."

Davina hesitated. She took his hand in hers. "You can't go wandering round the women patients' rooms, I can."

"All right." He wasn't going to argue with her. He was going to say yes to everything. "All right, you pinpoint the target and we'll move from there." He pulled her towards him and kissed her. "What did you say you wanted done?"

"My nose," she said. "And do you know what he said? The same as you said once; my jaw is too square!"

"It's the sign of a determined character," Lomax murmured.

"If I say something," Davina said slowly, "you're not to go overboard on it, will you promise?"

"Promise."

She pushed her hair back from her forehead; he knew the gesture well. "I'm frightened," she said. "It's all so white and clean and welcoming and everybody gives you their big smiles, but I'm more frightened than I've ever been. So you needn't worry, Colin, love." She kissed his cheek. "I shan't take any risks, and I'm very, very happy you jumped the gun on me and moved in too. I wouldn't want to be here on my own."

"You were never going to be, my sweetheart," he said gently. "But I've learned now not to argue."

The shuttle from New York disgorged its cargo of businessmen, government officials, and visitors. The tall, spectacled man hailed a cab and drove direct to the Press Club. His entrance into the bar brought acquaintances crowding round him. The word spread that Dave Benson had flown in, and that meant there was trouble for someone in official circles. He didn't drink alcohol; it had caused him problems when he was in his thirties. A broken marriage was the first casualty and his career had seemed likely to be the next. Benson gave up drink, joined Alcoholics Anonymous, and discovered social injustice. The self-destruction was channeled into fighting what he believed to be corruption and oppression, and the self-disgust changed to hatred of the status quo. Dave Benson agonized over the poverty of the Third World and wrote blistering denunciations of the genocide of primitive people in Central America. He espoused the lost and the hopeless because he couldn't identify with his own society any longer. He needed a lance under his arm if he wasn't going to take a glass in his hand. He genuinely hated and mistrusted the system that governed his country and the people in it. He was also bitterly opposed to the oppression of dissidents and Jews in Soviet Russia, but less motivated to go after foreign demons than the ones roaming the United States.

A veteran pressman bought him juice and asked him what he

had come down for. "To do a story on a security cover-up," Benson said.

"What kind of security? Or aren't you trading today?"

"I'm trading," Benson answered. "How long has Ed Fleming been out of his office and what's the matter with him?"

The other man eyed him for a moment. "What do *I* get?" he said.

"The truth," Benson answered. "As soon as I dig it out. What gives around town on Fleming?"

"Marriage problems. She's a lush. He's given out he's got a stomach ailment, but no hard medical evidence or statements from his office. And there's a lot of activity in his area, I'm told."

"What kind of activity?"

"CIA," was the laconic answer. "But you know Washington, somebody sees a new face at a window, and it's the CIA. I wouldn't bet on it."

Benson drank his fruit juice and set down the empty glass.

"I would," he said. "They're setting up a cover job on this guy. We can't have crap on the ground when the President walks by."

"What kind of crap?"

"We'd have to trade a little more for that," Benson remarked. "I'll buy you lunch."

"Doctor O'Farrell, can I speak with you a moment?"

"Of course, doctor. Come in. You can go get yourself some coffee, Anna, while I consult with Doctor Felipe."

Jaime Luis O'Farrell was a very dark-skinned Mexican. His grandfather had come from County Monaghan as an immigrant and drifted down on the tide of poverty to Mexico, where he eked out a miserable life as a casual laborer and married an Indian girl who bore eight children. His grandson owed his features and the dark pigment in his skin to the Indian, but his eyes were as gray as the skies over Monaghan. His own father had been bitterly ashamed of his Indian blood, and savagely determined that his children should be educated, to take their place in the world of white people. He had driven them with his fists and his feet towards escaping their background.

He had succeeded with only one, the dark-skinned son who reminded him too well of his mixed blood but was so brilliant that he won a scholarship to medical school in Los Angeles. At Mexico University, Jaime Luis had become politically committed.

When they were alone, Felipe said, "We have two new clients. A married couple called Maxwell. I saw the wife this morning, and I have Mendoza's notes on the husband. They make interesting reading." He handed them to O'Farrell. After he had read them he looked up.

"Yes. They are an unusual couple, aren't they? The man is in his mid-thirties, in top physical condition so far as we can judge. He refused to let Mendoza examine him. Says he has come to stay near his wife. Wants to play squash and swim, doesn't concern himself with diet. It sounds reasonable enough. But why is the wife here? She doesn't need to lose weight. From your notes she's a very healthy woman. Tired, you say here."

"On edge," Felipe corrected. "Very tense. She wants her nose changed. It doesn't need changing. I told her so, but she insisted. She wants to see you today. I said I would arrange it."

"Why not? It would be well to have a look at her myself. Did Mendoza say anything more about the husband than he wrote down?"

"What you'd expect," was the contemptuous answer. "Not much pickings to be had there. You know what he's like."

"A leech sucking on other leeches," O'Farrell said softly.

"I'd like to say to some of these fat pigs who come here, why don't you go to one of the villages and live with the people for a week or two? You'd soon lose weight!"

"You're too full of fire, my friend," O'Farrell said. "Remember our work here. Think of how many comrades have benefited from this clinic in the last five years—new faces, a chance to fight again. And now—Quetzalcoatl. The rest is unimportant."

"How is she?"

"Better," was the answer. "Still screaming for a drink now and then, but she's dried out. I told her this morning, the quicker you clean the alcohol out of your system, the quicker I can operate and you can go."

"It's a mistake," Felipe said. "I don't understand our orders."

"We don't have to understand them," O'Farrell said sharply. "We just obey them, that's all. We will run a check on these Maxwells. Photographs and fingerprints. Telex them through to New York immediately. Probably we are being too cautious, but as long as we have the Plumed Serpent here, we can't risk anything."

"What time will you see Mrs. Maxwell?"

O'Farrell glanced at his watch. "Two fifteen. Ask her to come to my office here. I'll get the fingerprints and a photograph. You deal with the husband."

Davina met Lomax in the grounds. They strolled towards the swimming pool.

"It's shaped like a horseshoe," he said. "All low-level bungalow-type buildings connected by corridors. And outside the perimeter of the horseshoe there's a smaller building; I'd say it was medical rather than residential. There are no windows outside, but probably a skylight."

"That would be the operating theater?"

"Could be, but I don't see why they'd bother with daylight. More like a studio. I didn't hang around. I jogged all over the place and took in as much as I could. But that place interested me. I'd like to take another look."

"You'd better not. I'll walk round there this afternoon. If there's overhead light and no windows, what do they use it for?"

"Perhaps our famous surgeon paints his subjects."

"I'm seeing him in ten minutes," said Davina. "I'll try and find out."

A nurse came to take her to the office; some of the staff were Mexican, but there was a high proportion of Americans among them. This was a pretty blonde girl with a Texas drawl. Davina slowed her pace and started to talk to her. The nurse said she'd been there for a year. "It's great training," she said. "I aim to go back home this fall, and open a clinic of my own. Daddy's going to finance me. Not surgery, but general beauty and health care—diet, massage."

"Do you get a lot of clients for surgery?"

"Oh, we sure do. But not so much this time of year. You know, Mrs. Maxwell, ladies like to have it done in the late fall or the winter. Then they come out looking beautiful and some say they've been on a cruise." The nurse giggled. "Or just lost a little weight, and my, just look what it's done for my chin. I shouldn't laugh about it; some of it's sad. I've been on surgery duty, and one or two of these ladies made me cry. They get divorced and they want to start life over with a new face. Doctor O'Farrell is just a magician when it comes to making a person look good!"

"So I've heard," Davina said. "Have you had anybody come in lately? I'm thinking of having something done myself, and wouldn't want to be the only one around."

The Texan said, "You wouldn't be alone; there's two here. Two ladies, both facials, as we call them. One's waiting for her operation, the other had it a few days ago and she's out of bandages now."

Davina's heart lurched with alarm. Don't, for God's sake, let it be the fake Elizabeth who's had the operation. If we're too late . . . "You mustn't mind me asking you all these questions," she said. She stopped in the corridor. "I'm a bit nervous, that's all."

The girl smiled and said in her treacle-coated voice, "Don't you worry, honey, you ask me all you want. What are you going to have done?"

"My nose," Davina admitted. "I'd like it shorter, more like

yours, actually. But how long do I have to wear bandages? How long before I could go out and nobody would notice?"

"Oh, for a nose, not long at all; say two weeks. Depends on how much bruising there is—it's not like a full face-lift, and Doctor O'Farrell does it so well there's never a scar left—but I don't think that kind of nose would suit you, Mrs. Maxwell. It wouldn't balance with your face. Hey, we're late already; he doesn't like people to be late." She glanced at Davina and said in a low voice, "For a Mexican he's mighty punctual. Here we are."

O'Farrell was sitting behind a plate-glass desk. The gray eyes were a shock in the bronze face, set like stones on either side of the broad Indian nose. He spoke with a slight American accent. Davina explained what she wanted while he sat, hands folded in front of him, impassive as an idol.

"I'm very nervous," she said. "I don't like the idea of surgery at all. But I've always wanted this done and if I don't pluck up the courage now, I never will. I want you to tell me everything, please, doctor, and before I decide to go ahead, I'd like to see the accommodation, and if there was anybody who's recently been done, perhaps it would help if I could ask them about it?"

"I have only one patient at the moment," he said. "This is not a busy time of the year. She has had some eye work done, the removal of pouches. I would have to ask her if she'd see you; we respect our clients' wish to be private, and some of them are very sensitive about having cosmetic surgery at all. But I can show you where the rooms are, and if you wish, the operating theater."

"Thank you," Davina said. "That would be a great help." She smiled slightly. "You must think I'm very silly making such a fuss over a small thing."

There was no answering smile. "Not at all, Mrs. Maxwell, I am used to nervous people and I have a lot of sympathy with them. If we are going to do this, we will need to photograph you from different angles. I would like to take two or three preliminary pictures and study them."

Davina got up. "I'd rather make up my mind definitely first," she said. "Then you can take pictures; otherwise it's a waste. Could I see the rooms now?"

He looked squat and heavy behind the desk, but when he stood, he was surprisingly tall. "I will take you myself," he said.

"He wouldn't show me the room with the glass roof," Davina said. They were sitting on the big terrace with the fountain in the center, and drinking iced fruit juice. Lomax had discouraged the attempts some Americans and a Mexican made to join them.

"I saw everything else, including the operating theater, but not that studio, or whatever it is. And there aren't any windows; all the light comes from above. I asked him what it was, and he said it was where he worked on sketches for clients with facial problems. Then he said, 'My real work is in my hospital in Mexico City. There I operate on really disfigured people, poor people who have suffered in fires and other dreadful accidents. This work here is my hobby. I bring my photographs and sketches from the hospital here, and I work in the studio. If I showed you that room, Mrs. Maxwell, and what is in it, you wouldn't want plastic surgery!' It was the same feeling I got with the young doctor. Hostility and contempt. I don't believe a word about the studio. That's where *she's* hiding out. And from what he and the little nurse told me, they can't have operated yet. He tried to take photographs of me, but I wouldn't let him. I saw a telex machine in that office."

"I put a stop on both our bedrooms. It'll be interesting to see if they've disturbed them."

"They won't find anything in my room," she said.

"Nor mine," he said. "Except fingerprints, and that won't help them. They wouldn't have any record. But they would have yours, wouldn't they?"

"And they'd be winging on their way if they dusted out my room. We've got to move very fast on this one. I told him I'd think about plastic surgery but I didn't sound very enthusiastic and he didn't seem surprised. Or perhaps I'm imagining the whole damned thing and they don't suspect . . ."

"Let's go and check on our rooms," he suggested quietly. "That'll tell us something."

They went to Davina's first; Lomax didn't bother with the door into the corridor. He strode across to the cupboard, Davina following.

"I can't see anything," she said. "What did you use, a hair?"

"That's for films, my darling," he said. "We have better methods. Yes—somebody's been in and opened it. Look." There were fragments on the floor. "Toothpaste," he explained. "Dead simple; you squeeze a bit on the lock of any door and shut it. It hardens; when you open it it flakes off. On an off-white carpet like this you'd never notice it unless you knew what to look for. There's some inside too. Now, let's just check on the chest of drawers."

Lomax opened the top two drawers and examined the clothes inside. "When you search," he said, "you make sure the top layer is exactly as you found it. I arranged one item on the bottom in each drawer. They've been moved. So that's it. They'll have been through my room too." He saw the question in her face and said, "I carry my equipment with me. All the time. They won't have found a thing."

"We'd better make our move tonight," Davina said. "We can't allow them time to check up." She noticed that he was balanced on the balls of his feet, swaying a fraction, and remembered the lightning attack in the Washington apartment that had saved her life. She knew at once what he was going to say.

"I think you should go back to Tula and wait for me. I'll get her out of here. If there's trouble, you'll only be in the way."

"We don't want trouble," Davina pointed out. "We want her alive and in one piece and if there is a shooting match, she'd be at risk. I know you, Colin. You go in like a rocket. I can cope with *her* if you're there to protect us. And when this is over, I want to go back to London and tell the Chief he can find himself another fool to manipulate. I want the last word on this, and if you really care about me, you'll let me have it. I know the risks and they're worth it to me. And there's another reason. You'll think I'm crazy, but ever since I've been here I keep thinking about Liz Carlton and what she must have suffered while they kept her locked up . . . The fact that I disliked her so much makes it worse. Can you make sense of that? I've got to pay her debt for her, Colin. Help me to do it. Then maybe I can think straight about my own life."

"If that's a bribe," Lomax said quietly, "it's the first dirty trick I've ever known you to play."

"It's not a bribe. And it's not a promise either."

Chapter Eight

DAVE BENSON looked around him, skimming over the diplomats and State Department officials with their wives, bypassing the French ambassador, who was talking to his Dutch and Swedish colleagues. Benson hated the smell of expensive scents and flowers, and the endless tinkle-tinkle of glasses full of champagne. He hated the affluence and the self-satisfaction on the well-fed faces; the false laughter and the loud voices offended him. He couldn't see integrity anywhere among his own people and he profoundly distrusted all Europeans. Benson raised his fruit juice to his lips when he saw Edward Fleming come in and shake hands with the ambassador. He set his glass down on a moving tray as skillfully as a football player passing the ball. He waited, watching, until Fleming had moved away from the ambassador's side. Then he stalked him round the room until he saw an opportunity when Fleming was not in conversation.

"Mr. Fleming? I'd like to introduce myself, I'm Dave Benson, *America Today.*"

Fleming knew the name and the reputation of the magazine. He stiffened. "Glad to know you," he said. He forced himself to sound friendly. No one in his right mind went out of his way to make an enemy of Benson. But only a fool stood around and talked to him. "I enjoy your pieces," he said.

"Thanks," Benson answered. He had placed himself directly in front of his quarry, so that Fleming would have to push past him to get away. "I hear you haven't been too well lately," he remarked. "You look recovered; are you? You don't mind my asking, but my editor would like me to do a profile on you sometime?"

"I'm flattered," Fleming said. He wondered if the journalist could hear the horrible judders his heart was making.

"What exactly has been the nature of your illness, Mr. Fleming? I've heard talk of an ulcer—is that correct?"

"No." Fleming managed a laugh. "Just a dose of food poisoning. I shan't eat shellfish again in a hurry!"

"Did you have it checked in the hospital?" Benson inquired.

"There was no need," Fleming answered. He felt the juddering accelerate and his hands dripped sweat. They warned me, he reminded himself, they warned me something like this could happen. He may be a plant or he may just be nosing round for something to pay his expenses down here. If he sees you're nervous he'll home in on you like a missile . . .

"I don't see your wife," said Benson. "Isn't she here?"

"No; she's away on a trip. Now, Mr. Benson, if you'll excuse me—there's a man I have to talk to over there."

Dave Benson didn't move. "Is it true that she's left you?"

Fleming felt suddenly so angry that his clammy hands bunched into fists. He longed to swing one of them into the middle of the prying, hostile face in front of him.

"No comment on my private life. Excuse me!" He stepped round the reporter.

"There are other rumors. Maybe I'd better ask you about them in your office. Can you give me an appointment, Mr. Fleming?"

Benson was walking step by step with him, dodging round

drinking couples as Fleming tried to escape. Edward Fleming stopped.

"I have no free time for interviews," he said. "I'm sorry, but your profile will have to wait."

"When will Mrs. Fleming come back to Washington? She's not sick, is she?"

Fleming didn't answer. He saw John Kidson and his beautiful wife at the other side of the room and he hurried to join them. Benson didn't follow him.

Fleming spoke in a low voice to Kidson. "I think it's started. What Jerry Barr warned me about. I'd better get in contact with him."

Kidson managed to control his alarm.

"They've sent in the journalist," Fleming muttered. "That's him over there. He grabbed me just now and started asking questions about Elizabeth. He's ruined a lot of people's reputations and he never seems to get it wrong. If you have a skeleton in the closet, that son of a bitch will dig it out. I'm going to excuse myself and go home. I'll call Barr from there." He took a drink from one of the embassy waiters. "The last thing I feel like is champagne," he said. "What the hell are we going to do?"

"Just keep calm," Kidson advised. "And keep away from him. Stall, do anything, but don't say another word. Let Jeremy Barr know and leave it to him. There's nothing you can do but wait. And hope."

"Hope for what?"

"News from Davina and Lomax," Kidson said quietly. "They're working on it. I don't believe they'll fail us."

Edward Fleming finished the champagne. "After what's happened to me," he said, "I don't believe anything anymore. If you'll excuse me, Mrs. Kidson," he said to Charlie, "I'll be going now."

John Kidson watched him make his way towards the ambassador and his wife to say goodbye. He looked a handsome, well-set-up man in the prime of his political life, with everything going in his favor. John Kidson took Charlie's arm. He had learned a lot about men from seeing them walk away.

"Whatever happens," he said, "he's finished."

"From what you've told me," she said simply, "he won't be any loss. Look, darling, isn't that Senator Kennedy over there? Do you know him?" He nodded and she tugged at his arm. "Do introduce me, I'd be fascinated to meet him."

"Not for anything in the world," John Kidson said firmly. "Introducing a beautiful woman to a Kennedy is like feeding a Christian to the lions. Come away, darling, and meet a nice dull Pentagon general."

On their way home in the car Charlie said suddenly, "If Davy gets this woman back, what will happen?"

"Whatever the CIA decides. It's out of our hands now. We should hear from her soon."

"How soon?"

"By tomorrow at the latest," he said. "Otherwise we know that she and Lomax are in trouble."

The embassy in Mexico received the message; its principal KGB officer had been on alert since the week before. So far, all his reports from the clinic at Tula indicated that the Plumed Serpent was progressing satisfactorily. Whether the code concerned a person or a project he did not know. He transmitted the reports to Moscow. The telex that reached him that afternoon was in a different vein. It requested urgent investigation of two clients at the clinic, whose fingerprints followed shortly on the teleprinter. The embassy was one of the most important in the Americas; it rated a high-grade ambassador and a very skilled intelligence contingent. The senior intelligence officer transmitted the details immediately to the communications center in the Lubyianka in Moscow. It was three A.M. Moscow time, but within the space of an hour the computers had filed the information and returned an answer. The man was on record as a member of the visa section at the British embassy in Washington. The woman was identified by her fingerprints as a former Soviet prisoner and a very important counterintelligence agent; this was confirmed by the photographs. Instructions would be telexed as soon as General Borisov had been informed.

Borisov was awakened in the small hours by the one telephone that put through emergency calls. His wife sat up in their double bed and asked him sleepily what was the matter. His response brought her wide awake. He slammed the phone down and shouted at her. "Disaster! That's what's the matter—go back to sleep, you stupid fool!" She heard him banging doors in the flat and getting dressed. She knew the significance of that telephone by the bed; it had only rung three times in the past eighteen months.

Borisov drove himself out through the back entrance and swiftly through the empty streets to his office in the Kremlin. There he had the use of a full night staff. He shut himself up alone and stared at the telephotos and the fingerprints. He swore furiously. In moments of great crisis, Borisov gave vent to his feelings; they were a safety valve for his judgment. When that was done, his self-control was total and his reactions as void of emotion as the great banks of computers in the communications center.

First he admitted his mistake. He should not have left the Plumed Serpent alive. She should have been killed as soon as it was known she had been questioned by the CIA. Her body, not that of the doped, dazed prisoner kept in readiness, should have been put in the trunk of Fleming's car. He had followed Soviet tradition and protected his operator. And left alive the one witness who could destroy his plan and expose the torturous and vicious trail of the Plumed Serpent and its Soviet manipulators. If that happened, he would not only lose his appointment, he could lose his liberty for thirty years in one of his own labor camps. He made his decision, and as soon as it was made, the machinery of sophisticated communications clicked into action and the message sped round the world to Mexico, where from the embassy it hummed through on the telex in the Quetzalcoatl Clinic.

Jaime Luis O'Farrell took the telex and decoded it. The instructions were stark and simple and one of them puzzled him. But he had a fanatic respect for orders. Unlike the hotheaded Felipe, he didn't question anything that came from Moscow. His clients had finished their dinner in the cafeteria; some would be strolling round in the cool evening, others taking a late swim in the heated pool. He had to know what the couple who called themselves Maxwell were doing, and he set out to find them. They were not in their rooms; a search of the patios and the common rooms was fruitless. It was too dark to see them if they were in the grounds. No one had seen them leave and their car was in the compound. Felipe joined him. O'Farrell walked through the clinic with the young doctor at his side. He stopped to speak to some of the clients he knew, and Felipe asked the normal questions about his charges' comfort and progress.

"We can't do anything until we find them," O'Farrell said. "There are three of us; send for Rose. We will look through the grounds. They're not in the clinic."

"What about her?" Felipe demanded. "What do we do about her?"

"We do as we have been instructed," the surgeon said. "We kill her. After we have taken the other two."

Outside the main terrace they separated. Rose, a Mexican woman in nurse's uniform, was with them. Each took a path through the grounds. The two men carried guns under their white coats.

"I'll open the door," Lomax whispered. "It'll be locked, but unless it's bolted I can fix it in a couple of minutes."

"She'll hear you," Davina protested.

He held up a thin twist of wire. "Not with this she won't. When it's open, you go in. I'll stay outside on guard. If she gives you any trouble, just call me. If I see trouble coming from my end I'll give you the signal to get out and run. You understand? You get to hell out of the place and go straight to the car. No arguments."

"None," Davina promised him. "But you can't have a shooting match—the whole place will come running."

"I hope I won't have to," he said. "Get in there and see if you can persuade her to come willingly. You know what to do if she kicks up a row."

She nodded. He had given her a round stone, picked up from their afternoon walk in the gardens. Fitted into the palm of the hand, it would make an untrained blow to the side of the neck as effective as a karate chop. Davina had been unwilling to take the stone. But Lomax had assured her it was a last resort, only to be used if the woman started screaming or tried to attack her before he could rush through the door. "Think of the real Elizabeth Carlton," Lomax had said.

They were hidden behind a screen of bushes when they saw the Mexicans in their white coats joined by a nurse.

"Three of them," Lomax murmured. "That's not too bad. They're fanning out in a search party. As soon as they pass out of the light along those three paths, we walk back inside. Is your watch right?"

"I think so. It's nine thirty."

"Nine thirty-three," he said. "Near enough. The lights go out at ten in the main rooms. The patients are encouraged to turn in at the same time. I reckon it'll take them half an hour to go right round the grounds and meet up together. By which time we should be on our way to the car park. Ready?"

"Yes," she said.

In the semidarkness he looked down at her.

"Scared?"

"Scared stiff," she whispered back.

"Good," he encouraged. "It's the best way to be; sharpens the reflexes. They're out of sight now. Come on."

They walked back into the clinic. Davina caught her breath as a voice behind them said, "Hi, Mrs. Maxwell—Dr. O'Farrell was looking for you." It was the pretty Texan.

"Oh," Davina said. "We were out walking. I suppose he wants to know if I've made up my mind about bobbing my nose."

"I guess so," the girl said. "Have a good evening."

"Thanks," Lomax answered, and they walked on. Inside the main building they separated. "Five minutes," he whispered to her. "You give me five minutes by your watch and then come. If I'm not around, don't worry. Try the door, and if it gives go in. If it doesn't, go to the car and wait. If I don't join you in another five minutes, go direct to the embassy and stay there."

"Colin," she began, but he interrupted her briskly. "Five minutes." Then he turned and was gone.

Davina went to her bedroom. She didn't turn on the light; she stayed by the window, with the stone weighing in her pocket. The time schedule was terrifyingly tight. Outside in the darkness three KGB agents were searching for them: Felipe, O'Farrell, and the nurse. Lomax had a gun, she had a stone. He was satisfied with the odds; she wasn't. The time was up. She opened her door, glanced up and down the corridor. It was empty. She went out.

Lomax didn't attempt to hide himself. He strolled out onto the patio, and turned towards the little building at the back. There was nobody near the entrance: he looked swiftly right and left, and then slipped inside. There was a light under the door on the left. The patient who had undergone plastic surgery was inside, as Davina had seen. Six other rooms were empty, luxurious bedrooms waiting for the winter influx. And in the center, next door to the operating theater, was the room without windows. Light blazed into the sky from the glass roof and a streak showed under the door. The night was very quiet. He checked his watch. Then he took the little twist of wire from his pocket and crouched in front of the door. First he tried the handle, turning it so slowly that the movement wouldn't catch the eye of anyone on the other side. It gave a faint click and he pressed gently forward but the door didn't move. He looked quickly round again and then inserted the lock pick. It was a simple mechanism; there was no sound as the bolt slid out of its socket. Lomax stood up. His gun, its silencer in place, was strapped round his waist. He saw Davina come round the corner and beckoned her. She hurried to him.

"It's open," he whispered. "No problem. Go in and I'll keep watch outside." Davina nodded. He noticed that she looked very white.

The woman was lying on her bed, reading a magazine. When the door opened she didn't look up. It's that goddamned nurse, she said to herself, with her orange juice and her sleeping pills. Davina closed the door quietly behind her.

"Hallo, Elizabeth," she said. "I thought I'd find you here."

It was O'Farrell who came into view first; Rose and Felipe were behind him. The girl from Texas was just going off duty when she saw him. She always tried to be helpful. She turned back and came up to him.

"You were looking for Mrs. Maxwell, doctor? Did you find her?"

"No." For a second the gray eyes glittered. "Have you seen her?"

"Yeah, about twenty minutes ago. She and her husband came in from the gardens. I told her you wanted to talk to her."

"Thank you, nurse," he said. He paused and the other two came up to him. He waited until the young girl was out of sight. "They're back inside the clinic," O'Farrell said. "Rose, try the recreation room. I will join you there if I don't find them."

"If we do?" Felipe demanded.

"Obey your orders," was the reply. "Then come to me when it's done. We will get rid of *her*."

He watched the nurse and the young doctor hurry away. He stood for a moment, his hands in his pockets, the right one curled round the butt of an automatic. It was a beautiful clear night, and the full moon was shedding her cold majestic light upon the Mexican earth. Five hundred years ago his ancestors sacrificed to the Moon Goddess at the top of the great pyramid at Teotihuacán. Human blood ran black at night; the Sun God saw it red. And the voices of his Indian ancestors spoke to Jaime Luis O'Farrell and they were louder than the words of twentieth-century reason and the Marxist philosophy by which he lived.

A few miles away from Tula, the double pyramid at Tenayuca pointed upward to the sky, surrounded by the plumed serpents symbolizing the bisexual god who unified heaven and earth. The Spaniards had thrown down the people's idols and replaced them with their Christian counterparts. The Indian woman who married Jaime's grandfather kept the image of the Plumed Serpent, feathered, taloned and ferocious, in a secret place. The Christ figure and the Madonna reigned in public but the old dark gods were worshiped still.

And that night, there would be human sacrifice again. A fitting sacrifice on the altar of the oppressed, enslaved Indian people's forbidden gods.

The woman on the bed had opened her mouth but no scream came. The beautiful face was blotched and haggard, with great dark rings under the eyes; the blonde hair hung down in an untidy mass. When she did speak it was in a cracked whisper and the words were vile obscenities.

"I was afraid I'd be too late to save you," said Davina quietly.

"Save me?" Elizabeth had got up, throwing the magazine aside. Her voice found its normal level and began to rise. "I don't know what you're talking about—I don't know what you're trying to pull but it won't work. You got in here, Miss Smartass, but you'll never get out!" She made a sudden quick movement and Davina guessed there was a bell that would summon help.

"They're going to kill you!" she blurted out. "Don't be a fool, Liz! I'm your only hope. Listen to me first."

The woman hesitated then, and the fear that had coiled inside her woke and stirred. Davina took her hand out of her pocket, without the stone.

"Why should they kill me?" she demanded. "I work for them, I'm one of them. I'm going to get a new face and a new life!"

"Do you really believe that, Elizabeth? Do you think they'll let the only witness get out of here alive? After what happened to the real Elizabeth, you'd trust them?"

It was a gamble, and Davina took it. She saw by the expression on the other woman's face that the gamble had come off. "Nothing happened to her! She's cozied up in a nursing home pumped full of dope—what's so bad about that? I know people who'd pay to live that way."

"She's dead," said Davina. "They took her to Washington and strangled her, and hid her body in the trunk of Fleming's car. That was the whole purpose of creating you, so they could set him up on a treason charge and bring it out as the motive for murdering his wife."

The woman had sunk back upon the bed. The face molded by O'Farrell crumpled up and the mouth went slack. "Oh, Jesus God," she muttered. "I didn't know—I swear I didn't know—I wouldn't have done it, if I'd known . . ."

"Maybe you can see now what's going to happen to you. I don't know why they've waited this long."

"He talked about tomorrow," Elizabeth jerked up in alarm. "He said they'd operate tomorrow. They dried me out, sedated me—why, if they weren't going to operate?"

"To keep you quiet," Davina answered. "To keep you in readiness in case you were needed again. Her body wasn't discovered until yesterday. They don't need you anymore. If you don't come away with me, you'll be as dead as the real Elizabeth Carlton by tomorrow!" She held out her hand. "Come on, Lomax is outside. We've got a car and we can be in Mexico City in an hour."

There was nobody in the corridor when Felipe came to the top of it. He walked on rubber-soled shoes and they made no sound on the tiled floors. He passed the room where the patient was recuperating; its light was out. She would be sleeping, he thought, and went on, past the operating theater and the two vacant bedrooms that adjoined the studio. He paused at the door, took the key out of his pocket and slipped it into the lock. It didn't click open and he froze. He listened and he could hear women's voices. He took the gun out of his pocket, slipped the safety catch and reached for the door handle with his left hand.

Lomax had seen him through the crack in the door to the empty bedroom where he was hiding. He heard nothing, but he saw the figure in white pass, and instantly he slipped out behind him. There was a distance of ten feet to cover; he didn't rush because the movement itself would have betrayed him. He waited until Felipe had tried the door and taken out his gun. Then he sprang forward. The blow caught the Mexican in the back of the neck; it snapped the spine and he died instantly, even before his body hit the ground. Lomax picked up the gun and pushed it into his waistband; his own was in his hand as he came through the door, and Elizabeth gasped out in terror.

"Out." he barked at Davina. "Quick. Run for it!"

Davina grabbed Liz by the hand; she was whimpering with fear, and she stumbled over Felipe's body and screamed and faltered.

"Shut up! Come *on*!"

They ran as fast as her pace would allow; she was uncoordinated and feeble, dragging on Davina. Davina didn't look behind but she knew Lomax was covering them till they reached the rear door. She rushed at it, grabbing for the handle. It was locked. She had hold of Elizabeth, who was panting and whimpering. Lomax was right behind them as she shouted to him, "We can't get out this way, it's locked!"

He didn't hesitate; he reached them and seized Davina by the arm. "Follow behind me; if anything breaks drop to the ground. We'll be all right once we're out of here." He sprinted along the corridor, glancing behind to make sure the two women were keeping up. The narrow passageway with only one exit was a deathtrap, and he knew it. He had to get them out into the open where they could take cover and try to get to the car.

O'Farrell had checked the two bedrooms, and Rose had looked into the common room; only two residents were there, playing cards. They met in the reception hall. "Nothing?" he demanded.

"Nothing," she replied. "We'd better go to Felipe."

"Wait," O'Farrell commanded. "You go to the car park. Stay there and watch. If they come, and *she* is with them, you'll know Felipe and I have failed."

"Don't worry," Rose said. "She won't get past me." She was a big woman with powerful shoulders and thick wrists. She was the resident masseuse and she could maim or kill with a blow. She hurried out of the clinic and disappeared into the darkness. O'Farrell slipped through the connecting door that led from the main building to the small reception hall of the surgical unit. The lights were out there; but they blazed overhead in the corridor and he heard the sound of someone running before he turned the corner and came into view.

He was a big man but he moved with the stealth of his hunting ancestors. He drew the Walther XPK out of his right-hand pocket, and slipped off the safety catch. Like Felipe's, his shoes were rubber-soled; it was the brief glimmer of his white coat through the screen of indoor plants that sent Lomax spinning back against the projecting wall. He shouted one word behind him. "Drop!" Davina literally threw Elizabeth to the ground and lay on top of her. For a moment the body thrashed and struggled and then subsided into total stillness. Davina could hear the rapid breaths of terror, or she would have thought she'd fainted.

O'Farrell made a cautious movement behind the shelter of the giant *Fenula glauca* that stretched its green branches and feathery leaves to the ceiling. He saw the two figures on the floor, and he knew that the man was very near although he couldn't see him. The woman calling herself Maxwell was acting as a human shield for the other one. A faint smile touched O'Farrell's broad lips. His special bullets would rip through both of them. But his orders were to take the agents alive. He would try to obey if he could. He knew his subject well; he knew exactly how to appeal to the mixture of cowardice and self-love in the worthless woman he had created in the image of another worthless woman. He was glad she had been sentenced to death.

"Quetzalcoatl!" His voice echoed from the walls. "Listen to me. They are going to kill you! Fight for your life—I will protect you. Come to me now! Push her off and come to me!"

They will kill her for me, he thought with ancient cunning. When she tries to run the man who is hiding will shoot her. In that way, the orders will be obeyed . . .

"Stay flat!" Davina hissed at her. "It's a trick."

From behind the camouflage of the plant, O'Farrell took another step, and saw the huddled body at the far end, outside the door of the studio. A hot rage surged up in him. Felipe was dead. Felipe, his pupil, dearer to him than a son. Lomax saw the gleam of white move among the green fronds of the plant. O'Farrell raised his Walther XPK armed with the lethal exploding bullets, and at the same moment Lomax swung away from the wall in a low crouch and his gun spat through the silencer. O'Farrell's reaction was equally fast; his body swiveled and his finger pumped a deadly stream of fire. There was continuous sound for several seconds, like a starting motorcycle, from the silenced weapons; twice there was a whine and a crack as bullets ricocheted off the walls. One dug itself into the tiled floor and exploded, showering Davina with tiny fragments. Elizabeth began to scream in thin little shrieks. Then suddenly it was quiet, and Lomax called out: "It's all right now. Get up and run for it, for Christ's sake!"

She knew when he spoke that he was hit. She scrambled up and ran to him. The body of Jaime Luis O'Farrell barred her way. It lay on its back with the arms outspread, and a pool of blood was seeping over the floor. Like the blood of the sacrifices made to the Moon Goddess, it ran away into the darkness like black water.

Lomax was kneeling on the ground; there was no blood but his body was hunched as if he had just been given a heavy blow. "Colin," she cried out, "Oh, God, he got you!" He managed a crooked grin that was tinged with pain.

"I got him better," he said. "Now be a good girl and get her to the car. I'll follow you in a minute."

Davina knelt beside him. She felt herself begin to shake. "Where are you hurt?" she asked. "It's bad, isn't it?"

"It's OK," he insisted. "I just need a breather and I'll be on my feet. Get going now. Come on, darling, don't hang about! I'll join you in the car." His color was changing; there was a gray pallor under the suntan.

Davina stood up. "I'm not leaving you," she said. "I don't care about her or anything else. You come with us, or we don't go at all." She turned and ran back to the woman huddled on the floor. She was crying and shivering. Davina reached down and heaved her up to her feet. She saw the mouth open and the eyes bulge with the onset of hysteria, and she swung her hand up and smacked her hard across the face.

"You pull yourself together!" she spat at her. "You help me get Lomax out or I'll bloody well leave you here! Come on."

It took the combined strength of the two women to get him on his feet. Blood had begun to seep from his chest and they slipped in the spreading pool on the floor as they struggled to support him. "Get his arm over your shoulder," Davina urged. "That's it, hang on to his wrist, I've got the other one. Colin, darling, please,

please try and take some weight. We can't hold you . . ." He didn't speak; his face was twisted with pain. He forced himself to stand and then to take step after step on either side of them. Davina kept on talking to him, pleading, encouraging. "Try, come on, just a bit further. Please, Colin, don't give in, it's not far now." On the other side of him Elizabeth made as much effort as she could; the blow had steadied her and she gasped out, "Don't worry, we'll get there."

They had reached the grounds when Davina realized that he couldn't go any further. He sagged, nearly bringing them down with him. He was still conscious when she knelt beside him. "I've bought it, my darling," he said. "I know I won't make it. You go now, and finish the job for me. Get her away, won't you?" He looked at her face in the clear moonlight, and whispered, "Don't cry, don't cry . . ."

"He's dying," Elizabeth mumbled to Davina. "For Christ's sake let's get out of here." Davina didn't answer. She held on to both his hands. They felt cold.

"Colin," she said slowly and clearly, "Colin, listen to me. I'm going to get the car. Do you hear me? I'm going to get the car and I'm coming back for you. I'm not going to leave you, so you better be ready. Don't go to sleep. Listen to me; don't go to sleep!"

He didn't seem to understand; for a moment she lost all hope as she looked at him and saw the signs of life draining away. Then he opened his eyes and said suddenly, "Watch out—there were three of them," before he lost consciousness.

The nurse had hidden herself beside a big white Mercedes, which was parked next to the car Davina and Lomax had rented. She seemed to have been waiting for longer than the half hour her watch showed. O'Farrell and Felipe must have settled it, she thought. I may as well go back and find out. She straightened up, easing the cramped muscles in her legs, and saw two figures running towards the car park. She drew in a sharp breath and swore. "Quetzalcoatl"—she never knew the woman by any other name.

She had massaged her body into shape and stood guard over her while she dried out; her powerful hands had held her down when she became violent, yelling for alcohol. They hadn't given her a gun. O'Farrell said she was more lethal without one.

Davina could hear Elizabeth panting for breath as they ran. She didn't look back. She didn't know or care whether she kept up. She had to get to the car. If I can just get him to a doctor, just get some help, he might have a chance . . . Where had the bullets gone—how many times was he hit? He was bleeding but not profusely. She felt the tears running down her face. Ivan. Colin. Oh, God, show a little mercy . . . And his words came back to her as she rounded the corner and came within yards of their car. "Watch out—there were three of them."

O'Farrell and Felipe were dead. But the nurse, the woman who had searched the grounds with them . . . A hand caught Davina's arm, and the frightened, breathless voice said, "Why are you stopping—where's the car?"

"The Opel, right in front of us," Davina said. Elizabeth pushed past her, stumbling blindly towards safety. The figure came out from behind the Mercedes; for a second she brushed so close to Davina that she saw her face. It was set and brutal with purpose. The target, Quetzalcoatl, was just in front of her, opening the car door. Rose had never realized how much she hated her until the few seconds before she struck at her to kill. Born ugly, built like a man, using her strength and her skill to keep other women beautiful, she had hated them all, and none more than the drunken woman who had screamed such personal insults at her. She shouted the Spanish word "Muerte!" before she sprang, the right arm drawn back, the hand rigid and perpendicular, lethal as an axe.

Afterwards Davina couldn't remember what happened. She couldn't remember reaching for the stone or throwing herself at the broad back and hitting out with all her strength. She only knew that by some miracle the blow caught the nurse on the back of the head. The slashing sideways stroke aimed at her victim's neck and the carotid artery lost its momentum, and the heavy body lurched and fell against the car before it slid to the ground. What Davina did was done by reflex; she didn't look at the nurse. She found the strength to thrust Elizabeth into the car, jump in and start the engine. She drove over curbs and through bushes and flowerbeds and screeched to a stop where she had left Lomax. He was still alive.

"Help me! Get out and help me lift him inside!" Elizabeth was speechless and shivering with shock; she obeyed like an automaton, beyond arguing, beyond panic. Lights were coming on in the clinic; the car had roared under the walls and scattered the loose stones like machine-gun bullets. A man's voice called out, "What the hell's going on out there?" But Davina didn't hear him. Lomax was a dead weight; she strained and heaved to get the upper part of his body into the back of the car while Elizabeth struggled with his legs. She propped him up as best she could; after the door was closed she put her hand on his chest to feel a feeble heartbeat. Her hands and her clothes were stained with his blood. She said, "You drive! I'll stay beside him."

"Where? Where to?"

Their rendezvous was in Mexico City. Davina dismissed it. He wouldn't survive that distance. "Tula," she said. "We've got to find a doctor. The place is waking up. We've got to get out fast! Hurry!"

The doctor was at dinner with his family when he heard the frantic knocking on the door; like all Mexicans, they never sat down to eat before ten o'clock. He saw the woman in the reflected light from his hallway; he heard the stumbling Spanish and understood. He shouted back into the house and his wife and eldest son came hurrying. They carried Lomax into his surgery. Davina and Elizabeth were left to wait in the parlor. A young girl came in with a bottle of tequila and two glasses. She spoke in Spanish, and before Davina could say anything, it was Elizabeth who translated. And while she did so, she took a glass and filled it to the top, so that it slopped over.

"She says her father will see us in a minute." She brought the glass up to her mouth and drained it. The young girl watched her in amazement. In Mexico only men drank like that. Tequila was offered to the *gringo* women because they were both in shock. Elizabeth shuddered like an animal. "Sweet Jesus," she muttered. "That was good." In Spanish she said to the girl, "Thank you. Leave the bottle with us, please." She poured a second glass and threw herself down on one of the red upholstered armchairs; her eyes closed and her face was the color of ashes. Davina could see that her whole body was shaking as if she had a violent fever. She had no sensation of anything; she didn't know that she looked the same bloodless color, or that her own hands and legs were trembling. Her dress was filthy with blood and dirt and there was a streak down her face where her reddened hand had wiped the flowing tears away. She didn't feel the tremor round her mouth that threatened to become a fit of uncontrollable weeping. She thought she was calm as she took a little of the tequila to steady herself and stood there waiting. She looked round the room, willing herself to keep clear-headed. Heavy lace curtains, red plush, ornate reproduction gilt frames contained garish pictures of Mexican scenery. A romanticized bullfight, with a matador triumphant in the sun-bright arena. The statue of the Madonna of Guadalupe above the fireplace. There was no Indian influence, no patterned rugs, no sinister carvings; it was modern Spanish Mexico, a house where Quetzalcoatl was just a pagan relic.

The door opened and the doctor came in. She saw him properly for the first time. He was fat and middle-aged, with a gray mustache that drooped either side of his mouth. "I have done what I can for your husband," he said. "He is bleeding inside. I don't think he will live. I must send for the police because it is a shooting. You understand, señora?"

"I understand," Davina said. "Will you let me telephone the American embassy in Mexico City before you speak to the police? Then I would like to see him."

"Of course." He glanced at her curiously. The American embassy. This was not a domestic quarrel then, as he at first supposed. "Come with me. The telephone is out here." Davina looked back at Elizabeth; she seemed to have collapsed into a daze after the tequila. She followed the doctor out to the hall and picked up the telephone.

Jeremy Spencer-Barr took the call. He had been waiting at the embassy since early that morning. He had bitten his nails to the quick, reverting to a childhood habit long since abandoned. The cuticles were raw and in some places bleeding. When the call came he seized the receiver. The chief intelligence officer in the U.S. embassy was with him; so were a picked group of action men. They heard Spencer-Barr shout in his excitement.

"You've got her!" His face flushed bright red. "They got her out! Yes, yes, in one piece—isn't that great? Well done, Davina—well done—what? Oh. Oh, that's too bad. All right, leave it with me. Sit tight there and we'll take it from now on. No, don't worry about the police. We'll get that organized. Just stay close to her, for Christ's sake!"

Lomax lay on the examination couch, covered by a rug. A tall angle poise lamp cast a brilliant light upon him, leaving the rest of the room in semishadow. A tube was attached to his left arm and blood dripped into it from a plasma container suspended above. The doctor said, "I had a supply of Group O Rh Negative, señora. There is a bull ring in town, and I keep this for emergencies. It can be given to any blood group. But he has lost much blood inside and it is draining into his lung. If you want, I will send for a priest? He has not much time left."

"No," Davina said slowly. "I don't think he'd want that. I'll sit with him."

"If there is a change," the doctor said, "in the breathing, or the color gets worse—call me! I think he will go gently, like sleeping."

She laid her hand over his; it was cold and still. His breathing was labored and there was a faint bubble in it; a dribble of red-stained froth was seeping from the side of his mouth. Outside the telephone began to shrill; she heard the rapid Spanish rise and fall. The phone rang several times; she didn't know how often, nor how long she sat there, holding his hand. She didn't pray; her mind seemed to have cast loose from her control. It roamed through the past, reminding her of the first time she ever saw him, at Marchwood. Surely, at odds with the civilian world; a soldier out of context. She remembered how they had squared up to each other like two antagonists before a word was spoken.

It had been easy for her; she was armored in grief. She had never imagined that anyone could pierce it and find her vulnerable again. When they became lovers she had held something in reserve. He had known it and suffered. Suffered as only the proud and sensitive can when they have given everything of themselves to another human being. With humor and persistence, tenderness and passion, Lomax had challenged her determination not to love him. He would die, she thought in icy calm, without knowing that in the end he had won.

John Kidson held Charlie in his arms. "She's safe," he kept repeating. "She's perfectly all right. And she's done the impossible. They've got that woman and she's safe in the embassy. My darling, you don't realize what this means!"

She disengaged herself; quickly, she blinked back the tears that came when he told her the news. "Of course I do," she answered. "But I'm thinking of something else, not just the political side of it."

"That's the price, I'm afraid," he said gently. "That's what Lomax's job entailed. He knew it; he knew the risks."

"John," she said, and the beautiful chin lifted and looked as square as her sister's, "John, I'd like to fly down to her. She must be feeling pretty miserable."

"You said she didn't love him," he reminded her.

"I know I did," Charlie answered. "But I want to be with her just the same."

"All right," he said. "I'll have to see this woman anyway. We'll fly down together. Now I've got to go. I have an appointment with Fleming. We're going to work out our strategy, before Mr. Dave Benson gets any nearer to the truth."

At that moment, Dave Benson was shopping in the Georgetown supermarket. He was actually pushing a cart and wandering round the shelves in the wake of Fleming's housekeeper, Ellen. He took a packet of cookies and a carton of root beer and maneuvered himself ahead of her at the checkout. Her cart was stacked with goods.

"Let me help you with those groceries. You've got a lot to carry there."

"I don't need help, thank you," Ellen answered. She had plenty of experience with reporters and she often told friends she could smell one a block away. He was another one, sniffing for news. Her dark face was very hostile as she marched out to the car, Benson following with a load of packages. He put them in the trunk for her and then he placed himself in front of the door to the driver's seat.

"I'm from *America Today* magazine," he said. "You work for Mr. Fleming, don't you?"

"I don't talk to journalists," Ellen said. "Would you just move away? I'm late home already."

"What does Fleming pay you, Mrs. Charles? Not the same as he'd give a white woman to take care of his house, I'll bet."

She flashed at him angrily: "That's where you're wrong, smart man! Mr. Fleming gives me the top wages, more than if I was white—you going to get out of my way, or I call a cop?"

Benson didn't move. "Mrs. Charles," he said softly. "Your boss is a lucky man. He's going to need friends like you. What's happened to his wife? Where is she?"

He saw the black eyes widen in alarm. "None of your damn business,' she said. She made a determined move towards the car door and he stepped aside.

He took a chance, and it was the kind of intuitive stab in the dark that made him a great investigative journalist. "She's dead, isn't she, Mrs. Charles? It's a cover-up, isn't it?" He saw the dark skin turn a muddy shade of gray and the panic in her eyes as she stared at him for a second or two, before diving into the car. As she drove away, he said to himself, "Dave, you just hit the jackpot. Right on the button!" He hunched his shoulders in his excitement and hurried away to his hotel. He spent the rest of the afternoon blocking out a rough draft for his first article, and then he telephoned the commissioner of police to ask for an appointment. If there was one way of digging out a CIA cover-up, it was to arouse the rivalry of the police department, and Benson was very skillful at playing on departmental jealousies. Before he went to the commissioner's office, he began a round of the private mortuaries in the city.

For Davina, the next few hours were a blur. Nature was kind and at times she slept; she woke when they came into the surgery to take Lomax away. Spencer-Barr was there, with three white-uniformed male nurses. The Mexican doctor was with them, and another man, who leaned over Colin's body and checked that he was still alive. He didn't say anything; he nodded and the nurses came forward. Davina found Spencer-Barr trying to pull her away, and she turned on him savagely, shouting at him to leave her alone, she wasn't going to let them touch him . . . and then she collapsed into bitter, hopeless weeping and let him lead her out of the room.

It was the parlor where she had left Elizabeth. It was empty now. Jeremy answered the question for her. "She's on her way to the embassy." He faced Davina and said awkwardly, "Look, it's no good upsetting yourself. He'll have the best possible chance. The Hospital Juarez is the best in Mexico. They've got a top surgeon ready."

She didn't stop crying immediately; rather unwillingly he gave her one of his expensive silk handkerchiefs, and then she looked at him and said, "You mean he isn't dead?" He wasn't sure afterwards whether she was crying again or laughing. But he did hear her say several times, "Oh, Colin, love, thank God, thank God . . ."

"I can't believe it," Edward Fleming mumbled. "I can't believe it's true—it's enough to send me crazy, just imagining . . ." He rested his head on his arm, and his shoulders heaved as he cried.

"I'm sorry," Humphrey Grant said. "There wasn't any point in harrowing you with the truth until we'd found her."

"What did they *do* to her?" Fleming raised his head, the tears were streaming down his face. "To hold her all that time and then murder her—God, it's unbearable—she was so gentle—she must have been so frightened and alone, and then to die like that." He got up suddenly and rushed out of the room. Humphrey heard him retching in the bathroom. After some minutes he knocked on the door. Fleming came out. His color was putty gray. "I'm all right," he said. He bit his lips and fumbled with a handkerchief.

"She was under drugs," Grant said. "She wouldn't have known too much of what was going on."

Fleming blew his nose and wiped his eyes. "Why didn't Spencer-Barr tell me when you found this out? Why didn't Kidson tell me?"

"Because we didn't know whether we'd find the double; the chances were she'd get away and the less you knew about the switch, the better chance you had of holding up when the storm broke. Nobody would have believed the story anyway. But Davina and that poor chap Lomax have pulled the hottest chestnut we've had for years out of the fire. You've got to go down there tomorrow and kill Benson's story dead. Your wife is in Mexico, and you're going to be interviewed and photographed together. The plane leaves at nine o'clock in the morning and you've got to be on it. Those are not my instructions, by the way. Spencer-Barr said this came for you by personal messenger from the Oval Office."

He handed Fleming an envelope.

Fleming saw the heading and ripped it open. The note was handwritten, and quite brief. The signature was bold and emphasized by a heavy upcurving line. Fleming folded it and put it in his pocket. "How much did you tell him?" he asked in a low voice. He didn't even look at Humphrey Grant.

"We told him nothing. Your own people are in charge now. They gave him some of the facts but certainly not all of them. He believes your wife has become a security risk because of her drinking. I think they passed some pretty broad hints about her morals too. His reaction was predictable, but I understand he was very sympathetic to you personally."

Edward Fleming caught the nine o'clock plane to Mexico City, a representative from the White House press office flying with him. Kidson and Charlie were well to the rear of the plane. She squeezed his hand. "Don't look so worried, darling. You've hardly said a word since you came back yesterday afternoon."

"I'm sorry," he said. "I've been rotten company, haven't I? Not much of a holiday for you, I'm afraid. It's just that there's something niggling at me, Charlie, and I don't know what it is. Something about the way this thing is shaping up that I don't like at all." He leaned his head back and sighed. "Never mind, we're only spectators now. Our part is finished. I just want to see Lomax pull through, and Davina safely back in England." He raised her hand and kissed the fingers. "Then I'm going to devote some time to you, my sweet, and Fergus. Have you missed him?"

"Yes," Charlie admitted. "Very, very much. He's got a way of worming his way into your heart that's just like his father. I spoke to Mother last night. She's not pressing me to come home at all. I don't think she wants to give him up."

"We could take a long weekend there if you like," he suggested. "I think I'll have had enough of Washington and Mexico and the whole stinking mess. A few days at Marchwood would be very healing."

Benson's interview with the police commissioner had gone very well. They were not friends, but they had been in contact over the years, and one thing Benson had always done was to defend the integrity of the police department, especially in Washington. For an antiestablishment crusader this was an unusual attitude, but the commissioner and his colleagues in other major cities were too thankful to wonder what his motive was. However many other facets of American life he showed to be a can of worms, the police forces came out clean.

The commissioner didn't deny that the CIA had taken over the routine security of Fleming's private residence. He hadn't been told the reason, and added sourly that one thing about the American secret service was that so far as his departments were concerned, they were sure as hell secret!

Benson became confidential and the commissioner smelled trouble for someone.

"There are rumors spreading in New York," Benson said. "My guess is they originated down here. And the rumors got to my editor. You and the department have always played straight with me, commissioner, and I'm a guy who pays his debts. Good and bad. We've heard that Edward Fleming's wife has disappeared. The word is she's dead and the CIA are covering it to shield her husband. Before I dig up any more dirt, I want to know what part the police have played in it. Or whether the boys from Langley have put you on the spot by hiding a murder."

The word galvanized the commissioner, as Benson expected.

His department had no knowledge of Mrs. Fleming's disappearance, and there had been no question of a cover-up so far as his men were concerned. He turned very red with rage and thumped the desk top, which secretly amused Dave Benson. It reminded him of an old James Cagney movie. Even the dialogue sounded period. "We know nothing about any cover-up of any homicide. You won't find a bent cop in my department!" After this it was easy to enlist his help in checking the exact date and time when the CIA threw their screen round Fleming's house. The commissioner hinted at a friend or two inside the Langley complex who might pass him information. Benson thanked him, and promised to make it clear that the police were blameless public servants.

Davina stayed at the British embassy. The ambassador was extremely helpful, putting a car at her disposal, and a young attaché to escort her to the hospital. Spencer-Barr called to see her the evening after they arrived. She had spent most of the day sitting in the waiting room while Colin Lomax underwent an emergency operation. The surgeon was honest with her; he was a kind man, but he refused to deceive his patients or their relatives.

"We have done all we can," he said. "But the damage was terrible—the bullet disintegrated inside and destroyed his right lung, apart from three upper ribs. There is extensive laceration of muscle and tissue and some of the fragments were very close to the right ventricle of his heart. He lost a lot of blood and suffered massive shock. If you hadn't found the doctor at Tula who gave him the transfusion, he would certainly have died." Seeing the expression in her eyes, he said cautiously, "But he is a strong man, señora. Now it is up to nature, and to him, if he recovers. I think it would be better for you to go home and sleep. Otherwise we will have another patient on our hands."

She couldn't sleep; images raced through her brain, and her heart hammered with anxiety. One lung gone, extensive damage, massive shock. The words mocked her and repeated themselves until she felt she couldn't stay alone another moment. She got up and went into the little sitting room they'd given her, and when the young attaché said that Jeremy Spencer-Barr had called to see her, she was almost glad. He was as smoothly self-confident as ever. She couldn't believe she had cried in his arms and blown her nose on his handkerchief only the night before. He was a dangerous man, deceptively stiff and British, in spite of the concessions to American clothes and the faint accent that crept in with certain words. A pale, fair tiger, with a tiger's heart.

"I called the hospital," he said. "They told me he's holding his own. I'm amazed. But it seems he takes a lot of killing." He hesitated, and fiddled with his shirt cuff. "You did a marvelous job. We've found out quite a lot about her in the last few hours. She's English-born, came to Hollywood when she won some talent contest, and never made the grade. Her name was Betty Russell, changed to Elizabeth Rowe. I remembered seeing her in one or two films; she wasn't bad."

"So we discovered," Davina said. "Is she sober?"

"Up to a point," Jeremy said, and his thin lips smiled. "She's more talkative after a few drinks. We've told her what she's got to do, and she agreed rather quickly. In exchange for certain guarantees."

"Her safety?" Davina asked sharply. "You made a deal after what she did and what happened to Elizabeth Carlton?"

"I made a deal," he answered smoothly. "In exchange for a press conference with Edward Fleming to announce their separation. He's arriving tomorrow. With your sister and brother-in-law, by the way. It's going to be staged with maximum publicity. I told her it would be her biggest role. She liked that."

"I don't want to hear about it." Davina turned away from him. "If she gets away with it, you're no better than the KGB!"

Jeremy shrugged. "Then don't concern yourself," he said. "She's our problem now. I'll tell her."

"Tell her what?" Davina swung round to him.

"She keeps asking to see you," he said. "That's really why I'm here. We feel it would help to keep her in line if she could talk to you. She's got some notion you're a friend."

"Has she really? She must be out of her mind." Davina lit a cigarette; her hand shook as she held the lighter.

"You won't help?"

She drew the smoke deep into her lungs. "I'll get a coat," she said.

There was a security guard outside the door of the room on the second floor of the American embassy. Spencer-Barr showed his ID card and the man opened up for them. Jeremy strode in first. "I've brought Miss Graham," he announced.

She was sitting in an armchair, with her legs tucked underneath her; she was smoking and there was a glass half full of whisky by her elbow.

Clothes and make-up had been provided, her hair was swept up in its normal style, and the voice when she answered was Elizabeth Fleming's. She was back in her role. But the face was haggard and strained under a coating of tan base, and the big blue eyes were bloodshot.

"I didn't think you'd come." She took her glass and swallowed greedily. "At least they're not trying to stop me having a drink if I want one."

"So I see," Davina retorted. "Why did you want to see me?"

"I want to know what the score is," she said flatly. "I don't trust that slimy bastard. Where do I stand with your people?"

"You don't stand anywhere," Davina said. "You're out of our hands now. As for not trusting Spencer-Barr, I think you're very lucky to be offered any deal at all. Whatever it is."

Elizabeth uncurled her legs and stood up; for the first time Davina noticed the small, elegant feet. "Oh, I'm getting the works," she said. "I give a press conference with my dear husband Edward and explain that though we still love each other, of course, we've got problems and we're separating for a while to see if we can work them out." She laughed suddenly; it was a coarse little chuckle. "What a lot of bloody hypocrites you people are. The lousy CIA and the rotten SIS. And the KGB," she added. "I trusted them. I worked for them and I believed they'd look after me. You stopped that gorilla Rose from killing me, didn't you?"

"Yes," Davina said quietly.

"I've thought about that," Elizabeth said. "I knew you weren't lying when you told me they were going to kill me. So I decided to save my skin and cooperate. And when I've played the big scene with darling Edward, I'm going to take a trip to Europe and fade out of view. And I'll get a new face and a new life. Funny, isn't it? The same payoff from both sides. And *they* have the gall to talk about morality and freedom! You know something? You were the only one I felt I could have trusted."

"Why didn't you?"

She laughed again, the same sneering giggle from the back of her throat. "Because I hated your guts," she said. She began to pace up and down the room, waving her cigarette about as she talked; it was like watching someone on a stage. "I learned all about her," she went on. "I learned about her home and her family; I knew the name of every bloody aunt and cousin, and all about life at that smart school you went to. The staff and the pupils, and you. You were the clever one, the bluestocking, she called you. 'Mousey.' Mousey Graham. And your sister; she was friendly with her, wasn't she? Oh, I read the script and I was word-perfect, wasn't I? You must admit, I took you in!" She stopped and dropped her cigarette into a flower bowl. "How did you find out?"

"You went wrong everywhere," Davina said evenly. "Except I didn't see it because they'd done such a good job on your looks. Liz Carlton was a charming, feminine woman as well as beautiful. She had taste and education. I kept thinking, what's happened, how could she have turned into a drunken, foul-mouthed creature like this? It was my sister Charlie who found the clue. She knew

Elizabeth Carlton's shoe size. It didn't match the shoes in your closets. Three sizes too small, I think they were. So we started thinking again."

The woman swore. She finished her drink.

"She had feet like soup plates," she said. "Nothing I could do about that. I hated her, you know? I hated everything about her. The more she talked about her background and her childhood, the more sick I felt listening to it. She was doped to the eyebrows. She poured it all out while we recorded it, so I could learn the part. And I kept thinking of the lousy town where I grew up. The dullest, meanest little place on earth. Nothing to look forward to but marrying some clown with a steady job and turning into a frump like my mother and my married friends. I wasn't going to end like that. I had looks, and talent. I *knew* I could make something of myself. She never had to struggle for anything. The good fairies were at her christening all right!" She poured herself another drink. The ice clattered into the glass and some of the whisky slopped over. She sat down and looked up at Davina.

"I didn't think they'd hurt her," she said slowly. "Before God, I never thought they'd do her any harm."

"Just turn her into a drug addict. Is that what you call not doing her any harm? I don't believe you; you just didn't want to know."

Elizabeth turned on her fiercely. "O'Farrell told me she'd be kept at the clinic," she said. "Listen, drugs didn't frighten me! I spent fifteen years in Hollywood. People pay thousands of dollars to get stoned. But I wouldn't have gone along with murder. That's why that Indian lied to me."

Davina didn't argue. It was possible she was telling the truth. "How long were you working for the Russians?" she asked. "I'm not asking for anybody but myself. What made you do it?"

"Money. I wasn't getting parts, I was running out of the few dollars I'd put by. It wasn't too difficult. I laid a few selected people and encouraged them to talk. That was the start of it. Then this came along. Quetzalcoatl, they called me. The Plumed Serpent. It sounded pretty dramatic; the acting part of a lifetime, learning to live someone else's life, marry the guy who fell in love with the other woman, keep it going for eighteen months, and lay the paper chase for your SIS at the same time!"

"No wonder you drank," Davina said. "It must have been a tremendous strain."

"It was. Not at first though; it was easy at first. Eddie was so crazy in love with me, I grew to like it. Can you imagine that? I started thinking how nice it would be to have a man like him and a life like hers. But it didn't last. He didn't love me for me; he loved the face they'd made for me at Tula. He loved the phony bits of me, the accent I copied from her, the mannerisms, the way she walked and dressed and did her hair . . . I never expected it to hurt, but it did. And then he started to hate me when I pulled the fake diary on him. I got frightened then." She took a hurried swallow of whisky. "I knew what had happened to his first wife. He stood by and let her burn. I could feel him hating me, and I kept thinking, he could do it again. And there's nowhere to run. You've got to sit it out till they tell you. I drank because otherwise I'd have lost my nerve and run out on the whole thing. You don't do that with my employers."

"And you'll be safe now?" Davina asked her quietly.

She sighed impatiently. "Yes, yes, they've promised. But it's not the life I wanted. Do you know how much money they were depositing in Switzerland for me? Half a million dollars! For the first time I was going to have all the things that people like you and *she* had from the moment you were born! Status, a background—"

"Money doesn't give you that. Liz Carlton wasn't rich; I live on my salary. You've got it all wrong if you think money is going to make you into someone different."

She wasn't really listening. "I was going to be an international star," she muttered. "They had a big French producer in their pocket. He was going to discover me, promote me—it's just packaging, you know—they make stars like that Indian made me into somebody else. All I needed was the money behind me, and the influence to set me on my way. That's what they promised me." She looked up at Davina. "That's why I did it. I wanted the spotlight to shine on me for a change. Now—I'll get a new face and a pension for keeping my mouth shut. And live in Europe. Not much, is it, for all I went through?" A tear streaked down one cheek, leaving a smudge of mascara. "Sweet Jesus," she mumbled, "what a lousy deal . . ."

Davina got up without saying anything; she tapped and the security man let her out. She walked slowly down to the main hall of the embassy and out into the bright Mexican sunshine. She felt quite sick.

The press conference was called at the Hotel Internacional. Elizabeth had booked in there late the night before, suitably accompanied by two CIA security men. The foyer was thronged with photographers and reporters; when Edward Fleming arrived just after midday, there was a rush to photograph him and journalists shouted questions. He looked pale and tense and his press officer fended them off with the promise that they could ask what they liked at the news conference. Fleming went up to the fifth floor. Spencer-Barr and John Kidson were waiting for him. Kidson had been driven ahead of him when the plane landed.

"Everything's set up," Jeremy announced. "How was your flight?"

"It was OK," Fleming answered.

"Would you read through this?" Jeremy handed him a typed sheet of paper. "See if you want any alterations made."

John Kidson watched him. He read it very quickly. "No changes," he said. "It's fine as it is. We've got twenty minutes before we meet the press. I want to ask you something, Mr. Barr."

"Certainly, anything I can do to help?" Jeremy said blandly.

"When we've gone through this charade, what happens next? What happens to the woman?"

"She takes a trip," Jeremy answered. "You never have to see or hear of her again; there'll be the announcement of a divorce some time later when all the interest has died down. We've been very lucky, Mr. Fleming. That creep Benson has been getting closer. The murder victim has been buried quietly upstate; we've covered all tracks, but he's liaised with another Washington press man and the police department have started asking questions. This morning is going to stop the whole investigation in its tracks. You'll have nothing to worry about then."

"No," Fleming said. "That's true. Where is she buried?" Kidson caught the look of anguish on his face. Whatever he is, he said to himself, he really loved that poor woman.

Jeremy said, "I'm sorry. That's classified. I should forget it, Mr. Fleming. Concentrate on the press conference."

"I'd like some flowers put on the grave." Edward Fleming turned for the first time to John Kidson. "Can you arrange that?"

"I'm sure we can," Kidson said. "I'll see to it."

Charlie found Davina at the hospital. Lomax was still unconscious in the intensive care unit. "There's nothing you can do by sitting here," Charlie said. "You look a wreck, Davy. Come on, let me take you to lunch somewhere. John's gone to this press conference thing and we can spend the afternoon together. I'll come back with you later and see how he is."

"Charlie, I don't think he's going to live." Davina put her arms round her sister and burst into long, bitter weeping. Charlie embraced her and let her cry. Davina had never cried, even as a child. Everything was bottled in, and sympathy was not invited when things went wrong. They had met her at the airport after Ivan's death. Charlie had expected tears, but there was an emptiness in her sister that was worse than giving way to grief. Now at least the emptiness was gone. She said gently, "You do love him, don't you?" And heard the sobbing, "Yes, of course I do . . ."

Charlie stepped back from her. "Here," she said. "Here's a handkerchief. Mop yourself up, darling. I think I'd like a word with the doctor. I won't be long." And leaving a wake of expensive scent behind her, she swept out in search of the sister in charge of the unit.

"You haven't let her see him?" she exclaimed, when the senior physician had been tracked down and badgered into talking to her. "Why not?"

He didn't know whether to be angry or admiring. "He is unconscious. He's on an IV and a heart monitor. It would do no good for her to see him like that. And he wouldn't benefit, I assure you."

"I'm not sure," Charlie said. "Sometimes when a person is unconscious outwardly, they still sense if someone they love is near. I know I did, the only time in my life when I was under anaesthetic. My father was holding my hand and I knew it. I didn't actually come round until a couple of hours afterwards. Please, doctor, won't you try it? What can you lose?"

He said, "What was the matter with you—an operation?"

She gave him a warm, mischievous smile. "Appendix," she said. "I was nine. But I promise you, it helped me get better."

As soon as he smiled back she knew she had won. "Very well," he said. "We will let her see him. I'll send a nurse for her. Perhaps you would take a cup of coffee in my office?"

"Thank you," Charlie said. "I'd be delighted."

It was imagination, of course. She'd been sitting for so long in the room that she was aware of the tiniest sounds, from the faint ping of the monitor measuring his heartbeat to the sudden creak when she moved a little in the chair. She didn't touch him. He was festooned in tubes and drips, connected to machines that recorded his struggle to survive. His face had shrunk and he looked small under the plain hospital cover. The noise that frightened her most was the ugly rasp of his breathing.

And then she heard it. It sounded like a whisper; the rhythm of each laboring breath was interrupted. "Oh, God," she said out loud, "I know what that means—he's going to die." She came right up to the side of the bed; the nurse sitting on duty in the side ward saw her move and hurried in. "Has he changed? Excuse me, you should go out now, I must check."

"He spoke," Davina said. "I'm sure I heard something . . . Oh, he's dying now, isn't he? Oh, Colin, Colin . . ."

The nurse put an arm round her shoulder and said kindly, "It is better you go. Please."

"Davina." They both whipped round to the bed. For some seconds his eyes opened.

"He is conscious," the nurse whispered. "That is very good. Very good indeed. He knows you are here."

"Yes," Davina said. "He does."

"I think you will go now," the nurse insisted. "I will send for the doctor. You should be happy; it is a good sign."

She walked back to the waiting room; mechanically, she glanced at her watch and was amazed to see that it was almost four o'clock. Her sister was in the waiting room, reading an American edition of *Vogue.*

"Davy? How is he?"

Davina came and sat beside her. She felt suddenly limp and weak. "I think he's better," she said. "He knew me. He spoke. The nurse said it was a very good sign."

Charlie squeezed her arm. "Seeing you did the trick," she said. "I told the doctor it would! Do you know, he gave me a delicious lunch while you were in there? Wasn't that kind?"

Davina managed a very weary smile. "If you went to Mars, Charlie," she said, "you'd find a little green man to take you out. Let's go now: I think I might sleep for a couple of hours. And thank you."

Charlie laughed. "I won't make snap judgments about you in a hurry! I swore you weren't in love with him. Nice idiot you've made me look!" She stopped a taxi and they drove back to the British embassy. But when they got inside, there was no question of Davina or anybody else taking a siesta.

Edward and Elizabeth Fleming made their joint statement and answered questions from invited members of the international press. The statement was short and dignified. Elizabeth Fleming answered all questions mildly and modestly. She blamed herself for the crisis. She felt her individuality had been swamped. She'd had to give up decorating her friends' houses, which was her hobby, and she spent long periods alone while her husband worked late or traveled. Nobody was near enough to get the whisky smell from her breath; she came across very well, and the tenor of the questions asked of Fleming were correspondingly hostile. He seemed dull and abstracted; his answers were mechanical and once when his wife touched his sleeve, he pulled his arm away. The session lasted just over twenty-five minutes. The Flemings went up in the elevator to the fourth floor, accompanied by Spencer-Barr, who had lurked in the background during the interview.

"Mrs. Fleming," he said, "you stay in your rooms here; nobody will be allowed to bother you. Mr. Fleming, you can catch a plane back to New York and the shuttle will get you home by eight o'clock tonight, if that suits you."

"I'd like to speak to my wife alone," Fleming said. "Just give us five minutes, will you? I want to ask her something private."

"We'll go inside," Jeremy said. The security guard opened the door and the three of them walked into the room where Davina had seen her that morning.

"Jesus," she said, "I could do with a drink." She bumped into a table in her haste to reach the bottle of whisky. Fleming looked at Jeremy.

"I'll wait in the bedroom," Jeremy said. "But make it five minutes, will you, please?"

Fleming didn't sit down or acknowledge her offer to fix a drink for him too. He stared at her and his eyes were dark voids in his face. "Tell me something. How much did she suffer?"

She took a swig, and faced him, one hand on her hip. "Is that all you've got to say to me? I was your wife, you know." The drink was lighting a fire in her eyes, making them as bright as his were dead. "You married *me*, not her—you slept with *me*."

"Tell me the truth," he said slowly. "Do one decent thing in your life and tell me. Did she suffer?"

"I was in love with you for a while," she said. "Not that you knew it; you didn't know anything about how *I* felt, the real me. All you could see was *her*. I was a *real* woman; she was just a spoiled little prick teaser. You really want to know if she suffered?" She took steps towards him until they were close. "I'll tell you. *She did*. She wasn't doped all the time, you know—there was a female gorilla in that place. Her name was Rose." She gave a sudden hoot of laughter. "She beat the hell out of her if she didn't behave . . ."

The bedroom door was left ajar. Jeremy had been listening and he had already pushed it open to stop her when Fleming took the gun out of his pocket and fired. He shot her twice in the chest at point-blank range. As Spencer-Barr came bursting in, Fleming put the barrel between his own eyes. Jeremy stood rooted.

"Don't!" he shouted at him. "Don't!"

Fleming said loudly, "You kill a snake by crushing its head." Then he pulled the trigger.

When Humphrey Grant arrived back in England it was early on Saturday morning. Sir James White's car was waiting for him. Lady White was at the wheel. She greeted Humphrey affectionately. She was the only woman he could bear touching him. She had been a surrogate mother when he was young; most of his holidays from university had been spent at the house where he was now going for the weekend.

"James is so looking forward to seeing you," she said. "He's been overworking since you've been away. He looks quite tired. You'll have to talk to him, Humphrey; he won't listen to me, you know."

"He doesn't listen to anyone," Humphrey Grant said. But he was glad to see the familiar pink-washed Georgian house, with its frame of June roses in the sunshine.

After lunch he settled into James White's study and gave him a long and detailed report of everything that happened. The brigadier lit a Turkish cigarette. He smiled. "A very satisfactory ending, my dear chap. All the ends neatly tied. A scandal, certainly, but not the kind of scandal Borisov had set up for us. Distracted by the breakup of his marriage, the President's personal advisor killed his wife and committed suicide. I gather poor old Kidson is blaming himself."

"Blaming me," Grant said. "He's a very shrewd fellow; I'm sure he suspects my reasons for filling in the details about the wretched Elizabeth Carlton. He hasn't actually accused me of inciting Fleming to kill Borisov's agent, but he's dropped some sharp hints. The CIA are furious, too."

"Naturally," Sir James agreed. "But we couldn't leave her in their hands, could we? I'm sure they meant to get rid of her, but this is much the best solution. You couldn't trust Spencer-Barr a yard; he'd be quite capable of using her himself if he saw an opportunity. The row will blow over, Humphrey; these things always do. What remains to be seen is what this will do to Igor Borisov. That's going to be interesting."

"Yes," Grant agreed. "The next few weeks of Moscow-watching should be very interesting indeed. By the way, what do we do with Neil Browning?"

"I've been thinking about that. I think we'll post him to Dublin. Moscow will promptly pick him up and we'll learn a lot from watching him. So will the Irish government. And he'll be nice and close whenever we decide he's no longer any use to us. What news of Major Lomax?"

"I went to see him in hospital. He's turned the corner, so I was told."

Grant's occasional lapses into cliché amused James White. His deputy considered himself rather a pedant about words.

"And the invaluable Miss Graham? What a splendid thing I did to get her to come back, wasn't it, Humphrey? And you said she never would."

"I wouldn't count on it," Grant said. "A lot will depend upon Lomax's recovery. I asked her when she was coming back to the Office and she said that she had no idea and didn't give a damn. I left her keeping vigil at the hospital."

"That's all right," James White dismissed it lightly. "She'll be back, all in good time. Now, how about a walk round the garden before tea?"

"You failed, Comrade General Borisov."

"Yes," Borisov said. "Yes, I failed. I wanted to report to you first." The heavy head lifted slightly; the general secretary of the Communist party of the Union of Soviet Socialist Republics. So much simpler, he thought, when they called the ruler of Russia the tsar.

"Why? What excuse have you to offer me?"

"No excuse," Igor Borisov said quietly. "I came to you direct, comrade, because you trusted me and had confidence in my work. I have failed you. I am sorry."

The older man regarded him silently for a few moments. "Sit down, Borisov," he said at last. "Let me tell you where you have made the serious mistake. Not the Plumed Serpent; intelligence operations of that complexity can often go wrong. This one did not entirely disappoint us. No." The thick hand came up as Borisov started to speak. "Listen to me. You hoped to destroy the new American administration. That is a young man's dream; you are an ambitious, clever young man. Men of my age are less ambitious, and therefore more often successful. Let me tell you about your mistake. Can you think what it is?"

"No." Igor Borisov shook his head. The interview was not taking the direction he expected. "Go to him direct," that had been Natalie's advice. "Speak to him as a father. He'll listen to you."

The older man smiled; it gave his ugly face a benign, yes, a fatherly look, Borisov thought.

"You underestimate the power of your position."

Borisov didn't know what to answer. He said nothing. The smile widened and then disappeared. A frown of reproof replaced it.

"You come here like a junior officer; you stand apologizing and being honest about what you have done wrong. Never do that again. Never stand in front of me or anyone else in the Politburo like a lieutenant caught smoking the colonel's cigarettes! You are in command of a quarter of a million men inside Russia: you are the guardian of our internal security. You control the Soviet state's most powerful weapon against its enemies from within and without. The KGB is not a counterintelligence agency alone. You have forgotten its other role in maintaining the safety of the state and the Soviet people. You are young for your position, Igor Igorovitch, and you have risked your reputation on a counterintelligence operation that had little chance of succeeding as you expected. I supported you in the Politburo when Rudzenko was attacking you. I hoped you would succeed, but I am not surprised you didn't. Nor disappointed. It has taught you a lesson, and it has achieved enough to beat back your enemies when they attack you. Prepare your case carefully, and I will continue to support you. You can make a case, I think."

"I can," Borisov said slowly. "There is a scandal; America has lost an able servant, and relations between the CIA and the SIS are very strained; each accusing the other of withholding information. I can defend myself, if you will support me."

"I backed your nomination for the post," the general secretary said. "I helped to put you in a position that is second only to mine. Nobody else is going to remove you. I need you to watch Rudzenko. We both have a motive."

"Yes," Igor Borisov said quietly. "I am your man. I will always be your man, and I will grow into my position, I promise you."

The gray head nodded. "I know you will," he said. "And you won't forget what you've learned today. So long as you have my trust you will defeat all your enemies. Including your own youth." He reached forward and offered Borisov his hand. He took it and held it for a long moment. No words were necessary. The alliance had been concluded between them.

"Thank goodness Davina's coming," Mrs. Graham said. "This house has been so empty since Charlie and John and little Fergie went home."

Captain Graham laid down his paper and said, "You're impossible, Betty. All you want is someone to look after. Why can't you run after me instead? I'd love to be fussed over!"

She laughed at him. "Oh, no, you wouldn't. The only time you had a temperature and I offered you the thermometer, you said something very rude indeed! I adored having the baby, he was so sweet." She sighed, but it was a contented little sound. "It's nice to see Charlie so happy," she said. "And such a good mother; I never thought she'd cope."

Her husband said quickly, "Whyever not? Charlie's a very loving girl, of course she'd love the baby." He didn't like his favorite daughter being criticized and he rustled the newspaper in protest. Betty Graham went on with her needlework; she belonged to a generation that had learned to sew beautifully.

"I wonder what this Major Lomax is like?" she said after an interval. "Charlie says she's in love with him."

"Charlie's an incurable romantic," her husband replied. "Davina said in the letter she was bringing a colleague down here to recuperate. He was very seriously injured out there and she wants him to have a rest in a private house. Much nicer than a convalescent home, that's what she wrote. Doesn't sound like a love affair to me. I thought it was a very cool letter, rather businesslike, in fact."

Betty Graham didn't answer; she bent over her embroidery frame and thought that Davina's father would never understand his daughter, fond of her though he was.

"This garden is the most peaceful place," Lomax said to her. He reached out and their hands met and clasped together. "Your family have been so good to me. I feel completely at home."

"You should," Davina answered. "You are at home. You won Mother's heart the minute you raved about the garden. And you're so much better since we've been here."

"Thanks to you. But I'll never be up to much. I can just about walk the length of the lawn and down here to the terrace and I'm flaked out!"

"It'll take time," she comforted. "And that's something we've got plenty of, thank God. I wish you'd been with me when I told the Chief I was resigning—you should have seen his face! That maddening look, as much as to say, there, there my dear, you'll see sense later on . . . And when he knew I meant it, I saw him angry for the very first time in all the years I've worked for him. That's why Humphrey's invited himself down. To try and make me change my mind."

"You should change it," Lomax said. "You're too good to go to waste. For a woman, anyway," and he smiled.

"I have a better life to live and a more important role to play," she said firmly. "And if all this is leading up to a nice bit of self-pity on your part, darling, you can forget it. I have you, and that is all I want. If you start saying you're a useless crock and I'm throwing myself away on you once more—I shall scream!"

"Then take a deep breath."

She turned, hearing her mother's dogs barking round the front entrance of the house. "Damn—that'll be Humphrey. I suppose I'd better go and meet him. Thank God John and Charlie are coming this evening; it'll take the weight off us. He's like lead to entertain. You stay quiet here."

Lomax eased himself in the garden chair. The roses were at the height of their flowering season, and the scent of them mingled with Mrs. Graham's beloved Madonna lilies. He had never had time to enjoy a beautiful garden. Now he had too much time. His enfeebled body was a prison for his spirit. He walked at the pace of an old man, railing against the weakness that defeated the urgency of his will. Not strong enough to make love to the woman who was so generous in her love for him. She wanted to marry him. He hadn't argued with her. There was nothing he could do but wait for Humphrey Grant to come.

It was a very cheerful gathering, Captain Graham thought, looking at his two daughters, his son-in-law, and his guest round the dining-room table. Charlie as always set everyone alight; he loved her gaiety. Davina was serene in her happiness. Clever Charlie had been right, of course. She was deeply in love with her major. A fine man, he thought contentedly. Just the sort of person his independent daughter needed to make her a little softer, more womanly. And the gaunt man who had come down from London was less lugubrious than his appearance suggested. He talked at length on world affairs with an astringency that the captain much appreciated. It made him feel less buried in the country to talk to someone who was in the center of things. He surveyed his family with a deep satisfaction. The silver gleamed on the table; his wife glanced at him and smiled; the sound of laughter was warm as the candlelight, and the Graham ancestors regarded them benignly from the walls. He felt himself a very fortunate man. They didn't linger at the table after dinner. Colin Lomax excused himself and went up the stairs to his room. It was a slow and painful progress, made a few steps at a time.

"He's getting on, though," the captain remarked to John Kidson. "We made a bedroom out of my study for the first few weeks. Davina's done wonders for him. I must say I never imagined she could be such a good nurse!"

"How much of it is pity, do you think?" John asked him. Captain Graham stared at him in surprise. "Pity? Oh, I never thought of that. She's in love with the chap. Not surprising, got the George Medal—badly shot up. Any woman worth her salt would fall for him. Come, my dear boy, I'll give you a glass of port. Where's Betty and the girls?"

"Making coffee and gossiping, I imagine. Humphrey's disappeared."

"He made his excuses," Captain Graham said. "Always goes to bed very early. Gets up very early too, so he says. I found him a most interesting fellow; Davy said he was terribly dry and dull."

"Perhaps she's never seen him out of the Office," Kidson suggested. "He certainly blossomed tonight. Let's go and have that port, then, shall we?"

"I couldn't come before," Humphrey Grant said. "The Chief wanted to give you plenty of time to think."

"I realized that."

"You did a very good job, Major Lomax; it can't have been easy for you."

"No," Colin answered. "Easy it wasn't. She trusted me, you see. That was what I found so difficult."

"Naturally; especially in view of your relationship. But that never colored your judgment, that is what is so admirable about the work you did for us."

"I didn't start the relationship with her till I was sure. Would you pass me a cigarette? Thanks very much."

Grant didn't show how much he disapproved of smoking. He struck a match and lit Lomax's cigarette. "It was a difficult decision to make," he said. "Nobody likes to set a spy on a colleague;

especially one like Davina who'd given such excellent service. But we just didn't know if we could trust her."

Lomax didn't answer for a moment. He drew reflectively on his cigarette. "She went into this last operation with a little question mark," Grant continued. "She has come out of it apparently unblemished, with a tremendous success to her credit. You knew what to look for, and didn't find it."

"I watched her every inch of the way, and she was faultless." Lomax took another puff. "She never put a foot wrong. She was everything a top operator should be. I hated the whole idea when you told me what I had to do. I didn't want to work with a woman, I didn't want to act as an informer on someone who thought I was there to protect her. The whole set-up stank to me."

"You made that clear."

"Then I changed my mind. I found she was marvelous to work with. A real challenge. And I got involved emotionally as well."

Grant nodded. "We were worried about that."

"You needn't have been. I was a hundred percent sure of her then. I still am. You've got nothing to worry about except for one thing."

"And that is?"

"You've been keeping tabs on the wrong person."

Grant's lips opened as if he were going to speak, then they snapped shut.

"I've put some facts together. A sort of appendix to my report on Davina. It's in the drawer there. Read it here if you like. I wouldn't take it to your Office."

Grant opened the few sheets of paper. He read what was written slowly and mouthed the words as he did so. Lomax stubbed out his cigarette; he couldn't take more than a few puffs. It was only a nervous habit now, forbidden by his doctors. To encourage him, Davina had given up completely.

He felt very tired, and closed his eyes. He opened them when Grant said in a croaking voice, "*My God—*"

"You see what I mean?"

"It's incredible!"

"Well," Colin Lomax said. "I leave it with you, Mr. Grant. I don't envy you much."

"No," Grant muttered. "I'll keep this." He folded the papers and put them into his inside pocket.

"I'm going to talk to Davina tomorrow morning, but I think it's a waste of time after her meeting with the Chief. She's retired for good. And it's a pity. We need her. Especially now."

Lomax looked at him. "I'm not going to hang round her neck," he said quietly. "You've seen the medical reports. Give it six months or so and she'll be back."

"I did see them," Grant said. "I'm very sorry. She doesn't know, of course."

"No. And she's not going to, either. I love her very much. But I could never sit back and be a burden to her."

"I can understand that," Humphrey Grant said. He cleared his throat and said awkwardly, "Being a bachelor myself I don't know much about these things, but if I were you, I'd let her have those six months to be happy. And make the most of them yourself. Goodnight, Major."

In their bedroom, Betty Graham switched out the reading light. She knew every creak in every board in the house; they told her that Davina was going down the passage to Lomax.

"Betty?" Fergus Graham said from the twin bed. "Not asleep are you?"

She smiled in the darkness. "No, darling, or I wouldn't be answering, would I?"

"What was that creaking noise—who's wandering about at this hour?"

"I think it's Davina. She sleeps in Colin's room, you know."

"Hmmm. He looked very tired tonight, I thought."

"Yes, he did, after dinner especially."

"But it was a very good evening," Fergus Graham said. "I thoroughly enjoyed it. And it was nice to look at our two girls and see them both settled and happy at last."

"Yes," Betty Graham answered. "I thought exactly the same thing."